JUST KILL

Also by Remi Kone

Innocent Guilt

For my grandmother and late uncle –
the best storytellers I've known.

Prologue

He slept like someone already dead. Face down. Not moving, except for the flare of his nostrils as the breath moved in and out. It was the heat that woke him, his T-shirt wet against his back. He sat up, eyes half closed, cotton sheets thrown carelessly to the floor. His mouth was heavy with the taste of sleep, and his body cried out for water to cool itself down. The room was covered by darkness, disguising morning as night, and he tripped on a shoe as he stumbled towards the door. Still in a daze, he felt his way down the stairs, resisting the light switch as he kept full consciousness at bay.

The journey to the kitchen was slow, and it took a while before he could angle his head under the tap and taste the cool rush of water in his mouth. Satisfied, he filled a glass and began the climb back to bed. It was only then that he heard it, soft and low – the hum of voices drifting from underneath the sitting room door. He sometimes forgot to turn off the television, and he approached hesitantly, his touch light as he pushed the handle down. It was almost completely black inside. He reached for the lamp, his eyes alert as they adjusted to the glow. The room seemed to be just as he had left it the night before – ordered without being tidy, his coat discarded on a chair. As he moved to retrieve it, he saw the shape – the crown of a head peeping above the back of the sofa, the hint of a body, perfectly still.

'Who's there?'

He barely recognised his own voice, strangled by fear.

'Who's there?' he said again.

No reply.

Eyes trained on the figure, he reached for the bookshelf that lay to his left. His fingers crawled silently along the ledge, wrapping around the spine of the first novel they found. He held it aloft, carefully feeling the weight in his hand. Then he propelled it through the air, praying it would keep flight. The book crashed to the floor before it reached its target, but the figure didn't flinch, continuing to face straight ahead. He grabbed the lamp as he edged towards the sofa, ripping the plug from the socket as he prepared to strike.

'Don't move . . .'

His voice faltered as his feet shifted forwards. He swallowed the bile creeping up his throat. As he rounded the sofa, he saw a man, sitting completely still, body slightly slumped. The intruder stared at the television, seemingly mesmerised, pale face lit by the glare from the screen, eyes not blinking, chest rigid under a thin shirt. There was no sign of life as the city waited for morning – an unknown stranger, dead before dawn.

PART I

Chapter One

Leah

I jolted awake, struggling to breathe. It was late. I had had another nightmare. The air was muggy and still as London embraced the height of a freak summer. I switched on the fan beside me, listening to the buzz of the blades as I reached for the notebook by my bedside, scribbling what I could remember before the details began to blur.

I had been recording my dreams for months now, convinced they held secrets from my past. I replayed the dream I had just had, straining for images I had already forgotten. I remembered there had been a wood, but the colours of the leaves kept changing; the moon shrank then grew; the trees multiplied. My phone screeched under my pillow, the volume dulled by the fabric above. I searched for it with my left hand, the pen in my right moving fast across the page.

'Ma'am?'

Randle, my detective sergeant, his voice calm and unhurried down the line.

'There's been a body. They found a suspect running away from the scene . . .'

I waited.

'He won't talk. The suspect – he says he'll only speak to you.'

Chapter Two

Leah

I dressed fast, pulling on a light leather jacket. The murder had taken place in another borough, but I had been requested by name. Randle had been told no more than that, and I walked out into the night, wondering what lay ahead. A group of boys loitered aimlessly in the courtyard, puffing out their chests through a haze of marijuana smoke. I had lived on the World's End council estate for over a year, so they knew I was police. They stared at me, daring me to approach, their defiance making them seem younger. I looked back, impassive – next time I wouldn't be as nice.

I heard Randle's motorbike before I saw him, midnight-blue helmet obscuring his face. He slipped it off as he pulled up beside me, pushing his dark blond hair back off his forehead. His blue eyes smiled when they found me, but his lips stayed neutral as he assessed my mood. Randle was confident without swagger in a way I had once found irritating but had slowly grown used to. He had shown his loyalty, but my boundaries remained. I tugged at the zip of my jacket, the small crease between my eyebrows deepening – we were colleagues; we didn't need to be friends. I reached for the spare helmet he held out towards me, climbing behind him without a word. Randle didn't need my encouragement – he was self-assured enough.

'How fast can you get us there?' I said.

He half turned. I saw the edge of a grin before he covered it with the midnight-blue shell.

'Hold on tight, ma'am.' The click of his visor closing. 'Wouldn't want you to fall off.'

Sarah Franks had rented a tiny flat above a newsagent's in a run-down part of Elephant and Castle. It was a depressing place to live, but a sadder place to die. The paint had been scraped off the door, exposing splintered wood, and a metal rubbish bin overflowed with fast-food wrappers spilling out of black plastic bags.

'Stop here.'

I had to shout to be heard over the engine. Randle tilted the bike towards the pavement, straightening effortlessly as we came to a halt.

I could see the circus of police and bystanders ten feet in the distance – the chaos of camera phones and overlapping voices as one person's tragedy became another person's sport. I assessed the picture in front of me: concrete building cordoned off to repel rubberneckers; all available exits sealed to secure the scene. Blue lights blinked in the darkness, announcing violence. Three police cars, badly parked, gleamed white in the street. There was no obvious sign of forensics. The crime was still fresh; the victim still here. The night was heavy and hot, and the officer standing guard shifted uncomfortably in his uniform as a drop of sweat slid down his neck.

'DI Leah Hutch and DS Ben Randle.'

I flashed my badge, striding past before he could delay us with questions. He opened his mouth, but I had already moved on. A woman in a grey, shapeless suit blocked our route to the entrance.

She had rolled up her sleeves, revealing heavily freckled arms; dark red hair pulled tight off a pale, unblemished face.

'DS Lu Hoffen.' Her voice was friendly, but her green eyes betrayed her. 'You don't remember me . . .' She stared through me. 'I heard you transferred back from Leeds last year.'

It took a moment, then an image, long forgotten, appeared in my mind. She had been called Louise when I first knew her – blonde, fuller-faced, more eager. Over a decade later, the dye had gone, along with the sincerity of her smile. There was a hardness to her, but life on the job could do that to a person – dead bodies and long days not everyone's dream.

'You've done well for yourself . . .' she said.

Her eyes were still speaking, but she swallowed the words before they came out. Her grip was limp when I shook her hand. We had trained together in my early days in London before I went to work in Leeds for ten years. I was now her superior on paper, but her expression told me it was a fact she would rather ignore. There were those who thought my promotion was about ticking diversity boxes, but I didn't let that bother me. I wasn't trying to win a popularity contest; solving cases sufficed.

'Thanks.'

I accepted the compliment she hadn't given. Lu Hoffen was free to think that her lack of advancement was because of the colour of her skin, but from what I remembered of our time together, she had struggled to get results.

'Welcome to Elephant and Castle,' she said. Again, her face and her words failed to match. 'We're honoured to have you.'

Her sarcasm didn't deter me. I hadn't chosen to get up in the middle of the night to encroach on another borough's case.

'I'm here to help, not to take over.' I nodded towards the building. 'What are we dealing with?'

She turned her back as she answered me. 'You can see for yourself. Let's get you kitted out.'

I took my time as I slid the first nitrile glove over my fingers, savouring the seconds before a new atrocity lodged itself in my brain. Lu hovered, her gaze flitting between me and Randle. She watched, eyes half closed as he slipped the loose, plastic sleeves over his boots. She wasn't the first colleague to show an interest in Randle, but I didn't see it myself – his features were too chiselled, his face too ordered, even with the slight break to the nose. He had an easy way with people; he didn't view the desire to be liked as a weakness – a few more years on the job and he would be in no doubt that it was. We followed in silence as Lu led the way down the narrow corridor. Randle moved carefully behind me, head stooped to avoid the low ceiling. A naked bulb hung from a cable, illuminating the trail of bloody footsteps painting a path to the front door of the victim's flat.

We entered a bedsit with a bath and toilet tucked into the far corner; a polyester curtain had been pulled back to reveal a sink, the ceramic chipped on the side of the basin. Soiled clothes and empty bottles lay in small mounds on the torn linoleum. The air was thick with the scent of stale beer and bad wine, and a poorly made bed was crammed into one corner, too large for the space.

Sarah Franks must have been crawling towards help when her body had failed her. Blood spattered her torso with lines of red flowing from a wound on the side of her neck. Her right arm stretched towards a mobile phone she would never reach. Her eyes were open, dulled by death. The floor was littered with shattered porcelain and pizza crusts – I imagined her panic as her final meal slid from her lap. She was half dressed in a vest top and tattered tracksuit bottoms, heavily stained and ripped at the thigh. My first thought was to hope I was suitably clothed if I were ever found dead.

'I heard there was a suspect fleeing the scene,' I said. 'Where is he?'

Lu nodded.

'This way,' she said.

We moved down the stairs, out through a narrow doorway. The street at the back was much quieter, with none of the fanfare we had seen at the front. A lone police car was positioned opposite, half-hidden under a plane tree. An officer stood guard by the passenger door, legs splayed, chin determined. Beyond him, I could see the outline of a figure, hunched behind the seat.

Lu's voice was too loud in the silence.

'We found him running from the scene with blood on his shoes and hands.'

She opened the door and took a step back.

A man in an expensive blue shirt sat with his head angled away from us. Thick, black hair curled into the nape of his neck. His hands tugged at the linen of his tailored trousers; his shoulders rolled inwards. His wrists were red where the handcuffs had rubbed, olive skin beginning to bruise. He didn't look up at first, then he turned towards me.

'Leah,' he said. 'Leah Hutch.'

Chapter Three

Leah

The last time I saw Sami Mograbi, he didn't have blood on his shoes. He wore box-fresh white Nikes with the laces loose; he had a face that was full of promise, a laugh that forced me to smile. I studied the man in handcuffs through the glass, fingers clenched between his legs, head bent to shield his eyes. The interview room in Lu's station was larger than the ones I was used to – Sami looked slighter, more vulnerable than he had seemed in the car.

'How do you know him, ma'am?'

Randle's voice behind me – loud enough to hear, but soft so as not to startle.

I didn't need to turn; I knew he was watching me. We had been working together for over a year, but sometimes I still caught him trying to read me like it was a fundamental part of his job. Nine months had passed since he had risked his life on a case. I had thought he had been killed; the depth of my relief when I discovered he hadn't had taken me by surprise. We had never spoken about that night. He never pushed it, and his questions hovered between us, waiting for answers or lies.

'We were at school together for less than a year,' I said, concentrating on Sami Mograbi.

I could hear the shuffle of shoes muffled by a cough, as Randle shifted his weight behind me.

'Do you think he's hoping you'll take it easier on him because you know him?'

'If he thinks that, he doesn't know *me*,' I said.

He waited for me to say more, but I was comfortable with the silence. The soles of his boots squeaked against the vinyl floor as he began to move away.

'DS Hoffen said she'll brief you shortly.'

I could tell he was relieved when I finally looked at him.

'Stay,' I said.

Almost twenty minutes passed before Lu Hoffen stepped in to join us. We were on her territory, and she didn't want me to forget.

'Sorry to keep you waiting, ma'am.' Again, her eyes said something different. 'I was getting to grips with what we know.'

Randle smiled warmly, and Lu's face softened. Then her features sharpened as she relayed the basic facts.

'Sarah Franks, the victim, was a maths teacher. Known problem with alcohol. She struggled to hold down a full-time job and did supply work in the local school. Neighbour said she heard some sort of scuffle. Thought she heard a woman crying for help. She's old and scared. She called the police. So far, no sign of the murder weapon in Sarah's flat. I've got a team scouring the area. They may need to start again when it's light.' Lu inclined her head towards the captive behind the glass. 'When uniform arrived, they found a man trying to get away. The suspect said his name is Sami Mograbi. It matches the information on his driving licence. Full name – Samir Wassif Mograbi. Posh boy. Lives in Eaton Square. So far, his name's all he's given us. Wouldn't tell us anything more unless he could speak to you.'

'OK. I'm happy to help.'

She nodded. 'Good. I'm happy for you to sit in.'

The fluorescent light made her skin strangely luminous. I could see a cluster of faint freckles hiding behind the layer of foundation on her nose.

'No,' I said. Her lips parted in protest. 'I'll take Randle. You and I can have a full debrief afterwards. I expect you'll be watching, so you can keep up.'

I could see Lu's mind searching for a suitable objection, but I was halfway out of the room.

Chapter Four

Leah

Sami Mograbi sat across from me for the first time in twenty-one years; his grey eyes moved everywhere apart from my face. I started with formalities. He let his lawyer answer for him, shifting in his chair whenever I spoke. His hair was much shorter than I remembered, so the curls were almost invisible. With his olive skin, he had always been hard to place. He had hung around with the Jamaican boys when I knew him, switching from patois to London street slang with an ease that had never seemed fake. His real accent was more polished, but harder to identify; it came out when he was alone with me or reading aloud in class. When I had first met him, I had thought he was also mixed heritage, but he told me his family was pure Lebanese. He had lived in more countries than I had thought possible, but he said he felt more at home in London than anywhere else. I had last seen him when we were both sixteen, simultaneously bored and excited by life. His family had moved back to the UK so his father could pursue a business opportunity. When the opportunity led to Dubai, Sami disappeared from my world. He had tried to maintain contact, but I didn't see the point. Even as a teenager, I wasn't sentimental about friendship. I had learned that from Margaretta, my adoptive mother – she had never let anyone get close, including me. Now, less than a year after her death, I wondered if I had known her at all.

Seeing Sami again cracked open a time in my life I had almost forgotten. I studied the man who had fled the murder scene. The soft chin from adolescence had been replaced by a more prominent jaw; the mouth which had once seemed too large, almost clownlike, looked more at home in his adult face. He swallowed as he felt me observing him, hugging his body tighter. It was hard to tell if he was overwhelmed by guilt or fear.

'Tell me how you know the deceased.' I kept my voice neutral.

He nodded at his lawyer before he answered, dismissing the warm-up act.

'We were friends,' he said.

He looked at me for the first time.

'How did you meet?'

'In a bar in our early twenties. We got on. She's been in my life off and on ever since. I hadn't seen her for a while.'

He had lost all trace of the faint accent I remembered from hours talking about nothing. It was like speaking to a stranger; it made things simpler somehow.

'Were you ever involved romantically?' Crimes of passion were a cliché for a reason; I had to rule it out.

'No.' His face was earnest. 'Nothing like that.'

'What made you go round to see her, if you hadn't been in touch?'

Sami rubbed at the line that had formed between his eyebrows.

'We'd spoken a couple of weeks before. She was a mess. I'd called a few times since to check in.'

'What made you think she was a mess? Did she say anything explicit?'

'She was panicky. Anxious. She was drinking a lot. She thought someone was watching her. She didn't know if she was being paranoid.' He gazed at the door behind me. 'The drink made her jittery. She said she couldn't trust what was real.'

'Did you have any reason to believe she was being watched?'

'She . . .' Sami hesitated. He pressed his knuckles hard against his jaw. 'I hadn't seen her for a while. How could I know?'

'Why call you . . . of all people?'

'I don't know . . . I guess she trusted me.' A small shrug of his shoulders. 'She wanted someone to listen. She knew I would.'

It was in keeping with the boy I had known as a teenager; the young Sami Mograbi had been generous and kind.

'What made you go there tonight? Why not just another phone conversation?' Randle said. His features had lost their usual warmth. Lean and broad behind the small table, he looked imposing.

Sami's whole body tensed as he pulled the air in through his nostrils. Shaking with the effort to control his emotions, he drew his hand down over his face.

'Why?' I echoed Randle's question. 'What was different about tonight?'

'She begged me to come over . . . She sounded scared.' Sami's expression was pained.

I pushed my elbows into the table, leaning forwards. Sami flinched, shifting back.

'Was she alive when you got there?'

He didn't answer.

'It's a simple question, Sami. Yes or no?'

He shook his head. His breathing quickened. 'I don't think so . . . I didn't get close enough to be sure.'

'Did you see someone? Did you feel threatened?'

His lawyer tried to silence him, but his words tumbled out.

'No. I didn't see anyone . . . but someone had been there before me . . .'

He clutched the table, squeezing hard until the tips of his fingers turned white. 'I didn't kill her. You have to believe me.'

'Then why run? Why not call for help? You said she was your friend.'

Sami closed his eyes – an act of shame or evasion.

'If you did nothing, Sami, why did you run?'

His breath was loud and measured, as if he were counting the seconds. I sat back, unfazed.

'I didn't kill Sarah.' His words came out as a whisper.

'That's not an answer, Sami. Why did you run?'

Nothing.

'How do you explain the blood on your hands?'

He exhaled slowly. 'I slipped . . .' Another whisper. 'She was bleeding . . . There was blood. On her body . . . on the floor.'

Sami looked at me, unblinking, as if there was no one else in the room.

'I didn't do it, Leah. Sarah was terrified . . . Whoever killed her got away.'

Chapter Five

Zed

Zechariah Okoro was longing for a growth spurt he knew would never come. At fourteen, it wasn't that he was short for his age; he had grown fast, and he had grown first, but Zed only had to look at his father to know he was destined to spend life as an adult constantly gazing up. He had spent hours hanging from a pull-up bar the previous summer, because he'd read it might help him gain an inch or two. He doubted it was true, but he had always been an optimist, and he preferred to live in hope. He had yet to fill out, but he was already athletic, lean muscle starting to form on his shoulders and arms. His resting face possessed the sweetness of a boy much younger, but he had perfected a look of bored indifference, so he seemed tougher, and the bullies left him alone. He had spent the last two weeks at camp counting the days until his real holiday began – time at home with his mother, relaxed in a way he never was with others, hanging out, having fun. His mother was conflicted about her working-class roots and middle-class lifestyle. She sent him to a predominantly white private school, where there was only one other black boy in his year. Then he came home to Ladbroke Grove, where he never noticed the colour of his skin. He knew he had more than the families in the estate up the street, but every summer, his mum made him go to a camp with inner-city kids, so he never forgot his head start in life was undeserved.

It was still morning, but it was already warm, and he wished he had worn shorts. His dark jeans felt like tents around his skinny legs; he could feel the sweat behind his knees. He stepped off the bus and stared up, squinting at the sun glaring back at him in the bright blue sky. Zed loved the sun, but it wasn't the heat that appealed to him – it was the only time he didn't feel weak when he was forced to look away. He hovered on the pavement, waiting for his mother to meet him as planned, keeping his stance wide so he took up more space. She had sent him a letter with a bucket list for the summer. She often had to travel for work, but this year, she had taken time off, and he felt a surge of excitement knowing she would be around. He would never admit it to another soul, but she was his favourite person in the world.

He pulled out his phone, dialling her number, but there was no reply. His rucksack felt heavy against his torso. He eased it off, so he could relieve the pressure on his back. His T-shirt was damp, and he wafted the fabric, peeling the material away from his skin. A stranger stopped to ask if he was OK; he scowled at her, shoulders set, until she gave up and turned away. He craned his neck, eyes searching for his mother. The sun grew hotter as he waited beneath it. She still didn't come.

Chapter Six

Leah

It was late morning when I headed to work. We had left Lu Hoffen in the early hours, but Sami hadn't said much more. I didn't want to believe that the boy I had known could be a killer, but I had no allegiance to the man he now was. I could see Albert Bridge up ahead, pink and white paint catching the sun. Joggers thudded down the Embankment wearing the minimum they could get away with, flaunting their flesh, desperate to get a tan. My phone rang. I glanced at it but didn't answer – it was the estate agent with news about Margaretta's house. Margaretta – my adoptive mother, whom I'd discovered was also my biological grandmother, but only after her death almost ten months ago. She had left me her house, but I didn't want it. Even though I knew she had been trying to protect me, it didn't make up for the lies. When I was eighteen, she had told me she had a son in prison – I had no idea he was my father until three weeks after she died. She let me discover the truth alone, taking the answers I craved to the grave.

I pushed my hands deep into my pockets. My cotton trousers were cut close around my hips, so my fingers pressed against my thighs. I could feel the tension in my body, and I put Margaretta to the back of my mind, my thoughts on Sami once again. It was hard to believe he was a killer, and I was glad it was Lu's case, not mine. The bridge shuddered under the weight of traffic as I made my way across the Thames. Battersea Park loomed to my left, a mecca for workshy sunbathers, subscribing to the common British fear that the sun might never return.

As I neared the station, I could see Akosua outside, eyes closed as she leant against the grey brick. Her dark skin had deepened in colour, and her afro was pulled into cornrows to keep her head cool.

'Don't let me stop you, DC Owusu.'

She stood to attention, her back so straight I almost expected a salute.

'Sorry, ma'am. Just taking a breather.'

I said nothing, heading for the door.

There was no air conditioning in the building. I wasn't an advocate of wasting taxpayers' money, but I struggled to believe the Met couldn't stretch to a few fans. The higher levels were almost unbearable, and we were stuck on the fourth floor. I could hear Akosua talking behind me, but I tuned her out. She had a habit of repeating herself – if it was important, she knew how to make herself heard. I caught sight of Kenny O'Sullivan, my DCI, in front of the lifts. He had his back to me, his large frame straining against his dark jacket. I wasn't in the mood for an interrogation, so I slipped through the entrance to the stairs.

Randle was finishing up on a call as I passed his desk, sleeves above his elbows so I could see the bruises on his arms. A year ago, he would have felt self-conscious, but I knew he raced his motorbike and sometimes took a corner too fast. His eyes were tired when he turned towards me.

'That was Lu Hoffen with an update, ma'am.'

My face frowned before I could stop it. 'I don't remember Lu being the chatty type.'

'I don't know, ma'am.' Randle's eyes were laughing. 'Maybe she's more of a morning person, and we caught her on a bad night.'

I continued to my office, so he had to follow behind me. He stopped by the door, head to one side.

'What did she say, Randle? I don't need a build-up.'

'Still no sign of the murder weapon. They're checking CCTV.'

'Anything from Sarah's phone?'

He nodded. 'Phone records show that Sarah Franks called Sami Mograbi earlier that night, so at least Sami wasn't lying about that.'

'You think he was lying about the rest of it?'

I read his face in case his words told a different story.

'I don't know, ma'am.' Randle shrugged. 'He literally had blood on his hands . . .'

The window was stiff as my fingers pushed up against the frame. It resisted for a second, then opened with a screech.

'I can find out more . . . if it's helpful . . . from Lu.'

I said nothing.

'She suggested we go for a drink.'

I eased into my chair and switched on my computer. There was a loud ping as the screen flashed to life.

'Your personal life's your business, Randle. If I need to talk to DS Hoffen, I think I'm able to pick up the phone.'

I saw the red creep across his cheeks before he turned to hide the blush. When he looked back at me, his face was earnest.

'Do you think Sami's capable of murder, ma'am? I know it was a long time ago, but you knew him once.'

I thought of the case that had almost broken me the year before – seemingly innocent people driven to do terrible things.

'I don't know what he's capable of,' I said, 'but you can't stab someone in the neck without a weapon. Sami was clean when they found him. If he killed Sarah Franks, where's the knife?'

Chapter Seven

Zed

Zed waited in the sun for close to two hours. He had used the last of his water to wash the sweat from his face, and his throat almost hurt it felt so dry. He had called his mother repeatedly from his mobile, but her phone was switched off. He rummaged through his rucksack for the bank card she had given him for emergencies. He couldn't see it at first and he panicked, then he felt the thin plastic wrapped in paper against his hand. It was still in the envelope his mother had placed it in – *URGENT USE ONLY* scribbled in black on the front. He took out the card, folding the envelope carefully. He didn't know why, but he felt it was important to keep. He tucked the paper into his pocket and hoisted his bag back onto his shoulders, shrinking under the weight.

The tube was crowded with irritable commuters. No one gave him a second glance, and he almost got caught in the doors as they slid shut. Born and raised in London, he was used to the Underground, and he found the sense of claustrophobia strangely comforting. He looked down at his trainers, avoiding eye contact with strangers. He couldn't believe his mother had forgotten to pick him up. He tried to remember whether he had given her the wrong date, but he was sure he had handed her the letter, and all the information had been right there. He wondered whether something had happened to her on the way to collect him. Then he put the thought out of his mind.

The mass of passengers had thinned by the time the train pulled into Ladbroke Grove station, and he felt a sense of anticipation as he climbed the steps towards the exit. A small man with long arms was playing the saxophone, his whole body vibrating as he filled the street with jazz. Zed had decided he didn't like that kind of music because his father always played it. He had never really allowed himself to listen, and he paused for a second, moved by the sound. He turned and walked up past Cambridge and Oxford Gardens, the song of the saxophone still loud in his ears. He was in a hurry to get home, but he kept his steps slow and deliberate – the rucksack screamed 'outsider', and he was keen to blend in. As he approached the council estate to his left, a group of older boys called out to him. He kept walking, lifting his chin in acknowledgement. They nodded, losing interest as they went back to their beers. Zed exhaled with relief as he continued past them. He didn't need any trouble; he just needed to see his mum.

A girl, roughly his age, was sitting on the wall further up the street, staring down at her fingers. As he got closer, he could see she had looped thick purple wool so it criss-crossed around each digit in an elaborate spider's web.

'It's a cat's cradle.' Her cheeks creased into a grin. 'They're really fun.'

Her pride in playing a children's game took him aback.

'Do you want a go?' she said.

Zed looked at her, surprised. He was popular in a way that didn't require friends – aloof and seemingly confident, he was admired by his peers from afar. He relied on his scowl to keep people at arm's length, but the girl was watching him expectantly, waiting for a reply. He gripped the straps of his bag and moved on without a word.

The gate was closed when finally he arrived at his house. He was comforted by the sight of the large white building with the heavy green door, and he lifted his rucksack off his back, pulling it behind him up the steps to the entrance. He and his mum had the ground floor and the level above. The basement flat was empty, and an elderly man lived at the top. Zed occasionally saw a carer, but the old man struggled with his mobility and seldom ventured out. Inside, the hallway was cool and dark, sheltered from the sun. There were a few envelopes scattered on the carpet. The sight of them made him uneasy; it was unlike his mother not to pick up the post. The door to their flat lay to the right a few feet in front of him. He had looked forward to this moment every day for the last week, but now he was afraid to go in.

The door squealed open as he turned the key, stepping into the familiar sitting room – L-shaped grey sofa on the oval navy rug, large flat screen for playing his favourite video games.

'Mum?' He waited. 'Mum? You here?'

No response.

The kitchen was immaculate, as always. The dishwasher was full, but it hadn't been turned on. Upstairs was quiet, and his footsteps sounded heavy. He pushed open his mother's bedroom door gently. She never slept during the day, but maybe she was ill and had lain down to rest. The room was empty, the bed neatly made.

Zed silenced the panic starting to rise within him, searching for his father's number on his phone. He couldn't remember the last time he had called it, and he almost hung up, unsure how the conversation would play out.

'Yes?' His dad sounded surprised. 'Zechariah, is that you?'

Zed nodded, then realised his father couldn't see him. 'Hi, Dad.'

'What is it, Zechariah? Have I mixed up the dates?'

He stayed with his dad one weekend a month, unless his mother travelled for work. He dreaded it, and he often wondered if his father noticed he was there.

'No. Did Mum call you?'

'Why would she call me?'

The click of fingers on a keyboard rattled in the background – he hated it when adults were pretending to pay attention but doing something else.

'Zechariah? Is everything OK?'

For a moment, he thought about sharing his fears, but his father had never shown any interest in either him or his mother, never said a kind word about the woman who had once been his wife. No. He didn't want his mum to get into trouble. Whatever had happened, he would deal with it himself.

'Everything's fine. Got to go. She just got back.'

He hung up, knowing his father would be too relieved to question him. The silence unnerved him when he put the phone away.

He stared at the king-sized bed with the cream cotton duvet. Maybe his mother had had to travel suddenly for work – it had happened before. She usually called him and made arrangements with his father, but maybe she had run out of time; maybe the battery on her mobile had died before the plane had taken off. He yanked at her bedside drawer, rifling through the notebooks and papers. She never travelled without her laptop, and he was encouraged when it wasn't there. Then he remembered she slept on the other side. He walked around the bed and pulled the drawer open, willing it to be empty, but the sleek, silver machine was stored safely inside.

Chapter Eight

Leah

'Akosua.'

Her head swivelled away from her computer screen. She moved too fast, her elbow bumping against a pile of Post-its, scattering the coloured squares across the floor.

'Yes, ma'am?'

She ignored the blocks of paper cascading around her feet, eagerly awaiting instruction. She hadn't paused the footage she had been watching, and the glare from the CCTV images reflected on her face. An old woman had been found dead in a nearby alley. A group of teenage boys had been caught kicking her on camera, before they stole her purse and spat in her face. It had taken two days for anyone to care enough to report the crime.

'I need you to give that to someone else and check some CCTV from Elephant and Castle for the last couple of weeks. Randle can give you the name of the street.'

Akosua grinned back at me. She welcomed mundane tasks she could excel at. I couldn't fault her keenness, but I wasn't convinced she had the imagination to turn her ambition into success.

'What am I looking for?'

'Randle will brief you. You'll know when you see it,' I said.

Sami had insisted Sarah had felt she was being watched. It wasn't my case, but something didn't sit right, and I owed it to Sami to ask the questions I knew Lu Hoffen would not.

'Ma'am . . .'

Randle was on his feet as I turned back towards my office.

'What?'

I know it's not our case, but just do what I say.

I stared at him, daring him to challenge me; I almost didn't see the envelope he was holding out.

'This came for you, ma'am.'

He pressed the paper into my hand. I glanced at it. I recognised the writing, and my body froze.

My biological father had been writing to me every month since I had last seen him. The first two letters had been brief, almost taunting. The next one had quoted lines from the Bible, even though he didn't believe in God. I had stopped reading them after that. I strode back to my office, burying the envelope in my bag beneath my wallet. Paranoid someone might find it, I slid it into my trouser pocket instead. I took pains to keep a line between the private and the professional, and I was furious with him for violating my code. I wanted no evidence of my association with him in my workplace. It was bad enough that he had once been a revered detective and had trained with my DCI, Kenny O'Sullivan. Kenny had no reason to suspect we were related – Margaretta had changed my name when I was a child – but my body tensed just knowing his letter was in my pocket. I was relieved when my phone rang before my anger could rise.

'Hutch?' It was Frank, the duty sergeant. *He* had rung *me*, but he sounded unsure.

'Speaking,' I said.

'Man on the line for you. Said it's urgent. Wouldn't give a name. Do you want me to put him through?'

'Sure.'

The hollow sound of nothing as he placed me on hold, then a voice, low and accusing, filled the void.

'Leah Hutch?' He didn't wait for an answer. 'This is Zikar Mograbi. You interrogated my son.'

Chapter Nine

Leah

I let Randle drive so I could familiarise myself with the basic facts about Zikar Mograbi – Sami's father, a man I had never met. He had made his money in the silver trade, then real estate; he gave interviews about his humble beginnings and the power of hard work.

'Why does he want to see you, ma'am?' Randle's touch on the wheel was gentle as he guided the car into the neighbouring lane. He looked completely at peace when he drove – leaning back, arm outstretched, fingers tapping whatever beat was playing in his head. Thick dark lashes covered his eyes; if I didn't know better, I'd have thought they were closed, but Randle was always watching, always alert.

'I don't know.'

Randle's lips curled into a smile. He glanced at me, quietly amused. I wasn't in the business of playing the hero. I took orders when I needed to – it made life simpler at work – but Zikar Mograbi wasn't my superior. I could have refused his request to see me and sent him to Lu without a second thought. The truth was, I was intrigued. I had gone to Sami's house during our brief acquaintance, but looking back, my visits had been stage-managed so his father was never around. Sami had spent more time at the home I shared with Margaretta. Margaretta was never warm, but she was welcoming in her own way.

'Does he know you know Sami, ma'am?'

Randle's voice interrupted my thoughts.

'It was a long time ago. It wasn't significant. I doubt Sami would have mentioned it.'

Randle manoeuvred the car around a sharp corner. His head was turned so I couldn't see his eyes. 'Maybe it was significant for him,' he said.

We turned into Eaton Square, with its characterless grandeur – five-storey townhouses with columns and white stucco façades, offering tranquillity in the centre of London for an unimaginable price. We were less than two miles from the estate where I lived, and I was struck by the contradictions of a city where such different worlds could co-exist. I remembered visiting the house for the first time as a teenager, shocked rather than impressed by the scale. I was surprised the Mograbis had kept it after the move to Dubai, but they were rich enough not to notice the cost.

Zikar Mograbi opened his front door himself, Burberry cardigan over cashmere crewneck that made little sense, given the weather, until we stepped inside. The house was invitingly cool, air conditioning set to the perfect temperature. Zikar Mograbi was barefoot.

'I don't know why Londoners are always surprised by the heat. It happens sometimes, albeit briefly. No excuse not to be prepared.'

He glanced at our feet and waited. Randle already had one boot off. I noticed Zikar Mograbi's perfect pedicure as I followed suit.

'You have a lovely house.' Randle's tone was polite without being obsequious. He had chosen his words carefully – the decor was tasteful, the furniture expensive, just as I remembered it, but the Mograbi residence had never felt like a home.

Zikar led us into a formal room with high ceilings and wide bay windows. An antique Rococo-style mirror dominated the far wall. The space had been designed to showcase wealth, instead of offering comfort; my toes sank into the plush carpet like they were moving through sand.

'I bought the house over twenty years ago. Sami's very fond of the place. He's always seen himself as British, even when others see something else.'

Zikar crossed to the mantelpiece and retrieved a remote control. There was a gentle whirr as the curtains drifted back, revealing an intimate garden behind with yellow roses and foxgloves around a small pond.

'The best view in the house. Sami has the same one from his bedroom. I converted the top floor into a flat.' He paused so we could acknowledge his generosity. 'I'm hardly here, but I appreciate my son needs his space.'

My eyes drifted to a photograph of Sami on the table in front of us, standing next to Zikar, eyes disappearing as he beamed with genuine delight.

'That was taken when he went up to Oxford,' Zikar said. 'So much promise, but potential's never been Sami's problem.'

'What has?' I couldn't resist the question.

'Sami's always been an idealist. I've tried to protect him, but maybe he needed toughening up. Please . . .'

He gestured towards the yellow sofa in front of us, large satin cushions propped against a mahogany frame. There was a low marble table in front – on it, an elaborate china tea set. Zikar took a seat in the armchair on the other side.

I perched on the edge of the sofa to stop myself from drowning in the dense fabric. Randle sat back, his long legs rooted on the floor.

'Thank you for making the time.' Zikar Mograbi hadn't stopped watching me. His dark eyes glistened with an intensity that raised my guard.

'It must be urgent. By all accounts, you're a hard man to meet,' I said.

'I can easily be found if you know how. I blame middle management. Getting in the way to appear more important.' His smile was almost charming. 'A good businessman will always see you, because he's always on the lookout for the next opportunity.'

'And what opportunity would this be, Mr Mograbi?'

The smile was forgotten as his face hardened. 'This isn't about business, Inspector. This is about my son.'

I sat up, ready to combat the coming aggression. 'As I mentioned on the phone, this isn't my case.'

'Humour me.' The smile was back, so polished it even reached his eyes. 'I flew into London this morning and was welcomed by a journalist, eager for my opinion on what happened to my son . . . what's happening . . .' he said, correcting himself. 'Update me, Inspector, if you would be so kind.'

'If you want an update, I'm sure DS Hoffen will oblige.'

I pulled out my card, checking my notes for Lu Hoffen's number before scribbling it on the back.

'It's not our investigation.'

I pushed the card across the table. Zikar didn't bother to look down.

'But it was *your* interrogation. *You* questioned him. He's still in custody. Forgive me for thinking that has something to do with you.'

I sensed Randle tense beside me. I flashed him a look that warned him not to react. Men like Zikar Mograbi existed in an echo chamber of assent; he wasn't used to being told no, but it wasn't a word I was scared to say.

'I'm afraid I can't help you. Sami won't be in the station much longer.' I smiled back at him. 'They'll charge him or release him. At the very worst, he'll be bailed or moved to a nearby prison. Police stations aren't known for having a lot of space.'

Zikar reached for the teapot, calling a truce.

'How do you like it?'

I watched him pour. 'No milk. No sugar. Please.'

'It's funny how the English avoid hot drinks during the summer. I find them refreshing.' His eyes fixed on mine. 'Don't you?'

There it was – he thought I would be sympathetic because I looked 'other'. I almost expected him to ask me where I was from, but point made, Zikar had already moved on. He held out the cup, half filled with brown liquid. His fingers gripped the saucer as I reached for it, so I was compelled to look at him. His eyes were dark, unlike Sami's, penetrating instead of kind.

'I'll be clear with you, Miss Hutch.' He had lost the 'inspector'. 'I need you and your colleagues to stop harassing my son. It won't look good for you if valuable police time is wasted, and the case gets thrown out of court.'

'I'm afraid police time often gets wasted, Mr Mograbi. It's an unfortunate hazard of the job.' I took a sip of my tea, missing the sharp hit I got from coffee. I gave up and put the cup down.

'DS Hoffen and her team will do a thorough investigation. If there's not enough evidence to charge Sami, he'll be released.'

'And in the meantime, people can say what they like about my family?'

'We're the police.' I kept my tone light. 'We don't work in PR.'

He sighed. The aggression was gone. 'My son doesn't belong in a police station.'

'If he's done nothing wrong,' my voice was gentler, 'he'll soon be a free man.'

I got up and reached out my hand in the space between us. Zikar ignored it.

'Thank you for the tea,' I said.

His eyes searched mine over his white china cup.

'Can I ask – are you looking for other suspects?'

'Even if I were allowed to tell you, I couldn't. I don't know the specifics of the case.'

'But you do know my son?' He had my full attention. 'Childhood friends. I hear you go way back.'

The phrase sounded forced in his precise, studied accent.

'I knew your son for a short period of time a very long time ago. That doesn't make us friends, and it doesn't affect my job.'

'Forgive me . . . I wasn't trying to imply . . .' He held up his hands in faux remorse. 'I didn't invite you here to offend you, Inspector. I want to help the fine institution you work for – save us all time, before this gets blown out of proportion and ruins my son's life.'

He reached under the tray and pulled out a thin paper file.

'What's this?' I took it and flicked it open: a mugshot of a woman I had never seen before stared back at me – red face, lank hair, eyes that had forgotten to hope. Behind the photograph were two sheets of A4 with snatches of information printed across each page.

'Sarah Franks was a drug addict, not just an alcoholic,' Zikar said.

I studied the woman in the file.

'Where did you get this?'

'Does it matter? If I want something, I get it, and I want my son freed,' he said.

'If that's all . . .'

I offered my hand; this time he took it. When I pulled back, he didn't let go.

'The woman in the photograph is called Tipper Wheldon. She's Sarah Franks' drug dealer. Goes by the name "Tip". Maybe your colleagues should be looking into her, not my son.'

Chapter Ten

Leah

We didn't speak until we were on the other side of the square from the house. Randle reached in his pocket, pulling out a lone cigarette.

'Do you mind, ma'am?'

I could tell he needed it. 'Be my guest.'

I watched him as his cheeks collapsed inwards, his jaw more defined as he pulled on the filter.

'What's up with you?'

He exhaled, watching the haze of smoke as it drifted away.

'He reminds me of my grandfather. Everything's a powerplay.'

Randle came from privilege. I had assumed he knew nothing of the London most people experienced each day, then he had told me about his mother, kicked out by his grandfather when she got pregnant with him. His early years had been spent on a council estate in North London until his grandfather had dangled the carrot of comfort and a private education, and his mother had returned to Hampstead for the good of her boy.

We arrived at the car, and I held up my hand for the keys. Randle flicked them over the roof, savouring the last drag of his cigarette before he crushed it under his boot. We drove without speaking, our thoughts filling the silence. Zikar Mograbi was a bully, but his efforts had been in vain. I didn't doubt that he loved his son, but he probably cared more about his reputation. He wasn't interested in Sami's guilt or innocence; he just needed the story to go away.

I preferred Sami to be innocent, but if he had killed Sarah Franks, he needed to face the consequences – our shared history wouldn't help his case. I lowered my foot on the brake and flipped the indicator, pivoting sharply in the middle of the road. Zikar Mograbi wasn't my problem. Lu Hoffen was welcome to him. I pushed down on the accelerator. I was feeling generous – she could have Tip Wheldon too.

'Nothing for ten years and then twice in twenty-four hours.'

Lu's eyes were cold as she sat behind her computer, a half-eaten sandwich in front of her, the tomatoes picked out. She leant back, watching us approach as the red pulp seeped into a napkin. The officer escorting us hesitated, unsure whether he had done the right thing.

'Thanks for bringing them up, Mikey.' Lu took her time to stand. 'I'll take it from here.'

A smile for Randle, nothing for me.

'Ben. Leah. How can I help you?' she said.

It obviously pained her to call me ma'am. She studied my face for signs I cared.

'Sami's father asked to see me.'

Her eyes were already offended. 'Zikar Mograbi? What did he want?'

I handed her Tip Wheldon's file.

'Gave us details about your victim's drug dealer. He thinks he's entitled to have his son released.'

'Does he now . . .'

She placed the file by her computer without glancing at it, barely avoiding the damp napkin, red with tomato juice. She almost smiled as she reached for her mouse. Directing the cursor towards a file, she clicked it open on the screen. The image had been blown up and was heavily pixilated. A figure in black, in motion, their face covered, appeared. I recognised the street behind Sarah Franks' flat.

'Balaclava doesn't help, but we've got a new suspect.'

Randle leant forwards to get a closer look. 'How do you know it's not Sami?' he said.

'We tracked them further afield than where we found Sami – he only made it a couple of streets from Sarah's house before we picked him up.'

'What happened to the figure in the balaclava? How far did you track them?'

'Not far.' Lu pulled out a printout of a map from under her sandwich, tracing a route with her finger. 'We got a visual up to here, then nothing.'

'The killer must have known where the cameras are,' I said. 'Sarah thought she was being watched. Have you checked the CCTV in the run-up to the murder to see if there are signs of anyone keeping tabs on the house?'

I had asked Akosua to look into it, because I suspected Lu wouldn't make it a priority. When she crossed her arms over her thin torso, I knew I had been right.

'Of course.' The words came out too sharp before she could soften them. 'Nothing unusual jumps out. Sarah was an addict; it's possible she was paranoid. We could be looking at a burglary gone wrong.'

Randle's eyes flicked between us. He kept his tone neutral when he spoke. 'There were no obvious signs of breaking and entering.'

'Doesn't mean it didn't happen.' Lu's voice was less defensive. 'Every good burglar knows how to pick a lock.'

'Was anything taken?' I said.

'Difficult to tell.' Her hands slipped into her pockets. 'You saw the flat. Sarah was hardly a fan of feng shui.'

It was a weak joke, but Randle acknowledged it with the lift of an eyebrow. Buoyed by the encouragement, Lu visibly relaxed. She turned to me, unsmiling.

'Thank you for your help, Leah, but I think we can take it from here.' Her gaze shifted back to the figure in the balaclava. 'Tell Zikar Mograbi it's his lucky day: Sami's in the clear.'

Chapter Eleven

Leah

It was well into the evening, but it was still light. I had forgotten to lower my blinds, and the glare from outside warmed my sitting room with a comforting glow. Sami Mograbi had come in and out of my life in twenty-four hours – a brief flirtation with the past. I could feel the envelope ruining the line of my trousers. I pulled it out, baulking at my name in black capital letters. I flung it on the pile of envelopes by the door with *LEAH HUTCH* in the same emphatic scrawl. A group of teenagers huddled outside the window, watching me with disinterest. I pulled down the blinds so I was no longer on display.

I moved through to my bedroom. My book of nightmares sat next to the clock on the table, the fore-edge crinkled from water spilt in my haste to record a dream. I eased the pages apart, scanning my incoherent scribbles – half sentences, vague sketches, phonetic sounds. I had taken to pointing the clock towards the wall, so I didn't torture myself on the nights I struggled to sleep. I swivelled it towards me, then immediately regretted it, conscious of the hours stretching before me until I could officially start the next day. Skipping helped clear my mind, tiring my body to persuade it to sleep. I rolled up my trousers, pushing my feet into a pair of trainers and headed for my skipping rope, nestled by the front door. As I reached for it, I caught sight of the small stack of mail, the most recent envelope taunting me. The words *LEAH HUTCH* shouted for attention in angry black letters. I ripped it open before I could overthink. The note was brief, as always, staccato in tone.

How's the rage? Under control? I need to see you. E.

Chapter Twelve

Zed

Zed woke up with his arms wrapped round his mother's pillow. No one could see him, but he pushed it away. He rolled over and straightened the covers, mindful of how his mum liked her bed made. As he folded the sheet under the mattress, he remembered a time when he was very small – there had been a lot of shouting and tears. One day his father arrived late to collect him from nursery; it was always his mother who came for him, and Zed had cried without knowing why. When they got home, his mother wasn't there. She didn't come the next day, or the one after that. He had sat on the stairs, watching the door. Another twenty-four hours passed before it opened, and his mother was standing there. She was sorry. She would never leave him again. She promised she would always come back. He remembered the tearful encounter as he reached for the pillow he had thrown on the floor, setting it carefully against the headboard. Something must have come up; his mum would be home in a couple of days.

He tried to think of the adults who had visited her. Even if he knew how to reach them, he was too afraid to call. There were kids at camp in foster care because their parents couldn't look after them. He had heard the horror stories about social services, seen the dead look in their eyes when they played games. He knew no one would understand if he told them about his mother, and he couldn't risk being taken away.

There was a box of eggs in the fridge and half a packet of poached salmon. He hadn't eaten the night before, but the smell made him nauseous, and he threw the salmon in the bin. He brushed his teeth and flicked a comb through his hair so he looked presentable. He made a mental list of essentials to get from the shop: milk, bread, ham, cornflakes, Skittles if they had them. Then he wrote the items on his palm in case he forgot.

London looked the same as it always did as he stepped onto the front step – a collection of individuals constantly in motion, oblivious to everyone else. No one looked at him with any interest – he just had to keep his head down, and everything would be OK. It was cooler than it was in the house, and he closed his eyes for a second to let the breeze catch his face. He felt for the bank card in his pocket, reassured by the gentle flex of plastic. As he neared the council estate, he could see the girl from the previous day on the wall up ahead. He crossed the road so she wouldn't see him, continuing towards the shop. She was still there ten minutes later when he walked back, the plastic bag of provisions bouncing against the side of his calf. She looked up as if she had been waiting for him, her fingers bent in a half-hearted attempt at a wave. Her heels kicked against the concrete – he was struck by how long and narrow her feet were. She was sitting down, but he had always been good with dimensions, and he guessed she was maybe an inch or two taller than him. She had a mass of curly dark hair that fell in a centre parting. Her light brown skin was peppered with faint freckles; the bridge of her nose was thin like her feet. She laughed when she noticed him looking at her. Zed bristled.

'Sorry.' She had the decency to blush. 'I do that when I'm nervous. I'm Seema. Seema Jackson. My mum's Indian, my dad's Jamaican . . . People always ask . . .'

He hadn't.

'What's your name?' she continued when he didn't say a word.

Up close, he realised she was younger than he had thought at first – twelve or thirteen at the most. Her 'Little Miss Busy' T-shirt was too small for her torso, her orange shorts slightly ripped above the hem.

'I normally see your mum running in the morning. She always smiles at me. I haven't seen her for a few days.'

Zed wrestled with the instinct to attack her with questions – *When did you last see my mother? Where was she heading? Did she look OK?* – but Seema's face was too open, her mouth too active; he couldn't trust her with his secrets, so he kept his questions to himself.

'Why are you nervous?' he said as he watched her. He noticed she blushed under his gaze. 'My name's Zed,' he said, to give her something else on which to focus.

Seema nodded, her cheeks still red. She slid off the wall, each limb moving like it belonged to someone else. She was easily two inches taller, but she dipped her head, reducing the gap by an inch. It had seemed like she wanted to talk to him, but now he had finally spoken, she looked like she wanted him to stop. Confused, he plunged his hands into his pockets and started to move away.

'Where's your mum?' he heard her say behind him.

He was grateful she couldn't see the panic in his eyes. He pushed his features into a scowl before he turned back towards her.

'She has a big job. She goes away a lot.' The words came out quickly.

Seema gasped in wonder. 'My mum would never let me stay on my own.'

'My dad stays the night when she's away.' Zed's pupils shifted; he had never been a good liar.

'Oh . . .' Seema glanced up under her lashes. 'I've never seen him.' She was looking beyond him. 'Is that him?'

They were about fifty feet from his house, but he could see the entrance clearly. A man stood looking up at the front window, completely still across the road. He wore a thin sweatshirt with a hood, his face hidden behind the material.

'Why's he just standing there? Why doesn't he go in?' Seema said.

Zed looked at her, his eyes pleading for silence. When he turned back towards his house again, the man had gone.

Chapter Thirteen

Leah

How's the rage? Under control?

I asked myself the same question every day, but now the voice in my head wasn't my own. I saw my biological father's face, blue eyes unblinking. The morning was pleasantly warm, the sun shielded behind a cloud. I remembered how Margaretta had loved the sun, even in winter, and I pictured the aviator sunglasses she wore every summer, replacing them with identical ones when the lenses got scratched. I had had moments of rage as a child, and more recently, under immense provocation. I hadn't had an outburst in months, but I hadn't been tested, and I knew the tension that simmered beneath the surface still threatened to explode. Exercise helped me stay calm, and the skin at the base of my fingers was calloused from hours spent gripping my skipping rope.

The street was relatively quiet as I turned towards the station. There was a man begging opposite the building, eyes focused on the grey brick around the door. He wore an orange scarf in a loose knot despite the weather, draped over a red string vest. No one gave him a second glance, but he seemed skittish. When he saw me step towards the entrance, he shifted his weight – ready to escape the moment anyone in uniform so much as looked his way.

Upstairs, the bullpen felt muggy, even though the windows were open. There were too many bodies, and the air struggled to move. My team barely looked up as I passed them, too much energy already expended sweating. Neither Randle nor Akosua were at their desks. I was greeted by a shiny afro when I reached my office. Akosua was crouched on the floor by the window. When she stood up, I saw she had plugged in a square fan.

'I had a couple spare lying around the house, ma'am.'

I didn't believe her – a thoughtful gesture, or an attempt to garner praise.

'You didn't need to, but thanks. Any progress on the Sarah Franks CCTV?'

'A figure in a balaclava can be seen outside the house a short time before the police arrived. I saved stills of the image . . .'

'I've seen them.'

A flicker of disappointment, then her eyes sparkled. 'That's not the only thing . . . There's a car driving past the house every day during the period you asked me to look at, but not the week of the murder.'

'Maybe the owner lives in the area.'

'Maybe . . .' Her brow furrowed as she debated whether to continue. 'It drove past two or three times each day with the windows up. Sometimes it slowed down, but never directly in front of Sarah's flat.'

'Did you get a registration plate?'

'No . . . Not for those days, but I checked the surrounding streets, and I caught it turning – I managed to get the plate . . .'

She paused, her face expectant.

'And?'

'It belongs to a man named Ray King. I have his details on my desk. Do you want me to email them to you or direct to the team in Elephant and Castle?'

'Just me – for now.'

I couldn't count on Lu Hoffen to prioritise the follow-up, and there was no guarantee this was part of her case.

'Do we know who was actually driving the car?'

'The windows were up when the car was in close proximity to Sarah's flat,' Akosua said. 'Further afield, there are images with the window down. We've checked – it's definitely Ray King.'

I was already moving towards the door. 'Tell Randle to meet me downstairs.'

Chapter Fourteen

Leah

He was standing exactly where the beggar had been. The first thought I had was: *You grew tall.*

He had seemed shorter hunched in the back of the police car; even smaller cowering opposite me in the bleak interview room, begging me to believe he had done nothing wrong. His black hair was wild and unbrushed. Lack of sleep had deepened the lines beside his mouth. Grey shadows had thickened under his eyes like smears of oil paint. It was the face of a man hardened by stress, then he saw me, and he was the sixteen-year-old boy again. He weaved through the moving cars with an energy that surprised me. He was two feet away when I finally spoke.

'Coincidence?'

'No.'

His shirt was made of good cotton, but traces of sweat had seeped through under the arms.

'You should try a T-shirt in this weather.'

He smiled, falling back into a long-forgotten rhythm. 'I'll bear that in mind.'

'What are you doing here?'

'I wanted to see you.'

'What makes you think this is a good idea?'

'I didn't think.'

Uncertainty distorted each feature, and his arms dangled awkwardly.

'How's Margaretta?' He grasped for something to say.

'Margaretta died.' It was meant to sound curt, but it came out broken. I saw my own sadness reflected in his eyes.

'I'm sorry.' He reached out, then let his hand fall. 'I know what she meant to you.'

I recovered quickly.

'Sami, what are you doing here?' I said again.

He shrugged. 'Saying thank you.'

My tone was harsh. 'I had nothing to do with your release.'

'Of course. I know. But I needed to say thank you all the same.'

'For what?'

'For answering the call, for coming.' He dropped his gaze. 'I wasn't sure you would.'

He took a step towards me. His limbs were long, and he was suddenly too close.

'Leah. Leah, I need to . . .'

His voice was urgent; I could see the spheres of his pupils dilating, then his eyes drifted over my head. I followed his gaze, watching Randle's familiar shape moving towards us – his long torso widening into broad shoulders, white shirt open at the neck. His face was wiped of all expression. I paused, expecting a smile to emerge, but he just looked out onto the street behind me. When I turned, Sami was walking away.

Chapter Fifteen

Leah

'I didn't mean to interrupt, ma'am.'

'You didn't.'

I pushed too hard on the accelerator. I touched the brake, bringing the car under control.

'What did he want?'

Even if I knew, I didn't owe Randle an answer. I pressed back into my seat, relaxing my hands on the wheel.

'He reminds me of boys from school.' Randle's voice was bitter. 'Brought up to believe that every mess can be cleaned up with charm.'

The car stumbled over a speedbump as we joined the queue of cars approaching Albert Bridge.

'Sami's not his father, Randle,' I said.

I flipped the temperature dial to the left, unleashing a wave of cool air. Randle eased up his sleeve, rubbing the ball of his thumb in circles over his wrist.

'Maybe you need to slow down on that bike of yours.'

He seemed relieved by the change of subject. The smile was back, his mouth falling into its favoured shape.

'Kind of defeats the point of racing, ma'am. It's worth it if I win.'

'And did you?'

'I don't intend to lose again.' He pressed deeper into his flesh, increasing the flow of blood to the soft tissue. 'You should come sometime, ma'am.'

I glanced at him, surprised by his boldness, then shifted my gaze back to the road. The sun's rays blazed through the windscreen, bleaching the dashboard. I flipped down the visor to shield my eyes.

'What makes you think I'd be remotely interested?'

'You've got more energy than anyone I know, and you never flinch on the back of my bike.'

The river lay to my right as London shifted and changed beside us – a series of bridges marking off each area as we moved past multi-million-pound houses overlooking the water in Chelsea, through Pimlico and Westminster, past Blackfriars into the city's core. The traffic slowed as we entered the square mile of the City of London – trades long forgotten immortalised as street names, history confronting the present in a battle for architectural supremacy. St Paul's Cathedral rose up on my left, its baroque dome curving upwards. Buses ejected an endless supply of tourists, expensive cameras pressed to their faces as if they'd lost the ability to use their eyes. I switched off the air conditioning and lowered the windows, listening to the wind as we drifted further east.

Ray King lived in a red-brick development five minutes from Stepney Green. A group of children dribbled a ball on the communal lawn, displaying an intensity and skill at odds with their chubby, little faces. Ray King's ground-floor flat had a prime view of the game. The main door to the block was on a latch, opening into a dingy hallway. A dark carpet hid years of stains and dirty footprints. The faint scent of lemon and vinegar reminded me of the homemade cleaning products Margaretta had favoured when I was a child. There was no answer as Randle's fist hit Ray's front door. He knocked again, but there were no footsteps on the other side. I walked outside, looking through the window – the curtains were pulled back to reveal a small room. There was a bed in the corner, sheets folded on the bare frayed mattress. The cupboard was open – three empty hangers spaced unevenly across the rail.

'Can I help you?'

A woman in her late fifties stood by the entrance, dark brown skin glowing with a thin sheen of sweat, jet black hair cut short, just covering her ears. Her clothes somehow worked with her stocky figure – a cheap leopard-print skirt elevated by confidence and sass.

'What you doing looking through that window?'

She pulled a battered packet of cigarettes out of a faux leopard-skin clutch bag, tapping the box with a polished red nail.

'Detectives Hutch and Randle.' I flashed my badge. 'We're looking for Ray King. Has he moved out?'

'You could say that.' She pushed a cigarette between pink lips but made no attempt to light it. 'Keisha Blake. He owes a month's rent, but lucky for him, he's dead.'

Chapter Sixteen

Leah

I stepped away from the window as Keisha held the orange flame from a matchstick up to her cigarette, watching the paper crackle then burn. She pushed out a thin stream of smoke.

'Are you the landlord?'

'No. My husband looks after this place, but he's more of a caretaker if you're looking for a job title. I'm a hairdresser.' She ran her eyes over my face and hair, making a silent assessment. 'Pop in some time.'

I looked beyond her as she pecked at the menthol cylinder, tipping ash onto the coir doormat, unabashed.

'Is your husband here?'

'He's doing the rounds. He'll be back soon. You can wait in the flat.'

Keisha led us into the block, to the door opposite Ray King's. She puffed at her cigarette as she rummaged for a set of keys in her bag. Her sitting room was small and perfectly ordered – freshly hoovered chocolate rug, surrounded by a matching sofa and two leather chairs. There were a handful of photos of family and friends – a young Keisha on her wedding day with a man who must have been her husband; baby pictures of a boy, who I imagined was their son or grandson.

'He gets paid peanuts, but we get a place to stay.' She disappeared into the adjoining kitchen, emerging with a metal ashtray. 'Don't tell Marlon.' One last drag, then she stubbed the cigarette dead.

There was a click as the door opened.

'Don't tell Marlon what?'

Marlon Blake was tall and dark with a neat grey afro. The sleeves of his shirt were rolled just beneath his elbows, the skin of his forearms covered in tightly curled hair.

'Keisha, love.' He shook his head at the sight of the ashtray.

She ignored him. 'They want to talk to you about Ray.'

A wave of sadness passed over his face. There were lines around his eyes I hadn't noticed when he entered the room. He eased himself into the wider of the two armchairs, the leather tightly moulded to his back.

'I need a beer,' he said.

It wasn't an order, but Keisha obliged, disappearing into the kitchen, returning with an open bottle, wet down the side. Marlon rested the mouth of the bottle against his lips, barely opening them as he sipped. He placed the beer on his thigh, holding the neck lightly with a strong finger and thumb.

'Ray King. It's a strange one,' he said. 'They say he died of a heart attack after he broke into another man's house.'

'Who's *they*?' I pressed my knees together so there was more space between me and Randle on the narrow brown sofa.

'Your people. The police.' There was no fondness behind the words. He spread his free palm across the surface of the armrest and took another slug of his beer.

Keisha handed Randle a long glass of water. I wasn't thirsty, but I accepted the second glass she held out in her hand.

'Thank you,' I said.

She moved back into the kitchen, leaving the door ajar. A moment passed, then the sound of a blade clunked against a chopping board. Marlon kneaded his jaw with two fingers, pressing into the bristles of his beard.

'They made out like he was trying to rob the place, then he dropped dead before he could get out.'

'Keisha mentioned he'd missed his rent payment.' Randle leant forwards. 'Could it have had something to do with that?'

'I'll be damned if I know. I'm a caretaker, not his wife.'

'Was Ray married?' I said.

'Widowed. A kid in Australia, but they weren't in touch.'

Marlon's eyes narrowed as the skin of his forehead became rumpled.

'Ray didn't have much, but he got by. Everyone knew Ray liked a drink. No one's going to judge a man for that. You get to my age, life deals you some blows. He wasn't an alcoholic or nothing; just fancied going on a bender every once in a while. Sometimes he got a little merry; sometimes he passed out. But breaking and entry . . .' He shook his head, taking a swig from the bottle. 'That's a new low, Inspector. A man's got to be desperate to go and do that.'

Chapter Seventeen

Leah

By the time we had reached the Embankment, Akosua had half a story. Her voice, amplified by the speaker, filled the car in excited bursts.

'Ray King just died of a heart attack after a break-in. He was ex-army. Thirty years plus service. Clean bill of health for years, then a history of heart issues after he retired. He had been hospitalised once before, but he recovered. He broke into a stranger's house, had another episode and was found dead in the early hours of the morning. The owner heard a noise at 2 a.m. Went into his front room and found a corpse sitting on his sofa.'

'Apparently Ray was having some financial issues. Was anything taken, Akos?'

I never understood Randle's use of the familiar diminutive – he pretended not to notice she competed with him, but they were far from friends.

'No. That's the thing . . .' Akosua's words sped up with enthusiasm. 'According to Gabriel McMahon, the owner of the house, nothing was taken. Ray's never been in trouble with the law, so the SIO at the scene reckoned the burglary was opportunistic. A desperate move by a drunk, desperate man. The investigation has effectively been closed – the perpetrator's dead, and the department's drowning in volume crime.'

'Let's notify Lu Hoffen. He was watching Sarah's flat. He could still have been the suspect in the balaclava,' I said.

'That's the thing, ma'am.' Akosua paused for an imaginary drum roll. 'Ray King can't be the one Lu's looking for – he died the week before Sarah Franks was killed.'

Chapter Eighteen

Leah

Kenny O'Sullivan understood that pragmatism, rather than passion, had been the key to his success. Optics were everything – he was a brilliant communicator, and an even better self-promoter. If a case went well, Kenny celebrated the team; if mistakes were made, you were on your own. He was nearing the end of an unblemished career, and he wasn't about to go out on a low. The door to his office was open, and the musky odour of cologne lingered as I approached. He sat back watching the entrance, fingers massaging the flesh of his stomach. He smoothed the fabric of his shirt over his belly, waiting for me to knock.

'You've been a busy bee. Not like you to be so keen, and it's not even lunch.'

'Sir?'

His delicate nose was like a small button, almost lost in the expanse of his face. His skin was flushed with sunburn, making his head seem even larger on his thick neck. I had trained under him as a junior officer before my ten-year stint in Leeds. When I had needed to transfer back, he had helped me, no questions asked. I should have been grateful, but I felt I owed him, and the debt hung between us, waiting to be repaid.

'What's all this about you playing with the other children's toys? Thought you were more the kid in the corner, reading alone.'

His nostrils flared, enjoying his joke.

'If you're talking about Sami Mograbi, sir, that's part of what I wanted to talk to you about.'

'Part of? It's not story hour, Leah. Crack on.'

I took a step into the room but remained standing. I noticed the thin film of sweat across his cheeks. He pressed his hands against the wooden desk in front of him, inching his chair back. The extra space seemed to provide relief, and he exhaled, a low growl through his lips. His eyelids drooped, but I knew he was still watching me – the flash of green beneath his short lashes gave him away.

'Sami Mograbi, the original suspect, specifically requested me, sir.'

'Why?' His eyes were still half closed, his forefinger resting on the tip of his nose.

'Because I knew him briefly a long time ago.'

Kenny's eyelids lifted in slow motion. I felt the weight of his full attention. Ten seconds passed before he spoke.

'OK . . . Anything that could compromise the case?'

His gaze didn't waver; I fought the temptation to blink.

'You tell me, sir. We were sixteen. He was at my school for less than a year. He tried to kiss me in the Cineworld cinema; I said no. He left school soon after that.'

Kenny's features folded together as his shoulders shook with a silent laugh.

'You broke his heart and ruined his education. Sounds like a motive to me.'

'I believe his father got a new job, sir. Probably that, not heart-break, that made him move.'

Kenny was still chuckling at his own joke.

'No self-respecting judge will think less than a year of being in the same class as someone over twenty years ago can have any bearing on a case. But that's not even the point now, sir. I hear he's been released, so there's no question to answer.'

Kenny shifted in his chair, extracting a pale blue handkerchief from his pocket. His initials were embroidered in white in the corner; he wiped his forehead with the 'K'.

'Leave DS Hoffen to it, Leah. No need to ask for extra homework. Let her find her killer and tie up her own case.'

He leant forwards, splaying his fingers across the keyboard at the edge of his desk. There was a low squeak as his stomach rubbed against the polished wood.

'There's something else, sir . . .'

'Of course there is . . .' He sounded bored.

'The CCTV shows someone was watching the victim's house.'

The sound of tapping was the only response Kenny offered, his fingers repeating the same pattern across the keys.

'We identified the man watching the house; that man's now dead.'

'And?'

'He died in bizarre circumstances.' I paused. 'Something's not right. It's just a gut feeling, sir, but—'

'The taxpayers aren't interested in your gut, Leah,' he said.

Kenny's greatest skill was avoiding bad publicity, knowing which grenade could cause the explosion that ended careers.

'I appreciate that, sir, but I'd like to rule out foul play.'

It was my turn to watch him; his entire body remained still, but the muscles of his nostrils pulsed visibly.

'Whoever killed Sarah Franks is still at large. Let me at least make sure there's nothing in it, sir.'

He pivoted on his heel, so his chair swung round, and I could no longer see his face. I focused on the view through the window beyond him – a part of the city that was neither suburban nor central, bustling with life.

'OK, Leah . . .' he said. 'I'll talk to DCI James over in Elephant and Castle. You've got seventy-two hours to show me this is something. I hate to disappoint you, but not everything comes down to murder. Sometimes people just die.'

Chapter Nineteen

Zed

Zed had hurried home after he had seen the man outside his building. Seema had called after him, but the words were lost before they reached his ears. He patrolled the ground floor of his flat lowering each blind in turn. He told himself he was over-reacting, but he didn't stop until every window was covered, and he was shielded from the world outside. He had tried to access his mother's laptop, searching for clues, but he couldn't figure out what her password was. He sat cocooned in his bedroom, his knees drawn up to his chest. He kept returning to the image of the man in his mind, but he hadn't seen his face. The chime of the bell startled him. He froze, hoping he had imagined it. Then he heard the sound again. He crept out of his room, his weight on his toes to dull the creak of the floorboards. He paused at the top of the stairs leading down to the sitting room at the front of the house. He could hear a soft tapping on the window, then a small voice repeating his name over and over. The tension slipped from his shoulders – it was only Seema, no need to be scared. He was tempted to ignore her, but he didn't want to attract unnecessary attention. He rushed outside. She stood there, her face pressed up to the glass, deep concern captured in her frown. He beckoned her over, pulling her into the building, slamming the entrance door when she was safely inside.

'What d'you want?'

She looked unsure of herself in the dark hallway. She winced, and he realised he still had hold of her arm. He dropped it, pressing his back against the wall.

'You just left,' she said.

He was puzzled by the hurt in her voice. He noticed she held a Pyrex dish, covered by foil.

'What's that?' His voice was gruff as he nodded towards it.

'Food. My mum made it . . .' She didn't elaborate.

'What did you tell her?'

Seema shrank back as Zed lifted his body away from the wall.

'Nothing . . . I just thought you might be hungry.'

'If you said anything, I swear I'll . . .' His voice wavered as he realised his total helplessness, threatening a little girl whose only crime was wanting to be his friend.

'I didn't say anything. I promise.' Seema looked down at her shoes, her feet bulging against the worn canvas; she pressed her big toe against the tip. 'Your mum's not working, is she?' The words came out in a whisper. Her teeth were small and crooked beneath her chapped lips.

Zed searched for another lie, but he couldn't think of one.

'It's OK . . . I won't tell anyone,' Seema said.

He raised his eyes to meet hers, and she stared back at him. She read the answer he couldn't hide on his face.

'Where's she gone?' He didn't know why she was still whispering.

'I don't know,' he said.

Seema's eyes blazed with a confidence Zed didn't feel. Her mouth opened wide in an awkward smile.

'It's OK,' she said again. 'I'll help you find her. Everything will be alright, you'll see.'

Her face glowed with childlike certainty. Zed's mother was gone, but he was no longer alone. He tried to ignore the question that had made his chest hurt when he had woken up that morning.

What will I do if she doesn't come back?

Chapter Twenty

Leah

The waiting room of Gabriel McMahon's GP surgery was full of sick patients scared of other people's germs. A cough or loud breath was met with a dirty look, eye contact seen as a declaration of war or certain infection. Gabriel McMahon looked uncomfortable when we were shown into his office. He was in his late thirties, but a receding hairline and too much sun made him look like he had seen forty long ago. There were traces of a once attractive man hidden in his features, but his skin was coarse and heavily wrinkled, his face bloated from too much rich food. Heavily muscled arms were testament to a once fitter body he was trying desperately to hold on to; his torso was bulky but soft, a small paunch spilling over an expensive leather belt.

'I have patients,' he said after we had introduced ourselves. 'Will this take long? I went through everything already with the police, right after it happened.'

He ran his fingers through strands of dyed black hair, tired eyes squinting beneath thick dark eyebrows.

'It must have been traumatic for you,' I said.

'Yes . . .' My sympathy softened him, and his gaze drifted as he remembered the shock of discovering a corpse on his sofa. 'I've seen dead bodies, of course, but this . . . this was different.'

'I've read the report,' I said, 'but can you talk us through what happened?'

Gabriel hesitated, pressing his teeth into his bottom lip. We stood like three points of an awkward triangle.

'Of course . . . Please take a seat,' he said.

His desk faced the wall, next to a blue canvas chair. He gestured towards it with a small tilt of the head. I glanced at Randle as I lowered myself to sitting. There was no other seat apart from the examination bed. Randle chose to stand, his back against the door. His tall frame filled the doorway; his smile reassured Gabriel as he pulled out his chair.

'Take your time,' I said.

Gabriel rubbed his scalp, his eyelids drooping as the action soothed him. He reached for a glass of water, holding it tight with one hand.

'I woke up in the middle of the night. It was too hot. I couldn't sleep. My throat was dry. I went downstairs to get a drink . . . I went to the kitchen, got a glass of water. You've got to understand, I was half asleep . . .'

'Of course. Then what happened, Mr McMahon?'

He took a sip of water, wincing as he replayed the memory.

'I had started to go back up the stairs,' he said, 'back to bed, when I heard a noise. I thought I heard voices coming from the sitting room. I live alone, so it alarmed me. I went to check and . . .' His breath hitched as he relived the fear. 'And he was just sitting there . . .'

'Just sitting there?'

'Yes. Sitting facing the screen. I didn't realise he was dead . . . at first.' He pummelled the skin on either side of his eyes, trying to focus.

'And did you recognise him? The deceased?' I said.

Gabriel's neck was wide and thick; he shook his head with surprising vigour. 'I'd never seen him before.'

'The victim was a man named Ray King. You have no recollection of him before that night?'

He downed his water like he was craving something stronger. His hand shook as he clutched the glass. 'I'd never met the man in my life.'

'Any idea why he would break into your house?'

Gabriel's voice was steady. 'I don't know. That's a question for the police. As I far as I know, he broke in and had a heart attack before he could rob me.'

'In your statement, you mentioned the television was on, and the voices were coming from there. Had you forgotten to turn it off?'

'I don't remember . . .'

Randle's interjection caught Gabriel off guard, and he tripped over his words.

'I've been under a lot of stress lately . . . It's possible I left it on.'

'But you can't say for certain?' I said, scanning his face for what was left unspoken.

'I – I don't know.' Gabriel bit his lip; his eyes looked tortured. 'A man broke into my house and died on my sofa. I don't need to know why it happened, Inspector; I just hope I can forget it did.'

Chapter Twenty-One

Leah

Ray King's corpse stared back at me from the wall in the police station – cheeks flushed from where the capillaries had burst after too many hard nights, loose skin in folds around his jowls where age hadn't been kind. Seated on Gabriel McMahon's linen sofa, he looked like a man relaxing at home, content after a day's work, but it wasn't his home, and he wasn't alive.

'Anything from the pathologist?' I said.

Georgina Harrison never kept me waiting long.

'Not yet.' Randle's hair was fighting a thin layer of gel; I wondered why he bothered. He flicked a tendril, frowning as it fell back onto his face.

'What d'you think, ma'am?' Akosua's deep Scottish drawl surprised me as she walked up to the board. She leant forwards, nose scrunched in concentration, scrutinising the photographs from the scene of the crime. 'Bit odd – breaking into Gabriel McMahon's house intending to rob it, then having a heart attack.'

'Odd doesn't make it untrue.'

I stepped back so I had a clearer view of the images. Ray King's bloodshot eyes and ruddy face pointed to a lifestyle of dissipation; his clothes had reportedly reeked of whisky, but there was still so much about him we didn't know. Kenny could ridicule my gut all he liked, but Ray's death, so close to the murder of the woman whose flat he had been watching, begged questions.

'Was there damage to the premises from forced entry?' I said.

'According to his original statement, Gabriel can't remember whether he left the side door open. Either that, or the lock was picked.'

Akosua's thick hair was parted in the centre, pulled tight into two neat plaits – with her wide, open face and smooth complexion, she looked more like a student than a detective trying to solve a case.

'What else do we know about Ray King?'

His file had been sent through whilst we were at Gabriel McMahon's surgery. Akosua had studied it in detail, keen to impress.

'Fifty-nine. Retired from the army. Had done odd jobs since. Did some work as an Uber driver. His private hire licence lapsed a couple of years ago, and it wasn't renewed. No known hobbies. Spent a lot of time in the pub. Keisha Blake said he was "drinking his pension away".' She exhaled, satisfied with her summary.

I scanned the wall of images. 'Any history of petty crime going back?'

Akosua flicked through her dog-eared notepad. 'No, ma'am. Not as far as we know.'

Randle massaged his jaw.

'Gabriel couldn't remember if he'd left the TV on,' he said. 'He could have left the side door open and forgot that too?'

Akosua scurried back to her desk, keen not to be outdone. She searched through the piles of paper, her expression triumphant as she handed me a page.

'Ray's flat was searched before the caretaker cleaned it out. Ray didn't own much. We were sent the index of possessions. Nothing jumps out.'

I glanced at it, turning back to the stills pinned on the board. Ray was dressed in a white shirt tucked into dark blue trousers; his appearance was neat and precise, befitting his military training; years of athletic discipline or good genes had kept his waistline trim, despite the heavy drinking. His sleeves were rolled up, displaying a collection of thin striped coloured bracelets on his right wrist – a man in midlife, grasping at youth.

'What did he have on him when he died?' I said. 'Did they photograph his personal effects?'

I watched Akosua rummage through her printouts. Her skin darkened when she handed me the photographs, embarrassed for making me wait.

Ray King had aged significantly since his days in the army – the face on his driving licence was of a much younger man. Other than his wallet, he had been carrying his house keys and a pen engraved with his initials. I paused on the keys – they were in different shades of silver and brass, around a black ring.

'Any mention of another property?'

'No, ma'am,' Akosua said. Her forehead puckered with concern that she had missed something.

Randle took a step towards me, studying the image I held in my hand.

There was a dull gold key, surrounded by three Banham ones, the metal dotted with tiny evenly spaced holes. I pictured Ray's front door when we stood outside knocking.

'Ray King's flat was hardly Fort Knox. There was only one

lock on the door. It was the same as the caretaker and his wife's.' I pictured Keisha Blake's door as she turned the key, allowing us in.

'So why all the keys?' Randle said.

'Ray carried so little. They must have a purpose. Maybe they opened a different door.' I turned to Akosua; she was poised, waiting for instruction. 'Check out what other properties Ray had access to or owned.'

Chapter Twenty-Two

Leah

My mobile rang as we approached the mortuary. Akosua's name filled the screen.

'Is it urgent? We're about to see the pathologist.'

'Sorry to bother you, ma'am. Sami Mograbi's downstairs.'

'What does he want?'

'He said he needs to speak to you.'

'Tell him to go home. There's nothing to say.'

I hung up before she could continue. Randle raised an eyebrow.

'What?' I said.

'I didn't say anything, ma'am.'

I turned down the corridor as he hid his grin.

Georgina Harrison was standing by a cabinet in the corner of her mortuary office, her head concealed by a large file.

'I hope you brought Randle.'

She glanced up. I could see her eyes were tired beneath the glint of mischief. I didn't need to look at Randle to know she had made him blush. He had his fair share of admirers; he wasn't shy around women, but every time Harrison performed her version of flirting in front of me, Randle couldn't look me in the eye.

'Georgina.'

His tone was strangely formal. Harrison's mouth twitched with amusement, but she stopped short of a smile. Affection wasn't a commodity she doled out easily – she found the living less reliable than the dead.

'You look jittery, Hutch. You know sleep isn't overrated. I could do with some myself.' She massaged the lines that marked her forehead, deeper than the last time we had met.

My eyes dropped to the snow boots she wore year-round, even though it was over thirty degrees in London – navy with a fur trim, thick red laces making her feet seem wide. Her arms were bare, tanned and lightly muscled – her upper body conceding it was summer, her lower limbs pretending it was not.

'Let's not go there with each other's quirks,' I said.

Her eyes shone as she debated whether to push the conversation. 'Let's not.'

'Tell me about Ray King.'

The atmosphere shifted as she followed my cue. All trace of amusement gone, she flicked open the file.

'What d'you know about the human heart, Hutch?'

'Never been a particular area of interest.'

The comment earned me a rare smile.

'What about you, Ben?' Harrison switched her focus, but he was ready for her.

'Not my specialty, but I like to think I paid enough attention in GCSE biology to get by.'

Harrison let out a low chuckle. 'Not so serious after all.'

She walked round to her desk. An X-ray of Ray King's heart filled her computer screen.

'Were you aware Ray King had a defibrillator?' She angled the monitor so we had a better view, indicating a small white shape on the right-hand side. 'It was fitted after his second heart attack.'

'My grandfather had one.' Randle squinted as he focused on the tiny device. 'He almost died at Christmas. It saved his life.'

My eyes filled with questions. He saw them and looked away.

'Why didn't it save Ray's?' he said.

Harrison's gaze travelled between us, then settled on Randle as she made a mental note. 'A defibrillator can correct an arrhythmic heartbeat – save a life in the face of sudden cardiac arrest. But it can't prevent them completely, and you can still die from a heart attack.' She turned to me. 'What's with the face, Hutch?'

'You tell me.' I relaxed the muscles between my eyes. 'It was the same the last time I checked.'

We had worked together when I was a trainee, before I went to Leeds. The snow boots had been plainer then, but they were still a fixture – her style subtly evolving over the last ten or so years. She looked at me – small eyes that intimidated so many but had only ever intrigued me, earning her respect.

'What's on your mind?' she said.

'The previous investigating team were looking to tie up the case because the borough's overworked, and they needed a quick win. The pieces fit so they drew a line under it very quickly. I want to know if they missed anything.'

She raised a heavily pencilled black eyebrow – the only trace of make-up on her narrow face. 'Like what?'

'He definitely died of a heart attack?'

'He did.'

'And there was no sign of a struggle?' Randle said.

She considered him for a moment. 'Why? Do you want there to have been one?'

He wilted when she flirted, but her professional coolness didn't make him flinch.

'The victim was fully dressed in the crime scene images. I wondered if there was any marking or bruising under his clothes?'

'No. He had a history of heart failure. He had a heart attack. He died. Full stop.'

'And there's no indication anyone else was there at the time?' Randle flicked the tip of his thumb with his forefinger as his brain worked through a possible scenario.

'The body was found in Gabriel McMahon's sitting room,' I said. 'It's the room Gabriel probably uses to entertain. There were bound to be multiple visitors. Unless they interfered with the body, it's impossible to link them to the time of death.'

'True, but I'm not sure it matters.' Harrison turned to me; the glint was back. 'Ray King's corpse was found in Gabriel McMahon's sitting room, but I'm pretty sure that's not where he died.'

Chapter Twenty-Three

Leah

I always marvelled at how quickly Harrison got changed into protective clothing – as if she couldn't wait to enter the world of the dead. We followed suit, walking behind her down the narrow corridor to the mortuary with its bank of silver fridges – like built-in wardrobes housing corpses instead of clothes. The mortuary technician blended into the room, as if he were part of the interior design. He had a ponytail of wiry silver hair, ivory skin, old but unlined. I had never seen him smile, but why would he? I doubted I would remember how to if I had spent years manipulating the dead. Ray King lay in the centre, naked on a metal tray. Rectangular panels of fluorescent light beamed down on a pale body that would never again see the sun.

'Look at this . . .'

Harrison gestured at the technician, making a signal only they could understand. He strode towards the body, turning it on its side. There was a darker layer of skin along the underside of Ray's neck stretching down along his back and legs.

'When blood stops circulating, the blood cells sink, and lividity sets in. If Ray died when he was sitting down, you would expect the skin to darken around the buttocks and back of the thighs, due to gravity. But the discolouration is all down the back of the body, suggesting he was lying down when he died.'

'But Ray King was found seated on a sofa . . .' Randle began.

I caught Harrison's eye. 'So he must have been moved after death,' I said.

She smiled. 'That's where it gets interesting.'

She moved gracefully around the body, indicating Ray's toes. They were long and gnarled like decrepit fingers, large gaps between each one.

'It's pretty hard to see, but there's a tiny puncture mark in the vein near his big toe that looks like it was made with a needle. The toxicology report's not back yet, but if I were a betting woman, I'd say he was injected with some sort of stimulant that induced a heart attack, making us think he died of natural causes, given his history.'

Randle stooped, straining to see the hole left by the needle. 'You think Ray King was murdered?'

Harrison stood back, observing the dead man in front of her. 'Quite possibly. Looks like he was killed, then his body was moved.'

Chapter Twenty-Four

Leah

Randle had a cigarette between his lips the moment we stepped outside.

'Sorry . . .'

It was a forewarning of the inevitable more than an apology.

He nodded towards the concrete cube that housed the mortuary behind us. His eyelids flickered as the sharp sting of nicotine filled his brain.

'D'you think Ray King and Sarah Franks' deaths are linked, ma'am?'

'Let's see what Harrison comes back with. The MO's so different, but it seems like too big a coincidence if Ray was watching Sarah's flat,' I said. 'Someone killed Sarah the week after Ray died. I suspect they must have been watching her too.'

I had asked Harrison to look into Sarah's autopsy on the downlow. I didn't have time for Lu Hoffen's attitude, and Harrison was on good terms with the pathologist on the case. We walked side by side in strained silence; Randle shortened his strides so we kept the same pace. The dark grey car glistened at the end of the street – the early evening sun bouncing off the windows in thin golden lines.

'I didn't know your grandfather had a heart attack,' I said.

His lips closed around his cigarette, pulling hard on the filter. His voice was devoid of emotion when he spoke.

'I made sure it didn't affect my work.'

His head was bent, so his hair crept across his forehead when he reached for the door handle. His dark lashes were so thick, I could no longer see his eyes. I enforced strict boundaries between the personal and the professional, but Randle had always seemed so open. I was surprised I hadn't known.

'Randle . . .'

He finally turned towards me. A flicker of pain, a sigh, then it was gone.

'Why didn't you say something?' I said.

His gaze shifted down as he drew a circle on the road with the toe of his shoe.

'It didn't seem relevant, ma'am.'

I watched as his foot returned to its starting place.

'It's none of my business, but for what it's worth, I'm sorry.'

'He's fine now.' He looked up, every feature lifting as a smile swept across his face. 'But for what it's worth, thanks.'

Chapter Twenty-Five

Leah

Kenny O'Sullivan was waiting in my office. He had never been a fan of natural light. The blinds were down, but the bulb overhead hadn't been switched on – just the lamp on the desk illuminating his upper body like a spotlight. It wouldn't have surprised me if the effect was deliberate. Kenny loved to make a statement, and when he did, he expected the equivalent of applause.

'You waiting to be interrogated, sir?' I played along, hoping he'd go away.

'Very funny, Leah.'

He said my name, but the words were self-congratulatory – the person who amused Kenny O'Sullivan the most had always been him. He sat tall in my chair, taking over my space like he owned it. His head was too large for his compact features, one chin tucked within another. His dark green eyes stared at me, set too close to the bridge. I had seen photographs of a younger Kenny in his early days in the police force – he had carried less bulk then, but he had the presence of a much older man. From what I had heard, he had understood the value of power – underneath the smooth amiability, Kenny had always been a pragmatist and a shark.

'Make yourself at home.' He gestured to the chair opposite, still enjoying his joke. 'Less than twenty-four hours – your gut didn't let you down this time. I would say well done, but we both know the work's just begun.'

I shrugged, letting Kenny's version of praise wash over me. My philosophy hadn't changed since I had trained under him – find the killer, solve the crime. I wasn't in it for the heroics, or the brownie points; I wouldn't be remembered like Kenny, but that was OK.

'You've seen the results of Ray King's autopsy, sir.' It was somewhere between a statement and a question.

'Of course. But humour me. Give me the Leah Hutch take.'

He swivelled the lamp round to face me, like an interrogator. I blinked at the sudden burst of light.

'Ray King's body was moved after he died,' I said. 'Gabriel McMahon swears he had never met Ray, but I doubt someone would go to all that trouble for some random prank.'

'Do you believe Gabriel?'

'Until I'm given a reason not to.'

'Why place Ray's corpse on his sofa?'

'That's the question we're asking, sir.' The conversation had already gone on for longer than I had hoped. 'The circumstances in which Ray died will help us determine a reason. The tox report hasn't come back, but—'

'Don't bore us both with caveats, Leah.' Kenny's green eyes flashed. He smoothed his shirt across his belly. 'Do us both a favour and get to the point.'

'It's likely Ray King died of an induced heart attack. I think someone killed him, sir.'

Kenny pressed his hands onto the desk, pushing himself up so he loomed over me. He puffed out his chest like a superhero revealing his true size.

'Looks like you got the murder investigation you wanted, Leah. Let's hope no more bodies turn up.'

Chapter Twenty-Six

Chris

Chris had just killed a man, but he felt nothing. It was as if it had never happened. One man's life reduced to zero, and he felt no emotion. Tomorrow, money would appear in his bank account – remuneration for a job well done. Then it would happen again, and again. He used to feel a sense of satisfaction. He could shoot a gun at close range or hit a target from a distance; he could break a person's neck with his hands or end a life with a single stab of a knife. A man of many talents, which he no longer enjoyed using – a practical set of skills to be deployed with care.

The sound of his phone cut through the stillness. He answered, listening carefully to each word. This time he wasn't required to kill. At least not at first. He sat back, wiping a speck of dirt from his glasses with his shirt. He was surprised to find he was relieved. No lives reduced to nothingness. No blood. No lack of guilt. He could save his best skills for another day. For now, all he had to do was watch and wait.

Chapter Twenty-Seven

Leah

The red brick of the World's End Estate looked almost brown in the evening light. The air felt warm as I arrived home, Ray King and Sarah Franks still on my mind. A huddle of tracksuits and oversized T-shirts dispersed as I approached, the smell of marijuana lingering in the air. I didn't have the energy for the paperwork, but I was bored of being challenged every day.

'Cut it out, or I'll arrest you,' I said.

No one liked submitting to authority, but it was tedious to rebel. I thought of Margaretta's silent disapproval of my childhood outbursts. She rarely chastised me, but one look, and I knew I was in the wrong. The oldest boy couldn't have been more than fourteen. He stubbed the joint against the wall, sloping off with unhurried petulance, his followers moving in sync behind.

We were several hours from darkness, and I knew I would struggle to sleep. I imagined my hands wrapped around my skipping rope, preparing myself for exhaustion. I was reaching for my keys when I saw him, bouncing his heel against the ground outside my front door. His head was bent, but his adult frame already felt familiar. He looked up, and I saw the uncertainty in his eyes.

'Twice in one day. I could arrest you for stalking, Sami. Probably preferable to murder . . .'

The word hung between us, reminding him we weren't friends.

'I didn't mean to make things awkward with your colleague . . .' he said.

'You didn't. How do you know where I live?'

He shrugged. His shoulders were still narrow, his body an elongated version of its teenage self.

'I heard you lived in World's End. I asked around. Figured there couldn't be many pretty, black police officers living on the estate.'

He spoke without thinking, lowering his gaze to hide his embarrassment.

'Sorry . . .'

'I heard you went back to the station. What do you want, Sami?' I said.

He dug his hands into his pockets, addressing the ground. 'Can I come in?'

'No.'

'Then can I buy you a drink?'

'I'm not a big drinker.'

He smiled. 'It doesn't have to be a big drink.'

He read the refusal in my eyes, then turned his back on me for the second time that day.

'Don't be so melodramatic. Come on, I'll walk you home,' I said. I reached for a card from my pocket. 'Next time you want to speak, call me. Don't turn up at the station unannounced.'

He slipped the card away and started walking. 'OK, Leah. Understood.'

We didn't speak for the first five minutes until we had reached the

Italian deli at the bottom of the road. Every now and again, Sami glanced behind us, searching for an invisible pursuer.

'You OK?' I said.

He nodded. 'Just cautious.'

If he had nothing to do with Sarah Franks' murder, I didn't blame him, after what he had seen, but if we were being followed, our shadow kept themself out of sight. The pavements were filled with people who had committed to enjoying their evening, faces flushed after several rounds of drinks.

'What's with the skipping?' Sami's eyes followed a chino-clad man who had barged past us. 'When I asked around, they said you're always skipping like a madwoman, or a boxer – take your pick.'

I shrugged. 'Probably a bit of both.'

He had relaxed into the rhythm of our stroll, his stride unhurried. I was reminded of walking back from school to Margaretta's house or Sami's home in Eaton Square.

'Leah Hutch, angel of justice.' He laughed – a soft chuckle carried away by the breeze.

'I'm not on a crusade to make the world a better place. I'd just rather killers were punished, instead of living their best lives whilst ending someone else's.'

'I'm not mocking you. We all want justice. It's the way we were made,' he said. 'I just never saw you as a detective. I . . .' He paused, turning to look at me with solemn eyes. 'It suits you. You always hated pretence. Makes sense you'd find a job that lets you search for the truth.'

I remembered Margaretta's words when I had felt aggrieved by some injustice. It was a sobering lesson for a ten-year-old, but Margaretta rarely made allowances for me being a child.

Be careful what you wish for, Leah. When the axe falls, your head will be on the chopping block, along with all the others whom you judge. Unless you put your faith in Jesus, your deeds will be judged as well.

Sami's voice cut across the memory. 'It feels strangely normal walking with you like this.'

He flicked his eyes in my direction, then back towards his feet.

'I hope so. It's a pretty normal everyday pursuit.'

'Do you remember the last time we did this?' he said.

'Walking home from college, playing eye-spy like a pair of five-year-olds.'

'That, yes.' He smiled. 'But it wasn't the last time.'

He turned to me, his face expectant. A flicker of hurt when he realised the memory was his alone.

'I had finally got up the courage to ask you out on a date. You said no, then called me at 1 a.m. and asked if I wanted to go for a walk instead.'

'Oh.' I focused on a woman in a red bandeau dress striding towards me. I could feel Sami watching me. I heard his feet drag along the pavement as he searched for the right words.

'Do you still have those dreams?' he said.

I turned to face him, saw the fine lines of concern around his eyes and mouth.

'No,' I lied.

'I'm glad. They sounded horrific, but . . . and I feel bad for saying this . . . but at the time, I was grateful. It was the only time you ever needed me, and I was glad.'

I hadn't always run towards my nightmares. They had terrified me before I was compelled to embrace them – violent images that jolted me awake, too frightened to go back to sleep. In those days, they had been brought on by stress: Margaretta had been ill, but we never spoke about it. She had recovered, and I sometimes wondered if I had imagined the whole thing. The night I first called Sami, he didn't ask for a reason. We walked and talked until my mind felt clear.

'I didn't kill Sarah. You've got to believe me . . .' His body deflated as he exhaled with a loud breath.

'Why? You've been released,' I said. 'It's not my case. It doesn't matter what I believe.'

'It matters to me.'

He moved ahead of me, thumbs gripping the outside of his pockets; I could see the outline of his knuckles as his fists clenched inside. We walked in silence as we approached Sloane Square station, a playwright's name illuminated in red letters across the theatre next door.

'You asked me why I ran?' His pace slowed as we weaved through middle-class literati and tourists. 'I said I was scared. But that wasn't the whole truth.'

Sami hesitated, waiting for a sign of encouragement, but I had interviewed enough suspects to know it wasn't the time to speak.

'I thought they would think I had something to do with it. With Sarah's murder. So I ran. I just left my friend,' he said.

'Fight or flight. It's a cliché for a reason – you're not the first person to run away.'

Sami sniffed bitterly. The shadows under his eyes had grown darker since the morning; his grey irises looked silver under the street light. 'I'm still a coward. The fact that there are others like me doesn't help, but thanks all the same.'

We veered to the right; Eaton Square loomed in the distance, white buildings dull in the darkness. I pivoted to face him. He stopped, surprised, holding my gaze.

'Why me? After all this time?'

Another shrug. 'I knew you were police. I saw you on the news when you were looking for that suspect last year. I didn't know who else to call . . . You're the only person I can trust.'

'How can you say that? You don't know me. We were teenagers before . . .'

'So?'

We stood there, neither of us speaking. The street was quiet, after the buzz of the main road.

'Why did *you* call *me*?' he said. 'When we were kids – when you couldn't sleep?'

You were the only person I trusted, apart from Margaretta, but I don't know the man asking me to trust him now.

'I don't know,' I said.

He blinked away a flash of disappointment, shaking his head as he spoke.

'It doesn't matter. It's not about me . . . Sarah shouldn't have died like that.' Sami's voice was urgent. 'She was killed without mercy. I need to know who murdered my friend.'

'Then what?'

The light died in his eyes but only for a second. Then the spark was back, and he was Sami again.

'Then it's up to the police. This is about justice, not revenge.'

He stared at me with intensity; his grey eyes seemed almost black. My mobile pierced the silence, and I was glad to look away. I reached into my pocket as I turned back towards the bustle. We didn't bother with goodbyes; enough had been said.

*

The voice at the other end of the line was imperious and impatient, as if I had been the one to call at a bad time.

'Selwyn Peterson.'

I had only met Margaretta's lawyer once, but the lack of warmth didn't surprise me. He would never contact me this late unless he had no choice.

'How can I help you, Mr Peterson?' I said.

'Your father, Eli Carson, has had a stroke. You're listed as his next of kin.'

Chapter Twenty-Eight

Leah

I told Selwyn I would call him back from the quiet of my flat. I noticed a piece of paper with Sami's name and number as I stepped across the threshold – he must have slipped it under the door before I found him hovering outside. My phone was on speaker as I waited for Selwyn to answer. For a second, I thought he wouldn't pick up, then I heard his voice.

'Selwyn Peterson.' It was obviously a habit.

'I'm sorry. You were saying?'

'There's not much more to report. Your father had an episode. He wants to see you.' Selwyn paused. 'But you already know that.'

'How would I know that?' I rummaged for my skipping rope. I made a mental note to buy a spare one. 'I had no idea he'd had a stroke.'

'I understand he was writing to you before that, but you ignored him?'

'If you're asking me to justify . . .' My fingers found the plastic handles as he interrupted me.

'That's none of my concern. Your father had a stroke. Whether you choose to see him is up to you.'

His tone was unsympathetic. He didn't think his job was to soothe me, and I preferred it that way.

'The prison didn't have your details. Eli used mine. I'm sorry to disturb your evening.'

Selwyn ended the call.

I was already shifting my weight onto the balls of my feet when the conversation was cut short.

Eli Carson – my father. The man who had murdered my mother and her lover, David Francis, thirty-two years ago – a fact I had discovered less than a year ago, after Margaretta died. David Francis' body had been dismembered and buried at the scene of the crime, but Eli had hidden my mother's body, never to be found. I was there the night she died, but I was only five years old, and I couldn't recall much of what I had seen. I had no love for the man who had slaughtered my mother, but the idea of Eli dying without revealing what he had done with her body stirred something within me that I needed to release. The courtyard was busy, but I didn't care if I had an audience. I grabbed my skipping rope and headed out. My feet were heavy in my shoes, and my legs moved fast to avoid the rope. With each swing, Eli's features faded, and my mind started to clear. I could feel the cramp build in my calves as I worked out my frustration. Almost an hour passed before the tension in my shoulders eased, and I returned to my flat, exhausted.

My file on Eli lay half open on the kitchen table. I never had guests, so there was no need to hide it away. It was a scrapbook of information Margaretta had left for me with her lawyer before she died the previous autumn – Selwyn Peterson, a man who dealt in cold facts, rather than emotions; the man she had chosen to witness my shock when I realised who my father was. I had read the contents so many times, I could practically quote them: the psychological evaluations of the brilliant police detective whose sudden capacity for violence his colleagues struggled to explain; correspondence between Eli and his mother – my grandmother, Margaretta; character statements from people who might have once called him a friend – my boss, Kenny O'Sullivan, one of the many who tried to understand the man he thought he knew. I was thankful that Kenny was unaware of my connection to Eli; his testimony was never far from my mind. It had been written over thirty years ago when they were colleagues, but I could clearly hear his voice.

We spend our days in the shadows, where the ugly becomes ordinary, and people do evil things.

Eli had surprised everybody, including Kenny, but I wasn't interested in playing judge. The file had thickened with pages of my own notes and research – timelines cobbled together from lengthy internet searches; snatches of information gleaned from newspaper cuttings and the police database; a photograph of my mother taken on the day she died, a scarf loose around her shoulders; pictures of Eli from the murder trial. I knew more than most about the case that had seen Eli convicted, but the question I needed to be answered still remained:

Where had Eli hidden my mother's body?

A few months ago, in a dream, I remembered following Eli into a wood, then the memory escaped from my grasp. I had been reaching for it ever since. All I remembered was Eli carrying my mother's body into a thicket; he turned, and I followed behind. I was convinced I had seen what Eli had done with her body. The memory would come back; it was only a matter of time.

The Eli in my dreams was always aware of my presence, but the Eli I saw in prison denied he knew I was there. My subconscious brain had played with different scenarios, but so far, my dreams had never taken me further than those first few steps beyond the trees. The last time I had been to see Eli, he had been dismissive. I hadn't been back since.

I closed the file, retreating to my room. I lay on my bed, thoughts of Eli and my mother going round in my head. I stared through the open window as the night swelled around me, counting down from a thousand until sleep finally won.

Chapter Twenty-Nine

Leah

The little girl had been walking for what seemed like hours, barefoot despite the rough ground. Her feet moved slowly, but she was breathless, the sound of wheezing filling her ears. She could see the silhouette of the man moving in front of her, and she tried to quicken her steps as he was swallowed by the thicket ahead. She followed, looking back as the sounds of night rose around her, until she was swept into the woodland.

She was surrounded by tall trees, long branches disappearing into the black sky. There was no one behind her; no one in front. Her tears fell before she could stop them, and she reached up to wipe her face. Her fingers felt wet as she rubbed at her cheeks, but when she looked at her hands, they were soaked with blood. She started to scream, the sound echoing in the stillness. She heard her mother's voice, quietly soothing, but when she looked up, she saw the man: Eli Carson, her father, singing softly, her dead mother limp in his arms. She heard wailing behind her, and when she turned, Eli was standing there, his finger raised to his lips. She could hear shouting in the distance, and when she turned again, she saw Eli, his palms covering his face. She heard the sound of her mother singing, then wailing, then shouting. The little girl kept turning from side to side. Three Elis surrounding her, taunting her; hushed voices calling her name. She opened her mouth to cry out, but she couldn't move her lips. The scream vibrated inside her until the sound ripped her mouth apart.

I woke with a start, reaching for my book of nightmares, recording what I remembered before the dream was lost to oblivion. When I had finished, my mind felt calm, one thought clear: it was time to see Eli again.

Chapter Thirty

Zed

Another day had passed. Zed was trying to stay positive, but he couldn't ignore the throb of anxiety in his gut. He tried to silence the part of his brain telling him he was foolish to think his mother was coming back. She would never leave him, but what if something had happened and she needed help? His only ally was a twelve-year-old girl he barely knew. Maybe he should tell his dad, or the police? Maybe he was making things worse keeping his mother's absence to himself? Then he thought of the kids at camp who had been taken away from their mums and not allowed to return – if he told someone, would he become one of them?

He rolled over on the bed, knitting his limbs together as he played through the different scenarios, but he couldn't find a clear path through his thoughts. He swung his legs onto the floor and massaged the muscles of his lower back, staring at the photograph of him with his mum on the chest of drawers opposite. Her hair was short, and she had her arms around him, laughing. He had refused to smile, but it had been a good day.

He was always happier after food, and he made his way downstairs, trying to feel more positive, reciting the mantra his mother had taught him whenever his spirits dipped:

My name's Zechariah Okoro and I'm a fighter. No one can break my spirit or steal my joy. My name's Zechariah Okoro and I'm a fighter. No one can break my spirit or steal my joy.

Downstairs was gloomy despite the bright weather, and the sun's rays struggled to penetrate the blinds. He tugged at each one, checking they were securely closed. He couldn't stop someone from watching the house, but he wasn't going to sit back and let them spy on his every move. The kitchen faced the back, so he flicked on the light. He had almost finished the box of cornflakes he had bought the day before. He emptied what was left into a bowl, submerging it in cold milk. He settled himself on the sofa in the sitting room, forgetting his troubles for a moment as he took the first bite. The crunch in his ears was strangely therapeutic, and he felt a sense of clarity he hadn't experienced since he had arrived back in London: if his mother wasn't back that night, he would go to his father – speak to him man to man. He spooned the last of the cornflakes into his mouth, chomping contentedly as he worked through his plan. At first, he thought the bell was a sound in his head merged with his chewing, then he heard knocking, brief but firm – hard knuckles pressing against the door that opened out to the street. He slid off the chair, unnerved by the unwanted guest. Seema he could handle, but somehow he knew it wasn't her. There was a force to this knock despite the muted sound. He was hidden from the window, crouched down by the table. He held his breath, waiting for the knock to come again. Thirty seconds passed, then the sound of footsteps fading. He half stood, knees still bent. A shadow appeared at the window, looming closer. He ducked down as a head pressed against the glass, flattening himself on the floor, his chest pounding.

My name's Zechariah Okoro and I'm a fighter. No one can break my spirit or steal my joy.

When he looked up, the shadow had gone. He held his breath until he heard footsteps, growing softer as the figure hurried away.

Adrenaline pumping, Zed sprang up and rushed to the door, slipping on a pair of trainers he had discarded on his way in. He hurried through the main hallway, desperate to catch a glimpse of the stranger whose face he had never seen. His eyes fixed on a broad back disappearing behind a crowd of confused tourists. The hood was gone, replaced by the shallow dome of a baseball cap tight against the man's skull. Zed recognised the wide torso, the angular shoulders; he knew it was the man he had seen watching his house.

His feet moved before his brain could stop them. Down the steps, then left down the street. He could see the man moving ahead of him. He plunged his hands in his pockets and followed behind.

Chapter Thirty-One

Leah

The body search seemed to go on forever – latex gloves patting and pressing my torso, sniffer dogs losing the glint of enthusiasm when they realised I had nothing of interest to find. The walls were peppered with monochrome posters advising prisoners about debt and disease. I focused on the stark warnings in capitalised text as I prepared myself for another round with Eli Carson.

Eli's face was even leaner than the last time I saw it. Deep lines were etched into his forehead; his cheekbones looked ready to pierce through his pale skin. According to Selwyn, the stroke had been serious, but his features appeared unaffected – if he had lost his sharpness, I couldn't yet tell. He sat in the chair opposite me, his back erect against the hard plastic, defiance undiminished by ill health. His eyes flicked to a fellow inmate handing out pre-ordered snacks with heavily tattooed fingers.

'No gifts for your infirm father?'

I shrugged. 'I thought my presence would be enough. Besides, I didn't peg you as a fan of crisps and cheap chocolate.'

'And you would be right, but they say it's the thought that counts.'

He bared his teeth, preparing for battle. I clenched my fists, concealing them beneath my thighs.

'I could have died.' His blue eyes shone with something far from amusement.

'You're not that lucky,' I said.

'*You* are, though.' It seemed like he would never blink. 'If I die, you'll never get the answers you so desperately want, Leah.'

'Oh, that . . .' I relaxed my fingers. 'And you've been such a help so far.'

'You're scared of the truth and yet you seek it. Maybe I'm helping by giving you what you need, not what you want.'

The family to my right sat in almost total silence – two teenage boys scowling at the clock, willing the visit to be over, their mother in tears as she struggled to find the right words. The heavily muscled inmate they were visiting barely glanced at them, stroking his triceps with love. Eli followed my gaze.

'We're the model of familial communication.' The tips of his lips twitched, but it wasn't a smile. 'I appreciate the bar is low, but it's a start.'

I leant back, increasing the distance between us. I noticed a slight droop to his mouth.

'Next of kin. A bit presumptuous.'

'Or simple biology.' His eyes flashed. 'Don't worry, Leah; I didn't announce you're my daughter. I needed to get your attention. It worked.'

'I almost didn't come.'

'Why did you?' He scanned my body for the answers he knew I wouldn't give him.

'You seemed desperate.'

He shifted forwards, his tone so intimate I fought the urge to look away.

'I didn't want to die with so much unfinished between us.'

I could smell cheap soap tinged with lemon. Everything inside me recoiled, but I didn't move.

'We both know you could speed things up and just tell me what happened, Eli.'

'And we both know you don't trust me, and you like to be in control.'

He sat back, enjoying the verbal sparring I found tedious. His elbows were like knives when he folded his arms. 'Let's call it fifteen all.'

His forefinger tapped against his bicep as he contemplated his next line of attack.

'Not a fan of letter writing?'

'I'm technically a millennial. Pen pals were never my thing.'

'Did you at least read them?'

'I stopped when you started quoting the Bible,' I said.

Something shifted in his eyes, but I couldn't read his expression. He blinked; I couldn't remember if it was the first time.

'Not a believer? You should be used to it from Margaretta.'

'Bit hypocritical from her atheist, killer son.'

He laughed. His teeth were bright white despite years of incarceration.

'How *is* the rage? Under control?'

'I was a child, Eli,' I said.

When I was five, soon after my mother's murder, I had hurt another little girl. I had buried the incident with the trauma of the past, but Eli had dredged the memory up.

'So?' He drummed the surface of the table with his slim fingers.

'What I did then has no bearing on who I am now.'

'People don't change, Leah. I should know; I've had plenty of time to think about it.'

'So have I. We're not the same.'

His cold eyes held mine, unwavering. 'Whatever you say.'

He looked at my long, straight fingers on the table between us, then down at his, a paler version of mine. I resisted the temptation to hide my hands back under my thighs, hating the similarity but refusing to let Eli know I cared. The woman to my left laughed as her partner whispered a joke – a sudden burst of joy at odds with the misery that filled the room.

'I can't make you talk to me, but I don't have time for games, Eli.'

'Maybe you should, Leah. It would do you some good.'

My palms were face down on the edge of the table. He mimicked the position, then drew his hands away.

'When you came here last, you said you remembered seeing me carrying your mother's body.'

He studied my face as my brain caught up.

'Then what?' he said.

I drew a breath, feeling my lungs strain against my ribcage. 'Then I followed you. We've been through this already. You insist you didn't know I was there.'

'I didn't know you were there *at the time*, Leah. Is that still all?'

I couldn't tell if he looked relieved.

'My memories are coming back; it's only a matter of time,' I said.

I clasped the edge of the table as I watched him. The smooth surface felt clammy against my skin.

'Why are you so interested all of a sudden?'

His blue eyes narrowed, the thin lines fanning them deepening. 'Maybe I saw death and had an epiphany.'

'Did you?'

'No. But what does it matter, if you get what you want?'

The guard behind Eli tried to muffle a sneeze. He mistimed the effort, spluttering all over his front.

'So what . . . ?' I watched as the guard rummaged in his pocket for a tissue. He gave up when he thought no one was looking, using his hand instead. 'After over thirty years of silence and refusing to talk about my mother's death, you're going to just . . . what? Just tell me what you did?'

'No . . .'

'We're going around in circles, Eli.'

'But I *can* tell you which memories are real.'

My arms were coiled around my chest, mirroring his body language. I didn't remember moving them, and I dropped them to my knees.

'And why do you suddenly want to help me remember?'

'I don't. But if you *do* remember, I need to know.'

'Why?' I kept my tone neutral. 'You're locked away. What difference does it make to you?'

He blinked twice, so slowly I held my breath, watching him.

'Why?' I said again. 'You won't stop me from finding her.'

'You've got no one else,' he said, ignoring the question. 'What have you got to lose?'

I looked down. I could feel the pace of my heart quicken beneath my breastbone. I counted to ten in my head before I looked up.

'So . . . How's this going to work? I tell you my dreams, you fill in the gaps?'

He grimaced as if the idea were distasteful.

'I'm not a teacher marking your homework, Leah. You describe what you think you remember; I'll tell you something in return.'

'About that night?

'About that night. About your mother. About the past. Let's see, shall we?'

'OK . . . Let's hear it . . .'

He laughed, his eyes sparkling. Merriment didn't suit him.

'Come back when you have something new to tell me,' he said. 'But Leah . . .'

His pale eyes locked on my dark ones.

'Margaretta wanted you to forget for a reason. *If* you remember, that's when the real nightmare begins.'

Chapter Thirty-Two

Zed

The man only glanced back once before he headed down the steps at Ladbroke Grove station. It was one of the few times Zed thanked God for keeping him short. Hidden behind a family of Americans, he kept his head down. The look was so fleeting, he still hadn't seen the man's face. The tube was rammed with sweating bodies; he tucked himself away at the far end of the carriage. He could see the man up ahead, his back to him, leaning against the door. Zed hadn't realised he was tired until his eyelids drifted downwards; the jolt of the train shook him awake. He panicked as he saw the man disembark. He took a breath to calm himself as he jumped off behind him, causing the doors to stutter as he pushed through them, his shoulders catching the edges before they shut. He had been slow to exit; the man was several metres ahead of him, separated by aggressive commuters obstructing his path. Zed drifted through the gaps, zigzagging between determined strangers, careful not to get too close.

He hung back as they emerged on the street. The crowd was less mixed, and he didn't want to stand out – one of the few black faces amidst a block of white. Across the road, a woman in a bright orange and red fabric moved briskly. Her dark brown skin glowed in the sun, but she didn't break a sweat. He crossed, walking a few paces behind her. To the lazy observer, they could have been mother and son. Up ahead, the man turned down a side street, lengthening his stride. Zed hovered, watching as the man approached a white house on the corner, glancing around to check no one was looking before he scurried down a set of steps to a basement door. The man barely looked at the woman in orange and red, failing to register Zed behind her.

Zed stood, hands in his pockets, watching, waiting for he wasn't sure what. Minutes passed. He didn't move. His fists clenched as he recognised his helplessness. This man could have information about his mother, but he couldn't just barge up and confront him. He could be a boyfriend or a predator. Zed's cheeks prickled with shame as he realised he didn't have the courage to find out. He had started to walk away when a sudden impulse made him glance back. The man had already crossed the street, his clothes changed, legs exposed under navy running shorts, ASICS sports trainers gleaming white. He set off in a fast jog, elbows jutting behind him, feet slapping the pavement with an uneven stride. Zed ignored the feeling of helplessness as curiosity led him towards the house. He hesitated as he neared the steps to the basement, peering down. If this was the man's house, why hadn't he used the front door? The curtains were open, but there were no lights on as far as he could see. He crept closer, conscious he only had visibility of one side of the building – the main entrance was round the corner. Everything seemed quiet; there was no sign of life.

The side gate was off the latch. He slipped through before his brain told him not to, moving quickly down the steps. His mother had disappeared; he didn't know where. He needed answers, and this might be his only chance. He looked up at the street above – the lower limbs of a pedestrian glided past. Zed's fingers curled around the handle of the door. He was almost relieved when it didn't budge. He squinted through the window into the basement. It was dark, despite the sunlight, and he gripped the wood beneath the glass to get a better look. He was surprised when the wooden frame shifted beneath his fingers. He held his breath as he pushed the window up and climbed inside.

He landed with a low thud. He bit his lip, swallowing the pain. He felt a sharp jab as his elbow collided with cool metal. It took a second for his eyes to adjust to the gloom. He was lying at the foot of a tall ladder. He reached for the lowest rung, pulling himself to his feet. The room was warm and smelt of mint tinged with lavender – a washing machine with a separate dryer was stacked against the far wall; a jumble of cotton shirts in a range of pinks and blues lay tangled in a pile. He recognised the hooded jumper the man had been wearing when he had first seen him outside. There was a wooden staircase in the corner opposite. Zed crept up each step hesitantly, listening out for the smallest sound. He found himself on the ground floor, with rooms off to the side and stairs leading up. He breathed hard into the silence, his brain fizzing with thoughts as he contemplated his next move. It would take too long to search every room, and he doubted his mother was there. Why would the man be spying if he knew where she was? No – the man must know something, want something; it was the only lead Zed had. He had no idea what he was looking for, when the man would come back, or if this was even his house. He had to act quickly. If he could find a name, it would be a start.

His feet sank into the soft pale blue carpet. He scanned the mat in front of the entrance, but there was no discarded mail. He glanced around each door – there was no one on the floor except for him. He reached for the bannister, his chest tight. Upstairs, the sun beamed through a narrow sash window on the landing, streaking the polished wood beneath him with long, golden rays. The creak of his shoe stirred a flutter of panic, and he quickened his pace as he approached the nearest room – inside, twin beds with pastel sheets and navy blankets. The chest of drawers between them was empty; he realised the room must be for guests. He moved back out onto the landing, glancing around him. The minutes were ticking, and he knew he needed to hurry up.

There was a bathroom opposite. Beside it, a closed door. He eased it open, stepping into a bedroom where everything was white or black. A giant bed dominated the centre. To his right, a wall of built-in cupboards stretched from the ceiling to the floor; to his left, a black leather chair rose up behind a plain white desk with drawers on either side. For the first time in days, Zed didn't feel helpless. Praying for answers, he took a step towards the desk. There was a shallow pile of unopened mail. He reached for it, each envelope bearing the same name.

Chapter Thirty-Three

Leah

Eli's voice played in my head as I emerged into the bright sunlight. I closed my eyes and let the breeze tickle my lashes, inhaling deeply as I tried to shut out the noise. I saw Eli with his finger to his lips, then his hands splayed across his eyes – whispering, singing, watching. Different versions of the man who filled my dreams flashed through my mind. I travelled back to central London, focusing on Ray King's dead body in an effort to block Eli out. The shriek of my phone was a welcome intrusion. I answered fast, my greeting too loud.

'Randle?'

'You were right, ma'am.' His voice was strangely reassuring as I marched towards the river.

'You'll need to be more specific.'

He laughed. 'About Ray King. The extra keys on his key ring – the ones he didn't need for the front door of his flat.'

A woman banged into my shoulder as she misjudged the space between us. She swore, but I ignored her; it wasn't an argument I wanted to have.

'Go on . . .' I said.

I turned down a side street, leaning against the building on the corner. The brick felt cool through the thin material of my blouse.

'Marlon Blake said Ray drank a lot,' Randle said. 'Ray was ex-military. He was used to being around people. Probably missed the camaraderie. I figured he might be a man who liked a pub, so I got the team to check out the ones in his area. Turns out Ray spent a lot of time in his local. Even rented a room upstairs.'

'You think the extra keys are for there?'

'Could be, ma'am. The pub's owned by a man called Stephen Campbell.'

I was heading back towards the station.

'Send me the address. I'll meet you there.'

Chapter Thirty-Four

Zed

Zed had started to move towards the bedroom door when he heard what sounded like the low patter of footsteps. He froze, straining to get a clearer sense of what was happening downstairs, but the silence had returned. He couldn't remember hearing a door close, and for a second, he felt relieved. Then he heard a soft tap of shoes advancing then retreating, and he knew he wasn't alone.

He lowered down to his knees, crawling into the narrow space under the bed. The slats of the frame sat an inch above his head. He rubbed his skull where he had banged it as he hid, fear dulling the pain. He had a clear view of the door from where he lay on his stomach. The duvet was curled neatly around the mattress, and he realised he was completely exposed if anyone thought to look beneath the bed. He flattened his chest against the floor. He could feel his heart pounding; he tried to calm his breathing as he listened for noise. Everything was quiet, but he didn't dare move. He lost all sense of time as he lay paralysed, ignoring the cramp in his leg. He closed his eyes and remembered the times he had struggled to sleep when he was little, recalling his mother's voice, the gentle feel of her hand as she stroked his head.

You're Zechariah Okoro and you're a fighter. No one can break your spirit or steal your joy.

The thought of his mother soothed him as he inhaled deeply, listening to the rhythm of his heart. He heard the soft slam of a door, then a scream downstairs. Everything stopped, including his breath.

Chapter Thirty-Five

Leah

The pub was a short walk from Stepney Green underground station – an old brick building curved round a corner from a main road into a side street, a choice of entrance on either side. Randle was facing away from me – the triangle of his back rose as he inhaled. He reached down to stub out his cigarette in a standing ashtray. He turned as I approached.

'Ma'am.' His lips twitched with a quick smile. 'The publican, Stephen Campbell, lives locally. Rents out rooms above the pub from time to time.'

'You been inside?'

'It's like an ad warning kids against the dangers of daytime drinking. I had a look through the window. Thought I'd wait for you so we could face it together.'

The man behind the bar looked up as we entered. The muscles in his arm tensed as he angled a glass under the beer tap, straightening it gradually to minimise the head. He was short and broad with powerful shoulders straining against a thin cotton T-shirt that was too tight. There was an image of a band I didn't recognise emblazoned across his chest. He had thick hair, almost orange, offset by a deep tan.

Two men in their fifties hung off stools, drinking in silence; three others sat alone at tables with dead eyes. I steeled my nostrils against the smell of stale beer as Randle took a step towards the bar.

'Stephen Campbell?'

The man in the band T-shirt stared back at Randle. His forehead was heavily wrinkled, but it was impossible to tell his age.

'I don't know about Stephen Campbell, but if you're looking for Steve, that's me.' He spoke slowly, his demeanour surprisingly understated, at odds with the image he portrayed.

'I'm Ben.' Randle reached for the man's hand across the bar. 'This is DI Leah Hutch.'

Steve's eyes passed over me. His gaze was meant to intimidate, but I didn't blink. He swallowed hard.

'You in charge?' He was still looking at me.

'In a manner of speaking.'

He jerked his head in Randle's direction. 'Why's he doing the talking?'

'Delegation,' I said.

He stared at me for a long moment, then his features melted. He laughed.

'Fair enough.' He placed two glasses on the counter, filling them with water from the soda gun. 'Do me a favour and drink something. Can't have you scaring the customers, even if you *are* in charge.'

My body relaxed as I swallowed the cool liquid. Ever since my meeting with Eli, every limb had felt tense.

'Now I know you didn't come down here for a glass of water. How can I be of service, Detectives?' Steve said.

'We understand Ray King rented a room from you . . .'

'If you can call it that.' There was a hint of Scottish in his accent, ironed out by years in the East End. 'There's a room upstairs I don't use for much. I let it out from time to time. Ray said he needed an office. The room was empty. He paid when he could.'

'What did he need an office for? I thought he was retired from the army.' The air felt too close, almost stifling. I reached for my glass, savouring the last drops of water in my mouth.

'He did odd jobs for people to keep himself busy,' Steve said. 'He said he needed a purpose after the first heart attack.'

'How long had you known him?'

'Since I bought this place.' He flicked his eyes up as he did the mental arithmetic. 'Coming on fourteen years next May.'

'I'm sorry for your loss.' The words sounded perfunctory, but Steve didn't seem to notice.

He dropped my glass in the sink behind him. 'What's this about, Detective? I've got a pub to run.'

I looked around at the paltry collection of customers.

'It gets busier in a bit,' he said, reading the scepticism in my eyes.

I glanced at the open doorway over his shoulder, the base of a staircase visible in the corner of the frame.

'We're just trying to clear up a few things. Do you mind if we take a look at the room Ray rented from you?'

Steve searched my face, as if weighing up whether refusing was worth the effort. 'Sure,' he finally said.

'Vanessa.' He barely raised his voice – a woman emerged from the back with thick silver braids. 'Mind the bar for a sec, would you?'

The floor above the pub was dark and airless, the faint odour of lager replaced by overripe fruit tinged with the smell of damp.

'I need to clean out the room, but I keep putting it off. Waste of time until someone else wants it,' Steve said, leading the way.

I noticed he had a slight stoop as he turned towards the door in the corner. The key in his hand resembled the ones from the photos of Ray's possessions, its perforated silver blade glinting in the gloom. The door opened with momentum, then abruptly stopped. Steve led us into a tiny, square room. Green and white checked curtains were pulled shut across narrow windows. The ceiling was within reach of my fingertips; it felt like the air had forgotten to move. I searched my pockets for a pair of nitrile gloves, blinking as Steve flicked a switch by the entrance, and Ray King's 'office' took shape under the fluorescent light.

'Give me a shout if you need anything,' Steve said, sounding more Scottish. He turned on his heel and left.

There was a heavy wooden desk pressed up against the opposite wall; a white plastic fold-up chair was positioned under it, with two cushions to soften the seat. A notepad and pen sat in perfect symmetry on top. There was nothing else on it.

'Not much to clear up, by the look of things.' Randle flipped through the pad with latex-clad fingers. The spine was weak where a clump of pages had been torn out.

Apart from the desk and chair, the room was practically empty. There was a six pack of carbonated water next to a heart monitor device on the floor. The door was at an odd angle, not fully open behind me. I pushed it shut so I could see what had stopped it from hitting the wall. A narrow wardrobe jutted out into the room. Inside it, a small stack of files was piled neatly in the centre. As I leant forwards to get a closer look, I could see multiple images in my peripheral vision – rows of photographs Blu-tacked to the back of the wardrobe doors: on one side, I recognised the newsagent's in Elephant and Castle – Sarah Franks' flat captured above it at various times of day. There were printouts of Sarah arriving and leaving, looking haunted – a zoomed-in image of her, anxious at a window, looking out onto the street below. On the other side, Ray King had captured a different London – fewer pedestrians, semi-detached houses overlooking pristine, tree-lined roads. There was a wide shot with a man in the corner, glancing over his shoulder; next to it, a close-up taken seconds before he had turned his face away. Dr Gabriel McMahon stared back at me, in miniature, dark brows sculpted at an angle, pale eyes stretched wide with fear.

'I found these in the desk drawer.'

Randle drew up beside me; the white cardboard rectangle looked tiny in his large hand. He flattened his palm so it was easier to read the navy lettering: a mobile phone number across the centre, above it the words *RAY KING, PRIVATE INVESTIGATOR*, printed in caps.

Chapter Thirty-Six

Leah

The car was too hot; the space felt claustrophobic. Randle reached for the lever, sliding back his seat so he could stretch his long legs out. The contents from Ray King's cupboard sat in an evidence bag behind him. I lowered the window, pressing the accelerator so the breeze brushed over my face.

'So, Ray King was working as a private investigator . . .'

'I don't think he had those cards printed for fun,' I said.

Randle ignored my sarcasm. 'Who do you think hired him to watch Sarah Franks and Gabriel McMahon?'

The steering wheel felt clammy against my skin. 'Let's speak to Gabriel before we jump to conclusions.'

Randle dipped his head, checking an email on his phone.

'The receptionist at his surgery says Gabriel's not in today, ma'am. She spoke to him earlier. She said we'll find him at home.'

He entered an address into the satnav. I flicked the indicator, following the arrow that appeared on the screen. Driving always helped me think. I pulled into the adjacent lane, replaying our encounter with Gabriel in my mind.

'Gabriel McMahon's hand shook when he held his water.' I recalled the unsteady tilt of Gabriel's glass as he struggled to control it, the way his eyes had tried to evade mine. 'I thought the memory of the intruder was what was troubling him, but that wasn't just it. He was haunted by what had happened. He wanted to forget it, but he couldn't because he was still scared.'

'Do you think Gabriel knew he was being followed, ma'am?'

'I don't know.' I pictured the image in Ray's cupboard – Gabriel glancing over his shoulder, checking for someone or something behind. 'We can ask the question. See the truth in his eyes.'

Randle leant his arm against the base of the window. His blue eyes looked blank, but the furrow of his brow gave him away. I didn't rush to fill the silence as our brains worked side by side. I visualised Ray King's corpse – the tiny prick where an injection most likely flooded his body with a dangerous stimulant; the darker skin at the back of his neck and legs that indicated he had been moved after he had died.

'Ray King was investigating something to do with Gabriel McMahon. Maybe someone didn't want that to happen?' Randle's fingers tapped at his jaw. 'That someone put Ray's corpse in Gabriel's house to send Gabriel a message. That's why Gabriel was so withdrawn. He was scared. He didn't want us to look into the break-in. He just wanted the whole thing to go away.'

I hit the brake as a grey van pulled out carelessly in front of me. The car jerked, snapping Randle's head forward then back.

'Sorry.'

He smiled. I wasn't known for my apologies. 'Let's hope he's more forthcoming this time around, ma'am.'

We had crossed the city from East to West London. The roads were wide and quiet as we entered Maida Vale. The neighbourhood prided itself on feeling more like a village. Colourful tables and chairs were clustered outside artisanal cafés; affluent Londoners sipped smoothies, posing in designer sunglasses, or walking dogs – furry kings pampered for life. Gabriel McMahon lived in a semi-detached house at the end of an avenue lined with trees, silver barks glistening in the sun. There were four steps leading up to a black door flanked by mini bamboo palms in terracotta pots. There was no answer when we rang the bell. I had always prized productivity over patience. I waited a second, then rang again. The house looked strangely deserted. I turned to Randle.

'You're sure the receptionist said he's home?'

'Yes, ma'am.'

'Do you have a mobile for him?'

Randle reached deep into his trouser pocket, pulling out a tiny notebook too small for his hand. I stared down the street as he flicked through the pages. The trees rose up in neat lines on either side. A toddler squealed in front of the house opposite as his mother tried to calm him down. He stomped a tiny foot on the pavement, drawing in as much air as his little body could tolerate, then expelled it with a piercing scream. The sound hit the back of my eardrums as Randle dialled Gabriel's number.

'No answer, ma'am.'

'Try again.'

There was a noise muffled beneath the toddler's misery – the low ring of a mobile behind Gabriel's front door. I flipped up the letter box and stared through into the hallway. A phone lay on the floor near a staircase, each vibration revealing a smashed screen. Small patches of red had sunk into the pale carpet beyond it – a haphazard trail meandering along the stairs. My eyes travelled up, following the red blotches, then stopped at the large handprint marking the white wall with blood.

Chapter Thirty-Seven

Leah

The muscles in Randle's back strained against his shirt as he wrenched the bamboo plant from the pot. He gripped the terracotta firmly, swinging at the sash window beside Gabriel's front door. The glass splintered and shattered in a pool around him. He balled his fist beneath his shirtsleeve and cleared the shards from the frame. Without hesitating, he lifted me, sliding me carefully, headfirst through the gap. I put out my hands to secure my landing, crawling forwards as my legs followed behind. I sprang to my feet and unlocked the door for Randle. He hurried in after me. I was already at the foot of the stairs, racing up three at a time. The landing above was completely silent – no cries for help, no strangled breaths. Red drops were smeared across the wooden floorboards. I followed the trail to a half-open door. I could hear Randle close behind me as I burst through into the room beyond. On the floor directly in front of me, Gabriel McMahon's body lay twisted, his eyes wide. His head had fallen back at an odd angle, exposing an angry wound where his carotid artery had been stabbed. The blood had stopped spurting, but waves of red coloured his neck so his collar was no longer white. Above us, crimson swirls stained the ceiling – a silent testimony to a brutal end.

'I'll check the rest of the house, ma'am. Make sure no one else is in here,' Randle said.

I nodded, my eyes on Gabriel as Randle slipped out.

Gabriel's chest was motionless beneath the thin layer of material that clung to it, but I checked for a pulse all the same. His skin felt cool beneath my fingers, but there was no movement: Gabriel McMahon was definitely dead. As I crouched beside his body, I heard a sharp intake of breath. I turned, listening intently, but the room had fallen silent once more. My gaze landed on a wall of wardrobes. All the doors looked closed, but when I moved towards them, I noticed one was slightly ajar. In the darkness beyond it, I heard the hitch of breath again. I nudged my foot into the crack, kicking the door back against the neighbouring wardrobe. My eyes moved slowly down. A figure sat curled with their knees pressed against their stomach, head bowed, hands clamped over their ears. Their lips moved, but all I could hear was a faint murmur. I squatted, straining to make out the words.

'My name's Zechariah Okoro and I'm a fighter. No one can break my spirit or steal my joy. My name's Zechariah Okoro and I'm a fighter. No one can break my spirit or steal my joy . . .'

A boy looked up at me. I saw the tears rushing down his cheeks, large eyes filled with fear. An image flashed in and out of my brain of a little girl kneeling behind a door, the sound of a woman screaming on the other side. A flash of metal, the drip of blood. I didn't realise my body had frozen until I felt Randle's hand gently pressing against my back.

'Ma'am?'

I couldn't control my breathing. I pushed past him and fled.

Chapter Thirty-Eight

Leah

I stood on the landing, my whole body trembling. My ears burnt with the screams of a woman in agony. I willed them to stop, but they just became shriller so the sound vibrated in my head. The bathroom door was open – I rushed in, slamming it shut. I could hear the deep rumble of Randle's voice through the wall. I saw the little girl kneeling behind the door, peering through a crack, terrified. I saw the silver blade of a knife crashing down, shining in the dark.

I stared at my reflection in the mirror. My eyes were wild; my face looked ashen in the dull light. I gripped the sink, trying to cling on to what was real. I curled my fingers round the edge of the basin. The ceramic was cool and hard under my skin. I shifted my weight from one foot to the other, clenching my hands round the handles of an invisible rope. I focused on the rhythm of my steps as I skipped faster and faster, imagining it swirling above my head. The flash of a knife, the little girl crying – the images slipped in and out of my mind. I listened to the tap of my shoes against the tiles, mimicking the steady pace of the beat with my breaths. I tightened my hold on the imaginary handles, pushing my nails into my palms until they started to bleed. The fear that clasped my chest slowly loosened its grip; the muscles in my shoulders relaxed as the screams began to fade. I closed my eyes. This time, when I saw a child, it was the frightened boy in the wardrobe in Gabriel McMahon's bedroom, not the little girl I knew was me.

Chapter Thirty-Nine

Zed

Zed stared at the man crouching in front of him – deep blue eyes trying to look friendly, shoulders curled inwards to disguise a muscular frame. He shifted backwards, wrapping his arms tighter around his shins, ducking his head so his face was hidden as he shrank further away. His first thought was that this was the man who had been watching his house, but the man squatting in front of him had fair hair; the other man had been dark. Zed wondered what had happened to the woman who had run from the room. He had seen the fear in her eyes when she had found him hidden at the bottom of the wardrobe – had she also heard the screams which had pierced through the door?

He didn't know how long he had been there. His right leg ached, but he didn't dare move. He needed to stay still until he knew what had happened, but he couldn't see past the fair-haired man into the room. He tried to salvage his memories, attempting to recall what had happened before he had covered his ears to keep the screams at bay. He had been under the bed; he had heard a door slam, the heavy tread of footsteps. He had made it to the wardrobe. Then the memory went dead.

Zed lifted his head, keeping his eyes down – it felt safer. The man's shoes were made of tough brown leather, scuffed at the toe.

'I'm Ben. I'm a detective. I won't hurt you.'

Ben's voice was soft and low. He was still squatting down, almost at Zed's level, but Zed was breathing so hard, he could barely hear what was being said. He saw the glint of the police badge, but he didn't fully register the details. The last police officer he had seen had stopped him for no reason; his mother had always told him trust had to be earned.

'I'm Ben,' the man said again. 'Are you hurt, Zechariah?'

He wondered how the man knew his name. Then he realised he was still muttering – his lips forming the words involuntarily, again and again.

'My name's Zechariah Okoro and I'm a fighter. No one can break my spirit or steal my joy. My name's Zechariah Okoro and I'm a fighter . . .'

'No one can break your spirit or steal your joy.'

There was something comforting about the man's smile – the way it lit up his eyes as he echoed the mantra Zed had learnt from his mother. Zed's breathing calmed, but his limbs still shook.

'I'm not going to hurt you, but I need to get you out of the room,' Ben said. 'Do you think you can manage that?'

Zed looked up, but the only words he could think of were the words of the mantra that comforted him when he was scared.

'Will you come with me, Zechariah? You don't need to say anything. Just nod if you understand.'

Zed tried to nod, but his head wouldn't move. He blinked, wondering what lay behind Ben in the bedroom. Ben's smile was gone, but his eyes were still gentle as he continued.

'I'm going to have to carry you out of here. I know you're not a baby, and you can probably walk on your own, but I need you to let me do that.' He paused. 'And I need you to keep your eyes shut. It will be for less than a minute. Is that OK?'

Ben didn't wait for a reply. When he reached out, Zed didn't resist, allowing himself to be scooped up into the man's arms. Zed couldn't remember the last time he had been carried; his cheek rubbed against the soft cotton of Ben's shirt as he kept his head turned away. He counted the seconds as he hovered above ground, willing himself to trust the man who had been sent to save him. He heard the creak of the door as Ben manoeuvred them through it, his head following his body out of the room. Curious, he opened his eyes, just for a second. He slammed them shut, but it was too late; he had already seen the blood.

Chapter Forty

Leah

My brain and body operated on autopilot as I played the role of a convincing senior investigating officer, giving orders as additional officers and forensics appeared at the scene. I could feel Randle's eyes on me, but he didn't comment. He drove us back to the station in silence, lowering the windows to give me some air. I sat in my office, waiting for the social worker. Zechariah Okoro had been checked by a medic. There was no blood on his body, and he was physically unharmed. Randle still hadn't mentioned my meltdown. My heart sank when I recognised his knock.

'Are you OK, ma'am?'

'Why wouldn't I be?'

He hesitated. 'Do you want to talk about what happened?'

I looked at him blankly.

'In the room. When I came in, you looked terrified.'

My brain was flooded with thoughts of Eli and my mother, but there was nothing true I could tell him. I had blurred the line between the personal and the professional, and the shame made me resent him, even though I knew he was trying to be kind.

'Any news on the social worker?'

Randle stared at me, his dark lashes highlighting bright eyes.

They were full of questions I couldn't answer. For the first time, I welcomed the sound of Kenny O'Sullivan's voice booming in the bullpen outside. Kenny didn't knock, but Randle moved as the door swung back and Kenny appeared, his face flushed.

'What's the story with the kid and the GP, Leah?' he said.

Randle glanced at me when I hesitated, playing the role of the enthusiastic sergeant speaking over their inspector to impress the DCI.

'The kid's OK, sir,' he said. 'The medic's given the all-clear, but the boy's still in a bit of a state. His parents are divorced, and we can't get hold of either of them – his mum's phone's dead; his dad's is going through to voicemail.'

He looked back at me for a second. I gave him a faint nod of gratitude. He dipped his chin as if to acknowledge it, turning back to Kenny.

'The social worker's just arrived, sir,' he said.

Kenny's eyes moved between me and Randle. If he noticed an undercurrent, he gave nothing away. He fixed his eyes on me as if I had been the one to give him the update.

'Tread carefully, Leah. I want a full debrief.'

'Yes, sir,' I said.

He walked out, leaving the door ajar.

The shrill sound of laughter came from the bullpen. I wondered who had made a joke, and whether it had been any good.

'Ma'am . . .'

'Yes, Randle?' My eyes dared him to continue.

'I can lead the interview with Zechariah, if you want.'

'Thank you. I appreciate the offer, but it won't be necessary.' My gaze was steady. 'I'm fine.'

Chapter Forty-One

Leah

Zechariah's clothes had been taken for testing. Huddled in the white paper suit, he looked closer to twelve than fourteen years old. His delicate features made him almost pretty. His limbs had started to bulk out, and his voice had begun to break. The social worker sat next to him, her body angled inwards so he knew she was on his side.

He looked up at me as Randle and I entered the stark interview room.

'You,' he said.

I had asked for the table to be removed to make the space less intimidating. We were left with two pairs of chairs facing each other, a low stool with a jug and four glasses to the side.

'You,' Zechariah said again. There was an even line of small spots running across his forehead, barely visible on otherwise smooth brown skin. His large eyes, rimmed by long lashes, appeared almost black in the dim light. 'You were there, then you left.'

It was more of a statement than an accusation.

'I'm sorry. It had nothing to do with you,' I said. 'I knew my colleague would take good care of you, but I apologise if it affected you.'

His expression was solemn as he considered my answer. He shrugged like he no longer cared.

'Whatever,' he said.

'We need to ask you some questions. Is that OK, Zechariah?'

'No one calls me Zechariah, except my parents.' He pulled back his shoulders, flexing his small muscles. 'It's just Zed.'

'I'm Leah. You've already met Ben.'

His skin darkened with a blush as he glanced down at his lap. I had no idea what had transpired in the room between them. Zed had been terrified, and I knew Randle would have been kind. I had seen boys his age who viewed vulnerability as a weakness. He raised his head to look at me, his features squeezed into a frown. I took the chair opposite him as Randle eased into the other one. I started the recording and went through the formalities, sitting back to give Zed more space.

'We want to talk to you about what happened before we found you in the wardrobe. If there's anything you don't remember, just say. OK?'

He drew back, pulling his left foot up in front of him on the seat. He rested his chin on his knee, his eyes far away.

'We just need you to tell us the truth, Zed, so we can find out what happened.'

His neck jerked up. 'I'm not a liar. You can ask anyone. I don't lie.'

'No one's saying you're a liar. It's important you tell the truth, that's all. Can you do that?'

He blinked. 'Yes.'

I inched forwards, softening my voice, but keeping my expression neutral.

'How did you end up in the wardrobe? Do you remember?' I said.

Zed tugged at the hem of his T-shirt, bunching then releasing the material. 'I didn't want him to see me.' He hesitated. 'It was the only place I could go.'

'You didn't want *who* to see you?'

'The man with dark hair.'

I sat back, keeping my tone light. 'Do you know the man's name?'

Zed stared back at me but didn't answer. His fist tightened around the hem.

'Had you seen him before?'

He didn't answer for a moment.

'Yes. Outside our house. He was watching. He kept coming back. I didn't know who he was.'

His eyes darted around the room, the words coming out faster the more he spoke.

I reached for a glass of water, holding it out between us, but Zed shook his head.

'Take your time, Zed. There's no rush.'

His fingers loosened as he trailed his foot on the floor between us. 'That's why I followed him. I just wanted to find out his name.'

'Did he see you?'

'I was careful. I don't think so. He kept looking around, but I was careful.'

'How did you get into his house?'

Zed's eyes snapped wider. He gripped the edge of his seat. 'I didn't do anything. I saw him go in through the basement. Then he came out, and I went to look. I didn't break in if that's what you're asking. The basement window was open . . . I just wanted to know his name. I heard him come back, and then I hid. That's all.'

'Is that how you ended up in the wardrobe?' I said.

He nodded. His eyes were pained as the memories returned. He grabbed the water, gulping down the liquid, inhaling hard as he placed the empty glass on the floor.

'I was looking through his post. I heard footsteps downstairs. I thought he had come back, so I hid under the bed.'

'You thought *who* had come back?'

Zed bit his lip, his voice quiet. 'The man with dark hair. I told you – I saw him leave the house . . . That's why I thought it was safe to go in.'

'You said you heard footsteps. Did you hear anything else?' I said.

'Not at first. But someone was in there. I didn't know what to do.'

'How long were you under the bed for?'

'I don't know.' He closed his eyes, rocking his body forwards and back. 'There were footsteps. They were getting closer. There was no way out . . . I got to the wardrobe before he saw me. The door slammed. Then I think I heard it open again. Someone else came in. Then . . .'

He stopped, his breath fragmented. Beside me, Randle ceased taking notes.

'Take your time, Zed. Then what?' I said.

Zed hugged both knees against his chest, his face in shadow. 'Then . . .' He paused. 'I just remember the screams.' He sucked in the air, holding his breath, trying to compose himself. 'You don't need to pretend. I saw the blood. Whose was it? Was it my mum's? Just tell me.'

'Why would it be your mother's blood, Zed?' I said.

His body heaved. I could see his eyes fill with questions, but he clammed up, clutching his body tight.

The social worker's voice was low beside him. 'Do you want to take a break, Zed? We can stop if you want to.'

His eyes grew wider. 'It wasn't me!'

'No one's accusing you of anything,' I said.

There was no blood on him. He wasn't a suspect.

'You don't understand.' His feet crashed to the ground. 'That's what he said.' Zed's tone was urgent. 'I heard a man's voice . . . when I was hiding. "It wasn't me . . . It was Chris." That's what the man said.'

Chapter Forty-Two

Chris

Chris took his time approaching the bar. He ordered a beer, even though he didn't drink. He chose Guinness, even though it tasted nothing like it did in Ireland – or at least that was what he had overheard at times like these, when he sat, watching, a lone man blending in with the crowd. A glass of non-Irish Guinness for the non-alcohol-drinker – a private joke that made him smile, even though he didn't have a sense of humour. He couldn't remember the last time he had laughed.

He paid the bartender and surveyed the room, looking past the sweaty bodies, perspiration sprinkled in tiny drops on bare skin, sun-kissed flesh glistening under the dim lights. It used to repulse him, but he was indifferent to it now. He walked close to pulsing limbs, never touching them. It was a game he played with himself: hovering over the scene – there, but never present. A silent spectator no one saw.

He made his way to the table in the furthest corner. There was only one chair, but he wasn't expecting company. He gripped the metal frame with his free hand, swinging it round so he had a better view. He nursed his drink, swaying gently to the beat – just another nobody, enjoying an evening in the company of strangers.

Bisi looked younger than Chris had expected. He hadn't been

told much, besides her name and age. He knew she was twenty-five on her last birthday – Pisces, not that it meant anything to him. He watched as she entered. She seemed more like a girl in her late teens. She wore a yellow crop top, so her skin glowed against the vibrant fabric, a tattoo of a snake coiled round her arm. She scanned the room, searching for admiring glances, but Chris was the only one looking, and he shielded his face with his hand so she couldn't see.

She sauntered to the bar with the determined energy of youth. Chris didn't remember being that confident at her age, but he preferred being older. There were no illusions, fewer disappointments, until this nagging numbness. He knew who he was.

The sun had made him thirsty. His fingers curled around his glass, but he didn't drink. His head was tipped downwards, but he was always aware of Bisi – where she was, whom she was with. Her long neck stretched above her collarbone – yellow top popping against chestnut skin.

'She's beautiful.'

The voice came from behind him, pensive and deep. He turned to see a tall boy – no older than nineteen or twenty, his body on the cusp of committing to a permanent frame.

'She's beautiful,' the boy said again.

His eyes lingered on Bisi, almost awestruck. He blinked in the murky light, waiting for a response in vain. People rarely approached Chris and he never engaged, but there was something about the boy's openness that he recognised from a time long ago, before he had chosen this life, which made the boy hard to dismiss.

'I'm Lemar.' The boy held out his hand, unfazed when Chris didn't shake it. 'I'd ask if you come here often, but you don't look like you want to talk.'

Chris followed the boy's gaze back to Bisi. She was speaking loudly, inviting others to watch. Her mascara had smudged in the heat, and she pulled out her compact mirror, nodding at her reflection, satisfied she still looked good. Her confidence bordered on arrogance, and he watched as she yawned with her whole body, drawing in her stomach as she stretched her arms above her head. Chris knew it was irrational, but he felt a strong flash of dislike for her. He wondered if he would lose any sleep if he was eventually asked to kill. He glanced back to see if the boy was still beside him, but Lemar had moved away.

Chapter Forty-Three

Leah

Ogechi Okoro hadn't come home for more than forty-eight hours, maybe longer. Zed had been too scared to report it in case he got his mother in trouble, lying to his father, convinced she would come back soon. It had taken several hours to prise the information out of him. He avoided my questions, then grew tired and gave up. We had finally got hold of his father. He had been in Paris on a work trip, rushing from St Pancras to claim Zed, furious with his ex-wife.

Alone in my office, I closed the door and slipped off my shoes. The floor felt warm under my toes. The room was hot and claustrophobic, and I was grateful to Akosua for the fan. I hit the highest setting, listening to the whirr of the blades rotating, the sound amplified by the silent office at night. The bullpen was practically empty except for a couple of stragglers, but if they were talking, I couldn't hear. I raised the blinds. Below me, pedestrians moved in and out of shadow, momentarily lit by the glow from the street lamps. Every time I thought of Zechariah Okoro terrified in Gabriel's wardrobe, I saw myself as a little girl crouching outside an unknown door. Then I saw Eli sitting across from me in prison, his eyes cold and challenging, his voice carrying a hint of a smile.

I needed a distraction – to forget Eli and my mother's murder. I wasn't in the mood for the solitude of my flat, but company wasn't an easy alternative. I had made little to no effort with my friends since I had returned to London, and now wasn't the time to start. I had never had the patience for the small talk needed to rekindle old relationships, and there was no one I could immediately think to call. I didn't want companionship, but I didn't want to be alone.

Outside, the night was heavy and humid as I turned in the opposite direction from the river. I drifted aimlessly away from the station, finding myself outside the brown-brick pub my fellow officers loved. I didn't get a kick out of drinking or socialising with colleagues. I had received the odd invitation, but I never felt bad saying no. I hesitated, regretting the choice I had made without thinking, but when I turned to head home, my only thought was the little girl trembling outside a door.

I stepped inside the pub, surprised to find it much busier than the first time I had been there. The air was clogged with the smell of summer, strong beer and sweaty bodies. Nineties anthems swept through the room, rousing tuneless nostalgia – low voices singing out of key. A couple from my team sat huddled, their noses almost touching, feet tapping subconsciously to the beat. The woman looked up, gesturing for me to join them. I shook my head, amused by her obvious relief when I said no. I recognised one or two other faces, but no one approached me. I slipped onto a bar stool, alone but content in the crowd. The barman looked up when he saw me. I flashed him a smile – warm enough to accelerate my order, but not enough to initiate a chat. The vodka bit at the sides of my throat as the first mouthful slipped down. The barman winked at me, his hazel eyes sparkling. I registered the extra shot with a nod.

'Looks like you've got a fan.'

I hadn't seen Randle when I entered. He had changed into a battered leather jacket over a navy T-shirt, but somehow, he didn't seem to be hot. He indicated the stool beside me.

'May I?'

'I can't stop you, but I don't want to talk about the case.'

He leant against the chair but didn't order, sliding his motorcycle helmet onto the wooden counter in front. 'We can talk about something else, if you like.'

Outside work, he wore his confidence differently, bolder without the chain of command. I looked for the flaws in his even features – the small scar on his forehead, the slight break in the bridge of his nose. He absorbed my gaze, unintimidated; I was the first to look away.

'I don't want to talk at all, Randle,' I said, concentrating on the pale yellow lemon in my glass. 'If you want scintillating conversation, I suggest you try someone else.'

I raised my drink to my lips, grimacing as the bitter liquid hit the back of my mouth.

Randle reached for my glass, placing it on the bar in front of us. 'I don't know what happened today, but this isn't the answer,' he said.

'What is then?' I was too weary to be indignant, and I wasn't sure he cared.

'I'll show you, if you like,' he said.

He stood tall, tugging at the collar of his jacket. I saw the flash of uncertainty as he ran a hand through his hair. He didn't say anything for a moment, then his mouth curved into a wide smile.

'Up to you.' He thrust his hands into his pockets. 'I'd ask you to trust me, but I'm not sure you trust anyone.'

I took another sip of my vodka. He turned and walked away. I looked up as the door swung shut after him. One more sip, then I followed him outside.

The sun had disappeared, but its rays hadn't been forgotten, and the air was still warm. Randle hovered a few feet ahead.

'Aren't you hot?' I nodded towards his worn leather jacket.

'No, and even if I was, it's a practical choice, not a fashion statement.'

I begged to differ – the cut fit too well.

Randle paused in front of his motorcycle.

'No way.' I locked my arms around my body. 'You've been drinking. I'm not getting on that with you.'

He took a step towards me, his eyes deadly serious. 'I never ride drunk. I had a sip of beer before I saw you. You can breathalyse me if you like.'

'I don't have the energy,' I said.

He eased off his jacket, holding it out between us – a long-sleeved navy T-shirt loose around his arms.

'Put this on. It will give you some protection. Do you mind waiting for a second? My spare helmet's under my desk.'

I watched him disappear around the corner as I swept the jacket over my back. It was several sizes too big. The material felt lighter than I had expected. I suspected it was expensive. That was the thing with Randle's wardrobe – his clothes were understated, the repertoire limited, but no matter how scruffy, they were always well made. A couple of minutes passed before Randle returned, walking briskly. He stopped when he saw me, suppressing a grin.

'I look ridiculous. I hope you know what you're doing.'

'You've looked better,' he said. 'But at least you'll be safe.'

Chapter Forty-Four

Leah

The journey was smooth as we travelled down the motorway, out of London. We pulled off down a side road, riding further into the night, until we arrived at a high wire fence. I watched as Randle jumped off the bike, pushing open the heavy metal gate.

'Don't worry,' he shouted above the engine. 'I know the owner. I called ahead.'

He climbed back on the bike, manoeuvring down a short path. Beyond it, I could see a large expanse of tarmac curving into a racetrack. He killed the engine. The silence was almost oppressive, but Randle was in no hurry to speak.

'What is this?' I said. 'Some kind of disused airfield?'

Randle pulled off his helmet, angling his body round so I could see his face. The front of his hair curled up as the breeze circled us. He raked a hand through the loose strands, pushing them down.

'I come here when I need a release,' he said. 'You look like you need to blow off some steam.'

'You want me to race your bike?' My voice was muffled beneath the visor.

'No.' He laughed. 'I'll do the racing. All you have to do is not fall off.' He turned back towards the track. 'I won't slow down until you tell me to.'

I gripped hard as the bike sped away. I couldn't see the dashboard, but I could feel the engine pulsing as the motorcycle moved faster and faster down the first straight. My nostrils filled with the sharp sting of petrol tinged with oil. I clung to Randle as the white lines of the track shimmered under the lights. His body dipped to the right as the bike accelerated. The wind squealed in my ears as the tyres spun. I could feel my heart moving beneath my ribcage – the murder of my mother a distant nightmare as I surrendered to the loss of control.

Chapter Forty-Five

Leah

I tried to hold on to the sense of peace as we arrived at the estate where I lived.

'Let me guess – you're going to tell me you could have gone faster?'

'I was trying to help you, not kill you. I like my job. I'm not trying to get the sack.' Randle's smile faded, the fine lines by his eyes disappearing. 'Did it? Help, I mean?' he said.

I didn't answer. Randle sighed, hitting the start button on the motorcycle. He turned towards the road as the engine swelled.

'Thanks,' I said.

I couldn't tell if he heard me. He pulled away, leaving me standing alone.

I stumbled through my flat, falling forwards onto my duvet. I buried my nose in the creased navy material – I had never understood the urge to iron sheets. Moonlight crept through the blinds, diluting the darkness. I started to count. Then everything went black.

The little girl crouched down, her cheek pressed against the wood. The door was slightly open, but she didn't dare look inside the room. The screams had stopped. The heavy thuds had faded. All she could hear now was the sound of laboured breathing, but she couldn't tell if it was coming from her. Her knees dug into the hard floor, pain shooting up both her legs. Her calves ached, but she couldn't move. She tried to forget the cramp, closing her eyes as a spasm ran through her. When she opened them, she was standing on the other side of the door. Her toes were wet, which confused her. She looked down at her shoes, but her feet were bare. Her toes curled in the shallow pool of water. Then the screaming started again, so close, she felt the vibrations. She was too scared to look up as the water rose around her. As it neared her chin, she realised it was red.

Chapter Forty-Six

Zed

Zed woke up screaming. He was startled by the crash of breaking glass. For a second, he didn't know where he was. He slowly took in his surroundings, focusing his eyes in the gloom: the rectangular shape of the flat-screen television; the bag of golf clubs he knew he would never use; the row of trainers in the cupboard which he refused to wear on principle, even though they were all his size. He had left his cupboard open, and he could see a pair of white tennis shoes shining in the dark. The bedside light had been left on; the metal base was heavy, and he suspected expensive, in keeping with most things in his father's flat. Remembering the sound of breaking, he looked down on the floor, staring at the smashed glass.

'Are you OK, Zechariah?'

His father stood in the doorway, a squat silhouette, head cocked to one side.

No! Zed wanted to shout. *What do you think?* But he ignored Isaac Okoro, burying his head in his hands.

He heard his father enter the room, flinching at the weight of his dad's hand on his shoulder – the awkward attempt at comfort making Zed resent him more.

'It's OK,' his father said.

Zed turned to him, his eyes wide with frustrated fury. 'Maybe for you.'

His father's hand dropped, but he didn't remember slapping it away. Isaac stood there, looking so helpless Zed almost felt sorry for him, then he remembered the rows when he was little, his mother's hidden tears.

'I just mean you're safe now.' His father sounded unsure of himself. 'No one can harm you. You don't need to feel scared.'

Zed shrugged. He stared at the pattern on his duvet – the familiar outline of *The Simpsons*, even though he had always hated cartoons.

'I cancelled my trip, so I can be around for you . . .'

It was the same tone his dad used on the phone when he was trying to placate a difficult client.

'I'm here if you need me. Do you want to talk about what happened?'

Zed looked at him, accusing. 'Do *you*?'

His father hesitated.

'I didn't think so.' Zed focused on Homer Simpson's yellow face. 'Anyway, talking's not going to bring Mum home.'

The mattress dipped as his father lowered his compact bulk onto the corner of the bed.

'I know you're worried, but you can't put yourself in danger. The police are doing all they can to try and bring her back.'

'Trying isn't enough,' Zed said.

He remembered the black detective's face when he had mentioned the name 'Chris'. She clearly didn't know who he was. The police would go through the motions, but they were no more use than his dad. The man he had followed had wanted something from his mother. He could have known something that would help Zed bring her back. Now the man was dead, and all Zed had was the name he had heard but no clues as to who the mysterious Chris was.

'We need to do something, Dad. We need to find her.'

He hadn't asked his dad for anything since he had walked out when Zed was six, but he couldn't stop thinking about the blood he had seen on the floor, the pain he had felt in his chest when he thought it belonged to his mum.

'Please, Dad,' he said again. 'I know you don't love her. But I do. She's all I've got.'

The mattress sprang up as his father shifted his weight to his feet.

'Get some sleep, Zechariah,' he said. 'The police will find her.'

Zed turned his back, hugging his duvet to his chest. His father started to say something, then stopped, the words suspended in his throat. The sound of them both breathing filled the air, but neither of them spoke. After a while, Zed heard wooden heels on carpet as his father retreated down the hall. Alone in the room, his vision was cloudy. Zed could feel the tears coming, but he refused to let them fall. If he had been braver, he would have kept watch through the crack in the wardrobe; he would have listened, instead of crying like a coward with his hands over his ears. If he had watched and listened, he might have seen who killed the man he had followed; he might have heard something which could lead him to Chris.

Chapter Forty-Seven

Leah

I woke with the sun, fully clothed, the next morning. The scent of oil still lingered in my nostrils; my trousers had ridden up, scrunched around my thighs. I stared at the ceiling, but all I could see were bodies – Gabriel McMahon, Ray King, Sarah Franks.

It was cooler than it had been for days, but the sun's rays threatened to break through the clouds. It was still early, and the streets were quiet: delivery vans on the wrong side of the speed limit; committed joggers with slimline backpacks, muttering their to-do lists on their commute to work. I crossed Albert Bridge, turning into Battersea Park. I trailed my hand along the railing as I walked down the path that followed the river. I could see the dense green of the weeping elm tree by the water up ahead. I turned down the track, past the bandstand and the outdoor gym. A shirtless man worked his triceps on the parallettes, gripping the frame with all his might. The chin-up bar was empty, and I slipped off my shoes, jumping up to catch the smooth metal bar. I pulled myself up until my chin rested above it, pushing down so it sat below my waist; then I lowered my body, before pulling myself up again. I lost myself in the repetitive motion – dipping down then jerking myself back up. I could feel the sweat gathering on my skin as my mind cleared and my heart rate quickened. I had to force myself to stop.

I lay on the grass to cool down, watching the park fill around me. I thought of Ray King watching Sarah Franks and Gabriel McMahon before he was found dead; Gabriel McMahon watching Ogechi's house before he was murdered in his bedroom; Sarah Franks with her throat cut, sprawled on the floor – an unknown figure in a balaclava watching her just before. It was clear the victims were connected, but how they were linked, I still didn't know.

Randle was standing outside the station when I turned the corner, grey shirt matching the ashy brick. His chin was tilted down towards his collar, so I couldn't see his eyes when he spoke.

'Morning, ma'am.'

The airfield was archived but not forgotten – we were back to the formality of work.

Randle exhaled deeply, waving away a trail of cigarette smoke. 'Zed's father wants to speak to you,' he said.

Isaac Okoro was sitting by the enquiry desk, watching the doorway. His son was next to him, but their bodies faced forwards, as if they were waiting alone. Isaac had the same delicate features as Zechariah, but in a larger face with a squarer jaw. His hair was receding above a slightly protruding forehead; his skin was without wrinkles, slightly lighter than his son's.

'Mr Okoro?' I said.

He shook the hand I offered, pulling himself up. His torso was long and broad under a well-cut suit. The tailoring flattered him, and I realised he was much shorter than I had thought.

'Leah Hutch. You wanted to see me?'

He steered me towards the door with our handshake, pleading with his eyes. 'Can we go somewhere?' He glanced at Zed without subtlety. 'I could do with some air.'

He looked at his son, as if he wasn't quite sure what to do with him.

'Randle,' I said. 'Can you get Zed something to drink, please?'

Zed glared at us but kept his thoughts to himself. I could feel his eyes boring into me as I followed his father outside.

Isaac nodded towards the turning ahead of us.

'I like to walk,' he said. 'Do you?'

He pulled a sleek silver vape from his jacket but just held it – an accessory or a comfort blanket, it was hard to tell. He set the pace, and I matched him. He didn't look at me when he spoke.

'The social worker said you found my son in a wardrobe in a room where a man was murdered,' he said.

'Yes. Gabriel McMahon. Zed told us he had been watching your ex-wife's flat. Did you know him? Has she ever mentioned him?' I kept my gaze straight ahead.

'No,' Isaac said. 'She didn't have many friends that I know of. A couple of colleagues. She never mentioned him.'

'What about someone called Chris?'

His mouth turned down at the corners as he pondered. 'Not as far as I can remember. No.'

We walked in silence as the road sloped upwards. Isaac glanced in my direction, then turned away.

'I didn't know his mother wasn't with him. You understand that, don't you, Inspector? She has sole custody. I don't see Zechariah much.'

At the junction, the lights changed from green to amber. He took my silence as judgement, gripping the vape.

'Zechariah lied to me, Inspector. He said Ogechi was at home with him. How could I know she wasn't there?'

'You didn't speak to her yourself?' I said.

'That would require a conversation.' His voice was spiked with resentment. 'Unless there's an issue, or she has to go away for work suddenly, we hardly speak any more.'

'Does she go away a lot?'

'It depends. She works in sales. Conferences. Overseas clients – that kind of thing. I know what you're thinking, Inspector.'

I watched the cars line up beside us as the lights turned red. 'Somehow I doubt that very much.'

'I mean, I realise what my relationship with Zechariah must look like.'

'I'm not here to judge your relationship, Mr Okoro,' I said.

He turned to face me, his eyes level with mine.

'I looked up to my father – trusted, even revered him. I always thought it would be that way when I had a son, but since the divorce, I can't get through to Zechariah.'

'How long were you married for?' I said.

'Six years.' His laugh was hollow as he finally brought the vape to his lips. 'It's funny to think we were so in love. I don't think Zechariah remembers. Sometimes I'm not sure I do myself. Ogechi's whole world is work and Zechariah. I always felt she was theirs more than she was mine.'

'Theirs?'

His lips tugged on the vape. The words came out bitter. 'Zechariah, her boss – Lance. I used to think she and he were lovers.'

'Were they?' I kept my stride even as Isaac's faltered.

'I don't know. I'm not sure I ever knew her. If anyone does, it's Lance.'

He stopped, pivoting to face me. Up close, I could see tiny lines etched at the corner of his eyes. 'Ogechi wasn't the best wife, but she's a good mother. She would never leave Zechariah. You need to find her. You need to find her for my son.'

Chapter Forty-Eight

Zed

Ben smiled at him like they were friends with history. Zed had only met the man twice, but Ben was less awkward with him than his dad. When Zed didn't stand up, Ben lowered himself into the chair Isaac had vacated.

'How are you?' he said, his voice relaxed.

Zed shrugged. He hadn't come to discuss his feelings. He was saved from answering when a large man approached with a determined stride, his button nose too small for his face. Ben rose, standing to attention like a soldier, but the man barely acknowledged him, marching past, his authority clear. Ben looked down at Zed – he was much taller, easily over six foot two.

'You want to get a drink, or you want to wait here?'

The hum of his phone interrupted him. He glanced at a message, then typed a swift reply.

'I'm afraid I need to take care of something, but Akosua will look after you until the inspector comes back with your dad.'

Zed neither wanted nor needed a babysitter, but he wasn't given a choice. Minutes later, Ben was replaced by a smiling woman with brown lipstick and her hair in Bantu knots. Her eyes were too friendly, and she looked nervous as she stood facing him. She introduced herself as Akosua, but he just stared at the floor.

They climbed four flights of stairs without speaking, making their way through a maze of corridors that led to a big open-plan workspace with a line of offices down the side. On the wall at the far end, he could see what looked like a grid of photographs, but he was too far away to make out anything more. Akosua steered him into the first office. There was a whiteboard and two desks, one with a glass of something orange next to a plate with three custard creams.

'I didn't know what biscuits you like.' She sounded apologetic.

'I don't like *them*,' he said, then immediately felt bad. He kicked out a chair, sitting down hard. He took a sip from the glass – the squash was too strong, and he pushed the drink away.

'I can get you a coffee,' Akosua said. 'Maybe not coffee. Water?'

Her awkwardness mixed with sympathy was grating.

'No. Thanks. I need to go to the loo.'

She nodded, glad to be tasked with something practical. She escorted him out of the room, back the way they came, then down a different corridor, until they arrived in front of a male pictogram peeling at the edges, stuck on a cheap door. When she made no attempt to leave, he looked at her, perplexed.

'I'm fourteen. I know how to go to the bathroom. You don't have to wait.'

He pushed open the door, without waiting for a response. When he emerged minutes later, he was relieved to find she had gone. He was sick of adults feeling sorry for him without doing anything useful. He took his time retracing his steps back to the room with the custard creams. The door was closed. He could see the board of photographs at the end of the walkway. No one was looking at him, so he kept moving towards it, drawn by the sight of his mother's name, *Ogechi Okoro*, printed in black on a white label underneath a photo of her smiling with a slight frown. He wondered where they had got it – she looked a lot younger. It wasn't a picture he had seen before. As his eyes roved, he was hit by a grid of brutal images. There were names under each photo, bloodied bodies cut and stabbed. *Gabriel McMahon* – the man he had followed; *Sarah Franks*; *Ray King*. He retched, clamping his mouth shut so he wasn't sick on the floor. He rushed back down the walkway to Akosua, waiting in the room. She sat at the second desk, holding out a mug towards him.

'I know it's summer, but I'm a fan of hot chocolate,' she said.

'Thank you.'

He reached for the handle, trying hard not to gag. His voice sounded small, but she didn't seem to notice, relieved to have got him on side.

'Good news. Your dad's finished with the inspector. A few more minutes and then you can go home.'

When he didn't say anything, she frowned, genuinely worried.

'Everything OK?'

'I'm fine, thank you,' he said.

He plastered on a smile, but his mind was filled with bodies. He prayed his mother wasn't dead too.

Chapter Forty-Nine

Leah

A timeline of death stretched across the wall: Gabriel McMahon's dead body, his neck and back butchered, next to Sarah Franks' pathetic, bloody corpse. Above them, Ray King, the private investigator, clothed and serene on Gabriel's sofa, then prostrate on a trolley, his pale skin lifeless and blotched. In the top left-hand corner, an enlarged photo of Ogechi Okoro; on the right, an empty white rectangle with *CHRIS?* printed in black caps.

'Do you think Ogechi Okoro's next, ma'am?'

Randle handed me a coffee I hadn't asked for – the kick of caffeine gave my brain a welcome prod.

'We don't know how they're all connected. You can't predict a pattern without some facts.'

'Point taken, ma'am.' Randle snapped open a banana – two bites and it was gone. 'We could be looking at three different killers.'

'Or two, or even one.'

We didn't know why Gabriel was watching the building where Ogechi lived, or why Ray had surveillance photos of Sarah Franks and Gabriel McMahon. If Ray was a private investigator, who hired him? Did they kill Sarah and Gabriel, or was it someone else?

'And who's Chris?' Randle said. 'The kid was scared. How can we be sure he heard the name correctly? Did Isaac Okoro know anything about him, ma'am?'

'No.'

'Could he be the figure in the balaclava?'

'Maybe.' I shrugged. 'Did Lu Hoffen get anywhere with the lead Sami's father gave us – Sarah Franks' drug dealer?'

'Tipper Wheldon? I don't know, ma'am,' Randle said. 'Do you want me to find out?'

'Sure.' It didn't hurt. 'And let's see if Chris' name comes up elsewhere. How are we doing with the contents of Ray's office? Any mention of a Chris?'

Akosua bounded towards us, eyes flashing with enthusiasm. Her hair was parted in even sections, each one crowned with a small, coiled bun. She tapped the two at the front, checking her vigour hadn't disrupted the knots.

'We're going through his files, ma'am. Nothing on Chris yet. Ray didn't have a phone on him when he was found,' she said. 'And there wasn't one in his office or his flat. We've got his records – we're looking at repeat numbers to identify the callers.'

'And?'

I wondered if she was capable of delivering facts without a build-up.

'Gabriel's number appears on the log – Ray King called Gabriel two nights before he was found dead on Gabriel's sofa.'

Randle's eyes moved to the bodies on the board. 'Coincidence or warning?'

His forefinger tapped against his thigh. His forehead furrowed as he thought.

'Gabriel insisted he had never seen Ray King before. Why would he lie to us?'

My eyes drifted to the image of Ray on the sofa, positioned so carefully it was meant to unnerve. I recalled Gabriel in his surgery, brittle and evasive – the way his hand shook when I said Ray King's name.

'Maybe Ray made contact with Gabriel by phone, but they didn't get a chance to meet . . .'

Randle was in front of the board in one stride, broad shoulders blocking my view. 'Until he turned up dead on Gabriel's sofa. That's quite some meeting, ma'am. No wonder Gabriel was on edge.'

I pictured Ray's corpse on Harrison's trolley – bluish-purple skin indicating his body had been moved. Then I remembered the surveillance photos of Gabriel, the fear I had seen in his eyes.

'Gabriel wasn't on edge, he was terrified,' I said. 'Whoever killed Ray wanted to give Gabriel a scare. Whatever Ray wanted with Gabriel, his killer made sure Gabriel wouldn't talk.'

Chapter Fifty

Leah

At first glance, the files from Ray King's office told us very little about what he had been investigating – just mundane details about his targets' lives. There were no names, so his notes were hard to follow, but the team was going through them all the same. The connection to Ogechi still eluded us. We turned to her boss to fill in the gaps. The rush-hour traffic tried my patience, and I regretted not letting Randle drive. He sat beside me, flicking through the pages of his notebook – there were never more than a couple of words scribbled on a page.

'Do you think Ogechi was involved in whatever got Gabriel killed, ma'am?'

I hit the brakes as a cyclist veered in front of me.

'I don't know. Let's see what Lance Elbourne has to say.'

Ogechi Okoro worked for a mid-sized medtech company specialising in orthopaedic devices. I pulled up outside a large concrete cuboid, with long windows covering the front in a grid. Lance Elbourne's office was on the third floor. The lift opened onto a large room with banks of desks and soulless office furniture. A man in his forties approached in grey trousers and a white shirt.

'Lance?'

Only photographs of the C-suite had made it onto the company website. Lance was senior but hadn't made the leadership team, running one of the divisions in sales.

'I'm Jimmy, his assistant.' Jimmy seemed determined not to smile. 'I'll take you to Mr Elbourne,' he said.

The City of London looked majestic through the floor-to-ceiling windows, old and new buildings rising up against the sky. No one looked up as we followed Jimmy to the office in the corner. He tapped the door, then waited.

'Come in,' a deep, melodious voice replied.

'Whenever you're ready . . .' Jimmy turned and walked away.

Lance Elbourne was standing by the window with his back to us, looking down at a car park enclosed by a high brick wall. He was a small man, with narrow hips in dark grey trousers, a navy linen jacket skimming the top of his legs.

'Just my luck,' he said, gesturing below him.

'I don't know. Sure, you missed out on a view, but I'm guessing you've achieved other things in life.'

He pivoted, grey eyes dancing with amusement. The paisley pattern on his shirt was surprisingly bright. He focused on Randle. 'Are you as sharp as she is, or just along for the ride?'

Randle just smiled as Lance's eyes moved back towards me. From the front, you couldn't tell he was balding – there was a slight frizz to his hair, disguised by its short length. It was light brown with wisps of silver, the potential for wildness tamed. His body was lean, but he had the beginnings of a double chin. He looked like a man in his early fifties, but his eyes betrayed an older age.

'Ignore me. Please do take a seat,' Lance said.

The office was small, and there was only one seat opposite his desk. The door opened and Jimmy appeared out of nowhere, brandishing another chair.

'Thank you, Jimmy.' Lance dismissed him with a nod. 'Please . . .' he said again.

I slipped into the chair opposite, looking at Randle to kick the encounter off.

'I'm DS Ben Randle.' Randle gestured towards me. 'DI Leah Hutch. We spoke on the phone.'

'Yes. You want to talk about Ogechi – how may I help?'

I found the lime-green paisley shirt strangely distracting. I forced my gaze back to his face.

'When was the last time you saw her?' I said.

Lance glanced at his watch with its frayed leather wristband. 'A week ago. She often works remotely. She's taken some time off over the summer to be with her child.'

'And you haven't heard from her?' I studied him unapologetically. 'I understand from her ex-husband that your working relationship was close.'

Lance leant back in his chair, giving us the full benefit of his shirt. His eyes were laughing. 'Isaac said that?'

'He thought you and Ogechi had an affair.'

Lance smoothed his collar against his shoulder. 'I'm flattered. I would say she's young enough to be my daughter, but when has that ever acted as a deterrent?' He glanced at the screen of his computer. 'It's a moot point, as it happens. Romance doesn't interest me – an unnecessary distraction from more important things in life.'

'Which are?'

'That's for another conversation, Inspector.'

'Does Ogechi feel the same way?'

'You'd have to ask her. What I do know is that she sees the value in her job. We're all trying to make the world a better place, do our bit for humankind and what not.'

'Are we?' I said.

Randle contained a smile.

'Isn't that the essence of your work, Inspector?' Lance ran his fingers along the lapel of his jacket. 'Ridding our streets of unsavoury types?'

'If you like, but it's a job, not a mission. It's not a crusade.' I pushed myself up in my seat so my eyes were level with his. 'And you haven't heard from Ogechi?'

'Not since I last saw her.'

'Do you have any idea where she might be?'

He studied my face, reading the question behind the question. 'I'm guessing on a little jaunt somewhere with her son.'

He stopped, grasping what I had left unspoken.

'You don't know where she is, do you, Inspector?' he said.

'She didn't turn up to pick up Zechariah. She's been missing for at least three days.'

'And there's no possibility she's travelling for work?' Randle's pen hovered over his tiny pad.

'I have complete oversight of her schedule. If she went away for her job, I would be the first to know.'

He eased himself forwards in his chair, settling his forearms on the desk.

'I've worked with Ogechi Okoro for a long time. She works hard; she has no interest in hobbies. She does two things in life – work and care for Zechariah. If she's not doing either, something's not right.'

Chapter Fifty-One

Leah

My phone vibrated as soon as we left the building. Georgina Harrison had sent me a text: a solitary exclamation mark, followed by her initials – lower case, because capitalising took time she didn't care to waste.

She was standing in the doorway of her office, arms folded, unsmiling, when we arrived.

'What took you so long?' she said.

The red laces on her snow boots were done up loosely – a grudging concession to the heat. Her navy shirt was rolled up above her elbows, a blur of letters swirled across the front. I squinted, attempting to decipher them.

'Don't bother trying to make them mean something, Hutch,' she said, watching me with small eyes. 'Some mysteries aren't meant to be solved.'

Her gaze travelled to Randle.

'See, Ben. I'm funny as well as smart.' She leant back against the door frame, bored of her half-hearted flirting. 'Which d'you want first, Detectives – heart or gore?'

'Heart,' I said.

'I never pegged you for a romantic. We'll save the bodies for the end.'

She turned back into her office, retrieving a thin cardboard file from her desk. The writing on the white label was illegible – a code only Harrison could understand.

'Ray King's full tox report's not back yet, but I was feeling generous, so I thought I'd give you a preview. Short version: I was right.'

'And the mid-length one?' I reached for the file. She held on to it for a second longer than was needed before she released it into my hand.

'Large quantities of cocaine were found in his bloodstream, but no traces of narcotics in his nasal passage, throat or on his gums. So . . .'

'You were right about the puncture wound. Someone injected him with cocaine to induce a heart attack; someone who knew he had a weak heart.'

'How do we know he didn't inject himself?' Randle said.

Harrison had always been serious about her work; there was no hint of flirtation when she replied.

'We don't – categorically – but there are no puncture or track marks anywhere else on his body so, if he did do that, it was likely the first time, and he's the king of bad luck.'

I scanned the notes she had given me – they only mentioned Ray King.

'Did you manage to get a look at the Sarah Franks autopsy?' I lowered my voice, aware I had put Harrison in a compromising position by asking for information about another detective's case.

'You don't need to whisper, Hutch,' she said. 'Lu Hoffen can't hear you all the way in Elephant and Castle. Even if she could, I reckon you could take her – on a good day.'

Harrison walked round her desk, so she could see her computer, attacking the keyboard with her forefinger and thumb. 'You owe me,' she said.

She looked up at Randle. He shifted his weight back onto his heels.

'Relax, Ben.' She flicked her eyes towards her screen. 'It's DI Hutch's debt. When I want something from you, you'll know.'

She angled the monitor to face us, scrolling through images of Sarah Franks sprawled on the floor in Elephant and Castle, clutching the wound on her neck. Harrison paused on a close-up taken during her autopsy. She appeared more peaceful than when we had seen her last – on her back, head straight, eyes closed. The wound to her neck was clearly visible – a brutal jab driven deep into her skin.

'She was stabbed in her carotid, but you already know that. She didn't stand a chance. Do you see this?'

Harrison traced the screen with her finger, indicating a thin red line across the front of Sarah's neck.

'It looks like a blade was held to her flesh, for long and hard enough to make an impact, without puncturing the skin.'

'Pretty efficient.' Randle's voice was soft behind me.

'You could say that.' Harrison swivelled the monitor back round. 'Very different from what happened to Ray King.'

'What about Gabriel McMahon?' I said.

I was still clutching the file. She glanced at it. Her brown eyes looked hazel under the overhead light.

'Put your homework away, Hutch. Talking will only get us so far. It's time for the fun part.'

*

Gabriel McMahon lay waiting in the mortuary – his pale corpse the central exhibit in the sterile white room. My gaze drifted to the silver fridges packed with dead bodies, stacked on top of one another like tins. I wondered where Ray King was shelved in his sterile metal coffin, now his place on the slab had been usurped. Gabriel had been positioned on his side, exposing a knife wound on his back, just above his shoulder blade. The skin was darker where he had been stabbed in his neck, but the blood had been flushed clean.

'What do you make of him?' Harrison said.

Randle didn't hesitate. 'Clean hit to the carotid artery, just like Sarah Franks.'

'Yes, but what did you see when you entered his house? What were the details? What were the clues? How do they help tell the story about how Gabriel McMahon died?'

I remembered the trail of blood up the stairs, the red handprint on the wall. I imagined a bloodied Gabriel McMahon trying to get away, being pursued to his bedroom. Harrison watched me intently – her voice was like a morbid voiceover as she described the scene of the crime.

'He encountered the killer in his home and tried to get away up the stairs. He was stabbed in the back to stop him. He tried to resist. He was overcome. Then he was stabbed in the carotid, just like Sarah Franks. The fatal wound was clean and precise. A quick strike with the knife, and he was as good as dead.' Harrison paused, holding my gaze as she delivered her final verdict. 'Both Gabriel McMahon and Sarah Franks were assassinated, Leah. The perpetrator knew how to get the job done. From the size of the wound, it could have been the same knife.'

Gabriel hadn't stood a chance; neither had Sarah Franks. Harrison was right – these were cold, clinical kills, likely carried out by the same murderer. But what about Ray King?

Chapter Fifty-Two

Leah

Kenny O'Sullivan listened without interrupting, his nostrils flaring. When I finished, he watched me without speaking, his small green eyes flashing as an internal conversation played in his head.

'So, what you're saying is that Sarah Franks and Gabriel McMahon's deaths could be related?'

I could tell from his tone he didn't want an answer. I focused on his collar, too tight round his neck – stiff white cotton digging into reddened skin at the end of a long day.

'What about Ray King – the mysterious TV enthusiast on the sofa?' His green eyes settled on mine. 'How does he tie in?'

'The murder was clever, planned, meticulous, sir. It was meant to scare Gabriel McMahon. Possibly to silence him. Different *modus operandi*, conceivably a different killer.'

'Or the same killer, wanting a different outcome,' Kenny said.

'Sarah Franks' drug dealer is a potential suspect for her death. Ray had drugs injected into his system. It's not out of the question,' I said.

I sometimes forgot Kenny had once been a shrewd investigator; he was so concerned with results, I was never sure how much he cared about a case. He rolled his fingertips over the contours of his belly, leaning back into the cushioned support of his chair.

'One killer's one killer too many, Leah. Two killers . . .' He puffed out a stream of air. 'More than most people can handle. The question is, can you?'

'We need a clearer picture, sir—'

'What we don't need, Leah, is word getting out about silent assassins planting dead bodies and slaying victims in their own homes.'

He didn't move, but the space between us felt smaller. 'You need to change the narrative . . .'

His familiar catchphrase – proof PR would always trump the needs of the case.

'No more bodies, and no more motherless children looking miserable in my police station.'

'Sir?'

He moved his elbows to his desk, interlacing his fingers to create a platform for his chin.

'I saw him downstairs with Randle, Leah. It sends the wrong message. The boy with the missing mother, trying not to cry. He thinks his mother's been murdered, but he's too scared to say it out loud.'

'There's no indication his mother's dead, sir.'

There's no indication she's alive.

I thought of my own mother, butchered to death by my father, her body still not found. I saw my younger self terrified, just like Zed. He still had a chance.

'You need a plan, Leah.'

'Yes, sir.'

'Put the father in front of a camera. Tug at the public's heart strings. Get the message out.'

Kenny stood up in slow motion. I heard the creak of his knees as he straightened to his full height.

'Step it up, Leah. No more bodies. I want her found, and I want her found alive.'

Chapter Fifty-Three

Zed

Bart Simpson's hair glowed in the darkness – a yellow shape on the navy duvet, lit by Zed's phone. He stared at the line of names on the screen, puzzled it wasn't longer. He had listed all his mum's friends he remembered, but there weren't many. He wondered whether it was because she was like him and didn't feel the need for company, or whether he knew her less well than he thought. At least now he could ask Isaac for their details – now his father knew she was gone. He suspected Isaac would refuse at first, but the guilt of being a bad father would push him to comply. There was a press conference the next day, a chance to beg for information from the public. He hoped his father would sound like he cared, so people would respond. Just before his parents split up, they used to pretend they liked each other when he was within earshot. It had been a convincing act until they started screaming and slamming doors.

He looked at the time on his phone – tiny digits reminding him that it was technically morning. He should have gone to sleep hours ago, but thoughts kept rolling over in his mind. He couldn't stop seeing the dead bodies on the board: the dark-haired stranger on the carpet he knew to be Gabriel McMahon; the woman whose name was Sarah, one hand clutching her neck; then, the one that terrified him most – the man sitting rigid on the sofa with death in his eyes.

Dissonant chords slipped under his bedroom door – his dad was still awake, listening to jazz. Zed's mind was overrun by pictures from the police station. A thought took hold – he had been working off the wrong list. He was wasting time trying to think of his mother's friends; he already had the leads he needed from the police station. He recited the names he remembered, recalling their position on the wall.

Chris?

Sarah – he couldn't remember her surname . . .

Gabriel McMahon

Ray King

Zed pulled up a search box on his mobile, typing in the full names. An obituary for Gabriel McMahon came up. He started to read, but lost interest halfway. There was a Ray King Instagram page with a couple of dozen followers – photographs of the dead man in military uniform, details of a tribute to be held in a pub. He scrolled down to find the address, interrupted by a knock on the door. He jumped under his duvet, pretending to be asleep. He could smell his father's aftershave – lime and cinnamon – the same scent from when his dad had lived at home. He squeezed his eyes shut in the darkness, trying to block his father out – all he could think of was Ray King dead on the sofa, staring straight ahead, eyes wide and blank.

Chapter Fifty-Four

Chris

Chris moved silently down the dark street, the rhythm of his steps dictated by another. It was like dancing with a partner who didn't know how to lead. He watched as Bisi left the club, tipsy on expensive stilettos. He stood back as she shouted at her driver, indignant down the phone. He followed her along a road lined with cars parked at odd angles. She had no idea he was behind her, hidden by the night. A couple of times, she turned her head, but he blended into the blackness. He could take her at any point, but there was a plan he had to follow, and it hadn't come to that – yet. He stayed in the shadows, waiting for her to walk a safe distance. She was drunk and oblivious, but he couldn't risk being caught. He was about to emerge when he heard loud breaths approaching – the sound of someone moving too fast for their body to cope. He held back, waiting, watching the lanky figure, not quite running. He recognised the tall boy he had spoken to in the bar, with his open, willing face. He looked on as Lemar approached Bisi, more confident than the first time Chris had seen him. Lemar glanced back as if sensing his thoughts. Chris stooped low behind a car so he wasn't visible. Bisi and Lemar spoke for a few seconds, eyes locked with intent. Chris couldn't decipher their words from where he hid.

Lemar touched Bisi's elbow, familiar. She looked down at his hand but didn't shrug him off. There was an intimacy between them that could become inconvenient. Somehow, he didn't want the boy to become involved. Chris' brief didn't include killing, but he had been here before, and it didn't end well.

Chapter Fifty-Five

Leah

I woke in the middle of the night. I couldn't remember many details, but I had dreamt about myself as a little girl again – my cheek pressed against a door, outside the room where Eli had committed his crimes, then inside. I couldn't get the screams out of my head.

I lay on my bed, staring at the sliver of moon visible through the window, unable to get back to sleep. I thought about skipping, but the courtyard was empty. The sound of rope hitting concrete would echo around the estate, drawing unwanted attention, and I didn't feel like putting on a show.

At times like these, Margaretta had read her Bible or counted out loud. I didn't have her faith, and I wasn't in the mood to listen to my voice droning on. I thought about Sami, those nights as a teenager when he would walk with me without asking questions. Before I could talk myself out of it, I found his number scribbled on the piece of paper and reached for my phone. I was about to hang up when I heard Sami's voice.

'Leah, are you OK?'

I didn't answer.

'What's going on? Is something wrong?'

'I'm sorry,' I said. 'Forget I called.' My voice sounded strangled. I hung up the phone before he could respond.

Frustrated, I forced myself out of bed and pulled on a vest and some old tracksuit bottoms. I retrieved my trainers from the shoe rack, devising a bodyweight circuit challenging enough to clear my head. I rotated through push-ups, lunges, squats and sit-ups – a hundred of each – then I started again. I was halfway through my third circuit when I heard knocking. I ignored it. The soft thuds continued.

I opened the door to find Sami standing opposite me, slightly ruffled, looking perplexed.

'You're sweating,' he said, like it was a new phenomenon.

'Why are you here, Sami?' I said.

'You had a nightmare.'

I couldn't tell if it was a question or a statement. I was still getting to grips with him being there.

He looked past me into my flat. Then his gaze settled back on my face. 'I wondered if you fancied a walk?'

'It's two in the morning.'

He shrugged like the time meant nothing to him. He must have dressed in a hurry, but he didn't look a mess: crisp blue shirt, navy trousers, slightly wild hair the only clue he had rushed out of bed. I thought about telling him to go home, then I saw the concern in his eyes, and I was grateful he cared. I grabbed my keys.

'OK,' I said. 'Lead the way.'

The night was heavy and humid, with very little breeze. Sami waited for me to speak first as we turned onto the street.

'How did you know I had a nightmare?'

'Your voice sounded strained,' he said quietly. 'Like it did that first time when we were kids.'

I had told him my dreams had gone. Witnessing his distress, I regretted the lie.

'How did you know I'd open the door?' I said.

'I didn't.' When I looked at him, he smiled back at me. 'I took a calculated risk.'

The neighbourhood was calm, the streets less busy. There were a few people about – unsteady on their feet, in a drunken haze.

'You haven't asked me what the dream was about.'

We turned onto a side street. My face was still hot from working out, my limbs tense, ready for more.

'Dreams can be revealing. Everyone's entitled to their secrets,' Sami said.

I raised an eyebrow. 'You sound like a man who has a lot of his own . . .'

He shrugged. His shirt was cut perfectly across his shoulders. 'Of course I have secrets. Who doesn't? You're not exactly an open book yourself.' His mouth curled into a grin.

We strolled in comfortable silence past a pub having a lock-in – the lights were on, the laughter and music loud. Sami looked up at the silhouettes dancing in the window. After a moment, he turned back to me. The buzz from the pub faded in the background. Sami's eyes were far from peaceful. I wondered what was going on in his mind.

'You haven't asked me about the case. You must be dying to?' I said.

He shook his head as a solitary car sped down the road. 'Tonight's about you, not me, not the case.'

'Those things aren't mutually exclusive.' I pushed harder.

'They're not. But why can't we focus on you? What are you scared of?' His grey eyes sparkled; they looked almost silver.

I turned away.

'Still the same Leah Hutch, evading personal questions.'

'Why change the habit of a lifetime?' I said.

Sami chuckled. 'Why indeed . . .'

We arrived at the main road. I could see the fluorescent lights of the petrol station up ahead, cars decelerating as they crept into the forecourt.

'What now?' I said.

'We could play eye-spy for old times' sake? Walk some more until you're ready to sleep? I've got no plans – we can walk for as long as you like.'

It was effortless being in his company, like we were teenagers again. A minute passed in which neither of us spoke. A man came towards us, striding directly into our path like a wrecking ball. I stood my ground, refusing to be intimidated. Sami took my elbow, steering me away.

'Easy, tiger. I know you're tough, Leah, but there's a killer out there.' He was laughing. 'No need to pick fights with strangers just because they get in your way.'

'I can handle myself, Sami. In case you hadn't noticed, I'm a police officer investigating murder.'

My tone was light, but the atmosphere instantly changed.

'I noticed.' Sami's eyes were pained. 'I saw Sarah's body . . . what they did to her. I just don't want you to get hurt.'

His eyes darkened, the intensity unnerving. The fact that I was with a former suspect in the early hours suddenly hit me. It felt ill-advised, even though Sami hadn't been charged, and it wasn't directly my case.

His hand was still resting on my arm. I shook it off unceremoniously.

'Sorry . . .'

There was an awkward tension between us.

'It's fine,' I said. 'Thanks for the walk, Sami. I'll make my own way home.'

Chapter Fifty-Six

Zed

Zed sat at the back of the room the next morning, studying his father's face. His dad's skin was fairer, but their features were the same – he recognised the long nose, the hidden nostrils, large eyes cloaked by heavy lids that could conceal a multitude of thoughts. The similarities were ironic, given his father was nothing like him – Isaac had nothing to do with the boy Zed was, or the man he planned to be. Isaac sat behind a table, beside Leah, the black female officer, and the large man who had walked past Zed downstairs in the police station the day he had seen the board. He was clearly Leah's superior, speaking twice as much to make his seniority known. In the spotlight, surrounded by cameras and journalists, his father looked less awkward than he did when he and Zed were alone.

Zed had never been to a press conference. Leah had managed his expectations – cameras, sombre faces, prying questions, urgent pleas. He wasn't supposed to be in the room, but he had insisted. His dad agreed because he didn't want a scene. He had been ushered in by Ben after the conference started; the plan was for them to slip out early before anyone noticed he was there. For now, he stared at his father's lips, pleading for the return of his child's mother, focusing on the pain of a son, rather than a husband who had lost his wife. Zed couldn't bring himself to listen to the specific words. Isaac Okoro had always been a hypocrite, but at least this time he was trying to help.

Afterwards, Zed was deposited in a room without windows, waiting for his father to collect him. Ben had left him in the care of a thin woman who seemed completely disinterested in him. He stared at another mug of milky brown hot chocolate, gagging at the sickly sweet smell. He thought of Seema, the girl from the estate, sure she would be delighted by the sugar overload. He was surprised by the sudden hankering for her childlike hopefulness. He barely knew her, but he found the adult world without his mother exhausting and sad. He sipped the drink, burning his tongue on the hot liquid. The door opened and Leah stood watching him. He guessed he was shorter than her, but only by a fraction. It was hard to tell because she appeared bigger than she was.

'Your father will just be a second,' Leah said, as if the words were supposed to comfort him.

He nodded, not wanting to appear rude.

'The press conference should help the investigation.'

She hovered, frowning, as if worried that the more she said, the harder it would be to leave. Zed spoke before he could censor himself, frustration spilling out.

'What else are you doing to find her?' His voice sounded too high in the bare room. He had a vague recollection of learning about acoustics in physics, but the thought died as quickly as it came to life.

'We have teams of people looking,' Leah said, matter-of-fact.

'How many?'

She sighed, accepting the inevitability of conversation. She took a step towards the table but didn't sit.

'As many as we think necessary.'

'What if that's not enough?'

'I'm not going to insult you by making empty promises.' She watched him for a reaction. 'But I want you to know we're doing everything we can.'

'What if that's not enough?' Zed said again. He was struggling to read her expression.

She placed her hands on the seat opposite. 'Let's not get too far ahead.'

Zed felt the doubt creeping up inside him. He hardened his features, willing Leah to leave him with the thin woman who ignored him, but she just stood there, holding on to the chair.

'Zed, your mother would never forgive herself if something happened to you. You can't put yourself at risk trying to find her. You need to trust us to do our job.'

She took a breath, as if it had cost her to reprimand him.

'Who's us?' He stared at her. He didn't know why he was being confrontational. 'You mean you and Boy Cop?'

Leah looked blank for a moment, then her lips twitched as she realised what he meant. 'I take it Boy Cop is DS Ben Randle?'

'Boy Cop and Black Cop . . .' He knew he sounded insolent, but it was too late to back down. 'Perfect for a black kid who lives with his mum – strong male role model, the female touch, hot drinks while we bond over our blackness. Got to say, it's a pretty solid play.'

He stopped, preparing for a rebuke or a comeback, but Leah just laughed, long and hard.

'You give us way too much credit.' Her face almost softened. 'We were just the first officers at the scene.'

He remembered the blood on the carpet, the piercing scream before the silence. His hostility faded as the horror filled his mind.

'When you ran out of the room, did you see anyone else in the house? Why was that man, Gabriel, watching our flat? Have you found who killed him?'

She frowned. 'Where did you hear that name?'

'I saw it on the letters. On his desk.' She didn't need to know he had seen the board of death in the police station.

Leah sighed again. 'It's an ongoing investigation.'

Zed balled his hands under the table.

'Ongoing's just another word for "no" . . . If you can't find Gabriel's murderer, why should I trust you to find my mother?'

He barely heard the scrape of the chair as she pulled it back.

'Who else are you going to trust, Zed?'

She sat, their eyes level across the table.

'What were you saying when I found you?' she said.

His fists felt like weights crushing his thighs. 'I don't know what you're talking about.'

'You were chanting something. What was it?' she said.

Her face held no trace of judgement, but he struggled to hold her gaze. 'My name's Zechariah Okoro and I'm a fighter. No one can break my spirit or steal my joy.'

'Where does that come from?' Leah said. 'Did you make it up?'

He shook his head, too exposed to be defensive. 'Something I got from my mum.'

'And how have you been since we found you?' She hesitated – awkwardness didn't suit her. 'Are you sleeping OK?'

Zed could see himself waking up screaming, but he had no recollection of the dream. Leah was looking at him intently, the concern in her voice unnerving.

'I know what you're doing, but I don't need therapy,' he said. 'My dad made me go when he left my mother. It doesn't change anything. It won't help me find my mum.'

'All I'm saying is . . .' – she continued as if she hadn't heard him – 'sometimes memories can be delayed. I'm not saying you did, but you could have heard something, seen something when you were hiding, which you can't remember, and then it suddenly comes back when you're not expecting it. If that happens, tell your father to call me.'

She pulled a slim leather wallet from her pocket, sliding out a small white card.

'Your father has my details, but here, take this too.'

She placed it between them on the table, but he didn't reach for it immediately. Once she had gone, he ran his fingers over the rough edge. He knew she was trying to help, but he couldn't sit back and do nothing. He was Zechariah Okoro. He had always been a fighter. No one could stop him from saving his mum.

Chapter Fifty-Seven

Leah

I could tell the boy wasn't listening, and I didn't blame him. At his age, I would have been the same. I imagined what I would have done if Margaretta had disappeared when I was a teenager – she had never been affectionate, but she cared for me, and I knew I would have been lost. I had a voice note from the estate agent wanting to start viewings of the house Margaretta had left me. I filed it in my mental to-do list for another time. I scanned a message from Randle warning me Kenny was in my office waiting. I didn't have the energy to deal with him; I turned around and headed out into the street. Zed was right, there was more that we could do. So far, I had avoided Lu Hoffen as much as possible, but it wasn't what was best for the case.

I wasn't familiar with Elephant and Castle, but the café was easy enough to find. The sergeant at the front desk at the police station hadn't asked many questions. He'd taken one look at my badge and told me what I needed to know. Lu Hoffen was facing away from the door, her lean frame hunched over a table by the back wall. She glanced up as I slid into the seat opposite, her knife and fork suspended above a plate of eggs, sausages, beans and fried bread.

'I'm eating.'

'I'm not stopping you.'

Her cutlery continued to hover. She was looking down, but I could see a blush spread across her cheeks.

'I don't like people watching me when I eat.' Her voice was low, as if she was confessing a long-held secret.

I angled my knees towards the neighbouring table so my body turned away.

'Better?'

'It will do . . . or you could go . . .'

I held up my hand and signalled to the waitress.

'Black coffee, please,' I said.

'How did you find me?' The scrape of metal against ceramic as Lu took her frustration out on her fry-up.

'I went to the station.'

'So much for confidentiality.' She snorted. 'Pass me the salt.'

I nudged the salt cellar towards her. I heard her reach for it. She chewed slowly, weighing her words.

'You know . . . if you wanted to take a look at Sarah Franks' autopsy, all you had to do was ask me.'

'I have no control over what Harrison chooses to look at,' I said.

Another snort. She swallowed her drink.

The waitress set a mug down by my elbow. Her hand moved too fast, and the brown liquid rose like a wave, spilling onto the white tablecloth. I could see Lu gearing up to complain, but the woman had already turned safely away.

Lu caught my eye as I mopped the coffee with a napkin. 'I come here for the food, not for the service,' she said.

'I'm not judging your choice of eating establishment, Lu. I came to see you.' I swivelled to face her. 'Anyway, I'm not a fan of eggs.'

'I remember.' She dropped her cutlery with a clatter, pushing away her plate. 'What do you want, Hutch? Come to waste more of my time?'

'What are you talking about?'

She made a noise, somewhere between a sniff and a laugh. 'Tip Wheldon? The dealer who supplied Sarah Franks with drugs?'

'What happened with her?' I said. 'Randle was going to follow up.'

'Well, she cried a lot.' Lu shrugged. 'Insisted she was helping Sarah keep her head above water, after she got hooked again. Supplying her with prescription meds instead of the hard stuff. Tip Wheldon's quite the girl guide. She doesn't touch Class As.'

'And?'

'Apparently she met Sarah through your boy, Sami.' She paused. 'But the most interesting part is that her alibi checks out, so it was a waste of time listening to her cry.'

'We follow leads,' I said. 'That's the job. Sometimes they don't work out.'

Lu stood. She was close to five foot ten, even with bad posture.

'Thanks for the career lesson, Leah. I need to get back.'

She pulled a ten-pound note and some coins from her pocket, laying them clumsily by her plate.

'Maybe I can help you,' I said.

Her arms stiffened. Resentment made her eyes small.

'We've been doing this for the same amount of time. I don't need you to draw me a diagram.'

'That's not what I meant. I have a case that may be related. That's all.'

For the second time, her face coloured, but she bit down any embarrassment. I pulled a slim folder from my bag, offering a truce.

'Autopsy results for a GP named Gabriel McMahon. We could be looking for the same killer.'

She flicked through the folder.

'We're looking for someone who knows what they're doing. A scuffle, then it was cold and clinical – just like Sarah Franks.'

She paused on a photograph, shaking her head at the senseless brutality. Whatever our differences, we were fighting for the same side.

'I'll share anything that seems relevant,' I said. 'What else have *you* got?'

She inhaled deeply, her shoulders rising towards her ears.

'What else have you got, Lu? This has to work both ways.'

'OK. In the spirit of open collaboration, you better follow me.'

She didn't speak as I walked behind her towards the station where Sami had been questioned. Her stride was surprisingly short, despite her long legs. Her hair was in a loose bun with strands escaping, the skin above her white collar burnt a dark red.

She led me down a narrow corridor, flinging open a door in the far corner.

'I'll be five minutes.'

She disappeared, leaving me alone. There were no windows, just a small space with four chairs and a table – a room for a suspect, not a superior officer, but I didn't have the energy to take offence. I waited outside for Lu to return. She strode past me into the interview room, unhurried, holding a plastic bag.

'What's this?'

I watched from the doorway as she held out a pair of nitrile gloves, limp rubber draped across her fingers, enticing me back into the room. I slipped them on, turning my attention to the evidence bag she had brought back with her. Inside, I found a roll of tightly knitted material. I eased it out, holding it up towards the light. At first, I mistook the black wool for an oversized beanie, then I realised I was holding a black balaclava, with two holes for eyes.

Chapter Fifty-Eight

Zed

Zed waited for his father to go to his meeting before he headed for the tube. As long as he sent Isaac regular updates, Isaac assumed Zed was in the Barbican flat. The tribute for Ray King wasn't for a couple of days, but it would be harder to get away in the evening when his dad was at home. He figured someone in the pub might know Ray, so it was worth the journey east.

East London felt like a different city. He had memorised the route to the pub so he could pass for a local. He walked with his legs astride, chest puffed out to mask his nerves. He could see the pub up ahead on the corner – baskets of flowers nesting above the sign, like his grandmother used to have on her terrace at home. He hesitated at the door – he knew he looked young, and no amount of strutting could make his face older. There were boys in his class with long bodies covered in hair. At least his voice had deepened over the past year. He scrunched his brow, reaching for the brass handle before his courage failed him.

There was no air conditioning inside, and the windows were all closed for some inexplicable reason. The air was tinged with beer – a smell he had never liked. There was a black and white poster on the wall with the photo of Ray King he had seen online. Blown up, Ray's eyes looked glazed, like they carried secrets; his hair was darker, greying at the front. Two men sat side by side at the bar, not speaking. A couple at a table nursed full drinks: the woman laughed; the man touched her leopard-print arm with affection. Zed couldn't remember his parents ever being that close. He stared too long; the woman caught him looking. Embarrassed, he turned towards the bar, but he could feel her eyes watching him. The red-haired man behind the bar looked up as Zed approached. His T-shirt was too tight – a faded image of a rock band stretched across the front.

'Don't even pretend you're eighteen, son,' he said, brandishing a dishcloth.

Zed's eyes flitted to the poster – the lie came before his brain caught up. 'That's my Uncle Ray,' he said.

The man laughed, the sound somewhere between a choke and a chuckle. 'More chance of me being your uncle, son.'

Zed tried to place the man's accent – he didn't sound like a Londoner.

'Ray King was an only child. He was always having a moan. Besides . . .' The man looked Zed up and down. 'One of you would have to be adopted. If I was you, I'd go back to wherever you got that nice posh voice from.'

Zed frowned. The man's T-shirt crawled up his midriff.

'I called him Uncle. He was a friend of my mum's.'

'What's your mum's name?' The barman's eyes challenged him. 'Better tell the truth, son, or I'll just kick you out, and you'll have had a wasted trip.'

Zed glanced at the poster, remembering the man on the sofa. He wondered whether the barman with small eyes knew how Ray had died.

'OK,' he said. 'You're right. He's not my uncle. My mum's

disappeared, and I think she and Ray knew the same people. I saw the poster . . . I thought . . .' His voice broke. 'I just thought someone here would know something . . .'

He dipped his hand into his pocket, pulling out his phone. He scrolled through his photos, looking for one he had chosen earlier. Ogechi looked happy, almost carefree.

'This is her. Has she been in here?'

The T-shirt man shook his head, barely registering the image.

'Please,' Zed said. 'Please – check again.'

The man didn't look up. Zed felt a pang of anger – it wouldn't cost him to show an interest.

'I'm here all the time, son. Never seen her,' the barman said.

'Cut the boy some slack, Steve.' A deep voice rose up behind him.

Zed's head whipped round – it was the man next to the woman in leopard print. He had a tidy grey afro framing a weary, drawn face.

'This is a pub, not a youth club, Marlon,' Steve the barman said, half smiling.

'Come here, boy.' Marlon, the man with the grey afro, beckoned him to come closer.

Zed moved towards him, cautious. He could feel the whole room watching each step he made.

'How d'you know about Ray?' Marlon said.

Zed recalled the photo on the wall in the police station. Marlon sat back, staring at him.

'You know what happened to Ray?'

Zed set his chin, but his voice came out weaker than intended. 'I know he's dead, if that's what you mean.'

Marlon's forehead furrowed. 'How can a dead man help you find your mum?'

The woman in leopard print touched his arm gently. 'You're not helping the boy, Marl.'

'He needs to know what he's sniffing around about, Keisha,' Marlon said. 'This isn't a playground.'

Zed bowed his head as the blood rushed to his cheeks, his shame concealed by the darkness of his skin.

It's the only lead I have! he wanted to shout at them. *I know it's not much, but I can't sit around like my dad and do nothing!*

'I just thought one of Ray's friends might know something,' he said.

Keisha, the leopard-print woman, angled her body towards him. She wore short leopard-print boots over wide ankles and bare legs. 'Show us your photo.'

Zed handed her his mobile, watching for any sign of recognition as she looked.

'Ray did odd jobs for people,' Keisha said. 'By the sounds of you, if he knew your mum, it was probably professional, not social, so he'd never bring her round here.'

'Look . . .' Marlon cut in. 'I hope they find your mother. But you're just a kid; there's nothing you can do. Running around London chasing shadows isn't gonna help no one. Let me call someone to come fetch you home . . .'

Zed was already heading for the door before Marlon had finished speaking. It had been a wasted trip. He had seen what had happened to Ray King, Gabriel McMahon and Sarah, the woman with the elusive surname. There was a space on the wall reserved for his mother's body, next to her smiling face. The photos from the police station kept him focused. He felt he was running out of time.

Chapter Fifty-Nine

Zed

As the train pulled into Ladbroke Grove station, the tension from Zed's neck seemed to fall off him. He knew he was imagining it, but the air felt lighter, and he could breathe with ease. He turned up the road towards the council estate. He had no idea what number flat was Seema's, and he hoped she would be in her usual spot on the wall. The brick building was set back from the street, with the pavement widening in front of it. As he drew closer, he could see a young boy doing wheelies on a battered BMX. Seema's wall was unoccupied, and there was no sign of her. He moved away, continuing up the road.

It hadn't been long, but he felt like he had been away for ages. The light above his bedroom was on, which meant his elderly neighbour was in his kitchen. The man struggled with his sight, so he relied on artificial light even on the brightest of days. Zed climbed the steps to the front door, casting a furtive glance over his shoulder. Gabriel McMahon was dead, but he couldn't shake the idea that there could be more people out there like him, watching. Inside, the flat was exactly as he had left it – closed blinds and darkened rooms, the empty cereal bowl with dregs of milk. He thought about what the leopard-print woman had said about professional connections – maybe there was an email trail between his mum and Ray King. He retrieved his mother's laptop from where he had moved it, safely hidden under his bed. He hoped there would be something on it which could help him find Ogechi, but he still couldn't figure out what her password was.

He sat on the edge of the bed, the laptop slanting across his knees. His gaze fell to the carpet. He remembered the blood as Ben carried him from the bedroom, imagined his mother dead on the floor instead of Gabriel McMahon. He ran onto the landing, retching, but there was nothing in his stomach. He rushed out of the flat, gasping for air. The heat from the sun was strangely comforting, and he sank onto the top step, squeezing his eyes open and closed as his breathing became normal again.

'Hello.'

It wasn't a voice he had heard often, but he recognised the pitch straight away.

'You're back.' Seema stood awkwardly by the gate. 'I saw you from my window. I've been watching to see if you'd pass by,' she said.

He smiled to himself, knowing she had been waiting for him. She blushed, talking too fast to hide her nerves.

'I saw your dad asking if anyone knew where your mum went. I thought he'd get you to say something, but I only saw him.'

'They said I was too young for the press conference.'

Her eyes blazed. 'That's stupid.'

Zed nodded. 'That's what I said.'

They watched each other in silence, Seema's blush deepening with every second. She looked at Zed expectantly, and he realised he had no idea what he wanted from her. He needed an ally, but how could a twelve-year-old girl help him? Then he thought of the pub of useless adults – he didn't have much choice.

'You said you'd help me.' He blurted out the words, then froze, embarrassed.

Seema's eyes widened, surprised by the loss of his usual cool. Her cheek dipped inwards as she chewed at the inside of her mouth. She bit her lip, breaking into a determined smile. She held her mobile phone aloft, moving closer to his face.

'What are you doing?' He turned away from the camera. 'Put that down.'

Her features crumpled as she slid the phone back into her pocket.

'Your dad seems nice, but my mum says people don't worry about grown-ups. Post a kid crying for his mum, that'll make people care. It's just the way it is.'

'What are you talking about?' Zed said.

Her voice sounded tentative, but he could hear the hint of excitement.

'We could do our own press conference. I'll create an account and post the video later.'

'OK,' Zed said. 'But I'm not going to cry.'

Chapter Sixty

Leah

The balaclava was being checked for DNA. In the spirit of my new-found collaboration with Lu Hoffen, we were cross-checking with the Gabriel McMahon crime scene. Gabriel had tried to run and had to be stopped, so there was a chance the killer had left evidence at his home. The sun had disappeared when I emerged from the police station. The balaclava had dominated my thoughts since Lu had revealed it, but I hadn't forgotten what she had said about Sami and Sarah's dealer, Tip Wheldon. I took a detour to the Mograbi household on my way home. There was an intercom with two buttons but no names. I remembered what Zikar had said about the flat he had created. I pressed the button on the top.

'Hello?' Sami's voice sounded tired and distant.

'It's Leah.'

An intake of breath.

I waited. A minute later, the front door opened. Sami stood there, barefoot, just like Zikar. His hair was dishevelled, black brows knitted together as he stared at me.

'What happened to automatic doors?' I said.

'My father doesn't believe in them. He has a thing about hospitality and welcoming guests yourself.'

'Am I welcome?'

I was still standing on the doorstep.

He frowned down at me, moving aside so I could go in.

'He gave you a flat, but he didn't give you a separate entrance?'

Sami laughed, the creases on his forehead fading.

'A flat's pushing it. He gave me a floor, but who am I to complain? If it's my dad you want, he's currently out of the country.'

He looked unsure of himself, but I wasn't there to boost his confidence.

'Can we talk, Sami?' I said.

He nodded, leading me towards the stairs. At the top of the house, there was a small landing with a metallic blue door. The door was new, but his teenage bedroom had been on the same floor. He pushed it gently, revealing a large, low-ceilinged room with a sleek open-plan kitchen that looked like it was never used. There was a door leading off to what I assumed was Sami's bedroom, and beside it, an ornate cabinet filled with bottles of alcohol, next to a heavy wooden desk. The décor felt slightly schizophrenic – much of it in keeping with the impersonal luxury of Zikar Mograbi's downstairs sitting room, with idiosyncratic flashes reflecting the character of his son. The far wall was dominated by a low bookcase crammed with leather-bound hardbacks – immaculate spines a sure sign they were only for show. Above it, a framed print of bright, coloured swirls dominated.

'Do you recognise it?' Sami said, walking up behind me.

As a teenager, he had been a fan of puzzles – anything that exercised his brain. The same 'Magic Eye' poster had been Blu-tacked above his bed when I had known him – a three-dimensional image hidden beneath two-dimensional shapes.

'It's the exact same one I had when we were kids. You never could see the face . . .'

I had never seen the point in wasting time on things I wasn't good at. My eyes drifted away from the picture to the mantelpiece – the only photograph in the room positioned in pride of place. It was the same picture of Sami and Zikar in Oxford that I had seen in Zikar's sitting room on my previous visit.

'My father put it there when they finished renovating,' Sami said. 'There's one downstairs too.'

'I know. I saw it.' I turned to face him. 'I thought you hated your father, yet you choose to live with him.'

'He's my father.' Sami shrugged. 'Whatever I do, he'll always be in my life.'

'Whatever works for you, Sami.' I hadn't come to talk about his housing situation. 'Why didn't you tell me you introduced Tip Wheldon to Sarah Franks?'

He looked directly at me, his gaze unwavering. 'Because it didn't seem relevant to any conversation we've had.'

'You introduced your dead friend to her drug dealer – I would say that's pretty relevant . . .'

He sighed. 'Tip's the daughter of an acquaintance of my father's. Her family owns a chain of hotels and restaurants. They're in hospitality. I knew she sold prescription drugs to friends, but I didn't realise Sarah was using again. She told me it was just the drink.' His eyes pleaded. 'Don't look at me like that, Leah – Tip's not even a proper drug dealer. She's just a trust-fund kid with no purpose and too much time.'

'What does that make you then, Sami?'

'Your friend.' He looked away, embarrassed. 'At least that's what I thought . . .'

'Then why do I get the feeling you're holding out on me?'

'Because you've always had a hard time with trust.'

He searched my face, looking for a reaction.

'I'm not here to talk about me, Sami. Let's stick to the subject,' I said.

'Tip Wheldon's not the subject, Leah. She's just a distraction. She had nothing to do with Sarah's death. My dad was just throwing around names, because he was desperate to get me off the hook.'

'Why is he so desperate?'

'Because he's my father, and he would do anything to avoid a scandal.'

'Is there something he's trying to cover up?'

'No. He doesn't know anything, and I don't know anything either. I don't know who killed Sarah. That's what I want to find out.'

'Does the name Gabriel McMahon ring a bell?'

I dropped it in lightly.

'No,' Sami said. 'Should it?'

I watched him closely. 'Not necessarily. No . . . Look, Sami, if there's anything you know which could help us find Sarah's killer, now's the time to tell me. No handcuffs. No police station. No interview room. It's just you and me,' I said.

'I'm not scared of your badge, Leah.' He held my gaze as he continued. 'I used to be a little bit scared of you.'

I swallowed. 'I know.'

Margaretta had often commented on it. It had kept a boundary between us I was never sure I wanted him to cross.

He looked at me, his grey eyes earnest. 'Then I got to know you, and I realised there were things you were scared of too.'

I remembered how the younger Sami would drop his gaze when he asked a question I chose to ignore. I was more open with him than anyone else at that time, but that wasn't saying much.

He moved to the desk by the window.

'I want to show you something.'

He rifled through the top drawer, handing me a photograph crumpled and faded with time. It was of a group of teenagers laughing, a younger version of Sami in the centre, a shaggy mop of black hair falling over his face. He had his arm slung around my shoulder; everyone was looking at the camera, except Sami, who was looking at me.

'What's this?' I said.

'A photograph. What does it look like?'

'This is a murder investigation, Sami, not some second chance with a first crush.'

His olive skin darkened as he took back the photograph. His voice was quiet.

'That's not why I showed it to you,' he said. 'It was a happy time for me. Something positive when everything else is . . . not. I thought maybe you had fond memories of that time too.'

'It doesn't matter why you showed it to me. That's not why I'm here . . . Look . . . I shouldn't have called you last night. I'm sorry if I gave you the wrong idea.'

We stood staring at each other in frustration. For a while neither of us spoke. I sighed.

'The night Sarah was murdered, you asked for me because on some level you wanted my help. I'm trying to help you, Sami,' I said.

'I know.'

He leant back against the desk, rubbing his hands across his face. I took a step towards him. When he glanced down at me, he looked like a little boy.

'If you can remember anything, Sami, anything at all about the night Sarah died or the time leading up to it, you need to tell me now. It doesn't have to feel significant to you, but it might help.'

Sami's eyes travelled to the gaudy drinks cabinet. His Adam's apple rose and fell in his throat. 'It may be nothing . . . but Sarah received a present. One night she came home. Outside the door was a bottle of gin.'

'And?'

'I don't know. She didn't go into detail. She clammed up. Said she shouldn't have said anything. It really freaked her out.'

'Why?' I said. 'Who did she think left it for her?'

'She didn't say. That's the thing – Sarah didn't have many friends, Leah. She didn't speak to her neighbours; didn't keep family around. That bottle of gin, for some reason, it scared her. She saw it as a threat, not a gift.'

Chapter Sixty-One

Leah

Sami was standing by the downstairs window when I stepped outside. He lifted a hand as I looked up at him, but I didn't wave back. I checked my phone, half expecting a missed call from Kenny O'Sullivan. I was relieved when I didn't see his name on the log. He had an unspoken rule never to leave voicemails, seeing them as demeaning pleas for a response. There was a message from the estate agent – she sounded like she was doing me a favour, and I was in some way letting her down. I was tempted to let her start viewings to stop the constant phone calls. Then I thought of Margaretta – protecting her dignity seemed even more important now she was dead.

I hadn't been to Margaretta's house for weeks. I'd told myself I had no reason to, but the moment I stepped into my childhood home, I knew I had been avoiding coming back. When I had lived there, I had known nothing about Eli Carson and the violence in my past. Now, as I stood in the hallway, all I could think of was a five-year-old girl who scared her adoptive mother with the intensity of her rage. The cleaning products were where Margaretta had always kept them, in a red bucket under the kitchen sink. The house was immaculate, but I dusted every surface, knowing how Margaretta felt about strangers in her home. I had already packed anything personal into suitcases and boxes, dragging them to the basement, away from the casual eye. I realised I had just dumped them down there, and I needed to tidy the mess. Prospective buyers would open every door, and I owed it to Margaretta to keep her standards up.

The basement was cooler than the floors above it. The windows hadn't been opened for weeks, and the smell of must filled the air. Boxes were strewn like pebbles, dotting a path across a room. I had stacked them, without caring about their contents – cardboard cubes commemorating Margaretta's life.

I had overpacked one of the boxes, so the contents strained against the sides, forcing the flaps apart. The green leather of a hardback jutted out, gathering dust. I lifted it up, wiping the spine with my sleeve. I was reminded my childhood wasn't unhappy, and I remembered Margaretta reading to me as a little girl. As I gathered the top layer of novels, so I could close the box securely, I noticed a white strip of card between the pages of the green leather book. Flipping it open, I was confronted by a photograph of Eli, the image faded. His face had more colour than the man I had met in prison, his blue eyes sparkling with genuine joy. Part of me wished I had known this version of my father; a larger part wished he had never been in my life at all. Beneath the photograph was another one of Eli lying under a cedar tree. His eyes were closed; his skin was unlined, almost glowing, a younger version of me sprawled across his chest, fast asleep. It was a picture of total trust between a father and daughter. On the back, the date – one week before my mother was killed.

Chapter Sixty-Two

Zed

Zed checked the account Seema had set up, hoping for a miracle. He cringed when he viewed the video of him, cutting it off before it reached the end. There were several comments from boys at his school congratulating themselves on knowing him – boys he sometimes talked to but weren't his friends. There were messages from adults he had never met before, offering condolences. All his life, he had flown beneath the radar; now he would forever be the child whose mother had gone missing – he hated the fact he cared.

There was a knock on the door. Isaac Okoro stood on the threshold like a vampire waiting for permission to come in.

'I have a meeting in the office this morning, but I can cancel it,' he said from the safety of the corridor.

'Why would you do that?' Zed said.

'We could do something . . . to take your mind off things.'

'Thanks, but I've got schoolwork . . . Just a holiday project I need to get done.' Zed lied to save them both.

Isaac looked relieved. 'I'll leave you to it. I'll be back for lunch. We can talk then.'

Zed watched his father's linen back retreat down the corridor. He raised his head, listening out for the slam of the front door. He stared at the list of his mother's acquaintances he had made on his mobile – the four new names at the top:

Chris?

Sarah???

Gabriel McMahon

Ray King

The visit to the pub hadn't helped, but Gabriel McMahon's obituary said he had been a doctor – Zed could go to the GP surgery and speak to people there. He would need to come up with a better story this time. He ran through various scenarios, chomping through a bowl of cornflakes as he paced around the sitting room. He never sat down when he ate in his father's flat, in case he dropped food on the designer furniture. He could think better at home – free from the pale blue chairs. He washed the bowl in the kitchen sink, counting the hours until lunchtime. He would go home and make a plan; he could be back before his father returned.

Seema wasn't on the wall, and he was almost relieved not to see her. He processed his thoughts better without noise, and Seema loved to talk. He checked his phone as he neared the approach to his house. There were more comments on the video – he skimmed them as he walked. A few unkind ones declared they would have left him too if he were their son. Others offered false sympathy, using too many long words. He put the phone in his pocket as he reached his gate. That's when he saw it – the large black suitcase sitting on the doorstep, the shiny, hard shell glinting under the sun. Zed turned back towards the street, searching for the owner. People ambled past, oblivious. No one looked his way. He climbed the steps slowly, instinct making him cautious. The suitcase was made of ridged plastic – he noticed there were no scratches, as if it had never been used. The old man upstairs rarely left his house – he would have no need for a suitcase. The solitary piece of luggage made Zed uneasy, and he wondered to whom it belonged. He wrapped his fingers around the handle. The case shifted an inch, but he couldn't lift it, the weight too much for his small wrist. The zip was open along the top, but he couldn't see what was inside. He reached for the pull tab, sliding it gingerly along the teeth. The plastic shell smacked open against the concrete, startling him with the sound. Zed almost tripped backwards down the steps, but he managed to steady himself just in time.

My name's Zechariah Okoro and I'm a fighter. No one can break my spirit or steal my joy.

He braced himself as he peered into the open suitcase, staring at the bundle of navy material and bloody flesh, left by his front door.

Chapter Sixty-Three

Leah

The photographs with Eli unnerved me – our apparent closeness colouring my view of the past. I was repulsed by the intimacy with a man I saw as a monster, but there was a beauty to the images I couldn't deny. Margaretta had cared for and protected me, but she rarely showed affection, and I recalled the photograph of the little girl clinging to Eli, capturing emotions I hadn't realised I had lost. Eli had claimed I had been the one to tell him my mother was leaving him. I had hidden in the car when he had gone to take his revenge. What had I expected him to do? Bring her back, not knowing he felt compelled to kill her? I needed to talk to someone about the night she died, but I couldn't face Eli, the lies, the games. That left Margaretta's lawyer – the man she had entrusted to deliver the truth to me. Margaretta had known I was a witness. Had she confided in her longtime lawyer? Told him secrets she had kept from me?

It had been too late to call Selwyn Peterson the night before. I tried him on my way to work, but there was no reply. I toyed with the packet of cigarettes in my hand but didn't open it. I hadn't touched a cigarette in years. I pushed the pack into my bag, sliding the zip firmly over it. I hated the taste of nicotine, but I felt comforted knowing they were within reach. I almost laughed at the irony as I rounded the street corner towards the police station – Randle, cigarette held down by his side, his face hidden behind a screen of smoke. His features emerged slowly, blue eyes trained in my direction. I had messaged him before I left my flat, updating him on the new information from Sami about Sarah Franks. I gave him the honour of communicating with Lu Hoffen, in no mood for her barbs.

'Did you see my call, ma'am?' He smiled – he couldn't help himself.

I had missed it when I was trying to reach Selwyn. 'No,' I said.

He killed the cigarette with the heel of his boot, stooping to retrieve it. He flicked it into a nearby bin with impressive accuracy, watching it slide through the slit. He wasn't looking at me, but I had clocked his frustration.

'I spoke to Lu Hoffen about Sami. She's sent an officer to take a statement. Apparently, Sarah's preference was whisky when it came to spirits. There was no record of a bottle of gin when they searched her flat,' he said.

'OK.' I made for the entrance. 'Is that it?'

'Zed's mum . . .' Randle was facing the sun. His hair looked brighter under its rays. 'We got a call, just now. She's been found . . . Ogechi Okoro's alive.'

Chapter Sixty-Four

Zed

Zed lay on his duvet with his knees tight against his chest. The clock by his bedside was ticking too loudly, but he didn't turn it off. He had struggled with the image of Ray King; now all he could think of was his mother stuffed in a suitcase, and he longed for the days when the worst thing in his head was a dead man on a sofa with wide eyes. He had called 999, then his dad, then sat on the step, staring at his phone. He had been too afraid to leave his mum alone, too scared to look at her in case she died while he was waiting. The ambulance had come, then his father; the details blurred into one after that. He remembered Black Cop and Boy Cop taking his statement, then his mum being carted away in an ambulance. No one had told him anything since. His father kept asking how he was, as if repeating the question would make everything OK. There was a knock on the door – Zed pretended he hadn't heard it. He didn't have the energy to make Isaac feel better by acting as if everything was fine. The knock grew louder – a small voice beneath the tapping, fighting for attention:

'Zed, it's Seema . . .'

He pulled himself off his bed and opened the door. She was standing there, holding a ball of wool, like a bar of gold.

'I thought you might want to learn . . . cat's cradle . . . My mum says it's a good distraction.'

He took it without speaking, so she felt forced to fill the silence.

'Your dad seems nice,' she said.

Zed shrugged at the useless piece of information. He wanted to be left alone, but Seema just stood there, waiting to be let in. It was more effort to turn her away, so he stepped back, watching her as she entered – he wondered whether he would ever stop being fascinated by the size of her feet. Her eyes widened as she considered everything he took for granted: TV, console, high-tech speakers, gaming chair. Her gaze travelled over the NFL posters, the chest of drawers covered by sports trophies, branded sweatshirts in a pile on the floor.

'Why don't you put your clothes away, or do you have too many?' she said.

'What do you want, Seema?'

Shame made him harsh. Ever since he had heard Gabriel McMahon being killed in the room whilst he hid, he had been unable to open a wardrobe.

'Now's not a good time.'

He hated that he sounded just like his father.

'Your mum's back?' It was as if she hadn't heard him.

'Yes.' He slumped down on his bed. 'They've taken her to hospital. They won't let me see her.'

Seema's mouth spread into a wide grin. 'She's back. That's all that matters.'

'Is it? They cut her badly. Stuffed her into a suitcase. You should have seen her . . . She looked like she was dead.'

The police had taken the suitcase, but he still remembered the smudges of blood inside.

'Do you think the video helped?' Seema said.

'I don't know. Maybe.'

His mind was still on the suitcase.

'How did you know my mum was back?' he said. 'Did you see the ambulance?'

'I heard it, but I saw the message first.'

'What message?'

Seema crouched down next to him, pulling out her phone so he could read the words for himself.

Glad your mother is back safely

'You'll get lots of those now,' she said.

Zed knew he should be thankful for the support, but the words meant nothing. He looked away, disinterested, then he froze.

'What's wrong?' Seema said.

His gaze moved back to the screen. He pointed at the timestamp.

'This was sent before the ambulance came . . . How did they know she was home?'

Chapter Sixty-Five

Leah

Ogechi Okoro had been off limits for almost twenty-four hours. We would have had to wait longer, but she agreed to speak to us, much to her doctor's annoyance and Randle's surprise. The car filled with the sound of the engine as Randle pulled away from the kerb. One hand rested lightly on the steering wheel, the fingers of the other flicked against his thigh. It was a habit he had when he was thinking deeply. I waited for the thought to play out.

'Do you think it's too soon, ma'am?' he said.

'It's not our job to decide.'

We were searching the CCTV of the area around Ogechi's house for suspicious vehicles. The cameras in her street didn't cover her entrance, but someone must have driven close by so they could deliver the suitcase without drawing attention to themselves. Then again, London was full of tourists, so the sight of someone with a large suitcase was unlikely to stand out. The shock of fitting a grown woman into a suitcase had worn off. I had seen the photographs – there was enough space. I wondered whether Ogechi had been given some form of muscle relaxant to make her limbs more pliable.

Even though we had parked in the shade, the car had overheated.

The air conditioning fought for dominance, but the hot air easily won. I lowered the window a fraction to allow the breeze to stream through. The hiss of traffic played like a soundtrack as I scrolled through the images on my phone, looking at close-ups of Ogechi's injuries: neat cuts to her arms and legs, short red lines lacerating dark flesh.

'Her wounds missed major arteries,' I said, flipping between the photographs and the accompanying email. 'Precise cuts, deep enough to hurt and weaken, but not deep enough to kill.'

Randle flicked his gaze down, then back towards the road. His usually amiable face was distorted with disgust. He took every case so personally – one day it might be too much.

'Do you think her attacker was trying to torture her, ma'am?' he said.

I peered closer, enlarging the image.

'Hard to tell. But whoever did this wanted to make Ogechi suffer, whilst keeping her alive.'

It was hard to tell how tall she was, lying in the hospital bed. She was positioned above the sheet to escape the heat, both legs bandaged around the thigh. Her torso was short in proportion to her lower limbs; a long-sleeved top covered her arms. She had been examined: she was weak and struggled with bright light; she hadn't eaten for days, but all things considered, Ogechi Okoro was fine.

I was struck by how familiar she seemed. It wasn't just that I had seen her photograph and spoken to her family; she had the kind of face that was inoffensive and unremarkable, the kind of face you felt you had seen before. Her features were evenly distributed, nothing too large or small. Her eyes were much sharper than in any photo. They followed us, unblinking, as we entered the ward.

'Ogechi?'

She didn't respond.

'DI Leah Hutch and DS Ben Randle,' I said.

'The doctors said you were coming.'

Her voice lacked power, as if she was out of practice using it. Her skin was darker than mine, but she looked paler – an outline of herself, waiting to be filled in.

'Do you mind sitting down?' The words came out slowly. 'It takes too much energy to look up.'

'Of course.' I pulled the one chair in the cubicle to the side of the bed, close to her legs. It always surprised me how hospitals often made allowances for only one visitor, as if they were saving on the cost of chairs.

'Have you seen my son?' Ogechi asked when Randle returned with a second seat.

'Yes.' Randle paused, choosing his words carefully.

'How is he?' Her voice was quiet.

'He's fine. He was desperate to find you. He knows you're alive and safe.'

Randle started to close the curtain around the cubicle; Ogechi's breathing became strained as the space shrank.

'I'm sorry.' He pushed the material back, his face stricken. 'I didn't mean to . . .'

'It's fine.' She shut her eyes. She looked calmer when she opened them. 'It's fine,' she said again.

'Ogechi,' I said. 'We can do this later if you're not ready. But the sooner you speak to us, the best chance we have of catching whoever did this to you.'

Her hand shook as she struggled to make contact with the glass of water on the table next to her. Randle rose quietly, placing it gently in her hand.

'I know.' She waited until Randle sat down beside me. 'I'm ready to speak.'

She lifted herself up with her free hand, gripping the bedsheet to keep from slipping down.

I listened until the rhythm of her breath became more even.

'What do you remember?' I said. 'Don't try to make sense of it. You can start at the beginning; you can start at the end.'

She lowered her head so her lips closed around the rim of the glass, holding it like a chalice, taking tentative sips.

'It was late,' she said. 'I normally run in the mornings, but I had to pick up Zed from camp the next day around lunchtime. There was a lot to do – I needed to get food, stock the fridge with his favourites. I don't bother with the supermarket when he's not home, just buy what I need, otherwise I just end up throwing things in the bin.'

It was a pointless tangent, but her voice grew stronger as she relaxed into the speech.

'Because I knew I wouldn't have time in the morning, I went for a jog the night before. I take precautions when it's dark – I don't listen to music so I'm always aware of what's around me. I know the area. I've never been scared.' She stopped, her mouth behind the glass barrier. 'I was jogging down by the canal. I don't know how it happened. I should have heard something . . .' Her voice trailed off.

'It's OK, Ogechi.' I softened my tone. 'You don't need to understand it.'

Her eyes were full of questions; she squeezed them with her fingers to shake them off.

'A man jogged past,' she continued. 'He was running just behind me at first. I don't like running near strangers. Their rhythm distracts me. I slowed down to let him overtake. He was about twenty metres in front when someone grabbed me round my neck. I couldn't remember any footsteps. I hadn't heard them come up. It was really sudden. I was running, and then my legs weren't moving, and I couldn't breathe. I tried to ease the pressure, to push them off, but my head was locked. I tried to scream.'

'Did no one hear you?'

Her eyes glazed over as her mind filled with the memory.

'The way they were holding me . . . I couldn't make a sound.'

Her teeth knocked against the glass as she took a sip of water. She focused on the liquid when she spoke.

'Before I could do anything, I was punched in the stomach.'

'From the front?'

'No. It can't have been. I'm pretty sure they were still behind me. I felt a hood go over my head. I remember being lifted up off the ground.'

'How were they carrying you?' I said. 'Like a baby?'

'No. I don't think so.' She closed her eyes, trying to colour in the details. 'My head was down. I remember my arms dangling away from me.'

'Like a fireman's lift?'

'Something like that. I don't remember how long I was carried for. Maybe only a couple minutes, but it felt like forever. I heard a beep, the sound of a car unlocking. A boot opening. I was lowered into it. I kicked. I must have made contact with the lid. I felt pain down my leg. Something soft landed on top of me. The smell of fumes. I don't know what. I heard a slam.' She glanced towards the door, as if checking there was an exit. 'I must have passed out. When I woke up, the hood was off, but it was still dark.'

The sun blazed through the window. She angled her face to avoid it.

'My legs and arms were stinging. I remember the pain. It was dark, but there was blood . . . I could see I had been cut.'

'Do you have any idea where you were?'

'No,' she said. 'Some kind of basement or underground garage, I think.'

'How do you know you were underground?'

She stopped like I had tricked her. 'I don't know. I just assumed . . . There were no windows . . .'

I nudged her back to the beginning of the story, trying to capture the image before it slipped from her mind.

'Do you remember anything else when you woke up? Was your attacker there? Did they say anything?'

She shook her head. Water spilled onto the bedsheet, but she didn't react.

'They never came in. They just took me, drugged me, cut me . . . left me. I thought they had left me there to die.'

'How did you get water? The doctors said you were kept hydrated . . .'

'There was one of those lifts, the small ones, like in a restaurant.' Her gaze drifted to the wall behind Randle as she rebuilt the room in her mind.

'A dumb waiter?' Randle said.

'Yes. That's what they're called.'

'Could you have been in some kind of kitchen?'

'I don't think so.' Her eyes were focused on the space above his shoulder. 'There could have been one on the floors above, or even below me. It felt like a cellar. Low ceilings. No windows.' Her tone was bleak. 'Empty. I was alone. There was one door. It was steel. I tried it every few hours, but I could never get it to budge. It was heavy, like it was moulded into the wall. No gaps. I tried to use the lift to get out, but it was switched off.'

'Then how did they get the water to you?' Randle said.

'There was a camera. They must have been watching me. I tried to stay awake. When I fell asleep, there was more water sent down . . . or up.'

'You were found in a suitcase. Do you remember being put in it, or how you ended up outside your house?' I said. 'Who opened the steel door and took you out?'

She turned her face to look at me. She had Zed's eyes, without his innocence. 'They must have drugged the water, just before. One moment I was drinking it. Then . . .' She trailed off.

Someone cleared their throat behind me. I turned to see a tall man in a creased white coat.

'I apologise, but I have to interrupt you.' He sounded far from sorry. 'We need to run some tests on Ms Okoro.'

'Of course. Can you give us a minute?' My eyes locked with his, holding his gaze until he left.

We hadn't got to Gabriel McMahon, let alone the mysterious Chris. I turned back to Ogechi.

'We'll speak again when you're better. Do you have any idea why someone would want to kidnap or hurt you?' I said.

'No, Inspector. And I try not to think about it. I just want to get on with my life.'

Chapter Sixty-Six

Leah

'It doesn't make sense, ma'am,' Randle said as we emerged from the sterile universe into the warm breeze outside. 'Why hold Ogechi and then release her? Do you think her attacker saw the press conference and had a change of heart?'

I could still smell the disinfectant masking the stench of sickness. I walked briskly; the scent had started to fade when I replied.

'If that was enough to panic them, it doesn't sound like the same person who murdered Sarah Franks and Gabriel McMahon.' We were looking for someone clinical, someone with a clear plan.

'What about the private investigator, Ray King, ma'am?' Randle said.

'What about him?'

'You said whoever put Ray King's corpse in Gabriel's house wanted to give him a scare.' Randle glanced at me. His blue eyes were animated as they caught the light. 'Maybe Gabriel ignored it, or he did the wrong thing, and he ended up dead.'

'What are you saying, Randle?'

He had almost stopped walking. I slowed my pace to match his.

'What if Ogechi was kidnapped to scare her? What if the victims are warned first before they're killed?'

I stopped, recalling what Sami had said about Sarah and the bottle of gin.

'Sarah was scared,' I said. 'That's what Sami Mograbi told me. She told Sami the gin was a threat, not a gift.'

Randle shrugged. 'It's not as dramatic as a body on a sofa, but maybe that was Sarah's warning – the gin. I checked the file – apparently the CCTV camera which covered Sarah's front door stopped working the day before the package was delivered. Coincidence or the mark of a pretty slick operation?'

He paused, waiting for encouragement. I waited to hear his theory in full.

'I realise it's a long shot, ma'am, but we know that the same knife that killed Sarah Franks probably killed Gabriel McMahon. We know Gabriel and Ogechi are connected in some way . . .' He hesitated. 'Breaking into a house and putting a dead man on a sofa is a pretty elaborate warning. Kidnapping a woman for a few days. Maybe that's a warning too . . .' He bit his lip, tapping his fingers against the fabric of his trousers. 'I'm not saying I'm right, ma'am. I just think it's worth considering,' he said.

'OK.' I squinted as I looked up at him, under the sunlight. 'But if Ogechi's kidnapping was just a warning, the killer's coming back.'

Chapter Sixty-Seven

Chris

Chris was used to waiting, but he was getting restless. He had been watching Bisi for a while now, waiting for the call. Her sense of entitlement irritated him, as did the way Lemar followed her, even though she had started to ignore him. But Chris was not paid to judge; he was paid to take orders, and the orders still hadn't come.

The phone rang – a rare sound in the quiet house, so low it was just a vibration. His body relaxed, but he didn't rush to pick up. The phone quivered on the table in front of him, screen flashing, number unknown. He answered but barely said a word. He had been told he had a talent for violence, not conversation, but his greatest skill was efficiency – never do more than you have to, always know your role. He hung up, placing the phone back on the table, rubbing his knuckles along the line of his jaw. There had been an unforeseen complication. It was time for him to take control and do what he did well.

Chapter Sixty-Eight

Zed

Zed wanted to stay in Ladbroke Grove, but Isaac refused to let him. They drove in silence back to his Barbican flat. Twice Zed tried to tell his father about the message Seema had shown him, but he didn't know where to start.

He woke up, famished, staring at the ceiling. There was a water stain in the corner, the only blemish in his father's otherwise immaculate home.

Glad your mother is back safely

They could have been the words of a concerned stranger, but Zed had been alone on the doorstep, his mother's body concealed inside the case. If they hadn't heard or seen the ambulance, how did they know she was back? He had tried to explain this to Seema, but she didn't understand at first. He showed her the calls to his father and the emergency services, made minutes after the message had been sent. Sometimes he forgot she was just a kid. He needed a stronger ally in a world of adults, but the only person he trusted was laid up in a hospital bed.

He pulled on a sweatshirt and walked out into the sitting room. His father sat on a pale blue chair, elbows on his knees, his head in his hands. Isaac's mobile rang twice; he glanced at it, then he noticed Zed standing there, watching him.

'You OK, son?'

Zed nodded. It was almost a reflex. Isaac's phone rang again. He looked down at the screen. 'What's up?'

Zed shifted his weight. He knew his father would be angry they had posted the video in the first place, but he had to tell him about the message; he couldn't keep putting it off. He lowered himself onto the pale blue chair, fidgeting with his pyjama trousers. Uncomfortable, he stood back up.

'What is it?' Isaac's face creased with concern.

'I need to tell you something,' Zed blurted out.

He took a breath. The phone rang again.

Father and son's eyes moved in unison.

'Who keeps calling you?' Zed stared at his father's mobile.

'Nothing for you to worry about. Mostly journalists. Since your mum came back . . .'

Zed bristled.

You mean, was delivered in a suitcase . . .

'They won't stop. The things they're writing about your mother. Don't pay attention. They just want a good story. You know that, don't you, Zechariah?'

Isaac's gaze travelled to the phone in Zed's hand.

'I've been thinking. Maybe you should come off that for a bit . . .'

Zed clutched his mobile as if Isaac had suggested cutting off his hand.

'You can't take my phone away from me.'

Isaac shook his head, frustrated. 'I'm trying to protect you, not punish you,' he said.

Zed imagined the rest of the conversation once his father had seen the message – Isaac overreacting, seizing his mobile, keeping him at home. Big gestures, concerned conversations, a social media blackout, but what would his father actually do to help?

'What did you want to tell me?' Isaac said.

Zed faked a smile. He wondered if Isaac would know the difference. 'I just wanted to say thank you for coming to get me.'

He tucked his phone away. He didn't need Isaac's help.

Chapter Sixty-Nine

Leah

A few phone calls and some hyperbole saw Ogechi moved to a private room in the hospital. A plain-clothes officer was placed on guard outside the door. Randle insisted on being there to supervise the transition. His name lit up my phone as I stepped into the darkness of my flat.

'What did you tell her?' I said, wishing I had bought a fan for the sitting room. I eased open a window. A neighbour shouted an obscenity. I silenced him with a look. I retrieved my phone from where I had dropped it on the sofa.

'Any problems?'

'No, ma'am.'

I stabbed the light switch with my elbow.

'What did you tell her?'

'Nothing.' Randle hesitated. 'But I didn't say we didn't have concerns.'

'Was your face concerned?' I made a mental note to buy brighter bulbs.

'I don't know. I wasn't looking in the mirror . . .'

'I'll take that as a yes then.' I slipped my feet out of my shoes, flexing my toes. 'Was she worried?'

'If she was, she didn't show it, ma'am.' He paused. 'I think she was relieved to have someone there.'

I wondered whether Ogechi meant him, or the constable on the door. Maybe she had meant both.

The hard floor was surprisingly cool under the soles of my feet. I lay down, staring at the ceiling, pressing my limbs against the wooden boards. It was too early to sleep. I checked my phone for messages. There was one from the estate agent asking when the house would be ready. I knew I owed her an answer, but I hadn't finished tidying Margaretta's basement, and I couldn't face going back, the photographs of Eli and me still fresh in my mind. I didn't want to think about him, but once he entered my thoughts, it was hard to push him out. Frustrated, I rolled onto my front. Planting my palms on the floor, I kicked my legs out behind me, dropping my chest between my arms. I pressed down and then up, cranking out push-ups without counting. I kept going until my arms shook, and I couldn't feel them any more. Only then did I drag my body to my bedroom. When I closed my eyes, I saw my mother's body covered in blood; me as a little girl crouched beside it, my face wet with tears. I squeezed my eyes tighter. Now it was Eli next to the body; the little girl was gone.

You're scared of the truth and yet you seek it.

Not tonight, Eli, I told the voice. *Not tonight*.

I got up and put on a pair of trainers. I walked slowly in the direction of the river, turning to the right. Albert Bridge lay ahead, an arc of lights hanging over the water. I didn't cross, just kept walking down the Embankment, trying to shift my thoughts away from Eli and the night my mother was killed. I thought about the brutal end met by Sarah Franks and Gabriel McMahon – carotid arteries slashed, no sign of the weapon, their killer still not caught. Across the river, Ogechi lay in hospital. A police guard had been deployed to protect her. She didn't need me, but I didn't want to go home.

Chapter Seventy

Leah

It was late when I reached the hospital. The walk had stimulated my muscles. I was swallowed through the gap as the automatic door slid shut. I paused, adjusting to the fluorescent light inside the building after the darkness outside. Two doctors in scrubs passed by, talking in hushed voices, playful bandanas at odds with the sombre tone. The woman on the information desk barely glanced at my badge when I presented it, absorbed by a video on her phone. I didn't have the patience to wait for the lifts, so I took the stairs up to the first floor. The stairwell had been recently mopped, the scent of disinfectant so strong I could taste it in my mouth. I emerged to see the cleaner up ahead, clinging to his trolley like a Zimmer frame, weighed down by the effort of life. He turned towards Ogechi's ward, tapping a key card against the electronic pad. He didn't look behind him as I slipped through the open door after him. A young nurse hovered by the nurses' station, his body drooped over a file. He looked at me with tired eyes as I approached, nodding with disinterest when I identified myself.

'That way,' he said. 'Up on the left.'

This time the nod had more purpose. I followed his gaze down the corridor. I could just about glimpse Ogechi's door. There was no one outside.

'Where's the police guard?'

The nurse was writing notes on a piece of paper, making clear I was low on his priority list. 'I don't know. He went for a cigarette earlier. Maybe he's gone again.'

'Stay here.'

The sharpness of my tone snapped him to attention.

'Stay away from that room. If you hear anything that alarms you, call 999.'

He nodded, weariness replaced by fear. I scanned the counter for a makeshift weapon – a jar of pens, a stapler, slim paper files. Half a dozen pink tulips sat in the corner. I grabbed the vase, ditching the flowers and water as I tested the weight of the glass in my hand. I moved towards the corridor, reaching for the pen in my pocket, flicking off the lid to expose the sharp tip.

Ogechi's door was ajar – I slipped through the opening, wincing at the creak of the hinge. The blinds were closed, the room in near darkness. I could see the outline of Ogechi's body on the bed under the sheet. Her face was caught by a sliver of moonlight, her breathing ragged through parted lips. A flash of white as her eyelids flickered. I sensed the movement behind me – a subtle change in the air. I didn't hesitate as I turned, lunging towards the creeping shadow. I swung the vase at the hooded figure stepping out from behind the door. They were ready for me, ducking out of the way. My elbow buckled, my arm falling fast through nothing. I felt a jab to my ribs, hard enough to wind me, but lacking sufficient force to bring me down. My fist tightened around the pen. I stabbed upwards, connecting with the soft flesh of a cheek beneath the hood. A cry of surprise mixed with pain. I swung the vase, then swung it again and again. The glass was thick and heavy. I didn't think where I aimed. I heard Ogechi shout, but her words were lost in the chaos as the vase shattered in my hand. The intruder went down. I heard shouts in the corridor. The door burst open. Strong arms wrestled with the body beneath me. A voice whispered my name.

'Leah . . .'

I looked at the police constable grappling with the intruder; his lips hadn't moved. I heard the muffled voice again. I peered at the figure prostrate in the darkness. I knew it was Sami before I peeled back the hood.

Chapter Seventy-One

Leah

Sami Mograbi was dragged to his feet in handcuffs as the police constable read him his rights.

'Where were you, Officer?' I said. My voice was devoid of emotion. I could feel the anger surging inside.

The constable mumbled a response but didn't look at me. 'I'm sorry, ma'am,' he said.

He held up a small object in the darkness – shining silver gleaming against black. 'I found this on him.'

I moved towards the doorway, fumbling for the light switch. The constable blinked in the brightness. His face was younger than his voice.

'What should I do with it, ma'am?'

He was so unsure I almost felt sorry for him. He held out a compact kitchen knife.

Sami watched me as I called for backup. His eyes pleaded, appealing to the embers of our friendship, but any allegiance I had felt completely died away.

'I can explain, Leah,' he said. His jaw was flecked with faint stubble, the olive in his skin dulled to a sickly shade of grey.

My gaze travelled to his handcuffs. 'Don't worry, Sami. You'll get your chance.'

I turned to the police constable standing behind him. He was gripping the weapon so tightly, the veins pulsed on the back of his hand. 'Get him to the station. I'll stay here and wait for backup.'

He nodded, desperate not to fail again.

'Word of advice: stop smoking, Constable. If this had been worse, it could have cost you your job and messed with your head.'

He started to mutter another apology, but my focus was on Ogechi. She cowered on the bed, her whole body shaking. She stared at me, working out if I was an ally or aggressor, then she seemed to remember me.

'Please get the doctor,' she said.

For the second time, I watched Sami trapped in the back of a police car, his legs folded behind the front seat. His face was pressed up against the glass, like he was trying to find a way through to me. I held his gaze without emotion, until the car pulled away.

Randle had arrived with the backup, and I had left him to deal with the hospital. Concern was written in the lines above his brow as he approached.

'All good, ma'am . . .'

It could have been a question or an update.

'How's Ogechi?' I said.

'Being seen by the doctors. They don't think she's hurt, but she's had quite a shock.'

I looked back at the building behind us.

'What was Sami doing there, ma'am?' Randle said.

'I don't know. We need a statement from Ogechi as soon as we get the all-clear.'

'And the knife, ma'am?'

'Get Harrison to take a look at it. See if it matches the wounds found on Sarah Franks and Gabriel McMahon.'

'What about Sami, ma'am?'

I was hit by a rush of tiredness. 'He's got some explaining to do.'

Chapter Seventy-Two

Leah

Sami's lawyer had got a tan since we had last seen him, the sneer of entitlement baked into bronzed skin. Sami was like a schoolboy beside him, waiting for his punishment to be over, head down, eyes on his lap, not saying a word. It was hard to tell if he was listening. He didn't move until I finished speaking. When he did, I saw the anguish in his eyes.

'I wasn't there to hurt her, Leah.'

'What were you doing then, after visiting hours? How do you explain the knife, Sami?' I said.

His lawyer started to interject. Sami spoke in a low voice, close to his ear.

'Sorry,' he said for my benefit. 'I'm ready for your questions. Ask me again.'

'We know you've been lying, Sami.' My voice was expressionless. 'The question is about what.'

His eyes tried to engage me in a private conversation, but I had drawn a line under our past.

'Do you know Ogechi Okoro?'

He nodded.

'I need a word, not a gesture.'

'Yes,' he said. 'We met at university. She was at Oxford with me. I saw the press conference. Someone mentioned the hospital online when they found her . . . I wanted to make sure she was OK.'

'So why not come like a normal person, bearing flowers and chocolates during visiting hours? Why the cloak and dagger? You literally brought a knife.'

Sami leant forwards, pressing his forearms into the table. His lawyer mirrored the movement, trying to keep sight of his client's face.

'I was scared,' Sami said. 'First Sarah, then Ogechi. Two people I know, both attacked.'

'You seem to be the common denominator. Maybe those attacks have something to do with you.'

'That's absurd.'

'Is it?'

His arms were crossed above his stomach, his chin tilted upwards. There was something studied about his defiance, as if he were scared his body would betray his mouth.

'DS Hoffen has a viable suspect for Sarah's murder.' The elusive figure in the balaclava. 'I wasn't charged because it wasn't me.'

I pushed my chair back, widening the space between us.

'Did Ogechi know Sarah?' I said.

'I wouldn't call them friends.'

'And you didn't know Gabriel McMahon?'

'I never met him. I wasn't lying to you, Leah.' His forehead creased with frustration. 'You don't need to ask me again. I didn't know Gabriel McMahon. I didn't hurt Sarah. I would never harm Ogechi. I don't know how many times you want me to say the same thing over and over again . . .'

'You can say them as many times as you need to, Sami. Words mean nothing without proof.'

'Then prove I killed them.' His grey eyes darkened. 'You should be hunting for the murderer, not wasting your time with me.'

There was steel to him that I hadn't seen before. He blinked and his face softened, recognisable once more. The door swung open, and Kenny O'Sullivan filled the frame.

'DI Hutch,' he said. 'Time for a break.'

Chapter Seventy-Three

Leah

Kenny strode down the corridor in front of me, his feet moving lightly. He turned without warning, his body looming. I was forced to retreat against the wall.

'My office, now.'

He stopped by the lift, hitting the button with an angry thumb.

'I'll see you up there,' he said as the doors slid shut, whisking him from sight.

Kenny had always been a fan of drama, so the exaggerated exit had little effect on me. It was a relief not to share a confined space, and I hoped the minutes alone would calm him down.

He was sitting behind his desk when I arrived in his office. The window was open, but the heat was stubborn, and the room was uncomfortably warm. Kenny dragged a handkerchief across the back of his neck. He tucked it into a pocket, looking at me for the first time since I walked through the door. His eyes were half closed, then they snapped open without warning, boring into mine.

'I've just had Zikar Mograbi on the phone, threatening to sue us.'

Sami's father was a man who made threats to feel important. Fear took up energy, and I had neither the patience, nor the time.

'He's been watching too much TV,' I said. 'He can't sue us for doing our job, sir.'

'He can make life hard if we put a foot wrong, Leah. What have you got on his son?'

Kenny's tone was almost conciliatory, but I knew better than to let my guard down.

'Potentially threatening behaviour. He approached the victim at night, carrying a knife.'

'Did he harm her?' Kenny's irises disappeared as he squinted, waiting for my reply.

'No, sir. He says he knows her and would never hurt her.'

'And the knife?'

'Harrison is checking to see if it could be the same one that killed Sarah Franks and Gabriel McMahon.'

'I thought Lu Hoffen had another suspect for the Sarah Franks murder. Any update on the figure in the balaclava?'

'No, sir. But maybe Sami was still involved in some way.'

Kenny shifted his weight from one side to the other. The chair creaked as it swivelled beneath him.

'All I'm hearing is maybe. Visiting someone after hours is hardly a crime.'

'What about the knife, sir?'

'I'm assuming he had a reason for having it?'

'His friends have been attacked. He said he's scared.'

'It's London. He's not the first person to carry a weapon. It doesn't make him a murderer, Leah; it just makes him a fool.'

'He's lying about something, sir.'

Kenny swallowed a chuckle, shaking his head.

'We're all lying about something, Leah. I lied to my wife this morning. Do you want to arrest me too? Do you have proof Sami's lying about the crime?'

'Not yet, sir. That's what the interview is for.' I tried to keep my tone neutral, but I could hear the sarcasm creeping into each word.

'Don't be smart, Leah, I know what's required.'

'Then you know we can't let Zikar Mograbi throw his weight around, sir. I know he's applying pressure, and there's a lot at stake . . .'

There were rumours Kenny wanted to move into politics once he retired, and Zikar Mograbi had enough reach to make the transition hard.

'Careful, Leah.' Kenny watched as I filtered my thoughts. 'Don't make accusations you'll regret.'

I bit down on my frustration. 'All I'm saying is that I'm not underestimating the power of Zikar Mograbi, sir. But first we catch his son running from a murder scene; now he's in a hospital room after hours, sneaking up on a kidnap victim, carrying a knife.'

His beady eyes locked on mine. 'I've asked you before and I'll ask you again.' His voice was slow and deliberate. 'Is there something personal going on here? Anything Zikar Mograbi could use against us? Anything I should know?'

'No, sir.' I held his gaze.

A question passed across his face, but he thought better of it. The screen of his mobile lit up on the desk in front of him. He picked it up before I could read the name.

'OK.' He glanced at the mobile phone. 'Get back to work, and Leah . . .'

With Kenny O'Sullivan, there was always a catch.

'If Harrison says it's not the murder weapon, give Sami a slap on the wrist by all means, then you've got to let him go.'

Chapter Seventy-Four

Zed

Zed walked behind his father down the hospital corridor. He had been awake all night, trying to reach the person who had messaged him about his mother, but the account had gone quiet, every attempt to connect failed. His brain was scrambled. It didn't feel like morning. He had overheard his father talking about an intruder trying to get to his mother the previous night. When he asked him if it was true, Isaac just told him not to worry, but how could he not? Someone had tried to hurt his mother again. Zed watched his father's shoulders as he followed him down the corridor, rigid and tense, inching up towards his ears. The last time Zed was in a hospital, his grandfather had been about to die. The scent of bleach curled round the edges of his nostrils. He exhaled for as long as he could to avoid inhaling the smell. He noticed the collar of his father's shirt was perfectly pressed. Isaac slowed his pace, so they were forced to walk in step, but Zed dragged his feet, dropping back behind him once more. He was desperate to be reunited with his mother, but his chest felt tight when he imagined seeing her. He recalled finding her stuffed in a suitcase – the stench of her, so unlike the smell he remembered, smears of dry blood covering her arms. He was about to see his mother, his greatest protector, but all he could feel was fear.

The corridor was busy with doctors and nurses zigzagging in and out of wards. He clutched a bag of his mother's clothes like a safety blanket as he approached the police officer creating a human barrier outside Ogechi's door. He almost expected to be denied entry, but his dad identified them. The officer logged their names, then dutifully stepped aside. Isaac hung back to let Zed enter first, but Zed's feet wouldn't move.

Isaac touched his arm. 'It's OK. Go on, son.'

When Zed looked at him, his eyes were kind. Zed filled his lungs – the air tasted of bleach and hand sanitiser. He was glad of the distraction as he stepped into the room.

Ogechi was lying flat, so at first he couldn't see her. He felt a surge of panic, then she eased herself up, and he caught sight of her face. Her skin was dry; lines had emerged under her eyes and deep across her forehead. Her arms were bandaged from her biceps to her wrists. She looked like an approximation of his mother he didn't recognise, with alien limbs that belonged to someone else. He stood, immobile, hovering at the threshold. Then she smiled, and he recognised his mother once again.

'You just going to stand there?' Her voice was weak, but it was comforting to hear.

This time, he went to her. His body felt light as he curled up by her side.

'I didn't tell anyone. They found me. I knew you would come back,' he said.

She didn't say anything, clinging to him like she did when he was small. Zed had forgotten his father was there until Isaac coughed. Embarrassed, he tried to move away from his mother, but Ogechi kept hold of his hand.

'Thank you for taking care of him,' she said to Isaac.

'No need to thank me, Ogechi. He's my son.'

Zed turned to his mother. He felt bad asking in front of his father, but he was conscious it might be his only chance.

'Can I come home now?'

He bit his lip when his mother didn't answer. Ogechi pushed down the covers – there were bandages around her calves and thighs. She swung her legs round, planting her feet on the floor.

'What are you doing, O?' It had been a long time since he had heard his father call her that.

'I'm going home, Isaac.' She faced Zed. 'Are you coming, Zechariah, or are you a fan of hospitals now?'

'The doctors won't like it. You're still weak . . .' Isaac started to protest as Ogechi reached for the clothes.

'As long as I'm still breathing, I'll decide what I do.'

The words were strident, but she seemed fragile. Zed thought of the cuts on her arms, the ordeal she had been through.

'It's OK.' The bandages gripped her forearms as she shook out her trousers.

Zed smiled, but something hardened inside him. Someone had dug a blade through his mother's flesh, then held her for days, and dumped her bleeding in a suitcase.

Someone had hurt his mother. Someone had to pay.

Chapter Seventy-Five

Leah

The envelope was waiting on my desk, tucked under the corner of the keyboard. I didn't see it until I had sat down and drained my coffee, sharpening my senses, ready for the day. The sun was shining, and a cool breeze swept through the open window. I had managed to make it to my office without being backed into a corner by Kenny O'Sullivan or being asked something inane. All in all, the world didn't seem terrible – then I saw the envelope. Eli's scrawl dominated most of the white rectangle, my name unnecessarily large compared to the address. I thought about throwing it away unopened, but I hadn't heard back from Selwyn Peterson, and I had too many questions without answers, even if I couldn't trust Eli to tell the truth. I pushed a pen under the seam, tearing open the letter. Inside was one sheet of paper, so thin the ink pressed through to the other side. I could hear Eli speaking as I scanned his note – his voice slow and measured, even though the words looked like they were written in haste.

Have you thought any more about my proposition? Come and see me. Your choice. The invitation has been made.

His words were followed by a verse. He had quoted the same words in previous letters, but I had skimmed over them, determined not to give Eli any more of my time. Now, as I took them in, I had a vague recollection of Margaretta quoting the same verse many years before.

Yea, though I walk in death's dark vale,

Yet will I fear no ill;

For Thou art with me; and Thy rod

And staff my comfort still.

The English was antiquated, but Margaretta had never been interested in appearing modern. Sometimes it had felt like she belonged to a period all of her own.

'Ma'am?'

Akosua hovered in the doorway.

'Good . . . You got the letter. I wanted it to be safe, but I didn't want you to miss it.' She looked at the sheet I clutched in my hand. 'I don't know anyone who still writes them. You're lucky, ma'am, they feel personal—'

'Anything from Harrison?' I cut her off.

'Oh, yes.' She teased her afro with her thumb and forefinger. 'Sami's knife's serrated. The one that killed Gabriel McMahon and Sarah Franks had a straight edge. So Sami wasn't carrying the murder weapon.'

She searched my face for signs of disappointment or relief. I gave nothing away.

'Go back over all the evidence. We're missing something. I want everyone on the team on this. Tell Randle to speak to Lu Hoffen about Sarah Franks.'

Randle appeared behind her, catching the tail end of the instruction.

'We got a call from the hospital, ma'am. Ogechi Okoro's discharged herself.'

If she was well enough to leave, she was well enough for more questions.

'Let's go and speak to her then,' I said.

'What about Sami? Do we release him or wait until we've checked his story with Ogechi?'

'Release him for now.' I didn't need Kenny O'Sullivan on my back.

Chapter Seventy-Six

Leah

Zed opened the door; his eyes were hostile.

'What do you want?' He puffed out his chest like an angry little man.

'We want to talk to your mother,' I said.

'Why? Your people let her down.'

He crossed his arms, trying to fill the doorway, struggling with his small frame.

'Zed,' I said. 'Please just tell your mother we're here.'

He looked from me to Randle, returning Randle's smile with a half-hearted scowl. Underneath the bravado, he was just a middle-class boy brought up to respect clear authority. He succumbed to the pressure of good manners and stood aside.

We followed him down a well-kept communal hallway into Ogechi's maisonette.

'Wait here. She's upstairs,' Zed said. He disappeared.

The sitting room was spacious with tasteful, lived-in furniture arranged carefully on the scuffed wooden floor. There was a fireplace with a white stone mantelpiece – a shrine to Zechariah at various stages of life. Most of the photographs were of Zed alone, but there were two of him with Ogechi, one in a large, silver frame. The boy we encountered was always so serious; the Zed in the photograph was laughing, every feature animated, the mask of defiance gone. One arm was wrapped affectionately over his mother's shoulder; he stared at the camera as she smiled at him, utter devotion in her eyes.

'She says to come up.' He paused. 'Maybe not Boy Cop . . . She's in her bedroom . . . She's not really dressed.'

'Of course,' Randle said.

I followed Zed up a narrow flight of stairs to the floor above. The door to Ogechi's room was open. She was sitting up against the headboard of a solid oak bed, curved shoulders prominent in a shapeless cotton gown. The sleeves stopped just below her elbows – the bandages were gone, revealing dark brown skin punctured by angry cuts.

'Do they offend you?' She glanced at her forearm. 'I can cover up.'

'No. Please. There's no need,' I said.

'Zechariah . . .'

'Yes, Mum.' His voice was gentler with her.

'Pull up that chair.'

She turned to me as he rearranged the furniture. 'Where's your partner?'

'We thought it was better if he stayed downstairs.'

Ogechi frowned. 'I'm in a *boubou*. It's not the nineteenth century. Zechariah, call him up.'

I lowered myself into the seat Zed had offered. 'I'm sorry.'

She looked genuinely perplexed.

'Why?' She trailed a finger along her forearm, dancing over one of her cuts. 'You didn't kidnap me and mutilate me. I'm not sure what you have to be sorry about.'

'I'm sorry for what happened in the hospital, Ogechi. The officer in question has been dealt with.'

She shifted on the bed so she could see me more easily. Her robe rose up, exposing a deep gash on her left shin.

'That sounds ominous,' she said. 'I'm fine. Nothing happened. I'm not looking for someone to lose their job.'

'I'm just saying that last night was an anomaly. You would be safe in hospital with a police guard.'

'I appreciate that.' She winced as she turned so she was facing me. 'But I didn't leave hospital because I felt unsafe; I left because I wanted to be home with my son.'

As if on cue, Zed appeared in the doorway, dwarfed by Randle standing by his side.

'Give us a second, Zechariah, would you?' she said.

'I'll be downstairs if you need me.'

There was a note of warning, a final glance, then he was gone. We could hear his footsteps lingering on the stairs. I waited until they started to fade, lowering my voice.

'Has your ex-husband spoken to you about Zechariah?'

'What do you mean?' Concern made her pupils large.

'Does the name Chris mean anything to you?'

'It's a common name. What's this about, Inspector?' she said.

She listened in silence as we explained what had happened with Gabriel McMahon. She closed her eyes when Randle described finding Zed in the wardrobe, cowering in fear.

'This must be an unsettling time for both of you,' I said. 'We can station one of our team outside, if it makes you feel safer. We'll be discreet.'

'I don't know.' She traced a wound on her arm with her fore-finger. 'What Zechariah needs now is normality, but yes, thank you, I think that would be good.'

'How did you know Gabriel?' I said.

She blinked at the change of subject.

'We had a fling in my twenties. I hadn't thought about him for years.'

'Did you stay in touch?'

'No. We weren't really friends before we got together. Once it was over between us, there was nothing to hold on to, I suppose.'

Her body drooped as her energy faded, but I didn't stop.

'How did Gabriel know where you lived?' I said.

'I don't know.' She rubbed her temples, trying to focus. 'I really don't know.'

I changed tack, watching her expression. 'Does the name Sami Mograbi mean anything to you?'

'I know him.' Her voice was quiet, but she didn't hesitate. 'I mean, I say I know him, but I haven't seen him since we were at university – years ago.'

'You know it was Sami in the hospital last night?'

A barely perceptible nod.

'Why do you think he would try to see you now, after all these years?'

Her face looked exhausted. She started to shake her head, then stopped.

'I have no idea.'

'Did Sami know Gabriel McMahon?' I said.

She thought for a moment. 'Not as far as I know.'

Randle was seated in the corner by Ogechi's dressing table. The stool was too low, and his knees rose up towards his chest.

'Have you got any reason to think Sami would want to hurt you?' he said.

'No.'

She exhaled loudly, rolling her fingers over her eyelids. I was reminded she had been through an ordeal, and I needed to offer her a way out.

'We can do this another time, if it's too much for you, Ogechi.'

I tried to sound like I meant it.

'No,' she said.

I hid my relief.

'You said you knew Sami at university. Did you study the same subject?'

'We both *read* medicine.'

She corrected my diction as if my choice of words mattered. Distracted, it took me a second to register what she had said.

'Medicine? But Sami was never a doctor . . .'

Sami and I were little more than strangers bonded by history, but it felt like something I should have known.

'No. He never practised. Neither did I.'

'Why?'

I could feel Randle watching me.

'I don't know . . .' She took a breath. 'Too much pressure. I was more suited to sales. I'm in medtech, so my medical background comes in handy. '

'So you and Sami were medical students together?' Randle said, stretching out his long legs in front of him.

Ogechi nodded. 'Yes.'

I thought of Gabriel McMahon in his GP surgery. The years had been less kind to him, but he would have been roughly the same age.

'Not just you and Sami,' I said. 'Gabriel McMahon as well.'

Chapter Seventy-Seven

Leah

Zed watched us file down the stairs, his face sombre as he walked us down the hallway.

'I know it's hard, but you've got to trust us,' Randle said.

'Right . . .' His lips parted. I waited for the sullen comeback, but he just closed the door quietly behind us.

Randle swept a hand through his hair, his mouth twisted in frustration.

'There's no point trying to reach him,' I said. 'We lost him when one of our team chose nicotine over his mum.'

'He's listening, ma'am. He's just pretending he can't hear . . . He's a vulnerable kid trying to tough it out. He needs to know there are adults he can rely on.'

'He's got parents who love him,' I said. 'That's more than some kids I know.'

He stared down at me. The top of his face was in shadow, sharpening the line of his jaw.

'I don't doubt his mother loves him, but what's the point if she's hardly around? His dad's part-time and might as well be a stranger. Don't be fooled by the fancy accent and nice house – even before Ogechi was kidnapped, trust me, that boy felt alone.'

He swallowed, retreating behind a wall of professionalism. It was as close to an outburst as Randle ever got. His face was neutral as he walked beside me, but a muscle twitched at the corner of his mouth.

'Zechariah Okoro's not one of your friends from childhood, Randle,' I said.

'I never said he was, ma'am.'

He said nothing as we arrived at the car. He slid back the passenger seat, watching in silence as I steered round the corner before he spoke again.

'What did you make of Ogechi, ma'am?' It was like his outburst had never happened. 'She was pretty chilled considering the circumstances.'

'What's your point, Randle?'

He adjusted the temperature on the dashboard. 'I don't know, ma'am . . .' he said. 'If acquaintances from my past looked me up out of the blue, then one got killed the week I was kidnapped, I'd be a nervous wreck.'

I remembered how I had lost control when I was coming to terms with my forgotten past, the constant struggle to keep Eli from getting inside my head.

'Maybe she's trying to keep her emotions in check, so they don't get out of control.'

'Maybe . . .' he said.

I lowered the window, looking out at the city of contrasts – boutiques selling expensive clothes no one wanted a hundred metres from bustling chicken shops; tourists from all nations awed by the history of one of the most cosmopolitan places in the world. My thoughts drifted back to the case as I turned off the busy road: Sami, Gabriel and Ogechi were peers who had all trained to be doctors;

seven years older, Sarah was the odd one out. It was conceivable she had studied medicine before choosing the path of a teacher, but somehow, I wasn't convinced. Maybe it was wrong to judge a person murdered at a low point, but death can provide a snapshot of who we are, as opposed to who we want to be. Sarah Franks looked like a woman with troubles, whose lot was to suffer, not heal. Sarah, Gabriel, Sami, Ogechi – I shuffled their names around my mental Venn diagram, then moved them around again. There was one area they all overlapped – each relationship had been formed in the past.

I heard the vibration before my mobile rang. Randle turned towards me as Sami's name lit up my phone.

'Do you need to take that, ma'am?' he said.

I killed the call. 'No.'

The phone rang again almost immediately. I reached out to silence it, then saw Akosua's name. Her voice filled the car, distorted by the speakers.

'Ma'am?' She took my silence as encouragement. 'I followed up on the Sarah Franks evidence with DS Hoffen. I'm at the station in Elephant and Castle. Are you able to get here?'

She finally took a breath.

The street was unusually quiet. I flipped the indicator, spinning the car round.

'It'd better be worth it,' I said.

Chapter Seventy-Eight

Leah

The sergeant at the enquiry desk in the police station regarded us with tired eyes. Minutes later, we were collected by a plain-clothes officer with a walk identical to Lu's. We followed her down the same narrow corridor Lu had led me down before; she had the same short, determined stride. Lu stood, propped against a door in the far corner, thin lips in a straight line.

'You're checking my evidence now.' She raised her voice before we reached her. 'I thought I was collaborating, not getting reviewed. I sent your team an inventory. We've already been through the contents of Sarah Franks' flat. There was no bottle of gin.'

I didn't respond until we were closer. I knew Akosua would have already explained what was needed, but Lu just wanted her frustration to be heard.

'Now we know our cases are connected, we need to understand how the victims are linked,' I said.

'Fine, but I don't need you to check my homework.' She crossed her arms, her body tense.

'This is about the case, Lu. How you do your job is no concern of mine.'

I had never understood the point of being chippy – it was just an excuse to get in your own way. Lu spent so much time imagining the world was against her, she ended up fighting herself.

'I appreciate your cooperation,' I said.

She had no comeback. She pushed the door open without another word.

Akosua was standing behind the table, looking like an underage drinker trying to fit in in a bar. Two dozen bottles of alcohol were laid out before her, most of them empty, a couple half full. She swept a hand across them with a self-conscious flourish that must have seemed better when she imagined it in her head.

'I give you a day in the life of Sarah Franks, ma'am,' she said. She lost confidence in her performance, trailing off at the end. 'All these were found in Sarah's flat.' Her voice was more matter-of-fact.

'Sarah liked to party.' Lu stifled a yawn. 'It's in the file. We already know this.'

Randle's eyes roved over the bottles. It was no secret he liked a night out. 'It's not really a party if you party alone,' he said.

Sarah Franks wasn't someone who entertained; she drank at home, and she drank a lot. She had been on the road to self-destruction; the killer had just sped up the clock. I eased a nitrile glove over each hand, picking up bottles at random – cheap whisky, dregs of vodka, a few stray cans of beer tucked away at the back. I paused over an old plastic bottle – two litres of water rising up like a tower of virtue in a city of vice.

Akosua indicated the battered bottle, full to the top. 'All the others were found in the kitchenette and living room. This one was found under Sarah's bed.' She paused, glancing at the door as if concerned someone would hear us. 'My uncle used to have a taste for hard spirits. I've seen bottles like this before.'

'We've been through this.' Lu sounded bored behind me. 'The woman was an alcoholic. She wasn't a fan of water. So what?'

I unscrewed the lid and brought the bottle towards my face. My nostrils flared as an unfamiliar odour landed at the back of my nose.

'What is this?' I pulled the bottle away.

'It's alcohol distilled from palm wine, ma'am,' Akosua said. 'It's called akpeteshie or apio.' She paused. 'It's basically moonshine from Ghana. There's a saying that if you drink it, it makes your lips red.'

She turned to Lu in earnest, not wanting to seem smug.

'That's why your team didn't find it, DS Hoffen. They were looking for a bottle of gin they recognised. But this stuff doesn't come in one. It comes in water bottles or jerry cans.'

I examined the old water bottle Lu's team had missed – the tiny red, yellow and green flag with a star in the corner of the label that belonged to Ghana.

'This is what Sami was talking about,' Akosua said. 'The surprise left outside Sarah Franks' door. The elusive bottle of gin.'

Randle nodded. 'But why did Sarah see it as a threat?'

I left Randle and Akosua to wrap things up with Lu and send the bottle for testing. I took the long route back to the car, pausing to enjoy the sun. The fresh air was a welcome relief after the windowless room and alcohol fumes. Someone had gone to a lot of effort to send Sarah Franks local gin from Ghana – but was it the gin or the country that Sarah had seen as a threat? I checked my mobile – there was nothing from Selwyn Peterson. I sent him a message, keeping it polite and brief. I had no missed calls, except the one from Sami. My finger hovered over his name, wondering whether I was being too harsh with him. The screen flashed with a number

I didn't recognise. My first thought was that it was Sami, trying his luck with a different phone. Relenting, I answered, prepared to listen, but all I could hear was wailing, punctuated by fractured breaths, then a cry so piercing, it seared my brain.

'It's Sami! He's gone . . .' Zikar Mograbi struggled to speak. 'My son . . . my son is dead . . .'

Chapter Seventy-Nine

Leah

The door to the Mograbi house appeared closed, but the sliver of light down the side revealed it was open. I hung back on the kerb as Randle made his way up the steps. He turned back, concerned eyes searching my face.

'You don't need to do this, ma'am. I can handle it.'

'I know you can,' I said.

It's just another body.

My legs felt heavy as I forced myself to follow him. My feet moved briskly, but time had slowed. The sound of traffic was loud in my ears even though there were barely any cars. I could hear a low whimper from inside the house, like an injured animal gripped by fear. I steeled myself as I entered.

The hallway was eerily silent. Then I heard the sound again. Randle moved towards the door to the sitting room with careful footsteps. I followed behind. The bay window opposite was covered in a wave of red, as if a hosepipe had burst in the room. The adjacent wall was spattered with a layer of uneven blood. Lines of chaotic crimson streaked the carpet. I recognised Sami's shoes, even though I didn't remember noticing them before. Expensive leather loafers peeked out from behind the sofa – fine black hairs on tanned ankles, his feet unmoving and flexed. Randle stepped further into the room. Joined by an invisible thread of dread, I was pulled in after him. Zikar Mograbi was draped over his son, his wide back shaking. I stared at Sami's legs, limp on the floor, as firm hands wrapped around his father. Zikar was a big man, but Randle's grip didn't weaken, even when the older man tried to resist. Grief had distorted Zikar's face. At first, he looked like a man ready to fight his way out of hell. Then his body crumpled, and he collapsed, screaming his son's name.

Sami's skin had blanched, so his face was a strange yellow. There was a congealed patch of red like a flower across his flesh where a knife had stabbed his carotid artery, an angry slash across his throat. I checked his pulse, even though I knew he would have died almost instantly. There was no kick against my fingers. I glimpsed the photograph of the younger Sami with Zikar – so full of life – and I felt a burst of rage. I closed my eyes so the emotion didn't overcome me. I wasn't sure it worked.

I could hear Randle speaking, but the words were scrambled. I fired out instructions to secure the room whilst we waited for backup, moving with an energy that was almost frenetic as I searched each room for Sami's killer. I paused outside Sami's flat at the top of the house, my anger cooled by a jolt of sadness. The space was smaller than I remembered. His aftershave lingered – the bitter lemon tang filled the air. The door had been left ajar, as if it had been opened in a hurry. The room looked much like it had done when I had visited before – the Magic Eye poster, the claustrophobic low ceiling, the garish cabinet of alcohol next to the oversized desk. The only difference seemed to be a full mug of coffee on the kitchen counter – a morning routine broken, but interrupted by what? I searched the bedroom and the bathroom, but there was no sign of an intruder. Defeated, I made my way towards the main door, passing the lone photograph on the mantelpiece – Sami with his arm slung around me all those years ago. I stopped. My eyes travelled back to the mantelpiece. The frame was the same, but the photograph was not. That night I had visited, there had been a different picture – Sami and Zikar, now replaced by the photo of Sami and me. I remembered Sami, pink with embarrassment when he showed me the photo of us as teenagers, before he slipped it back into a drawer. Now it was proudly on display. My eyes drifted to the poster he had owned since childhood, coloured shapes concealing a face I couldn't make out. I thought of Sami's love for puzzles, making me play eye-spy on the walks home from school.

What, Sami? What do you want me to see?

I took the photo frame off the mantelpiece, flipping it round. The clips attaching the backing were haphazard, as if the photo had been changed fast. I eased them to the side, holding my breath as I lifted the brown board, looking for a note or message, but there was just the back of the old photograph, frayed around the edges. Then I saw the desk, and the puzzle started to make sense. I opened the top drawer – inside it, the photograph of Sami with a proud Zikar, which had been framed on the mantelpiece when I had been there last. The photo was raised up by something underneath it. I pushed it to the side, revealing a black mobile phone. The screen was unlocked, the most recent messages short and innocuous. I flicked to the call history – the penultimate call, the one Sami had made to me. He had made one more, hanging up before it was answered. He could have been interrupted by the killer, but why put the phone in a drawer?

Why, Sami? What do you want me to see?

There was no name identifying the recipient of the final call, just a number. I pressed it. It rang once, then there was a small hollow sound. One word, laced with surprise, a name turned into a question.

'Sami?'

I knew the voice – Lance Elbourne, Ogechi Okoro's boss.

Chapter Eighty

Zed

Zed had considered about mentioning the message from the well-wisher to Boy Cop and Black Cop, but the thought of the intruder had diminished the little faith in the police that remained. He popped his head round his mother's bedroom door. Her eyes were closed but she said his name when she sensed him.

'I'm going to the shop,' he said.

'Don't be long.' Ogechi smiled weakly.

'We need milk. I'll be back soon.'

He closed the door softly, hurrying down the stairs.

Seema was not on the wall when he passed it. He continued to the shop, messaging her on the way.

The shopkeeper was planted on a high stool behind the register, watching as Zed placed a carton of milk along with a Mars bar and a packet of Skittles on the counter. She scanned the items slowly, offering a pitying smile as she tried to think of something to say. Zed grabbed an extra Mars bar, paying quickly. He shoved the sweets into his pocket, almost forgetting the milk as he rushed out of the shop.

He could see Seema leaning against the wall as he turned the corner.

'My mum asks more questions about where I'm going ever since they cut up your mum.' She kicked her heel against the brick, catching herself. 'Sorry. Is that weird for you?'

He looked down at her feet. 'No.'

'We've had more messages,' she said.

More messages of sympathy. He had hoped they would tail off soon.

'I can delete the account now your mum's turned up.'

'No,' he said. 'Keep it live.'

'For what?' She stared at him, her wide eyes flashing.

Zed perched on the wall. He had been debating his plan, but now he realised what he must do. Seema slipped up to sit beside him. For once, she knew better than to interrupt his thoughts.

'Let's ask if anyone knows anything about who took my mum. We could offer a reward.'

Seema brightened, then he saw her face fall.

'Where are you going to get the reward from?' she said.

'That's not the point.' She was getting hung up on details. 'We offer it and then if we get something good, I'll make my dad give me some money. He's always trying to buy me stuff to make me like him. He feels guilty for leaving us, and he thinks money can make up for being crap.'

'It's not nice to use people.'

Seema's voice was solemn. He was surprised by the disappointment in her eyes.

Zed sighed. 'My dad's loaded. He feels guilty. I might as well do something with the money that's worth it.'

When he thought about his mother's attacker, he felt his anger build. He didn't know what he would do to them when he found them, but he was determined to get revenge.

Chapter Eighty-One

Leah

'I'm sorry, ma'am.'

Randle's first words as I pulled away from the kerb too fast. I waited for the reproach, but he just looked at me, his eyes kind. I slowed the car, even though my foot itched to slam against the accelerator.

'For what? You didn't do anything.'

'Neither did you,' he said.

He stared at his fingers, resting on his lap. I could see them twitching as he stopped himself from speaking.

'I know . . . If I had, things might have been different.' I let out a bitter laugh.

'That's not what I meant, ma'am.'

'I know.'

The car in front of us wrestled with the speed limit, then burst forwards, giving up on the rules. I felt a surge of envy as I resisted the urge to press down on the accelerator, desperate for some kind of release. I cut across the main road, heading for the river. There was usually something soothing about the way the bridges punctuated the water, but this time the beauty didn't help.

Randle watched me, pressing his fingers together. 'It was probably too late by the time Sami called.'

'We'll never know now, will we?'

I pushed down on the accelerator, shifting my mind to Lance Elbourne as the car roared. Randle took the hint, and we drove in silence the rest of the way.

According to his PA, Lance was indisposed. His assistant, Jimmy, seemed taller in the brightly lit reception, the same grey trousers, starched white shirt one size too big, the slope of his shoulders slightly uneven. His eyes glazed over with disinterest when I told him we would wait. He turned without a word, marching towards the lift. Lance had said nothing more on the phone after he had uttered Sami's name. I had cut the call almost immediately. With any luck, he would have no idea who was on the other end of the line, and our visit would take him by surprise. The reception was situated by floor-to-ceiling windows. I paced backwards and forwards, looking at the concrete towers outside. Randle moved towards a cluster of faux leather seats around a low table.

'Jimmy didn't look to be in any kind of hurry, ma'am,' he said. 'We might be in for a long wait.'

Squatting into a chair, he nodded towards the one opposite. Reluctantly, I chose the chair beside him, so eye contact was a choice I could avoid. Randle glanced up at the receptionist, but she was preoccupied with her phone under the desk. He spoke softly, his words just for me.

'Do you think Lance Elbourne had something to do with Sami's death, ma'am?'

'I don't know. Sami wanted me to know they were connected.' Otherwise why leave his phone somewhere he hoped I would find it? 'It was a deliberately cancelled call. I don't think he wanted it to go through.'

'And Zikar Mograbi?'

'I don't know, Randle. Your guess is as good as mine until he's in a fit state to speak to us.'

Zikar's anguished wails pierced my memory. His clothes had been sent for testing whilst he received medical care. Randle had separated him from his son's body, but he had to be sedated – his grief so raw it couldn't be contained.

The tinted windows dulled the blue in the sky outside. With the fluorescent lights, it could have been any season. I welcomed the air conditioning, running over the facts in my mind. We would have been in a stronger position if I had waited for a proper briefing on Lance Elbourne's history. I didn't want to give him time to regroup, so all we had were snippets from the internet which Randle recounted, his voice low.

'First degree and doctorate from Oxford. He tutored undergraduates studying medicine there before he made the move to medtech sales. I guess academia has its perks but doesn't pay, ma'am,' he said.

It was possible, but Lance Elbourne's bank balance wasn't my concern.

The phone trilled; the receptionist answered, her face a picture of concentration, as if her sole purpose in life was to wait for its ring. We were sent up to the third floor without an escort. Lance's assistant, Jimmy, was waiting when we arrived. He made no attempt at small talk as he led us across the open-plan office. Lance's door was open. He didn't look up. He waited for Jimmy to close the door behind us, then he stood, morphing into the perfect host. He shook our hands with just the right amount of pressure.

'I hear Ogechi Okoro is home safe.'

'She's home,' I said.

His eyes searched mine. I wondered if he knew about the suitcase; if he did, he gave nothing away.

This time, there were two chairs opposite his. He gestured for us to sit.

'Where was she found, Inspector?' He sounded concerned.

I sat back, taking in the man opposite me – the same jacket he had worn before, with a different shirt, bright stripes instead of paisley pressed across his chest.

'Where and how she was found is the subject of an ongoing investigation,' I said. 'That's not why I'm here.'

'Of course.' He cleared his throat with a low cough. 'Delivering good news can't be a priority with criminals on the loose.'

'I'll get to the point.' I was in no mood for games. 'What's your connection to Sami Mograbi?'

'Sami Mograbi?'

The name sounded strange when he repeated it. I couldn't tell if he was surprised or playing for time.

'Yours was the last number he dialled before he was killed.'

Lance's pupils dilated for a second; the rest of his body was motionless. He exhaled sharply.

'Sami's dead?'

I watched his face, trying to read his expression, but Lance kept his emotions contained.

'He was murdered earlier today.'

'How?'

Sami's body flashed before me – the wounds to his neck, the blood on the wall.

'Why was Sami calling you?' I said.

Lance's body snapped back to life, his movements deliberate. He wasn't a man to fidget. He clasped his hands in front of him, elbows digging into his desk, creating a platform for his chin.

'Why Sami would call me in general is easy to answer. The timing, I suppose, is the question for you . . . I had a previous life in academia at Oxford, before I realised that money was more important to me than I care to admit. I tutored Sami as an undergraduate. It was a formative time. When he left, he kept in touch.'

My encounters with teachers had been unmemorable or unpleasant. Respecting authority had come slowly with age.

'Is it usual to have such a close teacher–student relationship?'

'We stayed in touch, Inspector. That's not the same as being close.'

He unclasped his hands. The tips of his fingers moved in slow circles at the edge of his cheekbones.

'Are you familiar with the Oxford system?' he said.

'I didn't go there, if that's what you mean, Mr Elbourne, but I'm sure Randle will be happy to indulge you with tales from his undergraduate past.'

Lance looked at Randle with something bordering on interest, then his gaze travelled back to me.

'I wasn't trying to patronise you, Inspector. If I was, trust me, you would know. All I was trying to convey was that tutoring one or two undergraduates every week can engender a more intimate understanding than in a classic classroom environment. I'm sure Detective Randle can testify to what I mean.'

Randle said nothing. He had lived on both sides of the line of privilege, but he wasn't ready to empathise with Lance Elbourne, even if he understood.

'Sami and I weren't close,' Lance continued. 'But we were familiar. He had a difficult relationship with his father. He looked to me for guidance at times.'

The Sami I knew was self-assured and confident.

'What did he need guidance for?' I said.

'He was one of the brightest students I ever taught, but he didn't know what to do with his talent . . . He dropped out before he had completed his practical training, near the start of his clinical years. He was hard on himself, because he wasn't up to it. He thought his father would see him as a failure. He needed someone to talk to. I obliged.'

'When was the last time you saw him?' I said.

'He came to see me recently,' Lance responded without hesitation. 'One of his friends had just died . . .'

'You mean Sarah Franks?' I said.

'I believe so. He was angry. He wanted answers.'

'And you were the man to give them to him?'

Lance's eyes dismissed my sarcasm.

'How could I? I didn't know his friend. Sami needed to vent. I just provided an understanding ear.' His lips curled into a slight smile. 'You're sceptical, Inspector. Your face betrays you.'

'I assure you, my face and my mind speak as one.'

Randle looked down, hiding a smirk, but I had already seen it. Lance Elbourne chuckled, quiet, almost soundless at the back of his throat.

'Of course,' he said. 'Of course.'

'If he looked to you for guidance,' I said, unblinking, 'why didn't Sami wait for his call to go through?'

Lance pushed his papers to the side, resting his forearms on the wooden surface. His face was serious, but there was no aggression in his eyes.

'Inspector, is this a conversation or an interrogation? I don't mind which, but just so we are all clear . . .'

'I ask questions. You answer them,' I said. 'Semantics aren't important. Not when a man's dead.'

Lance shook his head. 'Details matter. You know that as well as I do. I'm happy to be interviewed formally, but you will be wasting both our time.'

Randle shifted beside me. The move was subtle, but I understood the question. My nod was almost imperceptible. His tone was deferential when he spoke.

'You're right, Mr Elbourne,' he said. 'Details *are* important. You mentioned Sami dropped out because he wasn't up to it. Did anything in particular happen, or did the pressure just catch up with him after years of studying hard?'

Lance turned to Randle. 'I don't know. I've asked myself the same question. He went on his elective. He came back and decided to give it all up.'

Lance searched my face, hoping to see confusion, but the chance to patronise me would have to wait. I was familiar with the concept of a medical elective – a couple of months' placement done by medical students, often spent working in a hospital abroad.

'I thought electives were for Western kids to have fun whilst feeling good about themselves for helping the less privileged.'

Lance smiled, but his eyes were dulled by sadness. 'For some, yes.

For others, it makes them feel small and helpless. They see a world of need that's bigger than them, and they don't know how to cope. Sami had too big a heart.' He looked at me with meaning. 'It never helps to care too much about what you can't change.'

He sighed, louder than necessary – an oral full stop drawing the conversation to a close.

'I'd be very happy to come down to the station for a formal interview, but like I said, I had nothing to do with Sami's death. I only ever tried to support him. I don't know why he called me. Of course we can all speculate, but we shall never know because he cut the call before it came through.'

He stood gracefully, offering his hand. I took it, my eyes never leaving his. If Lance Elbourne was responsible for Sami's death, I would make sure justice was served.

'One more thing,' I said as I released my grip. 'Sami's elective. Where did he go that was so bad it ruined medicine for him?'

Lance chuckled again. This time the sound was louder. 'I wouldn't go that far, Inspector. It would be doing a disservice to a wonderful country. He went to Ghana. With Ogechi Okoro. She was my student too before she came to work for me.'

'Why didn't you mention that – when we first spoke to you?' I said.

'It didn't seem relevant.' He paused. 'And you never asked.'

Chapter Eighty-Two

Leah

I shut myself in my office, relieved finally to be alone. Sami was dead, and I had ignored him. If I had answered his call, he might still be alive. It was too late, but I couldn't get the thought out of my head. The heat made me jittery. The room was too hot. The blades of the fan moved slowly, stuttering until they finally died. Frustrated, I yanked out the lead, hurling it into the bin. I pushed up the window, letting out a silent scream into the still air. Sami had known Lance Elbourne, had done his medical elective in Ghana; Ogechi had been at Oxford with Sami, in Ghana at the same time. The facts darted around in circles, refusing to settle. My fingers twitched with pent-up energy, the need to skip the only clear thought in my mind. I burst out into the bullpen, making a beeline for the accessible bathroom. Akosua stopped me before I made it to the exit.

'The tests came back for the water bottle we found in Sarah's flat, ma'am,' she said. 'It's definitely local gin. The water bottle's from Ghana. No one else has smelt akpeteshie, but I'm pretty sure that's what it is.'

She tightened the hairband securing her bun decisively as Randle came up behind her.

'To most people here that's just a bottle for selling water,' he said. 'But didn't you say akpeteshie is sold in water bottles and jerry cans in Ghana?'

'Yes . . .' She stiffened, ready for a challenge.

'So whoever sent the gin was trying to make a point. If it was local gin, delivered in a local water bottle, they must have been confident Sarah would understand the significance.'

Akosua's shoulders visibly relaxed. 'You mean, she must have some kind of connection to Ghana?'

'I don't know.' Randle turned to me. 'Worth us checking, don't you think, ma'am?'

'Sure, and find out where Gabriel McMahon did his medical elective. I bet you anything's it's Ghana . . .' I said, my eyes on the door.

'And if it's not?' Randle said.

'What?' I was caught off guard by the interruption as I made to move past.

'Nothing. Just that that sounded like a bet.'

My eyes flitted to the exit in the far corner. I needed to get away. 'If it isn't, I'll go to one of your races,' I said.

'I found the hospital where Ogechi and Sami did their placement in Ghana.' Akosua angled her body towards me, shutting Randle out. 'I called them, but it's so long ago, no one seemed to remember them. I keep getting passed around departments, but so far, no one can help.'

'Keep calling until someone has something interesting to say.'

The phone on Randle's desk rang. They both turned, and I seized my chance to escape. I moved swiftly towards the exit, down the corridor, towards the bathroom. I had almost reached my destination when I heard Randle's voice call out.

'Zikar Mograbi's been processed. He's ready to be interviewed. Are *you* ready, ma'am?'

I turned, defeated. We needed to rule him out as a suspect. Skipping would have to wait.

'Let's get this over with,' I said.

Chapter Eighty-Three

Leah

I let Randle move ahead of me when we reached the door to the stairs. He usually bounded down, long legs covering multiple steps, but he hung back, his movements slow. When he reached the bottom, he turned, his back across the exit, his eyes a darker blue in the dim light.

'Zikar Mograbi was a mess when I was with him, ma'am. He's seen a doctor, but he was still pretty raw . . . I know you hadn't seen Sami for a long time, but with all due respect . . .'

'If you think that gives you permission to say something you shouldn't, I'd stop now if I were you,' I said.

A hint of doubt entered his eyes. He leant back, blocking the door.

'Zikar is grieving. So are you, ma'am. That's not a good combination for an interview. I'm happy to lead if you want to sit this one out.'

He pushed his hair back off his face as he looked down at me, his gaze unwavering. 'It's up to you.'

He stepped aside.

I reached past him, pushing the door open. I was halfway down the corridor when I stopped.

'OK,' I said. 'Run the interview, Randle. I'll be watching from behind the glass.'

Chapter Eighty-Four

Leah

Zikar Mograbi seemed smaller than the man I had seen clutching Sami's body. He was slumped with his head in his hands, wide palms pressing hard against his temples. His lawyer whispered something in his ear, but Zikar didn't react. There was a dull thud as he thumped his fist against the table, a low shout that morphed into a moan. I stood back, peering through the two-way mirror. If Zikar knew he was being watched, he didn't seem to care. The door swung open, announcing Randle and Akosua's entrance. Zikar looked up, red eyes following their walk in. Gone was Randle's usual, easy gait – he commanded the space as he strode into the room.

I watched as Randle went through the formalities. His face was kind, seeking to put Zikar at ease. Zikar nodded distractedly through the introductions. He looked like a man drowning in his thoughts, his mind far away.

'How are you doing, Mr Mograbi?' Randle's tone was warm and genuine.

'How do you think I'm doing?' Zikar's voice was laced with aggression. 'My son is dead, and you have no idea who killed him.'

Randle absorbed the blow, sitting back in his chair. Zikar's face hardened as he drummed his fingers on the table.

'When we first met, you thought my son was a killer. Now he's dead, you've shifted the blame to me. The incompetence and time wasting of the British police doesn't surprise me, but if your incompetence means my son's murderer walks free, I'll make sure this is the last case you do.'

Akosua shifted in her seat, but Randle didn't flinch.

'We won't keep you longer than we have to, Mr Mograbi. We just need to establish the facts, so we can find whoever killed Sami.'

Zikar's whole body crumpled at the mention of Sami. A sound escaped his mouth, almost like a whimper. Randle waited as the wave of grief rose then died before he carried on. Behind the glass, I watched Zikar listen patiently as Randle questioned him about his whereabouts.

'I arrived back from Paris on the Eurostar,' Zikar said, without expression. 'I was picked up by the same driver I always use. He dropped me at home. You can verify the times with the chauffeur service. When I went in, the sitting room door was open . . .' Zikar trailed off. 'I saw what I saw. I called Inspector Hutch.'

'How long did you wait between arriving and calling the inspector?'

'I don't know . . .' Zikar glanced down at his wrist, but his watch had been taken with his clothing. 'Seconds . . . minutes . . . Why are you asking me? You're wasting time. You can check all this. Every second you question me, you're not out there doing your job.'

Randle ran his hand along the thin file in front of him. He flicked it open but didn't look down before he spoke.

'Sami made several calls just before he was killed. One was to a Lance Elbourne. Did Sami ever mention him?'

Zikar's head snapped up, his eyes piercing.

'You said several calls. Whom else did he ring? Did he call *her*?'

Randle held his gaze. 'Who?'

'Don't play games with me.' Zikar's body was coiled, ready for an explosion. 'Where is she?'

He slammed his palm down, shaking the table between them.

'I understand this is hard,' Randle said. 'But I need to ask you to control your emotions.'

'Where is she?' Zikar said again.

His lawyer put a hand on his arm, but he shook it off, springing to his feet.

'Where is she? Is she watching? Get her in here now. I want to talk to her.' He didn't raise his voice, but his tone was chilling.

'Sit down, Zikar.' Randle's voice was steady. 'If you don't calm down, this conversation is over.'

The room was small – three angry steps and Zikar and I were face to face through the two-way mirror. He couldn't see me, but he stared, knowing I was there.

'Arrest me. Lock me up. I don't care,' he said. 'I'm not sitting down, and if you touch me, I'll sue. I will bring down this entire station unless you get her in here, *now*.'

I didn't wait for Randle's reaction; I was already moving. Out the door, down the corridor. I heard Akosua's voice introduce my entrance, but I was already speaking.

'Sit down, Zikar.'

Neither of us blinked.

He drew himself up, debating his reaction. Then he walked to his side of the table, scraping back his chair with a slow, deliberate motion. Randle stood so I could sit opposite. Zikar watched in silence, waiting until our eyes were level. He leant forwards with a long, deep exhalation. The anger had gone, leaving anguish in its wake.

'Do you know what it's like, Miss Hutch, to walk into a room and see someone you love with their body cut open? To hold them . . . to feel their blood on your skin and know they died in more pain than you can imagine?'

He searched my face for a reaction. My mother's body flashed into my mind, but I felt no emotion. I looked across at Zikar, but I had no words for him.

'That's all you've got?' I could hear the disgust. 'You sit there, and you say nothing.'

'I don't know what more you want from me. Help us find who did this to your son.'

Zikar snorted. 'You speak as if he's just another victim. What was it you said? He wasn't a friend, just someone you knew *for a short period a very long time ago*.' His eyes were full of contempt. 'I wonder, how do you feel now he's dead?'

I bit down on the rage rising up inside me. 'How I feel,' I said, 'is not relevant to this conversation.'

'You're right.' Zikar sat back, but the heat from his breath lingered. 'I don't care how you feel. But I'll tell you this, Leah Hutch – my son was your friend, and you were once his friend too. Sami came to you, and you didn't listen. I hope his bleeding body haunts your dreams. He was your friend. You owe it to him to find his killer.'

Chapter Eighty-Five

Leah

This time no one was stopping me. I walked fast, my nails clawing into my palms until I reached the peace of the accessible bathroom. I flipped the lock, pressed my back against the door. My heartbeat pounded in my head. I placed my phone on the floor, breathing deeply until the sound faded.

I shifted my weight, flicking my wrists – the dead bodies living in my brain swept away as an invisible rope twirled over me. Ray King, Sarah Franks, Gabriel McMahon drifted out of focus, but the image of Sami remained. I saw my mother, lifeless beside him – the same flowering of blood on her neck. My phone flashed with the name Selwyn Peterson. I reached for it, knowing he wouldn't call again.

'Hello?' I blinked away the thought of my mother's body.

'Selwyn Peterson.' The same dance he always led. 'You rang, Ms Hutch. I have an hour. If you still need to see me, that is.'

I was out of breath. 'I'm at least half an hour away.'

'Then you'll have half an hour of my time, if you move fast.'

Chapter Eighty-Six

Leah

Selwyn Peterson was standing in the doorway of his office, filling the frame with a well-cut suit. The pinstripe lengthened his torso, concealing a spreading waistline his ageing metabolism could no longer fight.

'Apologies. I got stuck in traffic.'

'You have seven minutes,' he said.

I nodded. 'I can think and talk fast.'

He shut the door behind me, motioning towards a sleek wooden chair. He remained standing behind the large desk in front of it, regarding me like a pupil he was about to expel.

'One message or phone call would have been sufficient, Miss Hutch. Saying the same thing several times only serves to irritate, not necessarily to get you heard.'

He sat, drawing his tortoiseshell glasses down the bridge of his nose. Despite the heatwave that consumed the city, his face maintained the same ivory sheen. He was the kind of man for whom a tan was distasteful – the kind who always wore a suit jacket whatever the temperature outside. He didn't look hot, in spite of the layers. There was no air conditioning. It was a mystery how he avoided sweat.

'Thank you for seeing me.' I tried to put us back onto an amicable footing.

Selwyn looked at his watch, then back at me pointedly. His nostrils were almost dainty despite the prominent nose. We had only met once before, but he had been close to Margaretta. He had been aware of me long before I saw him for the first time.

'Do you remember me?' I said. 'As a child? In the period leading up to my mother's death and immediately after?'

He blinked once, as if the question was tedious, lifting a silver fountain pen.

'It's not my job to reminisce.' He tapped the pen against a leather notebook. 'If you have a specific question, I suggest you ask it now.'

Last autumn he had revealed a photograph of me as a toddler, with the family I had forgotten I had: Eli, my mother, Margaretta – the woman who had brought me up with lies.

'I still have gaps in my memory,' I said.

'That's to be expected. You experienced something deeply disturbing when you were extremely young.'

'I'm curious about my relationship with my father. Did Margaretta ever mention that to you?'

Selwyn sat back as if the question physically repelled him. His tone was dry, verging on sarcastic when he spoke.

'I'm sure there are specialists you can employ to explore your family trauma, Miss Hutch. I'm a lawyer, not a therapist. Unearthing memories is not part of my job.'

I focused on the oak-panelled wall directly behind his earlobe.

'You're familiar with Eli's crime?' I said. 'Was there any evidence of me at the crime scene?'

'No witnesses were mentioned during the trial.' He watched me. 'Do you have any reason to believe you were there?'

My mind moved fast, but I kept my face neutral, conscious Selwyn wasn't paid to be on my side.

'I'm sure you know Eli is prone to mind games,' I said. 'I just want to be sure of the facts. What did Margaretta tell you about that night?'

Selwyn's fingers glided along the edge of the pen, then slowly glided back.

'As her lawyer, I only know what was in the file I gave you.'

'And as her friend?'

A rare smile that didn't travel past his mouth.

'It was over thirty years ago, Miss Hutch,' he said.

'But details are part of your job. You don't just turn that off.'

He removed his glasses, folding them slowly in front of him, his face on full display for the first time. His skin was smooth around his eyes and jawline – surprising for a man of his age.

'The police weren't looking for your DNA at the crime scene.' He chose his words carefully. 'So if you *were* there, no evidence was found. Given that it was over thirty years ago, it's not a question anyone is asking now.'

I gripped my thighs, fighting the urge to lean forwards. 'If there's anything Margaretta told you about that night, the trial, anything . . . I'm asking you – please tell me . . .'

'Miss Hutch.' Selwyn's speech was clipped and deliberate.

There was a knock. He looked past me to the grandfather clock by the doorway.

'I'm afraid we're out of time. I'm sorry I can't help you more.'

I stood, an involuntary sigh escaping me.

'I'm not a psychologist,' Selwyn said, 'but, in my experience, when someone is searching for a memory, location can sometimes help.'

He opened the notebook in front of him, scrawling a few words with the silver pen.

'What's this?' I accepted the sheet of paper he offered me.

'The address of the cottage where your mother was said to have died and David Francis' body was found . . . Personally, I wouldn't advise it. But sometimes, the only way to get answers is to revisit the scene of the crime.'

Chapter Eighty-Seven

Zed

Zed scrolled through the messages offering information in exchange for a reward. There were a handful, but none of them helped. He hadn't mentioned the suitcase in his original post, and when he probed, no one had any idea about the shiny black shell that had delivered his mother home. He pulled up the notes app on his phone, scanning the list of names he had made when he was searching for Ogechi.

Chris?

Sarah???

Gabriel McMahon

Ray King

He wished he could remember Sarah's surname, but all he recalled was the body in the photograph, her neck stained with blood.

Ogechi called out as he passed her bedroom. She was lying on her duvet, watching the door. He searched her face for signs of pain or anxiety, but she just looked tired and old.

'You OK, Mum?' he said.

'Come here, Zechariah.' She smiled faintly. 'Are *you* OK? We haven't talked about any of this.'

'Just get better first.'

He was ready to move off, but she patted the space next to her. He slid up onto the soft blue cotton, his legs dangling over the edge of the bed.

'I'm fine, Mum.'

'No. You're not, Zechariah, and you shouldn't be. I heard what happened.' There were tears in her eyes. 'I'm so sorry you had to go through that because you were worried about me.'

Zed stared at the dark green logo on his white leather trainers. 'Did you know that man? The one they killed?' he said.

Ogechi's head snapped up. 'Did you see who did it?'

He couldn't look at her. In his mind, he was back, hiding in the wardrobe. He shook his head. 'Did you know him?' he said.

'A long time ago.'

'He was watching the flat. Why?'

'I don't know, Zechariah.'

'Do you know why he was killed?'

'No.' She shook her head.

'Was it the same people who took you?'

'I don't know.' She gripped his hands, stopping his questions. 'Zechariah, look at me.' Her skin was warm against his. 'I don't have answers for you now. I may never have. But you have to promise me you won't put yourself in danger again. We need to leave it to the police now.'

He kissed her cheek.

'Don't worry, Mum. I won't do anything stupid.'

He stood, thinking of the bodies on the wall. At the bottom of the stairs, he glanced at his phone again. He saw the new message. The words made the breath catch in his throat.

Glad she's back safely. I know what happened to your mum

Chapter Eighty-Eight

Leah

It was a relief to close the door to my office and sink down into the hard chair behind my desk. The air was close, but I felt no urge to open the window. I angled my computer away from the glare of sunlight. Retrieving the address Selwyn had given me from my pocket, I typed the words on my keyboard. I hesitated before I hit enter, staring as an image of the cottage where my mother was murdered with her lover filled the screen.

You're scared of the truth and yet you seek it.

Eli's words hovered in my mind.

I could have found David Francis' house myself if I had wanted to. I had the means that came with my job. So why hadn't I looked it up?

You're scared of the truth and yet you seek it.

I hated the fact that Eli was right.

I studied the cottage. Surrounded by overgrown grass and forget-me-nots, my mother's lover David Francis' house looked like it had been abandoned many years ago. I zoomed in, hoping it would trigger a memory – was I in the room when my mother was killed, or was the image of me as a little girl on the inside of the door just a nightmare I couldn't shake?

I didn't hear Kenny's footsteps; the sound of his voice surprised me.

'I hear you pulled in Zikar Mograbi.' His face within a face was impassive. 'How did that go?'

'Fine, sir.' We didn't have enough evidence to charge him, and I doubted he would ever harm Sami. 'I think we can let him go.'

Kenny watched me. It was hard to tell whether he had seen the recording of the interview. If he had, he gave nothing away. He swallowed as if preparing himself to say something, then changed his mind as Randle approached.

'Yes?' Kenny said.

Randle scanned my face, checking I was OK with the interruption. 'I can come back, ma'am?'

'What is it?' I said.

'Sami Mograbi's post-mortem's in progress. Harrison says she can debrief us when it's over. She didn't think you would want to be there.'

I could feel Kenny's eyes on me, watching.

'Let her know I'll join,' I said.

Chapter Eighty-Nine

Leah

I couldn't see Harrison's eyes behind the plastic visor. Her head was down, the post-mortem well underway. Sami lay on the metal slab, his olive skin turned mushroom, sliced open down the middle, from the chin. I focused on the neat line dividing him in two halves, the small incision on his neck, pale pink where his carotid artery had been slashed. Harrison looked up as I stopped opposite her. There was a kindness in her eyes I had never seen before. I didn't remember telling her about my history with Sami. Harrison abhorred gossip, but I was often surprised by what she knew about the lives of the dead.

'I can always rely on you to time your entrance, Hutch.' Her voice sounded duller behind the plastic. 'We're just getting to the interesting part – the jab to the carotid would have killed him in a couple of minutes, but this . . .'

She motioned to a straight wound across Sami's throat. I imagined a blade ripping the soft olive flesh. I looked down – the drain was still wet from when they had hosed the body, no trace of the blood that had been washed away.

'It's hard to know which came first – the stab to the carotid or the cut across the trachea,' Harrison was saying.

'Why cut the trachea, if the wound to the carotid was guaranteed to kill him in minutes?' I said.

'Why indeed?' The edge of her eyebrow lifted above the face covering. She indicated the neat wound where the killer had pressed the knife into Sami's carotid. 'The killer knew exactly where to find the major artery. They didn't need an insurance policy with the trachea. So why cut it? There are several options. I'll give you two.'

She looked up to make sure I was following, her eyes darker behind the transparent shield.

'Option one,' she said. 'They did it because they could, and they enjoyed it, but if they were a sadist, they would have had more fun with the body, and there are only the two serious wounds.'

'What's option two?' I still hadn't looked at Sami's face.

'They specifically cut the trachea *before* the hit to the carotid,' Harrison said, 'to ensure the victim suffered before he died. It wasn't about the killer's pleasure; it was about the victim's pain.'

I tried to hold the image at arm's length, but it pushed itself into my mind – Sami clutching his neck in agony, knowing he only had minutes left on earth. I pulled my thoughts back to the room – the sterile metal counter, the set of butcher's scales, the empty viewing gallery beyond the glass behind Harrison, the glistening sheen of water above the drain.

'How long between the killer slitting his throat and stabbing him in the neck?' I said.

'Seconds, minutes. Too long a gap, and he'd already be dead.'

'He died in agony.' I remembered the call I rejected.

'Likely.' Harrison's tone softened. 'But we don't know for sure.'

She signalled to the limp-haired technician. He stepped forward, his face animated as he brandished the circular saw. He held the blade inches from Sami's corpse. His long limbs reminded me of Eli; I thought of the bloody axe the police had found with his fingerprints before they finally arrested him all those years ago. I felt the weight of someone's gaze on me. I glanced up – Kenny's eyes held mine behind the glass. I couldn't be sure when he had entered the viewing room, but I knew he would have been watching me from the moment he arrived. Without thinking, my eyes shifted to Sami's face. My breath hitched as I saw him for the first time since we had found him – the strong nose, the defined jaw that had surprised me. If his last moments on earth had been unbearable, it wasn't evident now. He looked calm, almost peaceful, unlike the anxious man who had sought my help. I closed my eyes momentarily, committing the image to memory. Then I heard the whirr of the saw preparing to drive through his skull. There was a crack. I couldn't watch. I knew Kenny was looking at me. I kept my gaze down as the bile rose up. I focused on Sami's torso, repelling the images of his murder as they rushed at me. The sound of the blade grew louder; I saw Eli standing above my mother's body, axe ready to slice soft flesh. My mother's body morphed into Sami's. I imagined the blade sinking into his neck. Without a word, I turned and left.

Chapter Ninety

Leah

Kenny was already in the corridor. He was surprisingly agile for his size. His substantial frame blocked my path to the exit. I tried to see past him to the stairwell, but he shifted his bulk, obscuring my line of sight.

'A minute, Hutch.'

He rarely used my surname. I unclenched my hands, bracing myself for an attack. Kenny pivoted, his wide back stretching across the narrow corridor as he strode away without turning round. He led me round the corner, out of earshot of anyone who could witness my dressing-down.

'What was that in there?' His eyes were piercing. He pinched the tip of his button nose.

'What was what, sir?'

Kenny closed the space between us. I drew myself up, aware of his height.

'It must have been hard seeing an old friend like that.' His green eyes watched me.

'As I said, he wasn't a friend, sir. Just someone I knew a long time ago. It's always hard seeing a victim when you feel you could have done more.'

His gaze travelled across my face, then moved back, as if reading my thoughts. I fought to keep my features neutral. Kenny made a clicking sound in the back of his throat.

'You should take a couple of days off, Leah,' he said. 'Call it a long weekend. DS Randle can hold the reins.'

My mouth dropped open in protest, but for a moment no words came out.

'I'm fine, sir,' I said.

A frown closed the gap between his neat eyebrows. 'A couple of days, Leah. It's just a couple of days.'

I saw myself through his eyes – fists balled, speech strained. I could feel my words die in my throat before they came out. My voice sounded pinched when I tried again.

'With all due respect, sir, that would be to the detriment of the case.'

Kenny folded his arms across his chest, elbows resting on the solid flesh of his gut.

'I watched the interview with Zikar Mograbi,' he said. 'He was understandably upset, so I'm going to give you the benefit of the doubt.'

'Sir . . .'

My dissent died when I saw his expression.

'A few days. It's a simple request, Leah. Let's not make it a demand.'

Chapter Ninety-One

Leah

I briefed Randle in staccato sentences, leaving before he could ask how I was. Outside, I realised I had left my jacket in my office, but it was warm, and I couldn't face going back. I crossed the river over Battersea Bridge, staring down the water at its grander neighbour – Albert Bridge, its pink arc clashing with the strident orange sky.

Sami had turned to me; now he was dead. Another person from my life, gone. I missed Margaretta; I was responsible for Sami; but when it came to my mother, I wasn't sure how I felt. Ever since Margaretta had died, the layers of my life had been scraped back, and I had no idea what lay at my core.

I looked out over the river. The colour fluctuated between brown and aquamarine under the intense summer sun. My nerves were raw. I couldn't predict my behaviour. My mind was filled with questions about the present and the past. I spent my days seeking justice for victims – now Kenny had taken that away. Maybe returning to the place of my mother's murder would help quiet my brain. I couldn't be sure that it would bring answers, but it was time to visit the scene of Eli's crime.

Chapter Ninety-Two

Zed

Zed walked to one end of his room and then back again. He paced back and forth across the small space. He checked the sequence of messages for the tenth time as he debated whether he had taken a foolish risk. He had responded to the initial message with a wary question mark. An offer to meet had been the swift reply.

Why didn't you go to the police?

Zed read his own words aloud as he continued pacing.

Nuf trouble with feds. U want to meet or what?

Yes

The only possible answer. What else could he say? It was the first real lead he had.

He slipped out onto the landing. His mum's bedroom door was slightly ajar. She was lying on her side, her eyes closed after a strong dose of painkillers. He waited by the door until he was satisfied she was asleep. He tiptoed back to his room, making a beeline for his computer. He pulled up his music and clicked on a retro hip hop track – not so noisy that it would rouse Ogechi, but loud enough to suggest he was next door, should she wake up. He slid a baseball cap over his head, his face in shadow so he appeared older. He closed the door quietly as he headed out.

Outside, it was hotter than he had anticipated. He wished he hadn't worn jeans, but he looked like a little boy in shorts. He glanced down the road – he could see Seema engrossed in her cat's cradle. She looked up expectantly, her T-shirt too tight round her arms. He approached slowly, apprehensive about telling her. He downloaded the information swiftly, so she couldn't interrupt. She nodded as he spoke, taking it all in.

'My mum says you shouldn't talk to strangers,' she said when he had finished.

'You were a stranger.' His tone was curt.

She dropped her gaze so he couldn't see the hurt in her eyes, but he had already glimpsed it.

'I mean, you were before,' he said.

He wasn't sure what she was now. At school, he would be embarrassed to be friends with a twelve-year-old girl in undersized T-shirts, but she was the only person he could talk to about what was going on in his life.

'Unlock your phone,' he ordered.

Seema didn't question him.

He pulled up her contacts, typing fast.

'She's called Leah. She's police, but she's alright,' he said. 'If I'm not back in an hour, call her. Tell her everything.'

Chapter Ninety-Three

Zed

Zed strode with purpose over the metal bridge that crossed the railway. There was a wall to his right, covered in swirls of graffiti, too high for him to peer over the side. A stream of cars fenced him in on his left. The purr of engines drowned out pedestrian footsteps in front and behind him. He moved fast, barely noticing the strangers he passed. There was a stairwell over the bridge, tucked between two buildings, shallow steps fanning down to the street below. He started to descend, then felt a presence encroaching. He looked back, but there was no one there. He removed his hands from his pockets, small fists clenched, ready to fight. There was no attacker, but he felt far from calm. He recited his mantra, walking faster as he made his way towards the meeting point.

He had memorised the route, so he didn't need to check the map on his phone. He turned down a side alley, conscious of the sound of his own footsteps. He stopped, reassured by the silence before he continued down the path. He emerged onto a residential street. For a moment, he was relieved to be out in the open, but every window seemed to hide an unseen spectator, and he felt totally exposed. He looked down to conceal his eyes. He took the next turning, spotting the T-junction up ahead. He felt someone close behind him.

His first instinct was to start running, but anxiety made him pause. He froze as a boy, a few years older, passed him. He stared at him, wondering if it was the stranger who had sent the messages, but the boy didn't glance back once. Zed quickened his pace, ignoring the squeak of rubber rotating on tarmac. He heard jagged breaths behind him. He moved faster as they grew louder, flinching as a bicycle screeched to a halt in front of him.

'Why didn't you wait for me?'

Fear morphed into annoyance as Seema caught her breath.

'What are you doing here?' Zed said, incredulous.

She sucked in oxygen, her bicycle glinting in the sunlight. Her tone was accusing.

'You just left . . .'

He looked at her, her whole face scrunched into a pout. He was about to tell her to leave, but he found her presence strangely reassuring.

'You can stay,' he said. 'If you promise not to speak.'

Seema nodded, keen to prove she could keep her end of the bargain. Her eyes bulged as a man in his early twenties approached. Zed followed her gaze, waiting for the slightest hint of recognition, but the man strutted past them, looking the other way. The road was quiet as they stood side by side, scanning for strangers. Zed could feel the weight of someone's gaze. He looked round, but there was no one there. They waited and waited, but no one came.

Chapter Ninety-Four

Leah

David Francis' house was two hours outside of London. I rented a car that struggled as straight roads became winding, and tarmac turned to gravel, then track. It was almost dark when I skidded to a halt outside the cottage. I opened the car door to the hum of insects surrounding me. My chest felt tight as I stood in front of the last place my mother had visited alive.

The path leading up to the entrance was overgrown with wild daisies and forget-me-nots. The front door sealed shut, the windows boarded up. I held my torch out in front of me, adjusting the beam of light. The door to the back was slightly open, the lock broken. There were signs of squatters – a bed of newspaper, half covered by a soiled blanket, and a small hoard of food in a box on the floor. I climbed the stairs, looking around me. The landing was unfamiliar. I entered each room, glancing around. There was no furniture, except a couple of camp beds and a fold-up table. I didn't recognise anything. I felt foolish for travelling all the way. The largest room was empty, cream wallpaper peeling. There was no bed, but I imagined it would have been the master bedroom. I closed my eyes, but I couldn't see my younger self crouching by the door. Frustrated, I walked back onto the landing, wondering if any of the images in my mind stemmed from truth.

I heard a noise below me. I rushed down the stairs, out of the back door. Outside, I could see no one. The car was parked where I had left it. My breathing became ragged, but it wasn't from fear. I saw myself as a little girl, hyperventilating – huddled on the back seat of a car, eyes full of tears. Over the image, I could hear singing, but I couldn't make out the words, and I didn't recognise the tune. A picture began to form slowly – me behind the driver's seat, a dark shape seated in front. I closed my eyes, clinging to what I was certain was a childhood memory. The figure turned – Eli looked back at me. I smiled at him through my tears.

Chapter Ninety-Five

Leah

I sat staring at the door in the visits hall. Five minutes passed, and still Eli didn't come. He had been the one to request my presence – another of the games he played. Fluorescent light filled the room – the artifice a grim reminder of the morning sun Eli and his fellow inmates would miss yet again. The couple beside me reached their fingers across the table, skin not quite touching, as if they didn't trust the lust reflected in each other's eyes. The man turned to me, mouthing obscenities. I stared back. Like a coward, he looked away.

'Picking fights with the big kids. I would have thought you'd know better.'

Eli stood in front of me. I hadn't heard him creep up. He lowered himself into the seat opposite, yawning without opening his mouth. He sat back, broad shoulders straight and angular, a trace of a smile playing on his lips. Even when relaxed, his posture remained controlled, his thin body long and strong.

'I'm glad you read my letter.' Eli's gaze was steady. 'I wasn't sure you'd come.'

The woman from the couple next to me coughed loudly. People turned accusingly. Eli's eyes remained on mine.

'I know you lied,' I said.

His irises flashed brighter, pale blue around large black pupils. His arm lingered on the table in front of us, fingers edging over the invisible divide.

'You know, not answering your questions and lying are two different things.'

'I'm not a fan of either, but you seem to be expert in both. Tell me the truth, Eli, or I'm not coming back.'

I was pretty sure what Eli felt for me was far from affection, but there was a satisfaction he derived from punishing me with the past. His hand retreated, moving back towards his side of the table. His fingers rested on the edge, tapping as he weighed the options in his mind.

'You need to be more specific, Leah – tell you the truth about what? I've told the truth about the person you were in the months following the death of your mother. The violent outbursts, hurting another child.'

'You also told me you didn't know at the time that I was there on the night of my mother's murder.' I didn't take my eyes off him. 'I know you lied.'

A flicker of surprise replaced by a glint of cruelty.

'Who told you that – the little girl in your dreams?' He paused, rearranging his features in an expression of sympathy. 'I told you, Leah. You heard your mother talking to her lover about leaving me; you told me because you were scared she was going to leave you too. You crawled into the back of the car when I went to confront them. I didn't know you were there. Accept it and move on.'

'I went to David Francis' house.'

The revelation hit Eli without warning.

'It triggered memories from that night,' I said.

'What memories?'

I drew myself up as the power shifted between us. There was always a pendulum, and I was conscious it would soon swing back towards him.

'I tell you what I remember; you tell me something true in return, or this . . .' – I waved my arm between us – 'whatever *this* is . . . these father–daughter reunions, where you show me how clever you are – they end today. It was your idea, Eli. Play fair or we don't play at all.'

He uncoiled himself, raising his head like a snake in search of a victim.

'So tell me . . .'

The air tasted bitter; I swallowed. 'OK,' I said. 'I remember hiding on the floor of the car on the way to the cottage, but there's another memory . . . from later . . . I'm sitting in the back seat. There are tears pouring down my face. You're in front, behind the steering wheel. You turn and look at me . . .'

'Then?'

You smile at me. I feel better.

'Then nothing,' I said.

On one side of me, the couple flirted in intense whispers; on the other, a teenager sat frozen, his father aloof.

'In the memory, I hear singing,' I said. 'I can't make out the words . . . In my dreams, it's my mother voice. But I'm pretty sure it was just you and me in the car . . . Did I imagine the song?'

Eli watched me, his blue eyes questioning. I remembered his letters – the words from the verse merged with the music in my head.

'It was you,' I said.

He recited the verse, caressing each syllable. His fingers danced between us, accompanying the tune.

Yea, though I walk in death's dark vale,

Yet will I fear no ill;

For Thou art with me; and Thy rod

And staff my comfort still.

'It's the hymn Margaretta used to sing to make you sleep when you couldn't. She sang it to me too when I was a child. She taught it to your mother . . . I sang it to you when I found you in the car that night. You were hysterical. You needed to calm down.'

'Is that why you sent me those words in your letters, to test how much I recalled?'

'If you like,' Eli said. 'We tried to help you forget, Leah. So you could lead a normal life—'

'And your secrets would remain buried,' I said.

'Margaretta only wanted what was best for you.'

'And what do you want, Eli?'

He ran his fingers through his thinning hair. 'For the past to stay in the past.'

You're scared of the truth and yet you seek it.

'Why was I upset?' I said. 'How do I fit into that night? Did you see me in the house? Was I in the room when . . . ?'

His cold eyes were unsympathetic. He stretched out his legs, tucking one ankle behind the other.

'I didn't see you get out of the car at the house, Leah. I'm not lying.'

I believed him.

'That's it.' It was clear for the first time. 'The games, the obfuscation . . . You don't want me to remember because you don't know what I saw.'

Chapter Ninety-Six

Leah

Eli's secrets lay tangled amongst buried memories. As I approached the estate, I did a mental search of my flat for my skipping rope, ready to exhaust myself until I collapsed on my bed.

Randle's back was to me, but the Suzuki logo caught the sunlight as the afternoon heat blazed.

'What are you doing here?' I said. 'Shouldn't you be at work?'

He slid off his motorbike, holding his mobile phone up.

'The wonders of modern technology, ma'am.' He glanced at it. 'Work moves with you these days.'

A hint of a smile threatened to light up his face, but he read my mood, killing the spark.

'Akosua looked into the elective, ma'am. Do you want the good news or the bad?'

'Bad first. Then give the good, quickly.'

He looked down at me, his eyes amused. 'The bad news is that you're not coming to a race anytime soon . . .'

'And the good?'

'Gabriel McMahon was in Ghana too – different hospital, but he was there at the same time.'

'OK,' I said. 'But what happened to the wonders of modern technology? You could have told me this over the phone.'

His blush was hidden under the shadow of his stubble. 'I wanted to check you're OK and give you this.'

He handed me my jacket.

I scanned his features for thoughts he wasn't voicing.

'What did Kenny say to you?'

His blues eyes widened. 'Just what you said. You're taking a few days off. I'm overseeing the case whilst you're gone.'

'Are you OK with that?'

He shrugged, his shoulders twitching forwards. 'I didn't come here because I was worried about work, ma'am.'

He leant against his bike, dipping his head. When he looked up, his discomfort was evident.

I took a step to move past him, so he was forced to address my back.

'I think you're right about Ghana,' he said. 'All roads lead there: Sami. Gabriel. Ogechi. Maybe Sarah. Something happened there that led to Sami and Gabriel's deaths. Maybe the connection with Ghana also helps us with what happened to Ray King and Sarah Franks.'

I turned.

'Keep digging. Keep asking questions.'

'No one wants to talk to us, ma'am. We call the hospitals, we get shunted around.'

'Keep calling then. Eventually someone will answer.'

'We need someone on the ground,' Randle said.

He looked at me through his lashes. 'Maybe you should go? Visit the hospitals in person . . .'

'I can't just disappear off to Ghana. Have you lost your mind?'

He stared down at me as if my words didn't make sense.

'It's like driving to Cornwall. It's a six-hour flight.' He thrust his hands in his pockets. 'It's just an idea, ma'am.'

'Let's hope you have better ones whilst I'm off.'

This time he didn't stop me from leaving. I heard the growl of the engine as I walked away. The estate compound was strangely quiet. I almost missed the petulant teenagers filling the space with attitude and marijuana smoke. Inside my flat, the conversation with Kenny hit me. The discipline of work brought order to my brain. My thigh tensed as my phone vibrated. An attachment – an e-ticket to Accra, Ghana, leaving the following afternoon. The return leg was booked for forty-eight hours later. I read the message: *It's like driving to Cornwall. I hope you find answers. Bx*

PART II

Chapter Ninety-Seven

Leah

I was asleep before the plane settled in the air. I had no recollection of what I had dreamt. I woke abruptly as the wheels skidded on the tarmac, aware I had had an intense experience, without knowing the details of what had passed. The airport was deceptively cool, but I could feel a thin layer of sweat creeping over me. I moved with the crowd of travellers past the smiling faces welcoming me to Accra. Through the bodies, I spotted a torn piece of lined A4 paper displaying my name in neat capital letters. The sign moved down, slowly revealing a square face, powder-dry. A man with a compact frame in a short-sleeved white shirt over crisp blue jeans, pressed with a line. The man's eyes glinted as I moved towards him.

'*Akwaaba.*' He was well-spoken with a strong Ghanaian accent. 'Pleased to meet you. I'm Kofi.'

He was a distant cousin of Akosua's. She had sent a message that morning saying he would take care of me during my stay. *He likes to talk, but you may need a friendly face, ma'am.*

I didn't have a chance to say no.

Randle had bought the ticket, refusing to give me details of his bank account so I could pay him back. Only the two of them knew I was in Ghana, and I preferred to keep it that way. Technically I was on my own time, but I could predict the quiet wrath of Kenny O'Sullivan if he ever found out.

'Pleased to meet you, Kofi,' I said.

Kofi reached for my case, but I kept hold of it. For a small man, his grip was firm.

'Please.'

He didn't let go. I gave in and withdrew my hand. Steering me through the crowd with expert precision, he secured my 'Visa on Arrival'. I had surrendered my passport to him, barely needing to say a word.

Outside, it was like someone had opened an oven door and clamped my face in front of it. Sweat drenched my body in seconds, pasting my shirt to my skin. People jostled behind a railing, trying to get a clear view of their loved ones. Wiry men reached for my luggage, uninvited, offering to help carry it to the car. Kofi batted them off with stern words in Fanti, a vice-like grip on my case.

'Down here, please.'

He guided me along the ramp towards the car park. In the distance, the neon signs of Airport City flashed in the dark. The humidity in the car was almost unbearable, the prospect of air conditioning the only thought in my mind.

'I'm sorry, mom. The AC doesn't work.' Kofi smiled, apologetic.

I hid my disappointment, turning to lower my window, angling my head to catch the warm breeze. Kofi grinned at me, sensing my discomfort.

'You will pay for this in London, isn't it?' he said.

I frowned at him, puzzled.

'You don't like sauna? Steam?'

He laughed as I caught up with the joke.

We moved away from the airport into the heart of Accra. We passed a large hotel, wooden beams glowing in the darkness, palm trees underlit by fairy lights; further down, a complex of beach huts topped with terracotta roofs – luxury at a price. It was a side of the country I would barely see on my trip in search of answers on behalf of the dead. The streets became quieter as we drifted into more residential neighbourhoods – white concrete houses peeking out above solid double gates. Randle may have refused money for the ticket, but I had insisted on paying for my own hotel. We drew up outside a pastel-coloured building next to a large colonial house. The reception was clean, and the wheels of my suitcase glided over the speckled terrazzo floor towards the wooden counter at the back. The man on duty introduced himself as Ebenezer, welcoming me with genuine warmth. Kofi finally relinquished my luggage – escorting me to my room a step too far.

'Tomorrow, we go to the hospital,' he said. 'I will come for you at nine o'clock sharp.'

I nodded even though it wasn't a question.

'Until tomorrow,' I said.

Ebenezer insisted on carrying my case up the stairs. I wondered who manned the counter when he wasn't there. He accepted his tip with an air of disappointment, watching me until I closed the door.

The room smelt of fresh mosquito spray. The air conditioning lacked power, and a standing fan blew hot air. I opened the louvre windows, staring through the netting at the alien city where Sami's secrets lay hidden.

I had forty-eight hours to unlock his past.

Chapter Ninety-Eight

Zed

Zed lay in bed, his hands lit by the glow of his mobile screen. He had lost track of the number of times he had checked the account.

You didn't come

His last message – unanswered. He closed the app, waiting a few minutes before he opened it again. He didn't have a compulsive personality, but he was frustrated to have come so close and have ended up discovering nothing. He refused to give up just yet. Downstairs, he could hear his parents talking in hushed voices. It was unusual to see his father in the house, but Isaac had been more attentive since his mother had returned home. Zed blocked out their conversation, huddling under the duvet. He thought of Seema – her tangents about her mother, her love of children's games. He heard her voice in his head. She had talked about 'manifesting', positive thoughts that made your dreams real. He zoned out when she started rambling, but he was desperate now, so he tried things her way. He squeezed his eyes shut, reloading the app as he visualised the message he wanted to become real.

He had been to Gabriel McMahon's GP surgery the day before, but no one had taken him seriously. He kicked off the duvet, thinking through his options as he recalled the bodies on the board. He could still remember their positions exactly.

Chris

Sarah

Gabriel McMahon

Ray King

So far, Gabriel and Ray were dead ends, and he had no information for Chris. That only left Sarah. He focused on the board in his mind, trying to see her last name. He remembered a memory trick his mum had taught him when he was younger – going through the alphabet until you recall a word. He mumbled his way through the letters, but Sarah's full name still eluded him – a blur of shapes at the fringes of his mind. He tried again, this time slower. When he got to the letter 'F', he could see the name.

Franks. Sarah Franks.

He finally remembered. Zed rolled over, pulling up the list of names on his phone. He updated it. He hesitated, giving in to the urge to check the account Seema had set up. There was a message. He held his breath.

You didn't come alone, it said.

He typed the response quickly, desperate to keep the conversation going.

She's just a kid I know. She can't do anything. I didn't tell anyone else.

A minute passed, maybe longer. He kicked himself for not leading with an apology, but now it was too late. Then a response came. Zed's body relaxed. He exhaled, relief flooding over him.

Kids have big mouths. I'm not looking to get into trouble with the feds.

OK. Zed chose his words carefully. *Let's meet again. I promise I'll come alone.*

He waited for a reply, but the conversation went dead.

Chapter Ninety-Nine

Leah

Kofi was standing by the car when I emerged the next morning – white short-sleeved shirt replaced by pale pink. He held up a portable fan in the space between us.

'Sorry about the AC, mom.'

The sun was low in the sky. The air felt cooler, but it was only a matter of time until the onslaught of heat.

'Thank you, Kofi.'

I clutched the fan like a secret treasure, flicking it on as I adjusted my seat. The air around my face was heavy and hot, inviting sweat to dampen my skin. The plastic blades created a gentle breeze, offering some relief. The radio was too loud. Kofi's fingers hovered over the dashboard.

'Do you like high life?' he said.

I shrugged, ambivalent. He flicked the channel when I didn't say no. Guitar strings filled the car, accompanied by a melodic male voice over a lazy drum beat that slowly gathered pace. We passed through Accra's Oxford Street, lined with stalls packed with leather goods and dresses in bright local cloth. Roadside sellers hawked their wares, balancing huge metal basins effortlessly on their heads. I imagined Sami blending in – just another of the many Lebanese in Accra.

The sun rose in the sky as we reached a large roundabout. Kofi swung off at the third exit, continuing down a narrow street. An off-white building appeared as we turned the corner, set back from the road. We followed the signs for reception, past the manicured lawns and neatly trimmed trees. Kofi knew the medical administrator. He was waiting by the north entrance as we stepped through the automatic doors. A born bureaucrat with an inflated view of his own importance, he puffed out his chest, trying to take up more space.

'You're talking about over fifteen years ago. The world's changed and so have our systems. You'd have to talk to someone who worked here back then.'

'Can you point us in the direction of someone who could help me?' I said.

'I can't give out that kind of information. I'm sorry you've had a wasted journey.'

From the UK . . .

'I'm sorry, mommy.' Kofi's lips turned down, mirroring my frustration. 'Please, brother, give us some help.'

'I'm not asking for employment history,' I said. 'I wouldn't want you to break any rules.'

He nodded. I mirrored him, forcing myself to smile.

'Try Sister Eunice.' Finally a concession. 'She's been here for twenty years,' he said.

'Is she a nurse?'

He smiled as if I had missed something. 'No. She works on reception. She is friendly with the doctors and medical students, especially the young ones on elective who need a kind face to show them round Accra.'

The reception was at the end of a narrow corridor. A man in round wire glasses stood behind the counter under a loud ceiling fan.

'Sister Eunice is not working until tomorrow.' His voice matched his movements, unhurried in the heat. 'Please, you can leave a message.'

His name badge said 'Yaw'. He handed me a biro and a sheet from a lined legal pad. I leant on the reception counter. A large photo frame was positioned near the edge. I reached for it, scanning the framed collage of young doctors in scrubs smiling for the camera, haircuts signifying the passage of years. I recognised a baby-faced Ogechi grinning next to a striking looking girl. In the corner of the photograph, an olive-skinned man had turned his head away. I could barely see his face, but the curl of black hair at the nape of his neck told me it was Sami. Sadness kicked me in the gut, then faded away.

'Please.' Yaw seized the photo frame from my hand. 'It's not for you.' He tried to usher me away.

A cleaner mopped the area around us, apologising repeatedly when the mophead licked the tip of Kofi's shoe. Yaw chastised him in a language I didn't understand. The cleaner's shoulders slumped as he turned away.

'Who took those photographs, Yaw?' I said.

'The doctors and students, madam. They send them to Eunice with thank you cards. She collected plenty for many years.'

'Do you mind if I take a photograph?'

I knew it was a step too far the moment I asked the question.

'Please. Come back tomorrow and speak to Eunice. I cannot help you,' he said.

We were almost at the car when I heard the voice behind us. I turned to see the cleaner, no longer hunched now he had no mop in his hand.

'Sorry again, sa.' He spoke fast to Kofi, then shifted his gaze to me. 'Please, madam . . .'

'Yes?'

His pupils were hidden behind a haze of cataracts.

'Some white man come here last month asking plenty plenty question about the young doctors. I dey clean dat side at dat time. He dey come with one black man with plenty white hair.'

'Did you hear their names?' Kofi said.

The cleaner scratched his head, his eyes suddenly blank as he looked at Kofi.

'Ah, no, sa.'

Kofi turned to me, embarrassed, rubbing his thumb and forefingers together – the international symbol for money. You could cross an ocean, but human self-interest remained the same. I pulled out my wallet, holding out a note. The cleaner reached for it, tucking it away without a glance. The sharpness returned to his face.

'The white man they dey call am Kin. The black man – 'e name be Blake.'

Without context, the names sounded alien, then I realised who he meant: Ray King, the private investigator found dead on a sofa, and the caretaker from his block of flats, Marlon Blake.

Chapter One Hundred

Leah

I sat on the terrace of a hotel bar filled with tourists, sipping bitter lemon as I looked out at the sea. Kofi was adamant I would regret leaving Ghana without at least seeing the beach. He insisted on waiting in the car, listening to the World Service as he baked in the heat. My eyes flitted to my phone, nestled behind the water jug. It had been a couple of hours since I had briefed Randle, and I was impatient for his call. A man roasted on a sun lounger below me, pale skin red raw. He didn't flinch as the sun's rays cooked him like meat on a barbecue – the will to tan at all costs. Mesmerised, I couldn't take my eyes off him, even when my phone finally rang.

'Is this a good time, ma'am?'

Randle knew I would have been waiting.

'As good as any. I'm watching a man kill himself to get brown.'

'Sun, sea and sights. What more could you want?'

I could hear the smile in his voice.

'To know what Ray King was doing in Accra?' I said.

The low sound of laughter somewhere in London. 'That too, ma'am.'

The sea was dull blue with ripples of gold where the water caught the light. The buzz of traffic under Randle's voice intruded – a reminder of the world to which I belonged. Randle couldn't talk to me from the office, as I was supposed to be taking a break from the case. There would be consequences if Kenny caught wind of it; Randle knew he was taking a risk.

'Marlon and Keisha Blake's son went travelling across West Africa with his childhood friend when he was eighteen,' he said. 'First time he had been outside the UK. Turns out it was also his last.'

'What happened to him?'

'That's the thing.' Randle's voice was full of feeling. 'No one knows. He disappeared into thin air.'

Shallow waves rolled into a blue expanse, fading into the sea as if they had never existed.

'What do you mean "disappeared"?' I said.

'They never found him or a body, ma'am. His parents flew out to Ghana to find him at the time. No joy. He was declared missing, presumed dead.'

'What was his name?'

'Lemar. Lemar Blake.'

I made a mental note. 'When was this?'

'The same year Sami and Ogechi did their medical elective, ma'am.'

I gulped down the last of the bitter lemon.

'What happened to Lemar's friend?' I said.

I heard Randle flip the page. I pictured him consulting his tiny book of notes.

'She struggled to get over his death, came back to England, had a breakdown, dropped out of university. Then went back to Ghana – her family's originally from there.'

'Where is she now?'

'She runs a yoga studio in Accra.'

'Are you being serious?'

'I would say "deadly", if it wasn't in such poor taste.'

I signalled for the bill. 'Let's pretend you never said that.'

'OK. What do you want me to do, ma'am?'

The sunbather had finally recognised he was a fighting a stronger opponent. He gathered his towel, retreating into the shade.

'Text me a name and address for the friend,' I said.

I could hear the cars navigating the streets of South London. Randle hovered at the other end of the line.

'What is it, Randle?'

The sound of rustling as he brought the phone closer to his mouth.

'It's been fifteen years since Lemar disappeared, ma'am,' he said. 'Why is Marlon Blake hiring a private investigator now?'

Chapter One Hundred and One

Zed

Zed stood staring at the newsagent's opposite. It matched the images he had found online. In the news, there had been police tape sealing off the building where Sarah Franks had died. The murder had been covered briefly by the media. Sarah had been killed in one of the flats above the shop. Looking up at the windows, Zed had no idea which one. Standing on the kerb with his hands in his pockets, he realised he didn't have a plan. The pain relief only made his mother drowsy for so long, and he needed to be back before she stirred.

He crossed the street, determined. The man behind the counter watched him as he entered the shop. Zed looked back at him, his confidence wavering. He headed to the confectionery aisle. The shopkeeper scrutinised Zed's hands as he grabbed a bag of skittles. Self-conscious, Zed reached for another packet he didn't even want. He made his way to the counter. Intimidation was all in the walk, and he dragged his feet to give himself more presence. The shopkeeper was flanked by a woman who could have been his wife or his daughter. Her lips curled downwards as she checked the name on the debit card Ogechi had given him.

'*O Okoro*? Is this you?' The woman squinted, her eyes accusing.

Zed kept his composure, refusing to blink. 'Yes.'

'What's the "O" for?'

He took back the card. 'Oscar.'

She repeated the syllables, her tone tinged with disbelief. He tried another tack.

'It's my older sister's card, but she's too scared to come in here because of the woman who was killed.'

Her head jerked up, her expression hardening. 'She didn't get killed in here. She died in the flat above.'

Zed tapped the card reader, pushing the skittles down in his pocket. The bell clanged softly behind him as he left the shop.

Outside, he pretended to examine the fruit and veg display as he watched the front door to the flats. It wasn't a large building and, for a while, no one entered or exited. He was about to give up when a skinny man drowned by a baggy T-shirt stopped, fumbling for his keys. Zed moved fast as the man disappeared into the building, preventing the door from closing with his foot.

Upstairs there were two flats on the same side of the hallway, their narrow plywood doors lined with mould. The door to the furthest flat slammed as Zed arrived at the top of the stairs, meaning the closest flat must have been Sarah's. Zed was reaching for the handle when he heard a voice.

'What are you doing?'

The shopkeeper stood behind him, wielding a cricket bat.

Chapter One Hundred and Two

Leah

Alice Addai taught Jivamukti yoga in an independent gym in a residential area. Walking into the reception was like arriving in another country – the air was chilled, and goosebumps rose up on my skin. Alice was teaching a class, followed by a short break. I said I was a friend from London and was invited to wait in the café outside. I sat on a hard plastic chair on a small veranda. There was a basic bar overlooking a well-kept garden with pink hibisci, a glass-fronted studio in the garden on the far side. Inside it, a tall, lithe woman circled pretzeled students, willing their bodies to bend with the power of their breath.

The minutes passed, and individuals gradually filtered out into the heat, convincing each other how relaxed they were, despite the pain they had endured.

'Can I help you?'

The South London accent was still strong, despite years spent in Ghana. Alice Addai floated towards me, muscled arms on display in a pale blue vest.

'I hope so,' I said.

She looked at me, calm eyes expectant.

'I'd like to talk to you about Lemar Blake.'

Her eyes filled with tears. She didn't try to hide them. 'I think I need a drink.'

We moved to a table in the corner, away from her students. She didn't say a word until she had downed a Campari, neat. She ordered another, watching the waitress set the glass down in front of her as I revealed the bare minimum about who I was and why I was there.

'A detective,' she said. 'All the way from London. Why now? After all these years?'

'We think Lemar's disappearance may be connected to a crime I'm not at liberty to talk about.'

She gulped her drink. 'I see . . . You people still don't care about him.'

She stared at the mango tree in the centre of the garden.

'I'm sorry about what happened to your friend,' I said.

Her eyes drifted back to me, anger behind the serenity.

'How can you be? No one knows what happened to him.' She tapped her glass with a long, manicured fingernail. 'I feel closer to him here.'

She pulled out a cigarette from the pocket of her loose yoga pants.

'Don't look so shocked, Inspector. Yoga only gets me so far,' she said.

'I'm not judging,' I said. 'It's never worked for me.'

She considered me for a moment. 'Somehow I doubt you tried very hard.'

'Maybe.'

She lit a cigarette, scarcely seeming to inhale before exhaling a gust of smoke with surprising force.

'You know it was my idea to come to West Africa?' she said. 'Lemar begged his parents. They only let him come because he was with me, and we'd known each other since primary school.' Her chest rose as she sucked in the nicotine. 'My parents are originally from here. I have family here. They thought he would be safe.'

'Apparently his dad was here recently,' I threw in, offhand. 'Did you see him?'

She shook her head. The tears returned. 'No. He reached out to me, but . . . I let him down. I couldn't see him.'

I didn't respond, letting her sit with the hurt.

'We started off in Cameroon – my dad has family there. Briefly in Nigeria, then Togo. Finally here. We had a lot of fun at first. Partied. No parents breathing down our necks. Lemar had never been outside of the UK. It was an adventure. When we got to Ghana, everything changed.'

She stared into her glass, swirling the liquid one way, then the other.

'He became infatuated with a girl he met in a bar.' She paused. 'He didn't have time for me. He'd just go to this bar each night, hoping she'd be there. Now I wish I had just gone with him, instead of feeling resentful and pulling away. Maybe things would have been different.'

'Who was the girl?' I tried not to sound too eager.

Alice shrugged, the petulant eighteen-year-old again. 'Some arrogant party girl. You know the type – doctor by day, hard at it by night.'

'Did you ever meet her?'

'I *saw* her – that first night. That was enough for me.' She looked away, embarrassed I had seen the flash of jealousy. 'You would think I would be over it after so many years.'

'Do you remember the name of the girl, or the hospital where she worked?'

'Bisi.' She paused. 'I never knew her last name . . . I told the police at the time, but they never tried that hard to find her.'

'When was the last time you saw Lemar?'

'He went out one night. Never came back,' she said. 'Marlon and Keisha flew over. We looked everywhere, asked all the right questions, but the police were never that supportive. The British High Commission gave up.'

A British citizen had disappeared fifteen years ago, but I couldn't remember the story from the news.

'It was like he never existed,' Alice said. 'One minute, we're laughing, arguing. The next, he's gone. I have no proof – but I always thought there was a cover-up.'

'Why?'

'I don't think Lemar was meant to be found.'

Chapter One Hundred and Three

Chris

Chris could feel his shirt plastered to his back. He could handle the heat, but he hated the humidity and the constant need to change his clothes. He slowed the car as he approached the checkpoint, the view ahead obscured by a red lorry in front. In his mind, he replayed the phone call that had set off this chain of events – the diversion he needed to deal with. Not his choice, but it never was. In his line of work, it didn't pay to get sentimental. In the world at large, people died every day. He looked back at the police officer as a torch beamed through the car window. He played the genial tourist, unfamiliar with the local ways. There was a fifty per cent chance the man would wave him through, but that day the odds weren't in his favour. More torches, a click as the boot flipped open, a cursory search, then it was closed again.

Driving away, Chris watched the police shrink then disappear in his rear-view mirror. His foot rested on the accelerator, careful not to increase the speed. He wondered how they hadn't noticed the boot was shallower than it should have been, concealing the body under the base.

Chapter One Hundred and Four

Leah

The red sun sank in the sky as Kofi dropped me outside the hotel.

'When you get upstairs, flash me,' he said.

I looked at him, shocked.

He laughed. 'Ring my phone. Then hang up. So I can tell Akosua I delivered you back in one piece.'

Inside, the lobby was quiet, and Ebenezer was not at his desk. I made my way upstairs, 'flashing' Kofi as I arrived on my floor. I could see the hotel entrance from the window on the landing, and I watched as his car pulled out onto the road. My room was at the end of a short corridor. As I neared my door, I noticed it was open. I pushed it hard so it slammed against the wall with force. If there was someone in my room, they couldn't have been hiding behind it, unless they had a high threshold for pain. I ventured inside, scanning for an intruder, but the room appeared to be empty. My clothes were strewn on the floor, my suitcase bashed open. The wardrobe had been upended in the corner, the TV on its side at the foot of the bed. The bathroom door was shut – a strip of light visible beneath it. I reached for the handle, gripping a pen in my hand. The cleaner had been – the shower gleamed, and the bathmat sat evenly on the rail. I could hear my heart beating too loudly.

I rushed out into the corridor, whipping my head round frantically, but there was no intruder to be seen. I retreated into my room, turning the lock behind me, my back against the door. It was only then that I noticed the neatly made bed, my passport resting in the centre of the pillow. The hotel notepad had been placed carefully beside it. Two words written in CAPS:

GO HOME

Chapter One Hundred and Five

Zed

Zed sat slumped in the police station in Elephant and Castle, waiting for his father. An 'appropriate adult' stood guard, sliding limp strands of hair behind a pointed ear. No one had told him what was happening beyond informing him they had called his parents. He stared at his wrists – he was not in handcuffs. No one had read him his rights. He didn't think he was under arrest. A spiky red-headed policewoman with a pale face had asked him some questions. She had left him with the pointy-eared man, promising to return when his father arrived. The door opened. A figure filled the frame, but it wasn't Isaac or the red-headed detective. Boy Cop stared down at him, concern in his eyes.

'Where's the other one?' It was all Zed could think to say.

Ben moved into the room. He was bigger than Zed remembered, more imposing, his hair fairer in the indoor gloom. He smiled, and his whole face transformed in a moment.

'If by "the other one" you mean Inspector Hutch, she had better things to do.'

'How did you know I was here?' Zed wondered if there was a secret police network.

'Your surname. DS Hoffen remembered the press conference

your dad did for your mother. She called me. She knew it was related to our case.'

'I'm not under arrest?'

Ben raised an eyebrow. 'Have you committed a crime?'

Zed looked down at his hands. 'No.' He had never entered Sarah's flat, so he couldn't be guilty of trespassing.

'There you go then. I've spoken to your parents. I'll give you a ride home.'

They drove without speaking. Zed stared through the windscreen as they passed through an alien part of the city he called his home. Ben ran his hand over his face. There was a slight break in his nose Zed hadn't noticed before.

'Go on then,' Zed said. He shifted in his seat; the silence made him uncomfortable.

'Go on then what?'

He could hear the smile in Ben's voice.

'Give me the role model chat you've been dying to give me. Man-to-man. I won't interrupt. Go ahead.'

Ben steered the car round a corner, two fingers controlling the steering wheel. 'I'm not a role model, Zed. There is no chat.'

'Whatever you say . . .' He lowered the window, staring out at strangers, wondering what his mother's attacker looked like.

'Look . . .' Ben sighed. 'I know you don't know me, and you've got no reason to trust me, but you can. You can trust us to do our job.'

Zed almost laughed. 'Did *she* tell you to say that? There's no point trying to impress her, you know.'

Ben glanced at him, blue eyes perplexed.

'It's never going to happen,' Zed said.

'What isn't?'

'Fine.' Zed fiddled with the controls on the door. 'Let's pretend we both don't know what I'm talking about.'

The engine groaned as they hit a line of traffic. A golden retriever with a sad face looked back at him from the car in front.

'Did you speak to my parents?' Zed tried not to sound nervous. 'What did they say?'

'They're worried about you . . . You can't keep tearing around trying to solve things when you don't know the big picture.'

'The big picture . . . Let me guess – I'm only a child, so you can't tell me what that is . . .'

Zed locked the door, then unlocked it, then locked it again. 'OK. Let's make a deal.' He turned back to face Ben, a scowl of determination etched on his small face. 'I'll stop "tearing around" if you promise you'll find the thug who hurt my mother and send them to prison so they can't get near her again.'

The cars in front were barely moving now. Ben clicked on the handbrake as the car rolled to a halt. There was a seriousness behind his eyes which made Zed look away.

'We'll do everything we can to find them, but you're not a kid – you don't need me to tell you, there are no guarantees.'

Zed lifted his gaze, his dark eyes burning.

'What if whoever hurt my mum comes back, and this time they kill her? Why should I stop trying to find them if I can't depend on you?'

Chapter One Hundred and Six

Leah

Kofi had come to get me as soon as I called him. He'd taken one look at my face and driven me to a new hotel. It was more than I had budgeted for, but it was worth it to stay safe. He had wanted to call the police, but I didn't need the attention, and I knew it would be a fruitless cause. I locked the door behind me, pulling the curtains shut. I lay on the bed, eyes open, waiting for morning to come.

Kofi arrived early. I wondered how long he had been waiting, leaning against the boot of his car – I sensed he didn't want me to know. I filled Randle in as we drove, trying to make light of the intruder. Randle's tone was urgent on the other end of the phone.

'Come back, ma'am.'

'I am. Tonight. *You* bought the ticket.'

'I mean, come back earlier,' he said.

'That's not possible.'

'Then stop digging. We can investigate from here. Someone doesn't want you there.'

The car jolted as Kofi hit a pothole. I clutched my phone as it threatened to slip from my grip.

'I've got to go, Randle.'

I hung up.

The hospital looked different in the early morning light. The grass seemed greener, the blades short and sharp. Yaw had been replaced on reception by a squat woman in her late fifties with a glossy, curled wig. She smiled at us as if she had just opened the door to her home, her face unlined, despite the wide grin. Even before I read her name badge, I knew it was Eunice, the queen of her domain.

'Welcome.' She was still smiling.

'I'm looking for Eunice,' I said.

Her eyes travelled over me, less friendly as she realised I was neither patient nor relative, the pieces coming together.

'You came yesterday,' she said.

'Yes. I'm Leah.'

Her eyes were more guarded. 'Yaw said you were coming back. You did.'

She observed me, her bottom lip between her teeth, waiting for me to say more. The automatic doors slid open and shut behind me, but her eyes didn't leave mine.

'My friend, Samir Mograbi, died recently. Suddenly,' I said. 'A group of friends are putting together a book of photos for his parents. His time in Ghana was formative. We tried to get in touch from London. I was coming to Accra for work, so I thought I'd try my luck.'

'He died?'

I was so focused on my story, it took me a moment to register her sadness.

'I'm sorry. He was a nice boy.' She smiled. 'He was always so serious. Kept himself to himself. His friend was more sociable.'

I took a punt. 'You mean Ogechi?' I said.

'Yes.' She relaxed when I mentioned the name. Her gaze drifted to the photo frame on the reception counter. 'Do you want to see?'

I moved round to examine the collage of photographs, pretending I was seeing them for the first time. My eyes were drawn to the photograph of Ogechi and Sami I had seen the day before.

'I don't know where that was taken,' Eunice said. 'Bisi sent it to me when she left. She and Ogechi became close. They liked to go out together.' She chuckled. 'Enjoy what Accra has to offer.'

Her eyes flitted over the doctors in miniature, pointing out a small striking woman waving at the camera, revealing a tattoo of a snake on her arm.

'Do you remember Bisi's surname?' I kept my voice casual. 'Sami mentioned her in passing. Maybe she would like to contribute too.'

'Akintola. Her father was Nigerian.' She chuckled at a memory. 'She wasn't shy that one. Kept sending me photos. I only printed a few. Let me see . . . I keep the best ones from each year.' She stopped, mistaking my silence for judgement. 'I like to remember my friends.'

Eunice took out her phone, scrolling through her photographs, a snapshot of her past.

'Do you remember someone called Chris from that time?' I said. He was the only name we hadn't connected. 'Sami mentioned him when he talked about Ghana. I'd like to get in touch to tell him the news.'

'Chris? No.' She sounded distracted as she flicked from image to image. She pulled up a selfie of Bisi posing in the canteen. 'There she is. I thought I had one with her and Sami, but I can't seem to find it.'

I looked at the photo of Bisi Akintola. Ogechi was beside her, her expression difficult to read. Opposite them, the blurred image of a woman I had seen before.

'Who's that with her there?' I said.

Eunice squinted at the photo. 'You mean Sarah? She worked in accounts in the hospital. Worked in Accra in her gap year. Fell in love with the country, got a job and stayed. She had a house in Cantonments. Rented out rooms to foreigners, because they paid more.'

'What happened to her?'

'She had a breakdown, not long after your friend Sami left. She got caught stealing oxycodone. The hospital agreed not to take it further if she went back home to the UK.'

Chapter One Hundred and Seven

Leah

Lemar Blake had disappeared in Ghana. Bisi Akintola connected him to Sami, Ogechi and now, it seemed, Sarah Franks. Outside, the air was thick – the humidity made my body feel heavy. The shelter of Kofi's air condition-less car suddenly felt inviting, but it wasn't where he had parked. I scanned the tarmac, searching for the white, lived-in Honda, but it was nowhere to be seen. My eyes travelled back to where I remembered it being – a silver Mercedes-Benz sat in its place. The windows were up, the dark tint obscuring my view. I turned back towards the hospital, retrieving my phone from my pocket as I dialled Kofi. The click of the car door opening was barely perceptible, but my senses were alert. The voice behind me was low.

'Leah Hutch.'

When I turned, a large man was standing in front of me. The passenger door opened, and another man stepped out. His white shirt was too tight around his muscled shoulders; neatly pressed trousers clung to his thighs.

'You need to come with us.' His voice was high and surprisingly genial, but there was no smile in his eyes.

'Why?' A wave of fear passed over me, but I kept my voice firm.

'You need to come with us.' He nodded towards the car.

I took a step back. 'I'm not going anywhere with you until you tell me why?'

The other man walked behind me. I felt the heat of his breath on my neck.

'Where's Kofi?' I said. My heart slammed against my chest.

'Don't worry, mommy.' The man in the white shirt flashed his teeth. 'Kofi is fine.'

He moved towards the back door, opening it as if it were an act of chivalry.

I weighed my options, walking towards the Mercedes with slow, deliberate steps. Inside, the seats were beige leather; the air was chilled. The seat belt felt too snug when I slid it across my chest. The whiff of stale sweat fizzed in my nostrils as the second man lowered himself beside me, instructing me to turn round. The slam of the door, then the rough feel of washed cotton as a blindfold was wrapped around my eyes.

Chapter One Hundred and Eight

Zed

Zed could feel the anxiety simmering as he opened his eyes slowly. So far, there had been no reprimand from his mother since Randle had dropped him home the previous night. She had just hugged him, whispering that she loved him as she sent him to bed with a sad smile. Zed took his time going down the stairs, enjoying the strong smell of bacon as it drifted towards him. His mother never ate breakfast; the clatter of cutlery against porcelain told him his father was there. Again.

Zed braced himself as he stepped into the kitchen. Isaac Okoro looked up, a forkful of scrambled egg stopping short of his mouth.

'What are you doing here?' Zed said.

Ogechi's voice was stern. 'He's your father. He was worried.'

Isaac pushed his plate away, ignoring the clang as the knife slid onto the marble worksurface. 'Zechariah, what were you doing at that woman's flat?'

Zed reached for the box of cereal, shaking flakes into a bowl.

'It was in the news. A woman was killed. A boy from school set a challenge to see if anyone could get into her flat,' he said, parroting the excuse he had prepared.

'Zechariah . . .' He could tell his mother didn't believe him. 'We think it's best if you spend a few days with your dad.'

'What? No . . .' He slammed the bowl down without meaning to, glimpsing the hurt in his father's eyes.

'You've been through a lot,' his mother said. 'You need time away from all this . . .'

'What's *this*?' He could hear his voice thicken. 'I don't need a break from you.'

'It's just for a few days, whilst I recover. Your dad will take care of you.'

'I can take care of myself.'

He felt bad even as he said the words; he couldn't bring himself to look at Isaac.

'That's not your job,' Ogechi said. 'You're just a child.'

'I was doing it for you.' He could hear the pleading tone. He hated it, but he couldn't stop. 'I saw her name in the police station. I thought going there might help me find out who did that to you.'

He saw the horror flash across Ogechi's face. She opened her mouth, but no words came out.

'Did you know her?' Zed said.

'I told you to leave it to the police.'

His father took out his phone. 'Maybe it would help to see Doctor Cole again?'

Zed blocked him out, his eyes fixed on his mother.

'Why do I need to talk to a therapist? I'm trying to talk to *you*.'

Isaac stood, moving round to flank Ogechi. 'We just want you to forget all this,' he said. Their unity sickened Zed – it should have been him standing beside his mum.

'It's hard to forget finding your mother in a suitcase, but OK, Dad, I'm sure therapy will fix it.'

Zed turned towards the door.

'Where are you going?' his father said.

'To pack.'

Zed stopped halfway up the stairs, gripping the bannister as he inhaled deeply. He held the air in his lungs, trying to quell the anger inside. He felt his phone vibrate against his thigh. He slid the flat rectangle out of his pocket. His breath hitched as he flicked to the message.

OK. Let's try again. I don't want trouble. This time come alone

Chapter One Hundred and Nine

Leah

The car shuddered to a stop. The grating sound of metal being dragged across concrete drowned out the engine. A sudden lurch forwards. Then the engine died, and everything was still.

'You can take it off now.'

The man in the white shirt.

I slid the blindfold down my face. My hands hadn't been restrained, and I wondered whether fear or good manners had kept me from pulling the blindfold down before. The door opened and the second man stood facing me, inviting me to step into the punishing heat.

I was in a small compound lined with avocado trees. A white bungalow with louvre windows and a brown metal roof stood a few feet ahead. The front door opened, and a woman in a pale blue cotton top with matching trousers beckoned me in. Inside, the house was darker and cooler than I expected, larger than it seemed from outside. I was in an open-plan space with a round dining table in one corner, a set of salmon-pink velvet chairs in a cluster on the other side. The chair directly opposite was bigger than the others. In it sat a small, smooth-skinned, bald man dwarfed by its high back, tiny, rimless glasses framing his eyes.

'Please, take a seat, Miss Leah Hutch.'

'Where am I?'

He smiled. 'Standing won't change the answer. You're a guest in my house. Please sit down.'

I chose the seat opposite him. The maid appeared again with a glass of cloudy grey liquid. She set it down on the table in front of me.

'Ekua makes the best lemonade in Accra,' the small man said.

'I don't doubt it, but I'm sure that's not why you brought me here.'

'No, Miss Hutch.' His voice was soft, almost deferential. 'But when in Rome . . .'

'. . . have your room ransacked and get forced into strange cars outside hospitals. Where's Kofi?' I said.

'My men gave him a small token and advised him to go home.'

'I want to speak to him.'

'Let's get the formalities over with, and then you can call him, if you like.' He stretched out his legs in front of him – they didn't go far. 'My name is Wesley Amponsah. I used to work for the British High Commission. I hope your journey wasn't unpleasant.'

'It's a bit late for hospitality now, don't you think?' I said. 'You turned my hotel room upside down and left a note telling me to go back to my country. I wouldn't call that pleasant, would you?'

He took off his glasses, sliding them into his shirt pocket. His naked eyes were more intense without the lenses.

'That had nothing to do with me, Miss Hutch, but you would do well to listen to the warning.' He leant forwards, pinning his palms to his thighs as his eyes bored into me. 'A word of advice – pack your bags and leave. Forget what you came here to find.'

'What does it matter to you?' I said.

He sighed. 'I'm trying to help you, Miss Hutch.'

'Why?'

He stood, cloaking his eyes with glasses once again. His torso was longer than his legs, making him even shorter than I expected. 'Kwame will take you back to your hotel and help you get on a flight tonight. Please don't ask any more questions.'

'Has this got anything to do with Lemar Blake?'

His body froze, his hand outstretched to usher me out. He recovered, dropping his arm to his side.

'Did you have something to do with his disappearance?' I said.

'Miss Hutch . . .' His voice was almost soothing, but there was steel beneath the lilt. 'You appear to be an intelligent person; it would help us both if you were smart. Go home and stop asking questions about Sami Mograbi and Ogechi Okoro.'

I watched him closely as I stood, assessing the man behind the façade. His glasses looked well-made but inexpensive; his shirt was neatly pressed, but the cotton was thin. His home was comfortable but relatively modest. This was a man with limited influence, who took what he could.

'Mr Amponsah, I'll be honest with you,' I said. 'I don't have the luxury of wasting my time or yours. You've been following me, so I assume you know what I do for a living. This trip is off the record – it's in my interest to be discreet.'

The air conditioning unit shuddered then died, but Wesley didn't shift his gaze from mine.

'Sami Mograbi was recently murdered.' I paused for effect. 'I have reason to believe his death is linked to events that happened here in Accra.'

'All the more reason to stop asking questions,' Wesley said.

'Why?'

He didn't blink.

'Because Sami Mograbi was a spy.'

Chapter One Hundred and Ten

Leah

We moved to the veranda, through a mosquito-net door that led to the back. Ekua placed a fresh lemonade on the table in front of me. My skin simmered in the heat, and I was grateful for the cool feel of the glass. Wesley waited for Ekua to retreat.

I took a sip of my drink. 'You weren't wrong. Accra's best.'

'Why would I lie to you?' Wesley flashed a toothy smile, then his face became solemn. 'I am telling you this for your own safety. You cannot tell anyone this came from me.'

'As I said, Mr Amponsah, Accra is outside my professional jurisdiction. Leah Hutch the detective was never here.'

Wesley nodded. There was a loosening around his jaw where middle age had caught up with him. He inhaled deeply. I could hear the quiver in his breath.

'I used to do some work for MI6 for a number of years. Low-level favours. They were good to me, for a time. I got a call about two medical students coming to Ghana for their placement. They needed to work at a certain hospital. I knew the right people. It was a simple job.'

I was still reeling from what he had said about Sami. I focused on the facts.

'You said *two* med students. Was Ogechi also MI6?'

Wesley nodded. 'Yes, but Sami was the lead.'

'Why were they sent here?'

His ran a finger round the rim of his glass. 'I was never told.'

'So your job was simply to organise their medical electives?'

'Yes.' He dropped his eyes. 'And to be a point person if something went wrong.'

'And did it?'

Another nod.

'What went wrong?'

'I don't know. I have my suspicions, but it's unwise to speculate, and you can't ask that of me, Miss Hutch. MI6 had a shadow guy waiting in the wings, if needed. I arranged his accommodation. If Sami called, I was to put them in touch with him.'

'What was his name?'

'I only ever had a first name – Chris.'

I recalled the name on the board in the police station with the question mark. The name Zed had overheard as he crouched, hidden in Gabriel's wardrobe.

'Where's Chris now?' I said.

'I don't know. I never met him.'

I took another sip. The lemon left a bitter aftertaste.

'Who was your MI6 contact, Wesley?'

He stared through his lenses. 'No more. Please. I've told you all I know.'

'If I'm right, you don't need to say anything,' I said. 'Was it Lance Elbourne?'

Wesley Amponsah's eyes opened wide. His lips remained firmly shut.

Chapter One Hundred and Eleven

Leah

Wesley Amponsah remained true to his word when I said I was leaving that night – Kofi answered his mobile after one ring. He was unharmed, apologetic for abandoning me. I understood he hadn't been given a choice. When he came to take me to the airport, he could barely look at me, and when he did, his eyes burned with shame.

I didn't sleep, even though it was night-time – six hours suspended in the clouds giving my brain time to work. From the moment the plane left the tarmac, I replayed Wesley's story, pondering the holes I couldn't yet fill: Lance Elbourne was a spymaster, Ogechi and Sami once his protégés. It seemed Sarah Franks and Gabriel McMahon were civilians, but whatever had happened in Accra involved them too. I had heard of spies being recruited at university, but I had never imagined them out in the field so young. Sami Mograbi – the boy from my childhood with the ruffled hair and easy smile – had been a spy from his student days. He had come back into my life, and I had had absolutely no idea. I ran through all our encounters, looking for signs I had missed. Sami had always been warm and seemingly open but, even as a teenager, he had kept parts of himself hidden away. As a child, he had kept me away from his father; as an adult, he had focused on nostalgia, revealing little about the man he had turned out to be. I looked out of the window as the plane dipped towards the ground – London was lit up below under the dawn sky. It should have been a return to normality, but everything had changed.

Immigration was quick, and I only had hand luggage. I wheeled my case through the arrivals hall, passing the cab drivers touting for fares. A familiar voice came from behind, surprising me.

'Over here, ma'am.'

Randle stood holding a sign, his shirt untucked. His eyes were tired, but the smile was still there.

Welcome back

'I would have added an exclamation mark, ma'am, but I know you hate them.'

I didn't remember mentioning that, but it was true – if you needed to embellish what you were saying, you hadn't chosen the right words.

I was relieved he had brought the car, not his motorbike. I sat back, plastering my body against the faux leather, tiredness finally catching up. Heathrow faded into miniature behind us.

'You survived, ma'am.' I could hear his relief.

'Just about,' I said. 'Yes. I did.'

Chapter One Hundred and Twelve

Leah

The streets started to get busy as we neared the World's End Estate. White vans and pedestrian crossings slowed our approach. I stared out at the road, contemplating how much to share. The stakes had changed now I knew we were dealing with the Secret Service.

I turned to Randle. 'Find somewhere to park.'

He glanced at me, curious.

'Let's take a walk,' I said.

We strolled towards the cemetery minutes from my flat, the majestic wrought-iron gates leading to the graveyard beyond. It was an oddly glorious setting – a place of beauty to honour the dead. Randle raised an eyebrow when I stopped outside.

'Here, ma'am?'

'Don't tell me you believe in ghosts?'

'No. It's just I had my first date here. Haven't been back since.'

'You know that's a cliché as well as creepy,' I said.

He stepped back to let me enter. 'What can I say, ma'am? I was a teenage boy – I thought it was cool.'

The cemetery was quiet and secluded, as I had hoped. There was a wide path down the centre, straddled by graves – entire lives boiled down to a range of dates and a handful of words on stone slabs. Randle's face remained neutral as I recounted what I had learnt from Wesley Amponsah. He didn't say anything when I had finished, staring down the line of yew trees that stretched up ahead. Eventually he spoke.

'So Ogechi and Sami were MI6 when they were med students. What about now?'

'I don't know,' I said. 'But seeing as Ogechi works for Lance in a sales job, I'd hazard a guess she still is.'

It was the perfect front to travel – I recalled what Zed had said about his mother going away for work.

Randle dug his hands deep in his pockets, kicking a stone up the path. It landed by a cedar tree, disappearing into the grass.

'What about Sami, ma'am?'

'I have no idea who he was.' I turned away towards a cluster of gravestones. 'He was trained to lie. He was lying to me all the time.'

'Maybe he was lying about some things, ma'am.' Randle drew a breath. 'But I think he thought your friendship was real. That's why he turned to you when Sarah Franks was killed. He needed someone he could trust.'

I laughed bitterly. 'Chances are a teenage boy died in Ghana, and Sami was part of the cover-up.'

Lemar Blake had never been found, his parents unable to bury his body, unable to grieve properly for their child. I wondered how many boys Lemar's age had ended up in the graves around me before they had the opportunity to grow into the men they promised to be. At least my mother had experienced more of life before hers was cut short. I could see the dome of the cream-coloured chapel ahead at the top of the avenue. I continued up the path towards it, Randle matching my stride.

'I still don't understand why Lance sent Sami and Ogechi to Ghana, ma'am. Was it sanctioned by the British government?'

'I don't know, Randle,' I said.

The sun had risen higher, making the blue in the sky brighter. A row of granite headstones glistened, hit by a ray of light. Randle glanced at me, his forehead puckered by a frown.

'What do you think the boss will do, ma'am, when you tell him what you found out?'

I had tried not think about Kenny O'Sullivan. I wasn't fazed by the prospect of his anger, but he was a consummate politician, and I couldn't be sure of his support.

'I wasn't planning on telling him just yet,' I said. 'He thinks I'm emotionally involved.'

Randle looked at me carefully. 'Are you?'

It was a fair question.

'I'm just trying to do my job.' I took a breath. 'Look, Randle. You're the only person I've told about Sami and Ogechi. I need to know what I'm dealing with before MI6 can shut this down, or worse.'

A heavy-set man jogged past us, his skin slippery with sweat.

'I think you should tell the boss, ma'am. This isn't a normal multiple murder. MI6 don't mess around.'

My fingers clenched. 'I'm not asking for your advice, Randle.'

He shook his head, staring at me, exasperated. 'If he made you take time off when Sami died, what do you think he'll do if you go behind his back?'

I planted my feet, looking up at him, the challenge in my eyes clear. 'I won't think less of you if you tell Kenny,' I said.

He chuckled at the irony. 'I didn't think you thought much of me at all.'

'I'm not telling him yet, Randle. What you do is up to you.'

He held my gaze, his decision clearly made. 'What's our next move, ma'am?'

I bit back a smile.

'I return to work. We carry on the investigation. Everything runs through the normal channels, except when it comes to Ogechi and Lance.'

'Do we bring Ogechi in for questioning, ma'am?'

'Not yet. She's MI6. Until we know what we're dealing with, we can't show our hand.'

Chapter One Hundred and Thirteen

Leah

Kenny O'Sullivan looked at me like he was reading my secrets. The skin was red around his small nose. I sat opposite him in his office, waiting as he typed. He took his time. When he spoke, there was an edge to his voice.

'You ready to come back, Leah, or do I need to worry about you?'

'You never need to worry about me,' I said.

'You. The case. Same thing.'

'No, sir, you don't. Randle and the team have made good progress.'

I told him about the electives and Ghana – how Ogechi, Sami, Gabriel and Sarah Franks had all been there at the same time, the first three as medical students, Sarah working in the same hospital as Ogechi and Sami, in accounts. I left out MI6, Lemar Blake and my trip to Accra, but I connected the key players, so there were questions Kenny could ask.

'You think the private investigator . . .' – he glanced at his computer – '. . . Ray King . . . was investigating something that happened fifteen years ago?'

'Possibly, sir.' I kept my expression neutral. 'It's too soon to say.'

He leant back, tapping his fingers on his stomach.

'Anything else you want to tell me?' he said.

I wondered if he knew more than he was letting on. Kenny was the king of political manoeuvres. MI6 had ransacked my room. For all I knew, Kenny could have friends high up in the Secret Service – whispers amongst the powerful, behind closed doors, always one step ahead. I took a gamble, steadying my gaze.

'No, sir,' I said. 'Nothing more for now.'

'OK, Leah.' He went back to his unconvincing typing. 'Keep me updated. You need to put this to bed.'

Chapter One Hundred and Fourteen

Leah

Randle and I had to divide and conquer. He was parked up near Ladbroke Grove watching Ogechi. He knew to keep out of sight, but we already had a police car stationed nearby, so if Ogechi saw him, he could pretend he was part of the protection team. I headed to the opposite side of London, arriving in Stepney Green. I slid my hands into my pockets as I walked up to the red brick building where Marlon and Keisha Blake lived. I had called ahead. I wanted them both to be present when I questioned them about their son. The heat was relentless. I could feel a creeping damp spreading across my lower back, but it felt like spring compared to the humidity in Ghana. Two teenage boys circled me on their bikes, laughing under the afternoon sun. I thought of Lemar Blake, not much older when he disappeared.

The main entrance was open. Keisha was at her front door. The leopard print looked more demure as a skirt with a white T-shirt, snug across broad shoulders. Her black bob looked more severe, pressed flat over her ears.

'We've been waiting for you,' she said. 'It's never good news with you lot. You better come in.'

Marlon was sitting in his chair, clutching a can of Guinness. His white hair seemed longer, the edges frayed.

I sat opposite him as Keisha handed me the obligatory glass of water. 'Thank you for talking to me about Lemar,' I said. 'I'm sorry about what happened to him – to you.'

Keisha stood by the door, arms folded. Her make-up was immaculate, but her eyes were weary and cold. 'We've had a lot of sorries.'

'I'm sure.'

There was pain behind her anger. Hostility spread across her face like a wave, hardening each feature in turn.

'Left to your people, it would be like Lemar had never existed.'

My gaze flicked to photographs in the room – young Keisha and Marlon on their wedding day; baby pictures of a boy I now knew was Lemar, but nothing of the man he had started to become. I could feel Keisha's eyes on me.

'Marlon doesn't like seeing him like he was before he—' she began.

Marlon cut her off. 'We deal with it in our own way.'

I nodded, not sure what to say.

I turned to Marlon, easing into the conversation that would poke at the pain of the past. 'You were in Ghana recently with Ray King?'

He looked at me as if I were the one who needed to do the explaining.

'Lemar disappeared over fifteen years ago,' I said. 'What made you start asking questions again, after all this time?'

He shook his head like I had missed the point of existence, the disappointment clear in his eyes. 'We've never stopped asking questions, Inspector. You don't just give up when someone you love disappears.'

I thought of my mother. I could barely remember her, but I needed to find her body and lay her to rest – whatever that meant.

'Of course,' I said.

Marlon drained his beer, gulping loudly. Keisha reached out for the can.

'We never stopped asking questions,' Marlon repeated as Keisha disappeared into the kitchen. 'But then Ray became a private investigator, started taking it seriously. He was always short of money. Convinced us he could help with Lemar. For a price. It was the first time in years anyone had offered to help us. Everyone was so unsupportive when it happened – when our boy disappeared. We tried the British High Commission, but there was very little support.'

Keisha re-entered the room, perching on the arm of Marlon's chair. 'Just another black boy whose life didn't matter. The British officials didn't care.'

Marlon took her hand. 'That would have been bad enough, but it felt like someone didn't want us to know about Lemar. Like something was being covered up. Then Ray starts asking questions . . .' His voice petered out. 'He was struggling to pay the bills, but to break into a house to what – rob it? That's not Ray.'

My throat was dry after the flight. I swallowed a hoarse cough.

'Did Ray find out anything, tell you much about his investigation?'

Marlon shifted to his feet. He crossed the room to the cabinet in the corner, retrieving a battered notebook with a pencil clipped to the side. He flicked through it.

'He had spoken to a doctor named Gabriel McMahon, who sounded like he was prepared to meet. Other than that, he said he had left a few messages, was following a few leads. We went to Ghana again, but we didn't find out much.'

'Why didn't you tell us about Ray and your investigation?' I said.

Keisha made no attempt to hide her bitterness. 'Do you blame us? The police did nothing to help. If anything, the authorities in both countries were obstructive. We couldn't let you get in the way again.'

Marlon's voice was tinged with sadness. 'Ray tries to help us, and he dies all of a sudden . . . Maybe he did break into that man's house and have a heart attack. But if there's something else going on . . .' Marlon's eyes were fearful. 'I don't want us to end up like him.'

Chapter One Hundred and Fifteen

Leah

I parked up the road from Ogechi's house the next morning. Randle was back in the office, taking the lead. The car was much too warm, but I kept the window up so it didn't look like there was someone inside. According to Randle, Ogechi hadn't left her home whilst he was there. The light was off in her bedroom, but the blinds were up. I had seen her silhouette earlier, then nothing, but I hadn't witnessed her leave, and the only exit was through the front door. I waited, prepared to be bored. I had brought a thermos flask for the occasion, but I was almost out of coffee, and I had barely started my shift. I had always found surveillance tedious, and I wondered what Sami was like as a spy. His face was so open, I couldn't imagine it, but I now realised I hadn't known him at all.

The front door opened suddenly. I sat up, hopeful. A woman in her sixties emerged in a starched nurse's uniform. I downed the dregs of coffee, prepared for a dull day. The taste was too bitter, and I reached for a bottle of water, almost missing Ogechi when she finally emerged. She was wearing dark chinos and a navy-blue T-shirt. Large dark sunglasses obscured half her face. She had almost turned the corner when I slipped out to follow her, her pace slow, her body still in pain. I was dressed in a baseball cap and trousers in breathable polyester, blending in with the West London ladies-that-lunched in their expensive athleisure wear. I kept my head down, so if Ogechi glanced back, she would think I was one of them – just another wellness aficionado trying to look the part. I kept a safe distance as I trailed behind, conscious she was trained in espionage. The road was packed with tourists, so it was easier to hide in the crowd. Ogechi seemed to walk without aim, as if enjoying a light summer stroll. As she turned down the path that led towards Holland Park, she paused to tie her shoelaces. I slowed my pace but didn't stop. The trees became denser, branches stretching over us, forming a canopy above. I stepped into the park, my eyes fixed on the entrance I had used, but I couldn't see her. I waited at a safe distance, obscured by the trunk of a tree. Minutes passed before she entered, heading across the grass. She looked weak, her trousers hanging off her, distorting the shape of her legs. She swivelled her head; I hid beneath the peak of my cap. A woman approached in fuchsia leggings, led by a sleek, black labrador. He pulled away from her, racing towards me with a yelp as the lead dropped from her hand. I had never been the greatest fan of dogs, and I moved fast, sidestepping out of its way. When I looked back up again, Ogechi had disappeared. Frustrated, I imagined myself skipping, shuffling my feet to work the annoyance off. Ogechi had probably known I was behind her all along, playing with me, letting me think she was oblivious as I followed her from her home. I slumped on a bench behind the tree, looking out at the park full of people – rich and poor basking equally in the sun. A little girl bowled a cricket ball with impressive precision. I watched as the ball ricocheted off her friend's bat, travelling low across the grass. That's when I saw Ogechi again, walking behind a sycamore tree, fifty metres away.

She paused for the briefest of moments as a man brushed past her, then continued on her way. I frowned. Something was troubling me, but I wasn't sure what. Something about her body language, so subtle, I almost didn't register it. Instinctively, I turned towards the man who had passed: his starched white shirt one size too big, grey trousers, shoulders that hung in an uneven slope. I had only met him twice, but I recognised him instantly – Lance Elbourne's assistant, Jimmy, walking away.

Chapter One Hundred and Sixteen

Leah

Randle stepped into my office, making sure the door was firmly shut. He leant against the fake wood, legs astride, so no one could interrupt.

'What have you got on Lance's PA?' I said.

There was a chance I was wrong, and Jimmy was just Ogechi's medtech colleague. But the brush in the park, as if they were strangers, felt odd. Isaac Okoro was jealous of how close his ex-wife was to Lance Elbourne; Ogechi would have known his assistant well enough to acknowledge him with at least a nod.

Randle produced a folder from behind his back.

'Jimmy Mann. Former police officer. Worked undercover with gangs. He was involved in a violent altercation. Arrested for GBH. The charges were dropped, but he left the job under a cloud. No secretarial experience prior to his time in the force. Minimal office work until he became Lance Elbourne's PA.'

I raised an eyebrow. 'Doesn't look like he was hired for his secretarial skills . . .'

'It's not out of the question he's on the books to do Lance Elbourne's dirty work, ma'am.'

'It's definitely possible,' I said. 'Anything else?'

He crossed the space between us. 'Ray King was part of a support group for ex-soldiers and former police officers. He had been going for years. Guess who starts attending the month Ray King was killed?'

'My money's on Jimmy Mann.'

Randle hovered – something I hated.

'What else? You know you don't get a pat on the back for doing your job?'

He grinned. He flipped open the folder, pulling out a snapshot of Jimmy leaving the office where he worked with Lance and Ogechi, carrying a slimline backpack, wearing a pair of shorts and a T-shirt.

'Jimmy sometimes runs home from work. It's usually a direct route door-to-door. Two weeks before Ray King was killed, he started taking a detour via Stepney Green.'

'Near Ray King's flat?'

'Closer to where he rented his office, ma'am.'

'You mean the room above the pub owned by Steve Campbell? Do you have any evidence Jimmy went in?'

'No, but there are no cameras at the back, so it's possible, but we don't know.'

He let me sit with my disappointment before he spoke.

'We got this outside a local café.'

He placed a CCTV still down on the desk by my computer – Jimmy Mann and Steve Campbell at a bus stop, standing side by side, looking straight ahead. He hesitated when I didn't say anything.

'I know it's not conclusive, ma'am . . .'

'. . . but it's enough to make Steve Campbell sweat.'

Chapter One Hundred and Seventeen

Leah

Steve Campbell looked up as we approached the bar. He was wearing a distressed T-shirt featuring another obscure band.

'What can I get you, Detectives?' He slapped a tea towel over his shoulder. 'I didn't think you were local. The ambience *must* be good.'

I lowered my voice to avoid a scene. 'Can we have a word in private, please, Steve?'

He realised it wasn't a question, sensed the edge behind my smile. For a second, I thought he would refuse. Then he turned to the woman we had seen behind the bar the last time, with thick silver braids.

'Mind the bar, Vanessa.' His smile was too warm.

He pivoted to face me.

'Follow me, Inspector.' He flicked his eyes to Randle. 'You can come too.'

He led us into a room behind the bar with a torn sofa and a couple of tattered bar stools. He made no move to sit down, so neither did we.

'How can I help you, Inspector?'

The tone he adopted was casual, but his body gave him away. His arms crossed his torso, thick fingers digging into reddened flesh.

I flipped my phone round, so the screen was visible to him.

'Do you know him?'

Steve stared at a zoomed-in image of Jimmy Mann, cropped to show only his face. Steve's eyes clouded over.

'Should I?' he said.

I returned my phone to my trouser pocket. 'The answer to that question is usually "yes" or "no".'

'May I look again?'

I could see he was biding his time. I had met enough Steve Campbells to know when to bluff. I seized my chance before the moment passed.

'We have images of the two of you conspiring together.'

'Let's see them then.'

The photo at the bus stop didn't prove anything. I didn't blink as I held his gaze. 'You're welcome to come down to the station . . .'

He ran a hand through his thick, ginger locks, his pupils dilating with fear. 'That won't be necessary.' He gave a thin smile. 'I've met him – once or twice . . . yes.'

'Look, Steve . . .' I perched on the edge of a bar stool as Steve fidgeted with his T-shirt, my tone unnervingly calm. 'Fascinating as you are, we're not interested in you. Tell me what you were doing with Jimmy Mann, and I'll try to leave you out of this.'

'Try?'

His pitch was high. I just looked at him.

'I haven't committed a crime.'

'Then you have nothing to worry about,' I said.

He slumped down on the sofa, pinching the skin on his chin.

'I never knew his name. I don't know what he does. He paid me to photograph the files Ray was working on.'

I waited to see if there was more.

'That's it,' Steve said. 'Ray owed me rent. I was entitled to that money. You can't arrest me for entering my own property. He hadn't paid for months, so he was more of a squatter than a tenant upstairs.'

I ignored his rant. 'You showed him the files, then what, Steve?'

His eyes were defiant, but I could see the guilt behind the glare.

'Then nothing . . . I haven't done anything wrong.'

'It wasn't nothing, Steve,' I said. 'Two weeks later, Ray King was dead.'

Chapter One Hundred and Eighteen

Leah

We arrested Jimmy Mann on his way to work the next morning. The evidence was tenuous, but I wanted to see how Lance Elbourne would react. Ray King had been digging into the disappearance of Lemar Blake fifteen years ago. Whatever happened coincided with an operation in which two of Lance Elbourne's junior spies were involved. We had nothing concrete to link Jimmy to the death of Ray King, but my instinct told me he was implicated somehow, and Jimmy worked for Lance. He sat in the interview room, his expression unchanging, shoulders sloped, back completely straight. He was flanked by a lawyer who had appeared remarkably quickly. There was no fear in his eyes. Randle rattled through the obligatory preamble. When he finished, I placed my elbows on the table, allowing the weight of the situation to sink in.

Jimmy took a sip of his water, waiting for me to speak.

'You understand you're being questioned about the death of a man named Ray King?'

He angled himself forwards, pivoting at the hip. His body had moved closer; the line of his back remained straight.

'No comment.' His voice was curt and clipped.

And so it began – the same answer to every question, the same blank expression in his eyes.

I knew there was no point, but I kept asking. Men like Lance Elbourne thought they were untouchable; I wanted him to know his acolytes were being watched. We took a break from the one-way conversation. The air lingered around us, heavy and hot. The corridor felt cooler after the windowless room. I was heading towards the water fountain when I heard Akosua's voice, coming from behind. I didn't slow down, so she had to project.

'DCI O'Sullivan wants to see you in his office,' she said.

'Can it wait?'

I turned, impatient, my mind still focused on Jimmy Mann.

Akosua didn't answer, but her eyes told me 'No'.

Chapter One Hundred and Nineteen

Zed

The meeting with the stranger had finally been set. Zed had moved the conversation to text, so Seema wouldn't know where it was. He had arranged a time when he was sure his father would be out working, so he could slip out with no questions asked. He knew he should brace himself for disappointment, in case it was another no-show, but the anticipation had been gradually building, and he felt something close to hope.

He had insisted they meet somewhere public. The stranger had agreed, suggesting a local theatre in North London near Finsbury Park. Born and bred in West London, North London was unfamiliar, but Zed agreed without hesitation, his mind fixed on his goal. If there was one thing he had learned from his father, it was never to let fear of the unknown prevent you from achieving your aims.

He emerged from the station, following the route he had memorised. The theatre was at the end of a street, up a gentle hill. He could hear dogs barking in the distance and, as he drew closer, he saw the sign for a dog home off to his right. An elderly man emerged from a side street with a thick metal cane. For a moment Zed wondered if this was his source, but the man was buried beneath a heavy tweed coat despite the heat, and Zed had been instructed he would be meeting someone in grey. The hill was deceptively steep and by the time Zed arrived at the top, his T-shirt was drenched in sweat and his jeans felt heavy around his legs. The door to the theatre was closed, a faded poster for Macbeth taped to the wood, the corners peeling off. The next performance wasn't until the following day, and there was no one in sight. Zed tried the handle, but it was locked, and he felt a tinge of disappointment at being led on again. He walked round to the side of the theatre, searching for another way in. The building backed onto a quiet road. He spotted another sign for the dog home; he could hear howls rising up in the distance, and he wondered how far away it was.

A cocker spaniel moped up ahead, eyes sad and wide, separated from its friends, its bark increasingly wild. Zed approached with tentative steps, troubled by the animal in distress. He recognised the feeling of helplessness, and he resolved to take the dog to the home, then return to Ladbroke Grove. The spaniel was moving in frantic circles, a red lead trailing in its wake. As Zed reached for it, a hand covered his mouth from behind. His arms were pinned down by his side, and he struggled to move. He couldn't breathe beneath the gloved fingers pressing against his face. He kicked out, but resistance was useless as he was dragged towards a car, the dog's barks growing louder all the while. Desperate, he bit down into soft flesh. The grip around him loosened. He didn't think; he just ran in the direction of the dog home. Stumbling, he fumbled for the phone in his pocket, hitting the digits 999. His throat had closed in panic. He could barely get out the words:

'Leah Hutch . . .'

Strong arms seized him. He kicked out in vain.

He opened his mouth in terror. The dog continued to bark.

Chapter One Hundred and Twenty

Leah

'Shut the door, Leah.'

Kenny O'Sullivan gestured towards the chair in front of his desk.

I did as I was told and sat opposite him – at least he was still using my first name.

There was an air conditioning unit beside him on the ground, so the room was pleasantly chilled. Kenny ran his hand across his face, as if I exhausted him. There was a light patch of sweat under his arm.

'We can't keep doing this,' he said.

'Sir?'

I was confused by the 'we'.

'This tired routine where you pursue lines of inquiry with little or no justification, Leah. You're an inspector; you should know better.' He squeezed the tip of his nose.

'With all due respect, sir . . .' I kept my tone even. 'I don't believe I'm doing that.'

'I don't care what you believe.' He gripped the desk in front of him, pushing his chair back with force. The wheels rolled half a foot before he stopped himself. I could see more of him, and I was acutely aware of his size.

'You have no grounds to question the man in that interview room. I have it on good authority he was never seen at Ray King's flat, nor at the pub Ray rented an office above.'

There was no way Kenny could have known the details so quickly unless Jimmy's lawyer had made a complaint.

My back was rigid with annoyance. I was relieved my voice was still calm.

'The pub landlord, Steve Campbell, has given a statement that Jimmy Mann paid him to photograph Ray King's private investigation files.'

'So?' Kenny's eyes flashed with exasperation. 'What aren't you telling me, Leah? I've just had a call from the superintendent telling me to shut this down.'

I looked at him, weighing my options – thin lips pursed in anger, hostility in his green eyes.

'It's up to you – you can tell me what you're up to, or enjoy your secrets without your badge, at home.'

The admission came out in a rush before I could change my mind.

'I think Jimmy works for MI6, sir, or at least he's on the payroll of a powerful spy.'

The words sounded almost ridiculous as I uttered them out loud. I took a breath, then told him all I knew. He listened without interrupting, but I could see his brain at work.

'You're making some big leaps, Hutch,' he said when I had finished.

'I have it on good authority, sir – I spoke to Lance's fixer in Ghana. He told me Lance, Ogechi and Sami were MI6.'

Kenny pinned me with his eyes. 'How did you find this *fixer*?'

I gripped my thighs, steeling myself for his wrath.

'*He* found *me*, sir . . . when I was there.'

'You went to *Ghana* behind my back?'

The quiet disappointment was worse than the outburst I had expected.

'I went in my own time, sir,' I said. 'You had put me on leave.'

Kenny's voice was cold and measured. 'I give you a lot of rope to manoeuvre, and you betray my trust. I don't know who you think you're working for, but I want Jimmy Mann sent home. Now.'

'You can't keep doing this, sir . . .' I said.

Kenny's head jerked fiercely on his neck; it was a wonder it didn't snap.

'Be very careful about what you say next, Hutch.'

His green eyes darkened, but I didn't flinch.

'I think it's a mistake to release Jimmy,' I said. 'It's in the interest of the case to question him. If there's nothing to charge him with, we'll let him go.'

Kenny's features contorted, his usual calm demeanour gone.

'I have tried with you, Leah. I have tried. I brought you back here after the mess with your boss in Leeds. I have made allowances for you, and yet you have the audacity to act as if I'm your enemy. If—'

A heavy fist pounded on the door. Ever the professional, Kenny rearranged his face. He cleared his throat.

'Come in.'

Randle stood in the doorway, his face stricken. He didn't wait for permission to speak.

'It's Zechariah Okoro,' he said. 'We think he's been taken. He left an SOS for Inspector Hutch.'

Chapter One Hundred and Twenty-One

Leah

I let Randle drive to Ogechi Okoro's. Kenny's reprimand had been cut short by necessity – find Zed, then I would hear my sentence in full. Randle's jaw was clenched tight. A muscle throbbed in his cheek.

'We let him down,' he said.

'He never trusted us.' I stared through the windscreen, my voice expressionless. Randle needed to get a grip on his emotions, or he would be of no use to Zed. We had tried to reassure Zechariah Okoro, but he had always acted like a boy who believed he was on his own.

'We need to ask Ogechi about MI6, ma'am.' Randle's mouth set in a thin line. 'There's no time for subtlety. We need to find Zed.'

We knew the last known location where Zed had used his mother's debit card – a ticket barrier at a train station nowhere near home. I had a team out searching for him in North London, another two knocking on doors in the neighbourhoods where each of his parents lived. A boy matching Zed's description had been seen walking away from Finsbury Park tube. Now Zed's phone was switched off, and we had no idea where he was.

Randle pulled up in the spot where I had parked to watch Ogechi twenty-four hours before.

'What happens if we don't find him, ma'am . . . ?' His voice trailed off.

I thought of my mother, her body missing for decades – the nightmares that disturbed my sleep.

'It won't come to that.'

Randle turned to me. 'We both know you can't promise that.'

'And we both know we'll do everything we can to find him.' I reached for the door. 'Let's hope that's enough.'

Ogechi Okoro insisted on listening to Zed's message. She barely breathed when she heard his voice – the panic when he said my name, the muffled squeal when he tried to shout out.

We sat at her kitchen table, a crystal vase of yellow roses in the centre, on the wood. Her skin looked ashen next to the flowers. Her hands were completely still.

'Zed got them for me when I came back from hospital. They're my favourite. He's always been thoughtful like that.'

I nodded.

'I have teams of officers out searching for your son, but you need to help us,' I said.

I slid the vase to the side so there was no barrier between us.

'Let's not waste time. We know you're MI6. We know the truth about your relationship with Lance Elbourne. We know this has something to do with what happened when you were in Ghana. We know Sami, Gabriel McMahon and Sarah Franks were all there, and it's related to the disappearance of Lemar Blake.'

'If you know all that, you know I'm bound by the Official Secrets Act.'

There was a coolness beneath the anxiety.

Randle's face was incredulous. 'Is that more important to you than your son?'

'Four people have been killed. I'm sure you know that,' I said. 'Your son is in danger. You need to tell us what happened in Ghana.'

Ogechi was silent for a moment, her face betraying no emotion – the pain we had seen when she had heard Zed's cries now hidden beneath the poker face of a spy.

I softened my tone, leaning forwards in my seat. 'What are you scared of?' I said. 'We're just trying to find Zechariah.'

'Lance likes games. It means he's always in control. If you're on his team, he's the best friend you could ever want. He's saved me multiple times, but he's not afraid to be ruthless. If you break ranks, there will be consequences; if you betray the cause, God help you.'

Her expression was blank, her voice a monotone, as if she were trying to keep her feelings at bay.

'The cause?' I said.

'Whatever mission he is running to protect alleged British interests. He looks like a mild-mannered academic, but he's a zealot. He won't let anything or anyone stand in his way.'

'I understand that, but we can't do anything if we don't know why this all started in the first place, Ogechi. What happened in Ghana that you're trying to cover up? You need to tell us the truth if you want us to find Zed. Time's running out.'

The mask faded. A mother's agony lined her skin.

'Promise me you'll find him.'

'I can't do that.'

'You need to,' she said.

She rose and walked to the window. I noticed she had already lowered the blinds. She was still facing away when she spoke.

'Sami and I were recruited by Lance Elbourne at university. Lance was a brilliant academic. He made the work sound exciting and important at the same time. I was young. The sense of danger appealed. Our first mission was in Ghana. In Accra. I didn't know then, but our government wasn't aware of it. Lance was flying solo – the mission was very much off the books. Lance had intel about a coup planned for Nigeria, being bankrolled by Femi Akintola, a Nigerian millionaire. According to Lance, Akintola's vision for Nigeria didn't align with global interests. He felt Akintola had to be stopped.'

Ogechi turned and walked to the kettle, flipping the power on to give her fingers something to do.

'Femi Akintola was very connected and had been an asset of Lance's before he had gone rogue. If the coup went ahead, not only would it not be good for British interests, Lance would end up with more than egg on his face.'

I remembered the party girl in the photographs – the junior doctor, Bisi Akintola; she had the same surname as Femi. The receptionist in the hospital in Accra insisted that she and Ogechi were close.

'Was Bisi Akintola Femi Akintola's daughter?' I said. 'What was the plan? To get to her father through her?'

'Akintola had gone to ground – no one could find him. Bisi was his greatest treasure in life. She was working as a junior doctor in Accra in Ghana. Lance knew she was in contact with her father. The mission was simple – Sami and I were placed on our medical elective in the same hospital. The mission was to get close to her and get information. Find out where Femi Akintola was.'

'Being a spy must be pressurised at the best of times,' I said. 'Quite a risk Lance took using students.'

'There are always risks, and they are always calculated. He needed the agents to be young to get alongside Bisi, or the mission would never have worked.'

The kettle screeched as it came to the boil. She ignored it.

'Bisi liked to party. I went out with her, shared a house. We got close. Sami was the studious one she talked to about work. It was a two-pronged approach. Sami hated clubbing, didn't drink. I built trust by being Bisi's wingman.'

'You lived with Sarah Franks,' I said.

A weak nod. 'You've done your homework.'

'How did the GP, Gabriel McMahon, fit in?'

Her skin darkened with embarrassment. 'We were in a relationship.'

I raised an eyebrow. 'A bit risky, considering your line of work.'

She flipped the kettle back on, pausing as the water hissed and bubbled. 'It was my first job. I didn't tell Sami. He wouldn't have approved.'

'Your love life isn't on trial here,' I said. 'Tell me about Lemar Blake.'

Her eyes glazed over. For a moment, I thought she might cry, then they were clear again.

'Lemar Blake,' she said. 'It's been a long time since I've said his name . . . Lemar had a fling with Bisi, became obsessed with her. She got bored and dumped him. He didn't react well. Tea?'

I shook my head, watching as she filled a dark brown mug with hot water, dropping the teabag in last, as if it were an afterthought. She sat down at the table, clutching the edge as she spoke.

'Lemar turned up at the house one night. Drunk. I was at home with Sarah watching a film. Gabriel was there too. Bisi was on call in the hospital. Lemar got angry. Refused to believe me when I said she wasn't home.'

Her eyes were blank as she relived the memory. Neither Randle nor I spoke.

'We tried to calm him down,' Ogechi said. 'It got physical. Gabriel tried to restrain him. It turned into a full-on fight. There was shoving. Fists were hurled. Sarah tried to help. Lemar fell. I don't know who pushed him. It was an accident. He broke his neck at the bottom of the stairs.'

Her voice was a whisper.

'No one meant to kill him.'

Randle looked at her, appalled. 'If it was an accident, why didn't you tell someone?'

She looked at him, incredulous.

'Gabriel and Sarah wanted to go to the police at first, but I persuaded them it was the wrong thing to do for all of us. Our futures would be over. We would end up in an African jail . . . You've got to understand – I was in the middle of my first mission. If they had gone to the police and there had been an investigation, it would have jeopardised everything. We needed to keep silent. The body needed to disappear.'

'Where was Sami?' I said. 'How does he play into that night?'

Ogechi bit her lip. Her pupils shifted.

'I called him. He was always the brilliant one. He told me to sit tight. Keep everyone in the house. Twenty minutes later, a man called Chris arrived.'

Randle looked up at the sound of the name.

'I didn't know it then,' Ogechi said, 'but Chris had been in Ghana the whole time – he was Lance's plan B and C. If Sami and I didn't get through to Bisi, Chris had more persuasive ways to make her talk. And if something went wrong—'

I understood immediately. 'He would know what to do.'

'Chris threatened Sarah and Gabriel. I don't know what was said, but the message was simple – we would never speak about that night again, or there would be consequences. Then Chris took Lemar's body away.'

'Before Gabriel died, Zed heard him or the killer say, "It was Chris,"' I said. 'Why would someone say that?'

'I don't know.' Ogechi's head hung limp on her neck. She looked drained. 'I never saw Chris again after that night.'

'Was Sami with him?'

'No. Sami never came into the house. He stayed outside in the car, but he had the worst job. He went with Chris to deal with the body. He never told me what they did.'

There were tears in her eyes.

'He saved me – my career, everything. He was always the better spy, but it destroyed him. He left the Service after that. Sarah self-medicated to try to forget.'

I remembered the hospital receptionist revealing that Sarah Franks had been sacked for stealing oxycodone.

'Gabriel left Accra straight away,' Ogechi said. 'We stayed in touch off and on. I got in deeper with Lance. Tried to prove my worth. I don't think he ever forgave me for losing Sami, his protégé.'

She blinked, shaking off the emotion. The tears were gone as she sat up.

'So, fifteen years ago, you and Sami were sent on a mission that had significant repercussions for Lance Elbourne's career.' The room felt warm as I delivered the cold facts. 'Lemar's death jeopardised your mission, and Lance's henchman at the time, Chris, made the problem go away.'

'Yes.' Ogechi's voice was soft but firm. 'And it did for fifteen years. Then that private investigator, Ray King, started digging.'

'Why? After all these years?' I said.

'We still don't know. Lance didn't like it at all.'

Randle hadn't moved from the doorway.

'You said Lance likes games,' he said. 'What do you mean by that?'

Ogechi looked at him intently. I couldn't read the expression in her eyes.

'He's not a straightforward person,' she said.

I recalled Georgina Harrison's confidence, after carrying out the autopsy, that Ray had been killed and his body moved to Gabriel McMahon's sofa after his death.

'Ray was asking too many questions about what happened in Ghana – he had to be silenced,' I said. 'He was killed. Then his body was used to warn Gabriel McMahon to keep his mouth shut. Sound like something Lance would do?'

Ogechi lifted the mug to her lips but didn't drink.

'I didn't think the British government was in the business of murder,' Randle said.

'It's not.' Ogechi was adamant. 'Lance gets results, so no one looks too closely at what he does. He's always been untouchable. It's a gift. There's always a Jimmy or a Chris to clean up.'

'So, Jimmy kills Ray King on Lance's say-so and leaves his body in Gabriel's sitting room in front of the television. The local police think it's a break-in, but Gabriel understands the warning and clams up?' I said.

Ogechi's mouth twitched in assent. 'It wouldn't surprise me. Gabriel had contacted me. He thought he was being followed. Lance found out. He would have seen that as a betrayal.'

The cuts on her arms had started to scab. She rubbed the skin near her elbow.

'Is that why you were kidnapped? To warn you not to break ranks?' Randle said.

'If Lance thought I was about to admit to what had really happened in Ghana, maybe. But I haven't said anything for fifteen years. He should trust me.'

There was hurt in her eyes.

'It can't have helped that Gabriel kept coming to your house,' Randle said.

'No.' Ogechi nodded. 'He must have panicked when I disappeared.'

I ran my finger along a crack near the edge of the table. 'Sarah Franks was murdered the week after Ray.'

Ogechi's poker face returned.

'Not long before that, a bottle of akpeteshie – local gin from Ghana – appeared on her doorstep. Sound like another Lance Elbourne warning to you?'

'Yes. Subtle but effective. With Lance, there's always a warning, always a test. He'll do whatever it takes to protect his interests. It's what makes him so good at what he does.'

'You make him sound like a hero,' Randle said.

She was unmoved by the accusation. 'Hero, villain – they're sometimes the same thing.'

'What happened in Ghana needed to stay buried,' I said. 'When Ray started digging, he was killed, and it seems you were all given warnings to make sure you didn't tell – Ray King's body on the sofa for Gabriel; the bottle of local gin for Sarah Franks; kidnapping for you. The others didn't heed their warning, so . . .'

'You think Lance had Jimmy kill them?' Ogechi said.

'Let's say he did for now.'

She shook her head. 'He loved Sami. It doesn't make sense.'

'Apart from speaking to Gabriel, did you give Lance any indication that you weren't loyal to him?'

I pushed my finger deeper into the crack. Ogechi dropped her gaze for a second, then her eyes found mine.

'No,' she said. 'I've worked so hard to prove myself since Ghana – he has no reason to doubt me.'

Randle took a step towards us. 'Maybe it's a test, as you say?'

'Possibly. Lance isn't above kidnapping and blackmail, but he's not sadistic. Having me lacerated is a pretty new low.'

'Do you think he could be behind Zechariah's disappearance?' Randle said.

'I don't know. If he is, he will never admit it. It's always on his terms. I'll do anything. I just want my boy back . . .'

She grabbed my wrist, her grip so hard her nails dug into my skin. I lifted my eyes to meet hers.

'If you're going to find Zechariah, you better be good at your job, Inspector,' she said. 'Lance is the ultimate game player. You can't beat him if you don't know what game to play.'

Chapter One Hundred and Twenty-Two

Leah

This time I drove because I needed a distraction. I took the back streets as I didn't have the patience to sit in traffic for long.

'Do you really think Lance had Sarah, Gabriel and Sami killed, ma'am, because they ignored the warnings he gave?'

'It's a possibility,' I said. 'But the modus operandi is very different from what happened with Ray King. We don't even know if Sami got a warning or what it was. And they were all killed after Ray, so there was no immediate threat that we know of, unless Lance was so spooked that he decided to clean house, just in case.'

I took a corner too fast, pushing down on the brake.

'Do you want me to contact Lu Hoffen? Check Jimmy Mann's DNA against the balaclava Sarah Franks' killer left?' Randle said.

'Sure.'

He pulled out his phone, tapping a message with fast thumbs.

We had almost reached Lance Elbourne's office. The long glass windows caught the sun, sparkling in the distance as we approached.

'So we're just going to march in there and confront him, ma'am?'

I wanted to see how Lance reacted. 'By now he must know we're on to him,' I said. 'He's a spy, after all, and we arrested his right-hand man.'

The engine hummed as we stopped at the lights.

'There are two ways to deal with men like Lance.' I closed the window, shutting out extraneous noise. 'Beat him at his own game, or come at him hard and see what falls when we shake things up.'

'Do you think we've put Ogechi in danger, ma'am?'

'No. Lance knows we're watching him. He's no fool.'

I had only met Lance Elbourne twice. I sensed he could be intellectually superior, not reckless.

Randle pulled a cereal bar from his pocket. He frowned, thinking as he chewed.

'I'm not sure I trust Ogechi, ma'am.'

I eased off the accelerator as we hit denser traffic. 'You don't have to. She's a spy. She deals in intelligence. Everything's a calculated risk, and right now she knows she can't trust Lance, which leaves us. She wants her son back. When it comes to Ghana, I'm pretty sure she's telling the truth.'

His phone flashed. I glanced down, saw 'Akosua'. Randle put the phone on speaker so I could listen in.

'Have you found Zed?'

I could hear the hope in Randle's voice.

'No.'

His shoulders slumped, eyes narrowing with frustration.

'Any news on the door-to-door?' I said.

Akosua cleared her throat. 'A little girl came forward called Seema Jackson. Zed's dad, Isaac Okoro, confirmed she had been to the flat. She set up a page with Zed after the press conference. They thought they could do a better job than us finding his mum. They kept the account active, even after Ogechi turned up. Seema said Zed was determined to find out who had hurt his mum.'

'Then what?' Randle looked appalled. 'Some kind of vigilante mission? He's a kid. What did he think he could do?'

'I don't know, Ben,' Akosua said, a bite to her tone. 'Seema didn't seem to know either. Apparently, someone came forward with information and wanted to meet. Seema gatecrashed the first meeting, but no one showed.'

'Did she know why Zed went to Finsbury Park?' I said.

'She swears no. Zed's source must have agreed to meet again after the no-show, but Zed switched to text message so Seema couldn't see the plan. We're analysing the account to check if there's anything we missed, ma'am.'

'Do you think Zed's source could be linked to Lance Elbourne?' Randle said, after he ended the call.

'I don't know,' I said. 'Zed's been missing for hours. The longer we take to find him, the less chance of finding him alive.'

Chapter One Hundred and Twenty-Three

Leah

Jimmy Mann escorted us to Lance's office as if our encounter in the police station had never occurred. I watched him, trying to reconcile the surly, quiet personal assistant with the ruthless killer who murdered on demand. He deposited us at the door to Lance Elbourne's office. As he turned to go, I saw a flash of contempt in his eyes.

Lance was in his favoured spot, at the window, looking down at the car park. He turned as we entered. A glimmer of a smile. The bright stripes on his shirt were distracting.

'Jimmy tells me you've been busy,' he said.

I pulled out one of the chairs opposite his desk. He watched as Randle followed suit.

'I can see you mean business.'

'If by "business", you mean trying to find a missing child.'

'Ah, that.' Lance drew out his own chair, lowering himself gracefully. 'Is Ogechi OK? I wouldn't wish that on anyone. Taking a child – that's a body blow.'

'If you had anything to do with Zed's disappearance—'

His eyes flashed. 'I didn't.'

'. . . tell me now,' I said.

He spoke slowly, annunciating each word. 'I had nothing to do with Zechariah going missing. His mother was sent back by whoever took her. Maybe they'll send the boy back too.'

The pink in his shirt looked almost fluorescent.

'I'm sorry I can't be of more help.' He framed his chin with thumb and forefinger. 'How did it go with Jimmy? He's never been a big talker.'

'I don't know. It's early days.' The sun poured through the window. I could feel its rays warm my face. 'We have evidence linking him to the death of the private investigator, Ray King.' It wasn't a complete lie. 'Maybe Jimmy doesn't have your luck.'

'I wouldn't call myself lucky, Inspector.'

'I don't know about that. For a while, everyone thought Ray King died of a natural heart attack – until we realised he didn't.'

'Is that what you wanted to talk to Jimmy about?' Lance didn't miss a beat.

I lowered my voice, so he had to lean forward to hear me.

'If Jimmy has committed murder, I'll prove it. If either of you had anything to do with Zechariah's disappearance, I'll make sure you pay.'

Lance's eyes twinkled. 'You see, at heart you *are* a crusader. All that talk about this just being a job.'

'A child is missing,' I said. 'If you had anything to do with it, make sure he comes home.'

'I'm not responsible for what has happened to Zechariah. It would serve you well to understand this, Inspector Hutch: everything I do is for the greater good. I serve the needs of my country first and foremost.' His expression was almost earnest. 'That's why I dedicated years to preparing the nation's future doctors. Sadly,

Sami Mograbi couldn't hack it, but you and I both know it takes a certain kind of person to do a hero's job.'

I was riled by the mention of Sami, as Lance intended.

'What's that exactly?' I said. 'Killing helpless victims and kidnapping children, so no one knows why and how you averted a coup that had nothing to do with you?'

Lance's face was inscrutable.

'If indeed a coup was averted, I would chalk that up as a win, whoever was responsible for the outcome.'

He was playing with me, saying everything and nothing.

'I'll ask you again,' I said. 'Do you know where Zechariah Okoro is?'

Lance looked at Randle, then back at me. He didn't blink.

'No. I don't.'

I scraped back my chair. He grimaced at the sound.

'We won't keep you any longer.'

I had almost reached the door when he spoke.

'You haven't asked me about Sami, Inspector. It was a shame he gave it all up. He was the best student I ever had. He got close to people but never too close to let them be a distraction. I sensed it wasn't always that way.'

I focused on his mouth as he spoke, concentrating so my face gave nothing away.

'He told me about you once. I needed to check what his attachments were before he went to Ghana. Sami said there was no one significant in his life – he had been in love once when he was sixteen. He wasn't sure the girl even knew how he felt. No one had come close since, and he doubted anyone ever would.'

Randle didn't look at me as Lance crept under my skin.

Lance tapped his pen against his desk, punching the tip against the wood.

'Good luck with Zechariah Okoro. I hope you find the boy alive.'

'Let's hope he fares better than Sami,' I said.

I watched Lance carefully. He looked away, but not before I saw the sadness in his eyes.

Chapter One Hundred and Twenty-Four

Leah

Randle's shoulders tensed in disgust as we left the building.

'He thinks he's untouchable because he's never been caught. He didn't even deny having Ray King killed.'

Ray was looking into Lemar's disappearance, but if he had discovered what happened, he would have found out about Sami and Ogechi's mission and the coup.

'What about the others? You think Lance had Jimmy kill them too?'

'I don't know, ma'am. He's certainly ruthless . . .'

I pictured Lance moments before – I couldn't get his expression out of my head when I had mentioned Sami. My phone rang before I could process the thought.

I recognised Lu Hoffen's prickly tone immediately. I hadn't bothered to save her number – after this case, it wasn't a relationship I planned to pursue.

"Leah . . ."

'Lu,' I said. 'It's not a good time.'

'It's never a good a time. But in the spirit of open collaboration, I've got some intel for you.'

'Thank you.'

'I'm not doing this for you, Leah,' she said. 'I heard the kid's gone missing. I'm doing it for him.'

I nodded, even though she couldn't see me.

'Remember that bum lead you gave me. Tip Wheldon? Trust-fund kid? Dealt drugs to Sarah Franks?'

'Yes,' I said. 'The drug dealer Zikar Mograbi tipped us off about, so we'd forget about Sami.'

'That's the one.'

It felt like weeks since Randle and I had first sat down with Sami's father, when he was trying to bully us into releasing his son.

I remembered Sami's words when I had confronted him about introducing Tip to Sarah Franks. I could hear his voice in my head. I shut it out. It felt too raw.

Tip's not even a proper drug dealer. She's just a trust-fund kid with no purpose and too much time.

'Tip's parents own a bunch of restaurants and hotels,' Lu said.

Sami had mentioned her family were in hospitality. I waited for Lu to say something of note.

'She just got arrested for possession with intent to distribute. She wanted a deal, so—'

I cut Lu off. 'What's she trading?'

'The usual. Information. She says she withheld facts related to Sarah Franks' murder.'

Finally, something I could use.

'What facts?' I said.

'Patience, Hutch. I don't have the full picture.'

'What has she told you so far?'

The seconds passed as Lu enjoyed having something I wanted.

'Her dad cut her off when she kept using. Eventually gave her a job looking after new developments, because Tip's mum made him feel bad. The Wheldons have bought a bunch of disused properties to develop into hotels – Tip's in charge of them. Tip uses a company that hires vets to provide security for the developments – keep squatters out, stop junkies from stripping the buildings, that kind of thing.'

'When you say "vets", you mean ex-soldiers?'

'Yep.' I could hear her swallow a sarcastic retort. 'But here's the thing – Tip's lost her trust fund; she has to make a living. She figures a lot of ex-soldiers have PTSD. She goes back to her old ways, decides to exploit it – uses the vets to tout drugs to their friends.'

'And this is relevant because . . . ?' I needed to find Zed, and there was a limit to my patience.

'Tip also dealt to friends of friends, like Sarah Franks. Usually delivered to those ones herself. All part of the service. But one of the ex-soldiers scared Tip into letting him deliver drugs to Sarah the night she was killed.'

'That's why there was no breaking and entry.'

'Exactly,' Lu said. 'The killer got into Sarah's flat because Sarah thought it was Tip. Apparently, she would just leave the door on the latch.'

I stopped, turning my back to the traffic so her voice was clear.

'What's the name of the ex-soldier who asked to deliver the drugs, Lu?'

I heard a rustle as she flicked through her notes.

'Some guy named Marlon Blake.'

Chapter One Hundred and Twenty-Five

Leah

Randle tapped his fingers on his thigh as he drove. 'Georgina Harrison was right – Gabriel, Sarah and Sami were assassinated. Marlon most likely killed them as revenge for what they did to Lemar.'

They were responsible for what happened to his son – that gave him motive. We now knew he had been a soldier with combat training – that gave him means. I turned over the facts in mind, trying to understand what had happened. Randle liked to process out loud.

'It makes sense of the different MOs, ma'am. Ray was a problem for Lance because he wouldn't stop asking questions about what happened in the past. He was looking into Lemar's disappearance, but he was getting too close to finding out about the coup. Gabriel was going to talk to Ray, so Lance gave him a big enough scare to terrify him into keeping silent. Maybe Sarah got a gentler warning because she hadn't spoken to Ray yet? Akpeteshie is not easy to come by. That must have been Lance too.'

'Ray was killed a week before Sarah's murder,' I said. 'Lance had no need to kill Sarah once Ray was out of the picture. Fifteen years had passed, and she had said nothing. There was no immediate threat.'

'So the figure in the balaclava – the one who escaped the scene . . .'

I finished Randle's sentence. '. . . was probably Marlon Blake.'

I thought back to that interview with Zechariah, when we had first heard the name 'Chris'.

Randle turned to face me as the car slowed down at the lights. The sun's rays cut across his face, making his eyes hard to see.

'It must have been Gabriel who said, "It was Chris," ma'am.'

The words Zed had heard as he hid, petrified, in Gabriel's wardrobe. I imagined Gabriel pleading for his life, blaming Chris for Lemar's disappearance so Marlon would let him live. Randle was silent for a moment, his frown deepening with each thought.

'I couldn't figure out why Lance would take the boy. He was so adamant when he denied it. He never denied killing Ray. But now it makes sense, if it was Marlon. The only thing worse than dying for a parent is losing a kid.'

'That's it,' I said. 'That's why Ogechi was released so soon after the press conference.'

I remembered Isaac's statement in front of the cameras – pleading with the public to help return a mother to her son, making clear Ogechi's greatest bond was with Zed, not him.

'What do you mean, ma'am?' Randle said.

'You were right when you thought the killer changed their mind when they released Ogechi. Her kidnap wasn't a warning. It didn't have anything to do with Lance.'

Ogechi had said mutilation wasn't Lance's style. She couldn't understand why he would doubt her loyalty and need to warn her like the others. She was right to question it, because it wasn't him.

'Marlon kidnapped Ogechi, planning to mutilate and then to

kill her,' I said. 'Then he realised she had a son she loved, saw the account Seema and Zed had made, and changed his mind. Why let Ogechi off with death, however painful? Take her child away, and she suffers for the rest of her life.'

Chapter One Hundred and Twenty-Six

Leah

There was no hint of a smile in Kenny's eyes as I stood opposite him. He didn't offer me a seat.

'Are you asking for permission or telling me what you've planned already?'

'Asking. I don't make a habit of going behind your back, sir.'

He snorted, his thumbs rubbing the sides of his belly.

'First it was Lance, now it's Marlon. Are you sure you know what you're doing, before you make a scene?'

'I need to find Zechariah. I'm sure it's worth a shot, sir.'

'We all want that outcome. If Marlon killed Sarah Franks and the others, how do you know the boy's not already dead?'

'I don't, sir.' My jaw set as I pushed the idea to the back of my mind. 'As long as there's a chance, I'll do everything I can to bring him back alive.'

Kenny's green eyes pierced mine. I could usually read his face, but not this time.

'Fight for the child by all means but make sure you don't cross the line.'

'What do you mean, sir? If you're talking about Ghana, I went in my own time . . .'

He pushed his fingers against his desk, flexing the joints, so the tips turned white.

'I'm not talking about Ghana; I'm talking about you.' He eased the pressure so the blood flowed again through his hands. 'Once we start looking for loopholes to justify our choices, we end up making up our own rules.'

I stiffened. 'That's not me, sir.'

'I hope not.' The sincerity of his tone unnerved me. 'Make sure it never is. Your father played by his own rules and look how that ended for him.'

The breath stuck in my throat. It hurt to exhale.

'What did you say?'

Kenny's eyes didn't move from my face. 'You heard me, Leah,' he said.

His fingers drummed the desk, his gaze fixed on me.

'How long have you known I was Eli Carson's daughter?' I struggled to keep the words steady.

Kenny gave a half laugh.

'Oh, Leah,' he said. 'I've always known. Why do you think I've cut you so much slack? Helped you when you wanted to transfer back after Leeds? Turned a blind eye when you behave like you do? You didn't have an easy start. It's hard to shake that kind of thing off. Margaretta came to me when you joined the force, asked me to look out for you. She knew I had worked with your dad.'

The kindness in his eyes surprised me. I gripped my thighs as a deep fear finally came true. I had always wondered if Kenny was aware of my relationship to Eli, hoping he didn't know. Now I realised he had always seen Eli within me. The thought sickened me. I willed the conversation to end.

Kenny sighed. His chest strained against the material of his white cotton shirt. 'Eli was once a brilliant police officer before he threw a great career away. I would hate to see the same thing happen to you.'

My voice was tight. 'I'm nothing like Eli, sir.'

'I hope not, for your sake.' Kenny turned his attention to his keyboard. 'Now bring me Marlon Blake.'

Chapter One Hundred and Twenty-Seven

Leah

The block of flats in Stepney Green had been contained. There were armed police at every exit. My body was hot under my flak jacket as I waited. Marlon Blake had been seen going into his flat, so we knew he was at home. I could feel the vibrations in my body as the officer swung the battering ram against the front door. The wood splintered as the door shuddered, then collapsed inwards. There was a thud of feet as police officers thundered inside. Marlon Blake stood by his chocolate-brown chair, eyes wide with shock. He raised his hands above his head as he was grabbed from the front and behind. He groaned when he was flung on the floor, cheek to one side as he was cuffed behind his back. His eyes didn't move from me as Randle read him his rights, arresting him for murder.

'Where is he?' I said.

'Who?' Marlon mumbled into the carpet. He had hit his head hard, and he was bleeding from his mouth.

'The child.'

His eyes flashed with fury. 'I don't know what you're talking about.'

I gestured to the officers to fan out and search the premises.

'You're wasting your time,' he said. 'There's no child here.'

Sweat pooled beneath his hairline. His breathing was ragged. I pulled my eyes from his, scanning the room.

'You can't keep treating us like this.' I could hear the anger and indignation. 'We deserve better. There hasn't been a child in this house since Lemar was a kid.'

I sensed the pain in his voice. My gaze drifted to a photograph of Lemar as a toddler, the promise of a life not lived. The adjoining kitchen was too small to hide Zechariah, but I stepped inside all the same. The room was immaculate, uncluttered – spices with labels facing forwards, stacked in a rack. There were photos in a grid on a pinboard opposite the cooker – more baby images of Lemar, Keisha on holiday, Marlon before his hair turned white. In the corner there was a picture of a younger Marlon in combat uniform, his arm slung around a muscular, baby-faced Ray King. Looking at them, I understood Marlon's sadness when Ray had been murdered – the investigation into his son's death had killed his friend. As I turned away, I caught sight of a familiar figure deep in the background, also in uniform. I strode back into the room.

'When was Keisha in the army, Marlon?' I said.

He didn't answer.

'When was Keisha in the army?' I said again.

'She did six years before Lemar was born. Special forces. It wasn't for her. She did a tour. Gave it up. Said she wanted to focus on raising our son.'

'Where is she now?'

Marlon closed his eyes.

'I don't know.'

Chapter One Hundred and Twenty-Eight

Leah

Keisha Blake wasn't at work or in the pub. No one had seen or heard from her and her mobile was off. Marlon Blake waited in the interview room. He didn't want a lawyer. For an ex-soldier, he had a surprising distrust of authority. Then I thought about what had happened to Lemar, and I understood. Trust had to be earned, and the authorities had let him down. He was a far cry from the powerful figure he had cut before. His hair was wild; dark shadows covered lined skin under his eyes. He looked up as I entered with Randle, his expression hostile.

'I didn't kill those people,' he said. 'Neither did Keisha, so you may as well let me go.'

'We'll get to that.'

I started the recording, following protocol. Kenny would be watching – everything had to be by the book if I wanted to find Zed.

'I didn't kill them,' Marlon said again, unprompted. 'I was in the army. I know what it is to take a life. We just wanted to look them in the eye and hear them admit what they had done.'

'We'll talk about that, Marlon, but first I need your help to find Zechariah Okoro.'

'No.' He shook his head with force. 'I'm not doing that.'

'Doing what?' I said.

'Letting you silence us again. You want to know what happened, I'll tell you, but you need to listen. If you had listened to us in the first place, we wouldn't be here.'

'OK.' I sat back. 'I'm listening.'

I gave him the floor he had wanted for years.

'After Lemar disappeared, things were hard in our marriage.' His voice quivered. 'Keisha and I were grieving in our own way, hoping he was safe somewhere, still alive, but knowing in our hearts he wasn't. We looked for him for years and then . . .' There was shame in his eyes as he continued. 'We kept asking questions, but we gradually gave up.'

'What changed?' I said. 'What made you restart your investigation? After fifteen years?'

'A man called Chris wrote to us. Asked us to visit him. He was dying. He had met Lemar and regretted what happened. He said he was disgusted by the life he had lived and wanted to make amends. He would die in pain, but at least he could give us peace before he did.'

I looked at Randle. We had been looking for a dying man.

'He confirmed that Lemar was dead. He had seen the body and disposed of it. It wasn't personal – he had even met our boy and liked him. Said he saw something of himself in Lemar, before he took the wrong path in life. He said he was just doing his job, but now he looked back and hated himself for what he had done. He told us what happened – Lemar's final moments on this earth. The way his body was thrown away like dirt . . . It was a relief to have closure at first, but I was so angry. I wanted the people responsible to face up to what they had done. Ray and I went way back – we had served together in the army. He told me he had become a private investigator. He had done the odd job, but business wasn't really catching on. I didn't take him seriously at first. He had never stuck at anything since he retired. Then I realised he wasn't playing. He needed the money. He was always good at strategy and surveillance. It made sense.'

'How did he know where to start?' I said.

'Chris had given us names; told us the role they had each played the night Lemar died.'

'Which names?'

'Sarah Franks, Gabriel McMahon, Ogechi Okoro, Samir Mograbi.' He recited them in a monotone. 'We had more than we had ever had before. We just needed to find them and say our piece. We just wanted to talk to them, Inspector. Even after what they had done, it wasn't our right to kill.'

'Why did you go back to Ghana?' Randle said.

Marlon shifted in his seat.

'I wanted to find the girl – Bisi. The one Lemar had a crush on. But she had moved to France.'

'Why did you want to find her?' Randle frowned. 'She had nothing to do with your son's death.'

'I know. That's what Keisha said. She felt it was an unnecessary distraction. It just seemed important to me. Lemar had cared for her once.'

'What happened after Chris gave you the names?'

'We wanted to confront them when they were most vulnerable. Ray followed each of them and reported back: Gabriel lived alone; Sarah was always high or drunk. Ogechi ran by the canal on her own. At first, we couldn't find Sami. He turned up later after Ray had started watching the others . . . Then Ray was killed by MI6, and everything changed.'

'When did you know it was them?' I said.

Marlon snorted.

'Chris told us who hired him. He said there had been some kind of MI6 mission and Lemar's death could have compromised it. Then Ray starts asking questions about Lemar fifteen years later and MI6 got scared he would find out what they had done all those years ago. They didn't care about Lemar, but if Ray found out what happened to Lemar, he would find out about the mission too – MI6 couldn't let that happen, so Ray had to go. They were sending a message. It was obvious. Well – message received.' His voice was thick with bitterness. 'I told Keisha we needed to stop. These are people who can disappear bodies . . . make a murder look like a heart attack. We were in way over our heads. Lemar is dead. Confronting those responsible won't bring him back . . . We weren't going ahead. I thought Keisha agreed.'

'What did you think when you heard Sarah Franks had been killed?'

'I thought it was MI6. It was in their interests to kill her.'

'Come on, Marlon,' I said. 'I know you're trying to protect Keisha, but you're not helping anyone. Ray was dead. The immediate threat MI6 had feared was gone. Why would they? There was no need to kill.'

Marlon looked down at his lap, pressing his knuckles into his face.

'Tip Wheldon arranged for you to deliver drugs to Sarah the night she died, so you could confront her as originally planned,' I said. 'You may have changed your mind and decided not to go, but you told Keisha, didn't you? Surely it crossed your mind that she could have gone and killed Sarah?'

'You don't know that.' He squeezed his temples.

I leant forwards. 'Four people excluding Chris were involved in the death and disappearance of your son, Marlon. Three are dead. One was kidnapped and then released, and now her son is missing. It just so happens that Ogechi is probably the most culpable – she was involved in Lemar's death; she made sure it was covered up. It makes sense that Keisha would want to make her suffer. MI6 have no reason to take her child. Can you say in your heart that Keisha's not behind this?'

I stared hard into his eyes, challenging him to look away.

'She wouldn't kill a child. Where's the justice in that? She knows what it's like to have your own child taken from you, not knowing whether they are alive or dead.'

'Maybe she won't kill him.' I shrugged. 'But she knows what it would do to his mother if she made him disappear.'

Marlon's eyes darted from side to side as his brain processed what he was hearing. His breathing quickened, but he didn't speak.

'Please, Marlon,' I said. 'A child is in danger. Surely that means something to you after what you went through?'

'I don't know where she is. I'm telling the truth,' he said. 'But Chris might know.'

'I thought Chris was dead – he told you the truth about Ghana because he was dying.'

'Dying, Inspector. Not dead. Chris is still alive.'

Chapter One Hundred and Twenty-Nine

Leah

Chris had been diagnosed with stomach cancer with less than a year to live. The diagnosis was still fairly recent. He had refused treatment, choosing to spend his final months close to his mother in Kingston, a suburb on the outskirts of London. Marlon and Keisha had visited Chris at home when he had first contacted them about Lemar. When Ray had died, Marlon had shut down about the past, but Keisha was still in touch with Chris.

Kenny insisted on sending us with backup, even though there was no guarantee Keisha would be there. I let Randle drive to give him another focus, but it didn't seem to work – he gripped the wheel tight with one hand, the fingers of the other tapping his thigh furiously. He had been increasingly tense since Zed had gone missing, full of nervous energy. His fair hair was unruly from raking his fingers through it – his default move when frustrated or stressed.

'I don't get it ma'am,' he said as we left central London behind. The windows were down, and the car was filled with a warm breeze. 'Keisha murdered Sarah Franks and Gabriel McMahon for killing Lemar by accident, but she lets Chris, the man who disappeared her son, live in comfort near his mother?'

I looked out as we crossed Kingston Bridge. The river was

emerald beneath us, the water glimmering in the evening light, dividing the city in two.

'Maybe she forgave him because he came clean and showed some kind of remorse?' I said. 'Maybe she decided to have mercy?'

Randle pushed back loose tendrils of hair, his whole body on edge. 'She just kidnapped an innocent fourteen-year-old boy, ma'am. She doesn't strike me as the merciful type.'

The air was still and stifling as we entered the heart of Kingston. According to Marlon, Chris lived in a terraced house in a less affluent part. We moved further away from the river – the houses shrank, the buildings became denser as we turned onto a quiet road, lined with lime trees. A police van was parked up ahead. The driver pulled away from the kerb when he saw us. We drove in convoy, no flashing lights, pausing just before the turning. Three officers poured out of the back of the van, moving further up the road. We turned onto a street flanked by neat, terraced houses. The van came to a halt outside a newly painted blue door. I had seen images before we set off – each house was almost identical, with a wooden fence in between and an exit through the back garden onto a narrow path. I checked my watch – the first group of officers would nearly be in position to contain the back exit whilst the rest of the team sealed off the front.

I got out of the car, waiting on the opposite side of the street as all access points were secured. Randle was with one of the officers, head down, going over last-minute details. My senses were on high alert as my eyes roved. A pedestrian approached then walked away, not wanting to get caught in the fracas. A dog barked loudly from the front lawn to my left. I turned just as a man in a baseball cap walked out of the neighbouring house, head dipped, trying to slip out unnoticed. We hadn't been able to find a recent image of Chris, but there was something about the physique of the man in the cap that caught my attention – hunched shoulders, a powerful frame, even though his body looked somehow diminished. It was possible to climb between the houses through the back gardens. If this was Chris, he must have made his move before the team was in position.

Instinctively I broke into a run, but the man in the cap had a head start. That's when I knew for a fact that it was him. Even with illness and age, he was still fast. I moved to catch up. I pushed myself, breathing through my nose as I drove my arms through the air. I could see his pace start to slow, and I hurled myself forwards, collapsing on top of him. I was strong for my size, but Chris had trained for maximum impact with minimum effort. Somehow, he flipped me onto my back, pinning me down with his thighs. His forearm pushed down across my throat. His eyes bulged, and he stifled a cough – he was evidently not in good health, but men like him never forgot decades of training, and I was in no doubt Chris could kill me if he wanted. Randle drew up behind us. I could see him raise the baton in his hand. My eyes widened, terrified about what would happen next.

'Stay back,' Chris said. He didn't turn round. 'I could snap her neck without a second thought, and you wouldn't want that, would you?' His eyes remained fixed on me as he continued to address Randle. 'Who's in charge here?'

Randle kept his voice even. 'She is. I'm her DS. We're looking for Keisha Blake. There's no need to do anything drastic.'

Chris finally turned his head, but only a fraction, so he could see both of us. He let out a hoarse cough. 'Radio your people. Tell them to stand down and not to follow, and I'll take you to her. If you try anything, I won't show you where she is.'

Randle did as he was told, watching as Chris released the pressure on my throat. He raised his hips so I could roll out from under him. The choking sensation remained, and I spluttered, still struggling to breathe.

Randle pulled me to my feet. 'Are you OK, ma'am?' His voice was gentle.

I felt better standing up, but my legs felt numb. Chris was already starting to move.

'Follow me,' he said.

He turned down a road, cutting across two parallel streets.

Randle watched him closely. 'We thought you were dead.'

His tone was flat. 'I will be by the end of the year.'

'And in the meantime?' I said.

He either didn't hear me, or he chose not to answer.

'I thought you were trying to make amends.'

'I am.' He looked back at us. The earnestness in his eyes surprised me. 'I'm helping a grieving mother find peace.'

'By helping her to kill?' Randle's tone was accusing.

'No,' Chris said. 'She knows you're coming for her. By giving her time.'

We arrived in front of a house three roads down. There were flower boxes with pink roses in the windows, fairy lights decorating the trees outside.

'Where are we?' I said.

'My mother's house. She's in a home. It's empty.'

'Where's Keisha?'

'Out the back. In the garden.'

He wasn't a man of many words.

'You said you wanted to give her time,' I said. 'Time for what?

'Time to bury the boy,' he said.

Chapter One Hundred and Thirty

Leah

I broke into a run round the side of the house. Randle overtook me as we arrived in the back garden. Keisha Blake was bent over, clutching a spade. She was almost unrecognisable from the woman in leopard print. She wore a mud-stained white vest over denim jeans cut off at the knee. She was standing next to a small mound of earth, shovelling brown clumps of soil into a shallow hole. The muscles in her arms tensed as she worked, powerful shoulders usually concealed on display in the sun. As we drew closer, I realised it was a makeshift grave.

We raced towards her. I went for the spade. Randle grabbed her arms, pulling them back behind her. Keisha barely resisted as he handcuffed her wrists behind her back, reading her her rights.

I jammed the spade into the soil, trying to empty the grave. Randle clawed back the dirt with his fingers, shouting Zed's name. I dug deeper and deeper, expecting to hit flesh or bone, but the deeper I went, the more it became clear that we weren't going to find a body in the grave. At the bottom, under a layer of earth, a framed photo of Lemar was just visible. There were football shirts, a teddy bear, mementos from his childhood – all buried in the shallow grave in Chris' mother's garden. I looked up to see the tears in Keisha's eyes. Then she blinked them away, her face full of quiet fury.

Chris had said Keisha was burying the boy; we had assumed he had meant Zechariah, but she was burying what remained of her son, finally saying goodbye. I sank down, sitting back on my heels, dripping with sweat, exhausted. I didn't know whether to be scared or relieved. I needed to catch my breath first.

Keisha watched as the realisation dawned. Randle was already on his feet, standing over her.

'Where is he?' he said.

'I take it you don't mean Lemar?' Keisha said. 'You people never cared about him. I just wanted to lay him to rest before you found me. Now it's all over.'

I climbed out of the hole, my body smeared with sweat and dried earth. 'Until you tell us where Zechariah is, this is far from over.'

Randle wiped the dust from his hands. 'Where is he?' he said again.

Keisha looked at him, her mouth set in defiance.

'I am sorry about what happened to your son, I truly am.' I tried to sound sympathetic. 'But it doesn't justify kidnap and killing, Keisha.'

'Says who?' Her eyes blazed. 'Who decides what's a just kill? You? Me? The so-called authorities? I may not have lasted long, but I did my time fighting for my country. I've killed people whose lives, whose dreams I know nothing about – all in the name of a war someone else decided I should fight. You tell me that's just and this isn't. My boy was killed and then chucked away like rubbish because someone in MI6 thought their operation mattered more than my son's life. The people that did that to him were never punished. How is that just?'

'I'm not saying it is,' I said. 'But it doesn't give you the right to kill.'

'Well, I'm done with listening to people who think they are in charge, who think people like me and my son don't matter.' Her voice was unnervingly calm.

'What you've done doesn't change what happened to Lemar,' I said.

'No. But we finally get justice, and I can live with that.'

She raised herself up onto her knees, her hands still secured behind her back, determined to get her message out.

'For years, we looked for Lemar, but we were doomed to fail because people more powerful than us had already decided *who* and *what* was important.'

'How is it different if *you* decide?'

Her eyes narrowed. She looked at me, but she was too consumed by hate to listen.

'You killed three people, Keisha.' Randle didn't hide his disgust. 'How is that justice?'

'I didn't plan to kill anybody at first. We were just going to confront them, so they faced up to what they did – take responsibility for destroying my family. Ray was only trying to help. He was the first person who gave us hope, brought Marlon and me back together. When they killed him. . .' She shook her head. 'They were trying to silence us. . . again. I had to get justice. For Ray. For Lemar. For all of us. Marlon didn't understand, but it's simple – you can sit around and let other people decide, or you can bring about your own justice. Ray had already spent time following them; I knew where they would be. All I had to do was turn up and finish this once and for all.'

I looked down at the photo of Lemar, the football shirt he must have treasured.

'Lemar shouldn't have died,' I said. 'But revenge isn't justice.'

'Maybe not, but it feels like it, and that's better than nothing.'

She smiled, but her whole being seemed weary. She looked from me to Randle, her eyes questioning.

'You know, I thought it was over when I dropped the balaclava after I killed Sarah Franks. I thought you would trace it back to me, before I could finish this, but that's the irony, isn't it? Lemar mattered so little to you, we weren't even on your radar. Well . . . ' She nodded towards the makeshift grave. 'It's done now. It's over. '

She looked from Randle to me. Sweat dripped from her brow, but she didn't seem to notice.

'You know Chris is too chicken to kill himself? Grown man like him who's killed others. He begged me to do it, but I don't need to. I'll let nature take its course. He'll die in pain, and he accepts that.'

Randle shook his head in disgust. 'You killed three people.'

'Sarah Franks. Gabriel McMahon. Sami Mograbi. Every kill was just. Sarah and Gabriel pushed him. It was an accident, but they went along with the cover-up. Sami deserved worse because he helped to get rid of my boy.'

I flinched at the mention of Sami's name. 'And Ogechi?'

'She made sure his body was never found. She's the one who decided. Because of her, we spent fifteen years not knowing what happened to him. If she hadn't been there that night and considered Lemar's life unimportant, there would have been no need for Chris or Sami.'

'Lemar might still be dead,' I said.

'Maybe. But we would have been allowed to grieve for him.'

I thought about Eli, my mother, my nightmares There was no peace without a body, but it didn't justify what Keisha had done.

I remembered Sami with his throat slit, the pain of seeing him – pointless, senseless deaths that didn't achieve anything at all.

Keisha's defiance faded into sadness, then she hardened herself again. 'Ogechi needs to feel a fraction of the agony that I've felt.'

'And what about Zed?' I said.

She looked from me to Randle. 'What about him?'

Randle kicked the earth with his heel. 'Why should Zed have to pay for what his mother did?'

She frowned. 'He's alive, unlike Lemar,' she said. 'But you can tell Ogechi this from me: I'll never tell you where he is, and she'll never see her son again.'

Chapter One Hundred and Thirty-One

Leah

The houses in Kingston were searched. We looked in every corner, but Zed was nowhere to be found. Chris was picked up by the police down by the river. He claimed he had no idea where Zed was, and somehow, I believed he was telling the truth. There were officers watching Marlon Blake's every move, but he insisted Keisha had left him in the dark; he had barely been out of their flat since the raid.

The moment Keisha entered the interview room, her speech was reduced to a series of *no comments*. We questioned her at length, but she didn't break.

I sat in my office, watching the clock. Zed had been missing for hours. I was determined to find him, but the odds were not looking good. I turned my chair to face the window, looking out at preoccupied Londoners.

What had we missed?

I moved to the board in the corner of the bullpen, staring at the images. My eyes roved over the victims. Sarah Franks dead on her floor. Gabriel McMahon, his throat cut a few feet from where Zed crouched hidden in a wardrobe. Ogechi smiling before her ordeal began; the black suitcase; her lacerated limbs before they were treated and dressed.

What was missing?

Sarah in her flat; Gabriel in his house – both photographed where they had been attacked.

There was something missing . . .

The place where Ogechi's wounds had been inflicted.

Keisha had changed her target. She had made sure Ogechi had no clue where she had been held. If Keisha believed we didn't know this, maybe she had kept the same location for Zed?

'What is it, ma'am?'

Randle had followed me, uninvited.

My eyes remained fixed on the board.

'What was it Ogechi said about where she was held when she was taken?' I said. 'Some kind of basement or underground garage?'

Randle pulled out his tiny notebook, balancing it in a large hand. 'She didn't know for sure, but she said there were no windows, a low ceiling. There was a dumb waiter lift like in a restaurant, but she wasn't in a kitchen. It could have been a cellar, she said.'

I turned to him.

'Tip Wheldon's family owns a chain of restaurants and hotels. Lu said they have bought up a bunch of disused properties and are using ex-soldiers to provide security – Marlon Blake is on their books. What if Keisha is too?'

Randle pushed back a loose strand of hair.

'You think Keisha could have hidden him in a disused hotel or restaurant?'

'Quite possibly.'

I moved into the centre of the room, firing off instructions at my team.

'Check if the security firm also hired Keisha.' I turned to Akosua.

'And get the floorplans of all the disused buildings Tip Wheldon's family have bought – we want properties with multiple floors, a room with no windows and a mini lift or dumb waiter. There's a chance Zed could be in one of them.'

Chapter One Hundred and Thirty-Two

Leah

Like Marlon, Keisha had been moonlighting as a security guard for the Wheldons' disused developments. The team had been working through the night. The sun had risen when Akosua knocked on my door, two large sheets of paper trailing behind her. Her hair was in a simple bun, too tired to bother with much more.

'I've got the plans, ma'am.'

I beckoned her in. She didn't sit, standing close to the desk instead.

'There are several developments that fit the bill – one in Edinburgh and two in London: one in Euston, the other in Balham. Apparently, the Wheldon Company is trying to get permission to knock down the building in Balham so they can rebuild.'

She placed the plans on my desk.

'According to the security firm, Keisha never worked for them in Euston or Scotland.'

She looked at me, her eyes full of expectation.

'OK, Akosua. Balham it is.'

Chapter One Hundred and Thirty-Three

Leah

This time, I drove. I glanced at Randle, looking out through the windscreen.

'Are you OK?'

He nodded, but his face was pale. His blue eyes were puffy with exhaustion. The building looked like a warehouse – a red-brick cube with multiple levels, set back behind a fence. The road was noisy; there was drilling at the junction, and I struggled to hear Randle above the din.

Inside the building felt cool; the smell of damp lingered. Picturing the floorplan, we headed downstairs to the basement.

The layout was exactly as I had expected – the compact metal lift diagonally opposite the heavy steel door. The room was cold and empty. In the corner, another door. I pulled it open, praying I would find Zed, but all I found was an empty larder – each wall covered with rows of bare shelves, no food or sign of life anywhere. I looked at Randle standing beside me – everything I felt was written on his face.

We turned back the way we came. Randle stopped, crouching low as something caught his eye on the stone floor.

'What is it?' I said.

He pulled a nitrile glove from his pocket, holding up a small plastic rectangle.

'It's a bank card – O *Okoro*.'

'Ogechi's?'

'Yes, but I remember the final numbers, ma'am. This is the one Zed used to get to Finsbury Park,' he said.

'He was here.' My voice was scarcely more than a whisper.

Where did she take you Zechariah? Where are you now?

I could hear the drilling outside from the roadworks. Underneath it a tiny sound I couldn't place.

'What is that, ma'am?'

I signalled for him to be quiet, turning towards the dumb waiter.

'It's coming from over there.'

I rushed towards the miniature lift, Randle close behind me. He moved ahead of me, prising open the silver doors of the dumb waiter. Crouched inside, his arms and legs bound, was a tiny, frightened Zechariah. His whole body was shaking; he was covered in sweat and dirt. His lips moved as he repeated his mantra, so soft, I could barely make out the words.

'My name's Zechariah Okoro and I'm a fighter. No one can break my spirit or steal my joy. My name's . . .'

He looked up at me, completely broken. I put my arms around him and held him tight.

Chapter One Hundred and Thirty-Four

Leah

Randle came to a stop outside my estate. I had been too tired to arc my body away from him as his motorbike navigated the streets, and I was still clinging to his waist as the engine died. I climbed off without a word, smoothing my trousers along my thighs. Zed had been taken to hospital to recover. He had been given the all-clear, but he was still on both our minds.

'You know he's going to be OK,' I said, facing Randle on the kerb.

He lifted his visor so I could see his face. 'We don't know that.'

There was no joy in his eyes.

'He's a tough kid,' I said.

'He's still a child.'

'A child with a future.' I thought of Lemar Blake, his life cut short. 'At least we found him. It could have been much worse.'

Randle pulled off his helmet. He looked older without his smile. 'What do you think will happen to Marlon and Keisha Blake, ma'am?'

'She'll go prison for a long time.'

'Not that. Do you think their marriage will survive?'

'I don't know, Randle.'

I squinted as I looked up at the sky – bright and blue, without a cloud.

'It survived the death of their son. Who knows if it will survive again?'

I watched as his face disappeared underneath his helmet again. He nodded, and then he was gone.

I turned back towards the estate, but I wasn't ready to go in. Without thinking, I began walking up the road, following the route I had taken with Sami not so long ago – up the King's Road, past the Royal Court Theatre into Eaton Square.

Zikar Mograbi's face was inscrutable when he opened his front door. He stood back to let me in without a greeting, gesturing to the room opposite the one where Sami's body had been found. The furniture was less ornate, the décor bland. There was a large television on the furthermost wall, the news on mute. Zikar closed the door behind us.

'I'm going to have that room redone,' he said. He didn't specify which room he was talking about, but we both knew.

An image of Sami's body flashed into my mind. I saw the pain in Zikar's eyes, and I knew he had had the same thought.

'Last time we spoke wasn't a good time for me,' Zikar said.

'Your son had just been killed . . .'

'Still . . .'

I nodded, accepting the apology he would never utter in words.

He sat back in his chair, his body disappearing into the dense grey cushion. 'Why are you here, Miss Hutch? I've been informed you've found the culprit. The case is closed.'

I realised I had gone there without knowing why – a subconscious decision which only became clear when he asked.

'I just wanted you to know that Sami *was* my friend,' I said. 'He was probably the closest friend I had. I hope he knew that.'

Zikar inhaled deeply, sinking further into the chair. For a moment he didn't say anything. I stood.

'I won't waste any more of your time,' I said.

Zikar planted his feet firmly on the carpet, drawing himself up to his full height. 'He knew, Miss Hutch,' he said. 'I'm glad you do too.'

I started to move towards the door, turning as I reached for the handle.

'Did you know?'

'That you were friends with my son?' Zikar gave a rare smile.

'No.' I swallowed. 'Did you know that Sami was a spy?'

His eyes darted from left to right as he contemplated which answer to give.

'Not at the time. No. He told me later that he had been recruited, but it didn't work out . . . I'm glad. As I said, Sami was an idealist. Cold, hard pragmatism wasn't for him. The life of a spy would have crucified him.'

I could feel the emotion rising up inside me. I turned back towards the door so Zikar couldn't see my face. He stopped me from leaving with his voice.

'His flat's open, Miss Hutch. You're welcome to take something – to remember him by.'

I didn't turn round.

'Thank you,' I said.

The journey to the top of the house felt longer than it had done before. Sami's flat looked the same – the mug still on the counter where he had left it before he went downstairs to his death. My gaze flicked to the mantelpiece, pausing on the photo of us as teenagers – Sami staring at me adoringly, the memory of laughter and fun. I reached for it before I changed my mind, slipping it carefully into my bag. Sami hadn't been back in my life for long, but it was strange being in his personal space, knowing he would never return. As I headed for the door, I caught sight of the Magic Eye poster out of the corner of my eye. I pivoted, squinting hard, but I still couldn't see the face.

Chapter One Hundred and Thirty-Five

Zed

Zed woke up in hospital, feeling drowsy. The fluorescent light above his bed was too bright after the time he had spent shut in that dark space. His mother was perched by the side of his bed, gripping his hand as if she were afraid she would lose him if she let go. His father was slouched in the corner, fast asleep in a chair. His mum forced her lips into a weak smile.

'Good. You're awake. I'm so sorry, my darling. There are things I need to tell you.'

His body felt cold, despite the heat. He was too scared to think about what had happened, unsure he could handle much more.

'OK, Mum.' He sounded fragile. 'But not yet. OK?'

Ogechi nodded. Her eyes were red, and he could tell she had been crying, even though she was trying to hide it from him.

'OK,' she said. 'But there's one thing I need to tell you now.'

Zed tilted his head towards her. 'What's that?' he said.

'I've quit my job.' Her voice was full of false cheer. 'We're going to have the best summer, Zechariah.'

He smiled, wanting to make her feel better, but gone was the child who revelled in summer adventures. Now he just wanted to sleep and forget.

There was a cough from the doorway. He looked up. There he was – DS Randle filling the frame.

'Ben.'

Zed tried to smile. He pushed himself up the headboard, sinking back against the hard plastic.

Ben took a step towards him. 'How you doing, Zed?

He tried to shrug, but it felt like more of a grimace. 'Never better.'

'You must be doing OK if your sarcasm's back.'

Zed knew his smile lacked power. 'It never went away.'

He looked down, gripping the bedsheet as he struggled to find the words. 'I didn't think you would find me,' he said.

'Zechariah . . .'

Ben said his full name so softly, for a moment Zed wondered if he had imagined it. He lifted his head. The kindness in Ben's eyes was almost more than he could bear.

'What did I say about trusting us to do our job?'

'You said there were no guarantees.'

'Maybe one,' Ben said. 'We were never going to give up until we found you.'

He reached out and briefly touched Zed's wrist. Zed hadn't realised he was shaking until Ben took his hand away.

'Am I interrupting?'

Leah stepped into the room.

Zed could never erase the memory of her face when she found him – so many emotions he implicitly understood. Her eyes were full of compassion as she looked at him. He held her gaze, not wanting to look away. He couldn't find the words to thank her; he hoped she understood.

His mother's eyes followed the silent exchange.

'I'll give you a moment,' she said. She turned to Leah. 'Thank you. I know I don't deserve a second chance with him.'

Ogechi moved towards Zed's dad before Leah could answer. She shook him gently, dragging him to his feet and out of the room.

Leah was watching Zed like she could read his thoughts. She slid into the chair his mum had left empty moments before. He felt vulnerable, conscious she was assessing him for a test he could never pass.

'Thank you for coming to get me.' His eyes flicked to Ben. 'Both of you. I should have trusted you,' he said.

'No point dwelling on that.' Leah leant forward, speaking in a hushed whisper. Ben hung back, giving them space. 'How are you feeling?'

Zed hesitated, nervous about revealing too much.

'Last night, I had this nightmare . . .' He trailed off.

Her face was sombre. 'You'll have more of them, I'm afraid.'

She rested her hand near his on the bedsheet, careful not to touch him.

'Don't let this define you,' she said.

'How?' His voice rose with the emotion he had been trying to control. He sounded like a little boy. 'How am I supposed to stop that from happening?'

He didn't mean to cry, but he could feel the tears hot in his eyes.

'I don't know,' Leah said. 'I can't pretend to have the answers, but you've got to learn to deal with it head on, or one day it will catch up with you, and destroy who you are.'

Chapter One Hundred and Thirty-Six

Leah

My words to Zechariah played in my mind. I returned to the place of my mother's death, determined to deal with my past. David Francis' house looked different in daylight. What had seemed eerie before now just seemed sad. The grass was overgrown, trampled in patches – a green wilderness nobody cared about. I was still processing the fact that Kenny knew my history, who my father was. He had known Eli when he killed my mother, had always seen me as a murderer's child.

As I walked to the back entrance to gain access to the cottage, visions of Eli carrying my dead mother into a thicket flashed into my mind. I had almost reached the door when I stopped – something didn't sit right with the image. I turned. My eyes swept over the green expanse. The grass was long, but there were only a few trees. There was no thicket, no wood. I rushed to the front, my head spinning. The house was situated in open land, surrounded by fields. I hadn't noticed when I came back the first time. It had been dark, and my mind was focused on the house. I looked out at the wild countryside. It was no wonder the police had never found my mother's body – they had been looking in the wrong place all along.

Acknowledgements

This book is for my grandmother and my late uncle, who captivated me with their stories when I was growing up.

I couldn't have done it without my family, friends and the talented team who worked tirelessly to support me.

Thank you to Camilla Bolton, an exceptional agent and thoughtful friend – your kindness makes working with you a pleasure, and your editorial skill makes your notes invaluable.

Thank you to my brilliant editor, Stef Bierwerth, whose care and support kept me on track when other commitments loomed large. Thank you for your patience and for believing in me and the Leah Hutch series.

Thank you to everyone at Darley Anderson: Georgia Schindler for your clear notes and attention to detail; Jade Kavanagh for your continued support; Georgia Fuller, Ilaria Albani, Francesca Edwards, Helen Dudley and Rosanna Bellingham for all your hard work. Thanks also to Sheila David from Catapult Rights.

Thank you to everyone who worked on the book at Quercus: Kat Burdon for your phenomenal eye and brilliant command of the English language; Andrew Smith for another stunning cover; Beth Wright, publicist extraordinaire, and the rest of the publicity team for promoting the book and organising events; Ellie Bailey and the rest of the marketing team for getting *Just Kill* out into the world; and Lucy Rostant for all your work behind the scenes. Thanks also to Katie Green and Lorraine Green for proofreading and copyediting.

Thank you to everyone who gave up their time to answer seemingly random questions to help with my research. Special thanks to Paul Ditta for always being on hand to discuss ideas and to offer advice, and to Sammy Warnakulasuriya for reading draft pages and suggesting little details.

Thanks to my two cousins for sharing motorcycle and local knowledge. Thanks to Eleanore Massey, Azeem Alam, Rajdeep Khattar, Jon Hutt, Andrew Sankey, Nicky and Jonny Brough for their professional expertise; and to Wes Illingsworth, Smita Rossetti, Caswell Barry, Lucy Martinez, Laura Meldrum-Carter and Phil Wheeler for being helpful sounding boards.

Thank you to the small army of cheerleaders who kept me motivated, often without realising they were doing so. I can't name you all, but I hope you know who you are. I particularly want to thank Ali King, Henry Swindell, Zemmy Momoh, Kylie Hutchison, Zarene Dallas, Myma Belo-Osagie and Christian and Theresa Goka. Thank you to Lucy Bruen and Andrew Brown for your hospitality, and to Lucas and Fabricio for all the coffees.

Thanks to Liz and Andrew Venz for providing me with a little haven in which to write, away from the distractions of city life.

Big thanks to my sister for being so supportive and such a champion of my work.

To Dominic Rose Price for being my first reader once again – your encouragement and belief helped me get over the finish line.

Finally, thanks to my mother who has been there from the start. Thank you for your valuable feedback and your unconditional love. You inspire me more than you know.

RAISING READERS
Books Build Bright Futures

Dear Reader,

We'd love your attention for one more page to tell you about the crisis in children's reading, and what we can all do.

Studies have shown that reading for fun is the **single biggest predictor of a child's future life chances** – more than family circumstance, parents' educational background or income. It improves academic results, mental health, wealth, communication skills, ambition and happiness.[1]

The number of children reading for fun is in rapid decline. Young people have a lot of competition for their time. In 2024, 1 in 10 children and young people in the UK aged 5 to 18 did not own a single book at home.[2]

Hachette works extensively with schools, libraries and literacy charities, but here are some ways we can all raise more readers:

- Reading to children for just 10 minutes a day makes a difference
- Don't give up if children aren't regular readers – there will be books for them!
- Visit bookshops and libraries to get recommendations
- Encourage them to listen to audiobooks
- Support school libraries
- Give books as gifts

There's a lot more information about how to encourage children to read on our website: **www.RaisingReaders.co.uk**

Thank you for reading.

hachette UK

[1] OECD, '21st-Century Readers: Developing Literacy Skills in a Digital World', 2021, https://www.oecd.org/en/publications/21st-century-readers_a83d84cb-en.html

[2] National Literacy Trust, 'Book Ownership in 2024', November 2024, https://literacytrust.org.uk/research-services/research-reports/book-ownership-in-2024